THE OTHER SIDE OF A MIRROR

C.K MULFORT

This is a work of fiction and loosely based on true scattered events. However, names, characters, and places are either a product of the author's imagination or used fictitiously.

THE OTHER SIDE OF A MIRROR Text copyright © 2020
Revised in 2022

No parts of this book may be reproduced, stored in a retrieval system, transmitted in any form or by any means, electronic, mechanical, photocopying, recording, or otherwise, without the permission of the author.

Cover design by Kenny Mulfort

Printed in the United States
Second Edition

Unless otherwise indicated below, images found in this novel were designed by C. K Mulfort.

ISBN: 9798565500592

"You'll experience events in life that make you reconsider everything. Don't ignore them! Believe in your moments."

C.K. Mulfort

Today…

CHAPTER 1

5:02 P.M.

NO ONE MAKES ME feel like I belong in this world more than someone who doesn't. That's the beauty of being a psychologist. I get to meet a lot of those people. Most of them struggle to find meaning in life because they're too busy measuring their worth through the perception of others. While the others are lost souls, crying out for help since they've somehow allowed their past to twist how they think and behave. By the time they arrive at my office, sit across from me on the off-white sofa, and reveal themselves through a scatter of words and emotions, it's usually too late.

Every so often, though, I encounter a patient whose story takes a toll on my conscience because even though I'm not supposed to, I find a little of myself in them. Taking deep dives into their lives in ways other professionals won't. Or perhaps, in a way, I shouldn't.

Like Mrs. Danielle Brown, a former patient of mine. In the depths of Mrs. Danielle Brown's harrowing past, her life was forever changed by a haunting event. It was an unimaginable tragedy that unfolded within seconds, just moments after she and her friend returned from a joyous wedding celebration. There, in a hotel room, while talking about life, Mrs. Brown witnessed her friend take her own life by shooting herself point blank in the head with a .45 caliber pistol. The echo of that pistol continues to sound off through Mrs. Brown's shattered existence. Haunted by the fragments of that fateful day, Mrs. Brown carries the weight of a belief that her friend had forsaken the pursuit of happiness, succumbing to a sinister presence that lurked beyond the realm of light. Colors dimmed in her world, eclipsed by an impending darkness that swallowed her spirit whole. When this happened, death became the only option for Mrs. Brown's friend.

If only her friend had grasped the depth of Mrs. Brown's love and devotion for her, then perhaps the tragedy would have been prevented. Unfortunately, now trapped within the confines of her own condition, Mrs. Brown is left to contemplate the agonizing "what ifs" that haunt her every waking moment.

Nevertheless, that defining moment left Mrs. Brown drowning in grief and despair and eventually into depression. Mentally, Mrs. Brown and I are nothing alike, but emotionally, we're both reserved and afraid to open ourselves to the world. Like myself, Mrs. Brown is a woman who would rather hide her inner pain because she is terrified of what others may think of her if they knew the truth. Every three minutes, she impulsively turns to her phone, hoping that someone is thinking of her at that moment. I know the feeling all too well because even smiling is something I've learned to do. The same could be said for Mrs. Brown, whom I've only seen smile once.

For nearly six years, I've diagnosed and counseled individuals with all sorts of stories that evoked thoughts and emotions from me. Some left me completely drained and discouraged, while others made me feel a little better about the woman I am today. However, never have I sat across from someone who genuinely caused me to question everything about myself… until now!

"I'm ready when you are." I slip on my full-rim glasses.

The woman sitting across from me on the off-white sofa remains unyielding, her silence piercing through the air. Her gaze locks onto mine, her arms tightly folded over her chest, and her legs elegantly crossed, right over left. There's an enigmatic quality to her presence, setting her apart from all the others, yet a sense of familiarity lingers between her and I. Madison, that's her name. I cannot fathom why, but her sudden appearance in my office feels somewhat expected. It is as though encountering her on this very day was destined to be.

Madison is a woman with enough flawless imperfections to make her seem perfect, and her pleasant voice, which comes out in whispers, comforts me. Then there's her scent. Deep inhale. *Mmm!* Oh my God, her scent, an earthy and creamy almond smell, opens the album of forgotten memories and pulls me to a place I haven't been to in a while. Back to the hotel lobby, where I first met David. Fuck! What is that scent? I know it, but I can't put a name to it. Think, Andrea. Think!

"Okay, Dr. Clarke. I'm ready." She whispers.

My stomach shifts as she slithers my name out of her mouth. Her deep-set hazel eyes, rimmed with long dark lashes, stare into mine and make me slightly uncomfortable. Her gaze isn't deliberately cold, but it's a look I haven't seen from any of the others. People don't often come into my office poised and pragmatic, but this young woman wears it like a second skin. She must have been the apple of her father's eye. That much, I can tell. There's no trace of anguish or pain on her gentle face, nor is there a burning stare or fidgeting in her hands and feet. The white in her eyes is like a blank page, softer than what I could imagine eyes to be. Almost as if they are the eyes of one who loves deeply. Now, this makes me wonder. Why is she really here?

"Okay. So, tell me then, how did this all begin?" I ask, my throat tightens.

Madison takes a deep breath, slowly uncrosses her legs, and

presses them together, gnawing at the inside of her cheeks as she looks over her right shoulder to the large window. The sun fading in the background rests on her reflection like sweet honey, and as I patiently wait, silence blankets us like fog over the hills. I wouldn't say I like silence because it tends to paralyze my thoughts while pulling me away from the mind-numbing reality I've grown accustomed to. At this moment—I can't think of anything other than what it must feel like to be Madison. To live unbothered and unapologetically. Bold and unafraid. Do as I want, say whatever the fuck I feel, and ignore anything that doesn't bring me happiness. The fact that I can't do exactly that makes me cringe with jealousy.

Oh yes, she's nothing like the others that have sat across from me on the off-white sofa. She's a total enigma with features I would kill to have—starting with those boney cheekbones that suit her hazel eyes exceptionally well. Her shoulders are seamlessly narrow. Her legs are so toned, yet they look soft. There are no scars or blemishes anywhere. Her lips, flush and glossy, are nothing like mine. It's no wonder why they would all fall for someone like Madison. Even as I close my eyes and listen to her voice, I can see her beauty, wants, and desires in an array of colors swimming through the windows to her soul. They must have seen the same thing.

Madison turns her back to me, smiling bashfully. I take a deep breath, bracing myself for what she will say next. Slowly, she recrosses her legs—left over right, and as her smile vanishes, I find myself drawn closer to her than I was before. Honestly, in a way, I haven't been with the others. Come on, Andrea! Get it together. Be professional. Yes! I must get ahold of myself. Besides, she's the client. Not me!

"Madison…?"

"Dr. Clarke, there must have been a time when no one needed a therapist, right? But at some point, something changed— making life much more difficult to understand and ultimately pushing us into the dark corners of our subconscious minds. Sometimes, I wonder what this world would look like if we were just honest with ourselves." Madison turns back to the large window.

"I guess there would be no need for someone of my profession." I offer a wry smile.

"Yeah. Perhaps you're right."

Madison thinks she and I have a lot in common. I find that hard to believe. In fact, it couldn't be farther from the truth. How can we? She sees opportunities and possibilities in every situation she encounters. Oftentimes, I struggle to see past the darkness of a world filled with deception and uncertainties. Madison's free-spirited soul guides her daring ways, and I, well, I am just a conformist. Most people would consider me a shy and reticent person. I doubt Madison has ever heard that from anyone. She seems like the woman who walks into a place, smiling and waving to everyone looking at her as if she were some sort of pageant queen. Furthermore, she's open-minded—always going with the flow, but unlike her, I need things to be systematically structured, organized, and thoroughly planned out. It tends to leave less room for errors in my life that way. We are entirely different, but deep down, I wish we were the same.

"You want to know when it all began, but Dr. Clarke, I'm not sure if I can answer that. Maybe when I was twelve? Eighteen? Twenty-five? Or maybe last year. See, I've always been a woman in control over my thoughts, urges, and impulses. Especially when it came to exploring my wants and needs. However, somewhere in between, I lost myself and became the woman you see today. So, telling you where it all began is a bit…difficult." She turns back to me.

"I understand. So, how about you start from the moment you feel like you lost control?"

The look in Madison's eyes vividly tells it all, yet like the blind living amongst the deaf, I'm unable to make sense of it. Before she opens her mouth to speak, her head tilts slightly to the right, closes her eyes, and then takes another deep breath. Madison doesn't know it, but I'm beginning to envy her.

Madison speaks as I listen…

I listen as Madison speaks.

"For the longest, I could only function throughout the day, knowing I would be in the arms of a man. Some women needed wine—some needed pills. I needed to be touched. Whether I accepted it or not, I knew the disease had taken control of me. Even to the point where I could care less about who I wound up with at the end of the night, just as long as they were touching me, holding me, and of course, fucking me.

What began as a simple thought, quickly grew into something beyond my control. When I was younger, I was what you would consider normal. So, I believed. The first time I touched myself, I was twelve. I overheard my teammate's mom, Mrs. Truitt, rambling over the phone about it to a girlfriend of hers. She had no idea I was listening to her speak about what she does in the bathroom during her showers. I never heard anyone talk about pleasuring themselves in the manner she did.

So, there I was in the bathtub, surrendering to a steady stream of warm water flowing down my body while the most intoxicating buildup brought me to my first orgasm. I had no idea what I had stumbled on that night, but I knew it was different yet conceivably sinful. So much so that I vowed never to do it again after that day. However, that was a miserable failure because I became unapologetically addicted to it, and I would not dare let anyone know. Especially my mother. She was always irrational when it came to taboo situations. So, it was my little secret. A secret that no one needed to know of, seeing as I was the intelligent and good girl who could never do anything wrong to everyone else.

I didn't get the attention from boys that the other girls received in high school. At first, I didn't mind it, but then, being normal became...boring. So eventually, I fed off it. I began to explore myself in ways the other girls weren't, seeking attention like a starving child. Mostly with older men. Some of them were twenty-five years my age. The more of them I encountered, the more my appetite grew. Going to bars was no longer enough because, at those spots, I had to have meaningless chats to seem normal when all I wanted was to be at their house or in a hotel room doing whatever I desired.

That's when I began to visit places most women would dare not go— dismissing any fears of danger. Places where prayers would never get answered, and exploring yourself, was all you could do. Some of them were not to my standards physically, but by then, I learned to detach myself from any feelings by remembering why I was there. Pleasure!

On the other side of town, between 27th street and 14th avenue, sits a black and white striped building. A unique massive structure with just two windows and a glass door. Some things happen in the building that goes beyond your imagination. Things that would have you question if you've experienced life. Fantasies, fetishes, all sorts of stuff go on in this place with people who all seem…normal. That's where I met him. A man who turned my world inside out and awakened the same spirit I encountered at the age of twelve. This man stood out amongst all the others I had ever been with, and what he did to me mentally, physically, and emotionally in just one night could not be considered ordinary. He became like some sort of drug— always leaving me to crave for his fix with a never-ending search for comfort.

The anticipation of us being together and needing to relieve each other made me want him more today than I did yesterday."

Madison takes a deep breath, shifts her body, and then takes me to the moment that has led her here.

"One night, while spending time with him, I felt like I was in complete control, yet I could not stop myself from allowing it to happen. I should have, though, because I probably wouldn't be sitting here. Indeed, I was tired. Tired of thinking, worshiping, and even fantasizing about him in a way that would be considered disturbing. It was to the point where deciphering between what was real and what wasn't had become almost impossible."

"It was a Sunday night, and by the time I stood at the doorstep of 511, the sky was dark, the streets were empty, and I was left entirely beyond myself. "I pulled into the driveway of a house on the corner of 41st and Robinson—just a few feet from the second stop sign. It's the red brick house on the block with a wooden door. That's what he told me. The wooden door was dented, with chipped gray paint and a brass-colored lock and doorknob, surprisingly in contrast to what I'd hoped to encounter once I was inside. But I knew it was too late to turn back. Besides, where would I go? Home? No. I couldn't do that. I had already driven nearly twenty-five miles across the county line to visit a man I barely knew anything about. The only thing I knew was that he was younger than me. His work required him to wear a suit and a tie. Oh, and there's that black leather bag with a decorative gold latch always hung on his shoulder. My guess is that he is an accountant. Or maybe a bank investor. Who knows? Beyond his pearly white smile and incredible physique, I didn't know much.

"Nevertheless, the moment of uncertainty was intriguing enough to place me on the doorstep of 511. I stood there for two minutes, waiting for the courage to knock on the door, but something kept holding me back. I wasn't sure what it was, but I could feel it all over my body. I even remember the time. 8:56 P.M. How could I forget? I had been waiting all day for that moment. Dr. Clarke, I was so close that I could hear him walking around inside—merely waiting for me to enter. There were so many questions circling in my head. What would happen once I walked through the door? Would there be any consequences to this encounter? Was it too late to turn around? Could I convince myself that night would be nothing more than a moment?

Then again, maybe I was reading too much into it. Perhaps we'd talk and share a few laughs over a drink or two. No, coffee. Drinks could cause clouded judgments, which would lead to uncontrollable situations. So, coffee it is. Yeah, I saw no harm in coffee.

"I took a deep breath, and with one foot closer to the door than the other, my right hand balled into a fist as my brittle knuckles finally knocked four times. Those four steady knocks turned me into a despairing woman, waiting on him to come to my rescue.

"*Click.*

"*Click.*

"*CLACK!*

"The door unlocked, and selfishly, time stopped, leaving me to endure a grueling wait all alone. I watched as the door opened to reveal him standing there. His face was masked with a smile obscured by a thick black beard. He had the eyes of a man I never wanted to cross, yet it didn't stop me from gazing into them. My heart fluttered, and with only anticipation keeping my feet planted to the ground, my body stiffened like a wet log, leaving me numb.

"'Glad you made it,' he said.

"I politely smiled as a response.

"'I was beginning to think you wouldn't show up.'

"His melodic voice carried chills down my spine whenever he

spoke.

"'Well, to tell you the truth, I almost didn't. But somehow, I'm here,' I replied, trying not to seem so eager as the muscles in my stomach involuntarily twitched.

"'Good,' he gazed into my eyes for a moment. 'Come in.'

"My feet felt like cold bricks with each step I took into his home, and I knew there was no turning back. He shut the door just as I entered the foyer, and quickly, I turned to him. He leaned against the door with a smile and folded his arms across his chest. His lips were delicate, smooth, and moist as he stood there, undressing me with his passionate brown eyes. His gaze upon my body was the kind that every woman secretly desired. It left me with disturbing thoughts and a void needing to be filled.

One second.

Two seconds.

Three seconds.

Four seconds…

"'You don't have a purse?' he broke the silence.

"'No. I don't,' I said. 'Why? Do I need one?'

"'Just an observation. It's kinda rare to see a woman without one. But then again, you're right. Why would you need it?'

"He smiled with intent as the silence once again became our guest. I turned away, and my eyes traveled around the room, desperately searching for the moment to indulge myself in the possibilities. Or perhaps a reason to leave.

"'You have a nice place.'

"'Thanks.'

"'So do you ever just—'

"My words were cut short when I turned and saw him taking off his shirt. At that moment, coffee was no longer an option.

"'You have no problem getting comfortable, do you?' I teased.

"'Why would you say that?' he asked. 'Is this an issue? Because I can always put my shirt back on.'

"It certainly didn't bother me in the way he may have suspected. He could have taken me right there, and I wouldn't have stopped him.

"'No! I'm just teasing you,' I said. 'Besides, this is your home.' I girlishly smiled. 'And your body is pretty nice.'

"Why I didn't stop at the smile, I'll never know. Your body is pretty nice? I still couldn't believe I said that. If I had to guess, I would say he was about six-foot-two and nearly two hundred pounds, with defining muscles surging down his shoulders, over his chest, and onto his flat stomach. The oil covering his body allowed the light to glisten off his skin like the sun setting over the waters. It reminded me of the times I'd sit on the shores of Lake Pontchartrain as a little girl.

"'Thank you. You look nice too,' he said.

"'If that were the case, you would have mentioned that the moment I walked in.'

"'Maybe it's not just your body that I was focused on.'

"I was putty in his hand, feeling like a little girl standing in the presence of her long-time crush. 'Right.'

"'But seriously, you do look great.'

"'Says the man wearing only blue pajama pants.' My words came out muttered as I focused on the outline of his dick resting between his legs.

"However, the thought did remain, why did I decide to wear this teal pleated skirt, which I got on sale, with this pink sleeveless blouse? I felt like such a vain sorority girl. I guess wearing anything too conservative might have screamed that I was dull and wearing something extravagant would have shown my eagerness. So, it was either wear this or show up on his doorstep with nothing underneath a Diane Von Furstenberg black pea coat.

"'So how was your day? Anything interesting? Say something,' I coyly asked.

"He chuckled and took a couple of steps closer. Oh, my goodness! It shifted to the left. His silk pajama pants left nothing to the imagination."

Soft inhale.

Soft exhale.

"'You're nervous, aren't you?' he said. 'I like it. It's like I get to see a side of you that others don't. But you don't have to be nervous with me.' He took a brief pause, smiled, and stepped closer. 'And to answer your question, my day was just another normal day, but now that you're here, I can end it on a better note.'

My right leg begins to fidget slightly as I listen to Madison go on with this story. I take a deep breath, hoping to subdue the urge that's starting to build. Then, I adjust my posture in my chair, crossing my legs left over right. Maybe that'll help.

"The more we stood in that foyer, the more I wanted to touch every inch of his body. But I had to control myself because that's not the woman I was.

"'Would you like a tour?' he asked. 'It's not much, and it's not in order at the moment, but so what?'

"'I don't mind. I'm your guest.'

"'Cool. Follow me then.'

His home stood as a testament to his impeccable taste, an embodiment of his enigmatic persona. It possessed an alluring charm, one that was a tranquil haven pulsating with a hint of passion. The open floor concept embraced a sense of serenity that easily invited me and made me feel safe. The pristine walls, dressed in pure white, held the weight of three massive abstract paintings, strategically positioned to adorn the house. A matte dark gray, like the shadows that whispered within, blanketed the wood-tiled flooring, harmonizing flawlessly with the rest of the meticulously curated space.

In the middle of the living room floor was a dark blue sofa commanded attention, anchoring the room with its luxury style. A white coffee table adorned with delicate golden accents stood as a testament to refined taste. An audacious mustard-hued accent chair, accompanied by a matching ottoman, exuded an air of boldness amidst the calculated precision. Everything in his place, the perfection of it all, prompted me to question his motives and secrets. I had never encountered a man so organized and perfect. It was enough for me to even question his sexuality.

"'And how was your day?'

"I trailed behind him, and as I went further into his home, I became more relaxed. It was strange, but something just felt…right. I can't explain it, but I felt I belonged there and nowhere else.

"'Uh, just another day. Woke up, went to work, got off. This. That. Blah, blah, blah. You can fill in the rest.'

"'Sounds like you need a drink.'

"'I don't drink so much, so I'll take your word for it.'

"The kitchen was large enough to host an episode of Iron Chef. Two ovens with a white granite island in the middle. Most women would die to have a kitchen like that. I mean, how was this man single? Or better yet why? Was it because he preferred a sporadic sexual lifestyle? Was he divorced? Or was he even single at all? There I was again, concerning myself with pointless questions.

"'You mind if I ask you something?' I said.

"'Sure. Go ahead.'

"'How old are you?'

"That's not the question I wanted to ask, but it's the one that came out. If I had to guess, I would say he was thirty. Thirty-two at most.

Then again, it didn't matter anyway. I was already deep within the comfort of his home. He paused, covered his face, and sighed."

"'Of all the questions you could ask to get you more comfortable, that's the one you chose?'

"'Hey, it's a simple question.'

"'Well then, let's just say I'm old enough.'

"Then, he approached me and asked if I wanted red or white wine, and when I asked if the wine was the only option, he told me there was water or vodka. We both laughed.

"'Red wine will be fine. Thank you.'

"He poured us a glass of wine. Mine first, and then his. Next, he handed me my drink and tapped his glass against mine before we took a sip, gazing into each other's eyes as we did so. The wine, smooth and sharp, traveled through me and touched parts that made my temperature rise.

"'This is good. What is it?' I inquired.

"'Castelvero Barbera. 2004. A friend of mine picked it up for me in Italy. I'm not a wine connoisseur or anything, but I know what tastes good and what doesn't.'

"'And tonight is the night you decided to open it?' I asked.

"'Special occasion.'

"I smiled nervously. Then, he placed his glass on the counter and stepped closer, closing the space between us. I could feel his cool breath with a hint of red wine.

"'It's my turn to ask a question,' he said.

"I took a deep gulp of air and braced myself. I can't explain why, but he had an indescribable hold on me. It was almost as if he had his foot stuck on the peddle of my self-control, steering my worst thoughts and behavior.

"'Sure. Ask away.'

"'What did you think was going to happen once you walked through my door?'

"'I didn't think it all the way through. So, whatever happens, I guess it just happens.'

"'Well, when you say it like that,' he leaned in, biting his lower lip, and gazing into my eyes. 'Can I have you now?'

"My breathing softened, and my body squirmed from the thought of him being inside me. He couldn't tell, but I felt a rush starting to occur between my thighs and then spreading throughout my entire body. I was connected to him in a way I shouldn't have been, and there was no point in hiding it anymore. I wanted him, and he wanted me.

Without saying a word, he grabbed hold of my left hand and pulled me in tight. I closed my eyes.

"'No! I want you to look at me,' he demanded.

"I opened my eyes at once and felt an intense rush flowing through my body as his demeanor soothed my sexual spirit. *Stay calm, girl*, I whispered internally to the place where I needed to feel him the most. I wanted him so bad that my insides were clenching without anything to grip onto. For him, that might have been another night. However, for me, I wanted it to be a night where I could fully explore every thought I've ever had about a man—even beyond all my other experiences. I had no idea what was happening, but I was not that woman who walked through that front door. There's no way that woman would have those feelings for a man she barely knew. She also wouldn't have—"

6:22 P.M.

"Dr. Clarke?" A voice calls my name.

I inhale deeply, hoping to soothe the feeling swarming throughout my body as I try to control my nerves. I can even feel the chills forming over my hypersensitive skin—especially around my neck. Not only that, but there's also a feeling of emptiness yearning to be filled between my legs. Madison's encounter with this man started to get the best of me.

"Dr. Clarke, are you in there?"

I quickly snap out of it, turning my head to the door where Rachel, my secretary, has her head poked into the room with her braided hair covering half her face. What the hell is she doing?

"Rachel, what is it? my voice quivers. "I'm busy."

"Sorry, Dr. Clarke. I didn't realize you were still here."

Rachel looks at me with puzzled eyes, but her stare feels like she just caught me naked with my fingers between my legs. We then turn to Madison, and for a moment, there's a silence that goes beyond acceptable. I hate silence.

"Rachel," I interject. "Is there something else I can help you with?"

"Oh, no. I'm sorry about that." Rachel's eyes squeeze together as she steps back and shuts the door.

"I apologize. I can assure you it won't happen again."

"It's fine. You want me to continue?" Madison asks.

What? There's more? It's bad enough I'm shattered by impulsive thoughts, but now she wants me to endure more of it? Everything about Madison that I am not makes me cringe with jealousy. And as I sit here wondering why she's even here in my office, it becomes more apparent that no one will understand Madison as I do, and yet I barely understand her at all.

CHAPTER 2

7:00 A.M.

I LIE IN BED, my eyes tightly shut, and face pressed against the satin pillow, attempting to drown out the relentless barks of Duke, the neighbor's dog. Each bark resonates with a profound sense of loneliness and desperation, an insistent cry for attention. I understand this yearning all too well, for dogs are not so different from us. Like humans, they strive for connection, resorting to extraordinary measures to be seen, acknowledged, and loved. It is our shared desire for validation that defines our very humanity.

Dr. Frank Lanier, my colleague, insists that the longing for acceptance arises from a failure to understand one's purpose in life. I cannot help but agree. The treacherous path of losing oneself becomes all too tempting when we are drifting through life, unsure of our own identity or the desires that stir within us.

Those who know me often consider me insane because of my resilient approach to being perfect. Sometimes I think my colleagues do too. It doesn't matter, though, because sanity is a system built to make sense to others, and I'm not like them. I am something different. While most people think in questions, my thoughts are full of answers. I am not someone who subscribes to the contemporary views of what is considered normal. If it's raining, I'd rather risk getting wet by finding out for myself than allowing someone to offer me an umbrella before I step outside.

Chewing my fingers off would be better than walking blindly in the fears of others. My logical sense of reality tiptoes within the line of sanity, while my unwavering behavior refuses to accept anything less. I am a woman, yet I am something different.

At last, I turn over on my back. My eyes remain closed as a tingling sensation rush throughout my body and lingers there for a moment too long. It's painless, but it feels like a million ants crawling inside of me and then slowly disappearing into the pit of my stomach. It's not the first time I've felt this strange feeling. In fact, for the past few weeks, it has covered me like a warm fur coat during the winter. Almost as if my body wants me to refill my soul with something that brings me purpose, but what could that be? This feeling has nothing to do with that time of the month because I've never felt this before. Nor is it any sort of medical issue. A recent visit to Dr. Chandler's office would confirm that. So, it must be something else. But what?

My college professor, Dr. Gonzalez, once stated that we instinctively know the day we will die because our lives mysteriously feel unfamiliar. As the explainable becomes inexplicable, normality seems surreal. Some of us choose to ignore all the signs that tell us that today, at any moment, we will die. Dr. Gonzalez described this as a cognitive aspect of thanatology. I always wondered if he was right. If he is, I hope today isn't the day I find out.

BEEP! BEEP! BEEP!

7:10 A.M.

The sound of my alarm clock goes off, but I remain in bed, drifting to a memory. The beeping fades to an eerily unnatural silence the further into the memory I wander off. This is what happens when you're awake for too long with your eyes shut. You begin to imagine things you never thought you could, and sometimes…things you shouldn't.

"Good morning, beautiful." Daniel pops in, carrying a breakfast tray—omelet, croissant, and a glass of apple juice.

"Daniel?" My voice is low and groggy.

"Here, I made this for you."

I sit up and look into his brown eyes, smiling over the breakfast Daniel has prepared for me. No woman could love a man more than I love Daniel. He isn't the tall, flashy, and suave guy that most women dream of finding, nor is he the type of man you'd see leaving the gym on his way to Nordstrom. He's a caring, intellectual, and charming man that wakes the pure side of me, the best side, all the parts of myself that require love and care. We're not married, but everything about us feels like we are. Or maybe that's just something I tell myself to justify my thoughts. I met Daniel at a time in my life when I had given up on the thought of love. In the darkness of this world, he came walking through with a flashlight. There I was, having lunch at my favorite restaurant when he came strolling in. We immediately noticed each other, but it wasn't anything more than a simple head nod and smile. However, I'll admit, I felt a tingle for a moment. But then he disappeared, returning ten minutes later with his drink and food. Rotisserie chicken, steamed vegetables, and warm potato salad. That's what he had on his plate. I still remember him sitting in front of me, eating his food as if he and I came to the restaurant together. He took a bite of his food, looked me in the eyes, and said…

"You want some? It's pretty good."

I chuckled, and I couldn't stop smiling. Yet, this man's sudden appearance left me torn. On the one hand, it was impressive of him to insert himself into my alone time, where I could reflect and enjoy my food. Then again, I couldn't help but think he'd be the same as all the others I have encountered. The type of man who would rather waste time creating a false sense of reality that even they couldn't believe in. When in fact, they could just be themselves. However, he wasn't like them. He was faithful to himself, genuine, and marched to the beat of his own drums.

"No, thank you. I'm good. My food should be out soon." I replied.

"Blackberry pineapple sidecar?" The female waiter said as she handed over the glass to me.

"Um…thank you," I answered her and then turned to him, blushing more than I should have. "How'd you know?"

"Well, during lunch hours, wine tells me you'd be the type to ask others random personal questions. And you don't mind sharing a few of your secrets, too. However, we both know that isn't you."

"You're right about that."

"Of course, I am. You're eating lunch alone. Secondly, a classic Martini says you are mysterious, clever, and know how to get your attention. That could be true of you during the nights, but right now…I doubt it."

"Go on…" I smiled.

"So that leaves us with the fun and interesting drinks. Like a blackberry pineapple sidecar. A drink that says you like to have expert knowledge talks on deep subjects, and you are the kind of woman everyone asks for help cause you're so good at giving advice." He then smiled and took another bite of the chicken.

"Either I'm that obvious, or you're that good."

"Both."

He smiled and introduced himself. Very confident, open, and straightforward. It was raw and unexpected. He even explained how he didn't feel comfortable seeing me sit alone for lunch. I told him this was nothing new for me, and he replied by saying…

"Just because you're used to it doesn't mean you have to be used to it."

His assertiveness, the look in his eyes, and the way he spoke caught me off guard. From that moment, he and I sat at the table on a Wednesday afternoon, talking and laughing for nearly three hours. We had cut our workday short to spend the rest of the day together. 10:41 P.M. That was the time when he and I finally went our separate ways. From eating lunch to bar hopping and then to dinner—we had developed something in just nine hours that I had never done with anyone else in my thirty-six years. That was two years ago.

"Let me know what you think. I tried something new." He places a piece of the omelet in my mouth and waits for my response. "So, do you like it?" he asks as his brown eyes twinkle.

"Yes. I love it. Thank you."

"You're not just saying that, right?"

"No. I mean it. You did a great job."

"Okay. Good." His chiseled jaw twitches to a pleasant smile.

Suddenly, his phone vibrates from his pocket, and just like that, his smile disappears. He looks up at me, smirks, and then quickly glances down at his screen. I'm not even sure he saw who was calling. That's strange.

"I need to get going." Daniel leans in, firmly wraps his arms around me, and kisses me on my forehead. Kindly, I plant my face in his chest. God, even his heartbeat is in rhythm with mine.

BEEP! BEEP! BEEP!

Daniel exits just as the harsh sound of the alarm clock goes off, and again, I silence it at once. This time, I climb out of bed, slip into a pair of slippers next to the nightstand, and wait. Duke continues to bark, but as frustrating as the bark may be, the faint sound of running water coming from the bathroom is what has my attention. Daniel must have left it running. He usually does this when he's in a hurry.

The moment I open the bathroom door, a thick fog of steam whooshes by as if it were waiting on me. I turn the water off, step out of my nightwear, and then walk over to the wall-mounted mirror that hangs above the vanity. It's a mirror that I seldomly look into because it can be deceiving, and it has a way of showing me parts of myself that I tend to ignore. Instead of noticing everything I love about the woman in the mirror, I tend to focus on the things I don't. That feeling of inadequacy. Blemishes. Lack of confidence. Anything that reminds me of the things that I despise in others.

The mirror is foggy, so I can't see enough of her to say she looks the same today. Those sad, warm brown eyes are familiar, and she could certainly use some rest, judging by the dark circles forming beneath her eyes. Doing something with her hair wouldn't be a bad idea either. Lord knows she's outgrown her short brown hair rich with shades only time can bring. Not to mention her eyebrows aren't doing much for her cheekbones either. Yet, none of this explains why the woman in the mirror looks like a stranger.

Shit!

That tingling sensation runs throughout my body like a free-for-all track meet once again. This time, it's sharp and pulsating, starting in my pelvis and seamlessly rushing to my breast. God, I hope today isn't the day that I die. There's so much that I need to get done.

8:24 A.M.

According to my watch, I have seventeen minutes before my first session. That's enough time to grab a cup of caramel macchiato with a hint of almond extract and watch the people walk up and down Second Avenue. That's all I do most mornings. Stand outside the massive forty-seven-story building, with my cup in hand, and stare at people with a life, wondering what it's like to be them— Not all, but some.

On Wednesday, I watched a young couple, holding hands, walk down the avenue without a care in the world. Mondays are typically the days I see this couple, and I notice something different about them every time. For the average person, the couple would appear to be perfect. However, that day, it was evident that the man loved the woman more than she loved him. I could tell by their meek interaction. He was sweet and attentive to her, like a happy puppy. Meanwhile, she seemed more occupied with the people walking around and posters hanging on the wall than noticing all the attention thrown her way. I watched them come to a stop at a bakery on the corner of Second and Third Avenue. That's where she works. Before she walked in, he pulled her in and gave her a long, loving kiss. Soon after they pulled away, she quickly looked left, right, and then back at him with a forged smile. Without saying another word, she walked into the bakery. He waited a moment, hoping she'd turn around for another kiss, but she never did.

On Thursday, a woman with long red hair, a petite frame, and the eyes of the devil came walking down the avenue. I don't know her name, so I call her Bridgette. There's nothing special about the woman, but she's someone I admire and don't know why. Every Thursday, at the same time, I can expect to see Bridgette, and when I do, I notice something about her that makes me consider everything about myself. From how she dresses to the way she glides down the street in long strides with her shoulders back to the ocean— always so poised and graceful. Every time she walks by, she stops in front of the mirrored building and stares at her reflection. Some might see her and think she's a self-absorbed narcissist. However, I see someone attempting to forge a persona that everyone she comes across that day would love to meet again tomorrow. We all do it. So, why not Bridgette?

Last Friday was all about the elites. That's what I like to call them.

They're always on the move, swarming with confidence, and dressed as if they stepped out of a Vogue magazine. It's almost as if they see themselves as someone chosen by a higher power to be some sort of false god. Most of them believe their status in life will excuse them from any sin. Therefore, they live their lives as such. Take advantage of the less fortunate. Waste funds and resources for personal gains. Flirt with everyone that comes their way. They live in their little bubble with a few others they can control. Despite all that, I know the truth. And the truth is that while they may appear superior, they all feel inadequate, masking the issues that make them feel secretly insecure. That false sense of reality and lack of humility takes away their ability to tell a gift from heaven from the bribery of hell. It's a shame, and it's sad. Yet, and still…I envy them.

8:31 A.M.

Now, this is interesting. A man with captivating features wearing denim jeans, a dark shirt, and a yellow hard hat crosses the street ahead. His African roots are chiseled into his face and carved from granite. He waves, and like a high school girl, I offer a dry smile and turn away. Luckily, my phone rings just in time. It's Ms. Chapman. A forty-four-year-old client of mine who's been married three times and is now working on her fourth. However, that's not why she's calling. It's her fear of dying that makes her my client. Simply put… she's a chronic hypochondriac.

"Good morning, Ms. Chapman. How may I help you?"

Ms. Chapman begins to ramble about a visit to her nutritionist, but as she does, my attention drifts to a woman standing at the front of the mirrored building. Her cheekbones are fierce, her skin is golden, and her pecan-shaped hazel eyes show no emotion. There's a brief flash of her inability to fully recognize herself before the image matches the one in her head. Immediately, I'm taken away by her natural look and glossy black hair pulled back into a ponytail. We're the same height, but she's a bit slender. Even beneath her skinny denim jeans, brown hipster jacket, and white v-cut shirt, I can see how perfect her body is. The woman appears out of nowhere with a beauty that no other can compete with, and at that moment, I begin to go through all her lies, truths, and secrets as she stares at her reflection in the mirrored window. No one else notices the woman as I have, but I feel like—

"Dr. Clarke? You still there?" Ms. Chapman snatches my attention from the woman at once.

"Yes, Ms. Chapman. I'm still here."

Ms. Chapman doesn't skip a beat as she continues to ramble on. Too bad for her. My attention remains on the woman. The woman is nothing like the others I've seen walk past the mirrored building. With the others, I saw a struggle between the woman they are and the woman they want to be. But not with her. She's exactly who she wants to be with no excuse. I can tell this simply by looking into her mysterious eyes.

Then, she turns and looks at me, and for a moment, her stare feels like an act of violence, causing my heart to skip a beat or two and then erratically speed up. I'm not afraid, but how the woman looks at me makes my stomach knot up.

"Excuse me, ma'am," a man's voice calls out.

I turn around and look into the eyes of a vagrant man whose face resembles misery and whose breath smells like tobacco and rum. Before he says anything, I quickly disclose that I have no cash.

"That's okay. I just want the time," the vagrant man says.

The time?! Why would a man in such a condition be so concerned with time?

"8:33," I reply, puzzled.

The vagrant man nods with a smile and then walks off, pushing a cart full of trash.

Skerrrt!!

The sound of rubber tires screech against the pavement of Second Avenue, and immediately, I turn my head to a black Range Rover parked along the curb. Directly across from the mirrored building. The car door opens, and out steps a distinguished gentleman who forces time to stop. My eyebrow raises in curiosity, my mouth becomes dry as it's left open for too long, and my brain shuts down for a moment. If it were anyone else, I would turn away, but with him, it feels different. He has me drawn to him in some strange way that I cannot explain.

Lord, have mercy!

He has the skin of my father but much smoother. It's not just one feature about the man that makes him unique, but his ecstatic brown eyes, which tell a story I am desperate to read, do come close. With a firmly built body like a soldier, he is undeniably handsome. His hair is neatly low cut, matching his brown eyes perfectly. Where he walks, the wind flows, and where he breathes, the trees sway to his gentle breath. If it weren't for the swarming in my stomach, I would not have believed this moment was real.

"…and yesterday was no different. I think I ought to come by…" Ms. Chapman continues.

A charcoal gray suit, a white shirt with a racy blue tie, and brown oxfords sure do look good on the distinguished man. I'll call him Derek. Yeah, he seems like a Derek.

Oh crap!

He's coming my way. I wonder if he'll notice me. They rarely do. So, I bask in his presence and gaze freely at every step he takes. Besides, he's a stranger—a stranger with kindness in his faint smile and a tender soul that shines through his eyes. Like Daniel, I can tell he's also an honest man with no motives or hidden agenda. There's something about the man that reminds me of my better self. Never have I stared at a man in the manner I am doing now. It's innocent, but a small part of me feels ashamed. The sad part is that I still can't turn away.

He's headed into the mirrored building when suddenly, he turns to me, grins, and kindly tilts his head up.

Shit!

He caught me staring. Not that it matters, but I don't want him thinking I admire him that way. My hands slightly raise to an awkward wave. What was that? I could have at least smiled. My mother told me to always smile because nobody wants to be with a woman who doesn't.

The man strides towards the double glass door, his steps purposeful. Just before entering, he halts, leaning into the woman standing before the mirrored window. Their proximity is unnerving, as their eyes lock in a silent exchange. A smile grace her lips, coupled with a seductive flutter of her lashes. It is evident that this is not their first encounter. Perhaps such a potent connection comes effortlessly between a woman of her allure and a man of his intrigue.

RING!

Once again, my phone rings and swiftly snatches me away from this mortifying moment. I was so focused on my disturbing thoughts that I accidentally ended my call with Ms. Chapman.

"Sorry about that, Ms. Chapman…" I recover.

"Good morning, Dr. Clarke. It's Rachel."

Rachel? Wow. Did I lose myself in my thoughts of the distinguished gentleman? What was I thinking?

"Sorry about that, Rachel. Morning. How may I help you?"

"I was checking to see what time you'd be in today. Angela Adams is here to see you."

"Really? She's early, isn't she?" I glance down at my watch. Oh shit! "Rachel, I'm on my way up now."

8:56 A.M.

Great! Now I won't even have time to grab my caramel macchiato. I dash to the elevator and repeatedly push the button, hoping the doors will open quicker. Nothing happens. Come on, hurry up. Why would this be happening to me on the day I'm running late?

Ding!

The doors finally open nearly a minute later, and I promptly step into the wide elevator with steel walls and charcoal marble flooring. I'm alone, headed up to the seventh floor. Then, a deep dulcet voice catches my attention just as the doors close.

"Hold the door!" the voice without a face demand.

My left arm quickly slips between the door, and *Oh my God*—it's him! Derek— the distinguished gentleman. It's just he and I, alone, in this elevator. My ability to speak forsakes me as my stomach flutters with butterflies. I can even feel the vibration of my heart thumping against my chest like a gong. Why is he here? Why wouldn't he be, Andrea? Well, what do I do now? He's so much more desirable up close. From his jaw structure to his broad neck, he is worth every immoral thought that comes to mind. My heart hammers away at my chest, and although it's a struggle, I keep my composure steady.

On top of everything, I can't help but think that my hair is a mess. Or maybe I have something stuck in my teeth. I'm sure there's a stain somewhere on my clothes that only I can't see. Did I put on deodorant this morning? Please let someone else walk in to ease the unsettling feeling that has taken over me.

"Thank you for holding the door," he politely says.

Deep inhale.

I suppress the fear of fumbling over my words by responding with silence. He reaches past me and presses the sixteenth-floor button. His leather oak scent tingles my senses and holds me in a place of comfort, where it's acceptable to be who I truly am. I could smell on him forever.

The door closes, and the silence embraces us like lovers in the night. Where I move, the silence follows—like my personal shadow. Quietly, I sigh, realizing that my prayer has gone unanswered. It's just him and me. Alone! No one else. Just him…and me.

Soft exhale.

"It's going to be a great day, huh?" he says.

I nod my head. But I doubt he notices, seeing how I am standing behind him. The elevator pulls up from the ground level, and my heart jumps to my throat, threatening to leap out.

"You okay?" he asks without turning.

Once again, I nod my head. But this time, I step back and firmly press my back against the wall.

Third Floor…

The man casually fixes his suit jacket and tie off the blurry reflection that the steel wall provides. I wish the elevator would hurry the hell up. What floor is he getting off again? Sixteenth-floor, Andrea. That's right—the sixteenth floor.

He turns to me, smiles chivalrously, and then turns away. I wish this elevator door would open right now. Come on! I hate silence. It's disturbing and causes me to have meaningless thoughts that bond me to the moment. Like right now, I can only imagine what type of man Derek might be. Is he the emotionally unavailable man who never shows up and is always full of excuses? Perhaps he's the type that loves to talk about himself because that's the only thing that matters to him. No. He doesn't seem like that type. He's much too calm and focused for that. I don't know, but whatever the case may be, he's cast a spell on me, and now I can even envision him doing things to me that he shouldn't be doing. Thoughts of him handling and kissing my body—especially in the places I desire to be touched the most. His virile hands embrace me while he squeezes and kisses areas of my body worth pleasing, starting from my shoulders down to my inner thighs. I can practically feel his hands, and it's making me feel quite uncomfortable. He's a biter too.

He bites on my collarbone.
He bites on my arms.
He bites. I moan.
Fourth Floor…

Oh shit! Daniel! Yes. How could I have forgotten about Daniel?

"I guess you didn't hear me when I asked if you were okay," he says as he turns his attention to me again.

"Me? Yeah. I'm fine."

His eyes pierce right through me, but like a Royal Guard, I make no eye contact. It doesn't matter anyway because my eyes drift to his muscular ass that seems to defy gravity. It looks so firm and round. Touching it would probably be giving my hand a massage. Dammit, Andrea! Stop it!

Fifth Floor…

"Okay. That's good to know. Just wanted to make sure."

Why is this elevator moving so slowly? I need to think about something else to keep my mind distracted. Think about something else! Think about something else! Think about…our lips passionately press against each other as our tongues intertwine. No! Not that. I wonder what cologne he's wearing right now because it smells so—

Ding!

At last, the elevator comes to a stop on the seventh floor. So desperate to escape, I slip by the man before the doors even fully open.

However, I must quickly gather myself, seeing how Rachel's desk sits directly across from the elevator. I can't let her see me looking flustered.

"Have a good day, Andrea." The distinguished gentleman murmurs.

I promptly turn to him, catching a glimpse of his smile as he disappears behind the closing doors. He knows my name? And the way he said it didn't sound platonic or flirtatious. It sounded more… endearing. As if he knows who I am…

CHAPTER 3

4:09 P.M.

I PATIENTLY SIT in my chair, facing a pale-skinned woman clad in a long blue sleeve shirt with gray sweatpants that is unflattering to her skinny frame. She looks like a dead body sitting on the off-white sofa with her shoulders slumped and her indigo ocean blue eyes cast down at her Max Mara loafers. She never has on makeup, but even if she did, it would be gone from all the tears. Judging from the heavy bags under her blood-shot eyes, chapped lips, and brown messy hair that is blown out and dry, this session is long overdue. Yet, and still, I think today would be considered a good day for Mrs. Salters. It's a good thing she's my last client of the day.

"How are you feeling, Mrs. Salters?" I ask.

Mrs. Salters adjusts her full-rimmed glasses that are too big for her face and looks up at me, lips trembling as if she's fighting the urge to cry.

"May I?" Mrs. Salters reaches for the box of Kleenex.

"Yes. Of course."

Finally, she looks up at me, takes a tissue and then slowly looks away. Her eyes roam the room, waiting for the moment where she can let it all out. This is what she does during every session.

Three years ago, Mrs. Salters met the love of her life—Paul Salters. Four months into their relationship, Paul decided to make an honest woman out of Mariah. Six months after their wedding, Mrs. Salters was struck in the back by a semi-truck while driving on I-95, causing her to flip several times across the highway. After ten grueling hours of surgery and a two-day coma, she survived the horrific accident. However, if it were up to Mrs. Salters, she would have rather died that day.

The operation left Mrs. Salters in bad shape. Both mentally and physically. Bad hip, painful scars all over her body, and no type of confidence. If that weren't bad enough, Mrs. Salters had to have her bladder removed, leaving her with an ostomy bag attached to an opening in her abdomen. Now, in the mind of her husband, Mrs. Salters is as worthless as a knife cutting water.

Things changed for Mrs. Salters once she left the hospital. Her husband became aggressive and less affectionate, and as the passion between them died, his love for control and power grew. No longer did he cherish her company because he was busy spending time doing God knows what. She never could say for sure what he was up to, but whatever it was, Mr. Salters didn't want her knowing about it. According to Mrs. Salters, it has to be another woman. That's the only thing that would make sense to her.

The times Mr. Salters did spend with Mrs. Salters would always turn into a fight, ending with his hands squeezed around her throat or palms swinging across her face. Mrs. Salters is convinced that if her own husband didn't look at her in a way that made her feel validated, then it's possible that no man would ever. By the time she realized that she simply needed to validate herself, Mrs. Salters had slept with four different men—all of whom left her still coveting that love from her husband. That's according to Mrs. Salters. So, as a result, she's in my office, in this moment, sitting across from me.

"Mrs. Salters?"

"Yes, Dr. Clarke?"

"So…how about we get started?" I ask in a warm and sympathetic tone.

She blows into the tissue, and then stares up at the ceiling. The walls begin to close on me as I dreadfully wait for her to say something. Anything. Had it not been for the large window looking out to the city, I would have lost my mind by now. The window often helps me to deal with the paralyzing silence and think beyond the scope of what I am used to. Sometimes, I even turn to the window and see my reflection, but rarely is it the person that others see.

I wait…

And wait…

"How about you start by telling me how you feel? Is there anything new since the last time we spoke?"

"No. Nothing at all. I was beginning to see a light at the end of the tunnel, but now I'm just tired and frustrated."

Her arms are folded across her flat chest as her left leg begins to shake uncontrollably. This is a sign that she is isolating herself to the dark corner of her mind. A gloomy place with no smell, no taste, and absolutely nothing to cling onto.

"Well, you look much better today."

"I do?" Her voice perks up and her leg stops shaking.

Looks like that helped.

"Yes. So, you should feel good about that."

She nods her head and then looks away for about two seconds…

One second.

Two seconds.

She turns back to me with her blue polished fingernails tapping against each other. In a quiet room, the sound can be as demoralizing as the endless drips from a leaky faucet. Then, she takes a deep breath and shields her face with an unusual smile. Some wouldn't even know she was smiling at all, but after all the sessions, I've come to finally identify it as one.

"Mariah…"

Mrs. Salter looks up at me, takes a deep breath, and begins to vent about how she feels alone and complacent in her non-existent world. But as Mrs. Salters speaks, my thoughts spontaneously drift to images of the distinguished gentleman from this morning. I can't help but wonder how he knows my name. Maybe I met him before, and I foolishly forgot? I wish that were the case because that would explain these random thoughts. Thoughts of the man kissing the back of my legs—directly behind my knee in a spot where I never knew such a feeling existed. It's like I can feel it. So much so, my nipples harden from the thought of it. Whew! It's a good thing that I have on this cashmere sweater, or else Mrs. Salters might notice. Wait! What am I doing? I shouldn't be thinking about this right now. I need to get a hold of myself and stop fantasizing about this stranger.

"…it's like no matter what I do, I can't get over that feeling. I know it's something that I need to work on, but I just can't seem to…" Mrs. Salters cries.

Oh my! Now, in my mind, his warm tongue brushes against my inner left thigh, making its way to the spot where I'm entirely moist. Stop it, Andrea! I internally scold. Great! Now, there's an increasing dampness building between my legs to the point of frustration. I shouldn't be thinking about any of this, but here I am, thinking about only my complete desire to be filled. Immediately, I cross my legs, right over left, and squeeze tight, hoping to ease some of the tension that's building. Hell, I need to take my mind away from these thoughts and onto something of substance. *Hmm…I wonder what Daniel is up to right now.*

"And I thought about killing my husband," Mrs. Salters unexpectedly blurts out.

Wait! What the fuck! Did I hear that correctly? My brain stumbles as I try to comprehend what I just heard from Mrs. Salters' mouth.

"Excuse me?" I reply, recovering from my immoral thoughts.

"I'm not proud of it, but for the first time, I thought about killing him. And for some reason, it keeps playing in my mind repeatedly. Sometimes I can vividly see it."

"This is, um…not what I expected Mariah. What makes you say that?"

"I'm not sure. Maybe because Paul doesn't want me anymore? I don't know what else to do. I mean, I come home, yet I never feel like it's my home. Yes, saying I want to kill him sounds extreme, but honestly, that's the only thing on my mind. What would you do if the man you loved suddenly didn't want you anymore, Dr. Clarke?"

I never thought about what I would do if the love I had for Daniel wasn't mirrored the same way. Would I try to work it out? Leave him alone? Or perhaps, be left in the same position as Mrs. Salters? Love can be painful just as much as it can be precious and delicate, and there's no telling when you'll face either emotion.

"Mariah, let me first say this. I know it wasn't easy for you to say that, but it takes bravery to bring your thoughts to these issues."

"Yet the rewards never seem to return the favor." She covers her face.

Just when I thought this session was going to be a typical sixty minutes, she goes and throws a curveball my way. Displaying signs of being callous or lacking empathy is unlike Mrs. Salters. Also, she's never shown any signs of violence, and I can tell by the look in her eyes that this is not a random thought. The burning hard stare of scorn with no trace of tears is how I know. It's also the exact look I saw in my mother's eyes as a young girl on many nights.

"Well, let's talk about that. Can you explain why you've been feeling this way?"

Mrs. Salters shrugs and then looks at me with a face of utter nonchalance. It's as if she were merely thinking about what she was going to cook for dinner. Not only does Ms. Salters explain the rationale behind killing her husband, but she also gives me details of how she would execute her plans—even considering how she'd get away with it too. There is a moment when my face registers shock, and there's nothing I can do to hide it. Andrea! You're a professional. Act like it. Yes, I must get ahold of myself before Mrs. Salters notices.

"I see. And if I were to ask you how likely are you to carry out this idea, what would you say?"

Mrs. Salters shrugs her shoulders once again and then pauses for a moment. Suddenly, a grin sneaks onto her face and stretches from one side to the other. Is she smiling? She hardly ever does that unless she's reached a breakthrough, or she stumbles upon a moment of clarity. Fuck! I'll certainly be here longer than I anticipated. Then again, I could call the police, but that would also involve more of my time and a lot of paperwork. I'll just hear what Mrs. Salters has to say before I take on my duty to warn.

That's when she tells me everything. According to Mrs. Salters, her husband's death would be slow and painful. That's what she desires. She'd kill him outside their home on a Saturday night, is what she tells me. I stare into those blue eyes as my heart falls silent, not because of what she says but how she says it. Cold, stern, and very matter-of-factly. Indeed, this is no random thought. That much I can tell. Mrs. Salters describes how she would add a small amount of temazepam into his drink to get him woozy. She claims that part would be easy because her husband has the same drink every Saturday afternoon—rum and ginger ale. I'm no expert in how to murder someone, but for a man of Mr. Salters' stature, Mariah would need a lot of temazepam to get the result she's looking to obtain. Perhaps, mixing it with diazepam would be a better choice for Mrs. Salters, seeing as diazepam helps with relaxing and sleeping. Not only that, but it's also more of the common benzodiazepine drugs out there. I would never tell Mrs. Salters this, but I must admit that the thought of knowing this information is exceptionally provocative.

Mrs. Salters then says she would send him to the store to buy brown sugar for the sweet potato pie he loves so much. The store is precisely twelve minutes away. That's just enough time because it would take the drug seven minutes to settle in. Once that happened, Mrs. Salters says her husband would pass out behind the steering wheel and crash in the middle of Highway 826.

The more details Mrs. Salters offers, the further I fall into my thoughts. So much so that I begin to envision Mrs. Salters' thoughts playing out in my head, and although it's her words, it's me that I see. It's strange. I don't feel concerned or frightened. Instead, I am intrigued and full of adrenaline. It tingles in me like electrical sparks on the way to my fingertips and toes. I can even feel my heart racing from the anticipation of what she will do next.

"That's what I would do, Dr. Clarke."

There is no trace of tears in Mrs. Salters' cold and narrow eyes as she continues her story. She tells me that she would hop in her car and follow Mr. Salters because if he didn't die during the crash for some reason, she'd want to finish him off herself. Her voice is even colder as she reveals how she would hop in the back seat of his car, wrap a belt around his neck, and pull back as tight as she could until he was no longer breathing. The frozen gaze in her eyes complements her slow breathing, and as she sits across from me on the white sofa, I can't help but think that those details aren't just a plan…but perhaps it's a memory.

"What are you thinking, Dr. Clarke?"

The room is rather cold, but I'm beginning to sweat throughout parts of my body where I don't usually sweat. Am I nervous? Eager? Or maybe the mixture of the two. Why am I so fascinated by Mrs. Salters' thoughts? I shouldn't be. Everything about this type of situation should have me worried and telling her all the things I'm supposed to. Validating her emotions and expressing my genuine concerns. Or perhaps, seeking further help. Instead, my body is heating up from the anticipation. For goodness sake, I no longer hear sounds outside the large window— just heartbeats and the ticking of a clock. Every natural body movement I possess is left on hold. However, I must get a hold of myself, remain calm, and carefully consider my next move. On the one hand, I can dig deeper and explore how Mrs. Salters fell to this point, but then on the other, I could warn the police. That would mean I have to decide between my job and her trust.

"So, how would you feel if it happened? Your husband dying." I ask.

"I'm not sure. I guess I'd eventually be okay with it. Maybe."

There's something that Mrs. Salters is not telling me. The question is, do I want to know what that something is?

"Why maybe?"

"Because…I don't know where that would leave me mentally and emotionally. But I doubt I could feel any worse than I do now."

Whew! That I can work with because at least it sounds like it's just a desired thought and not a memory. On the other hand, how could someone so fragile and petite as Mrs. Salters process a scenario with no hint of distress or hurt in her eyes?

"I'm worried about you, Mariah."

"I appreciate that, but that's nothing new, Dr. Clarke."

"I know, but this time it's more concerning. This is unlike you to have these types of thoughts. And so suddenly too. Last week there was no talk of this."

"Yeah, well, some people can do that to others."

"Do what?"

"Reveal a side of themselves they never knew about."

Mrs. Salters sits motionless, unaware of time passing us by as she stares into an empty void. I always knew she had pain inside, but now it's visible on her face as well.

"Well, Dr. Clarke, I should get going now."

Now is the time to make the decision, Andrea. What are you going to do? Let her go and wait to find out if she kills her husband? Or initiate an involuntary hospitalization and possibly inform her husband or the police? But God, am I intrigued by what she will do more than I am genuinely concerned.

"Mariah…you should come back in on Monday. I think it would help."

Her shoulders slump over, her lip quivers, and her eyes glimmer with a teary gaze. Then, she sighs and looks away.

One second…

Two seconds.

She turns back to me like clockwork and walks to the door. And just before she exits…

"I'm fine, Dr. Clarke. I'm going to leave town for a couple of weeks. I'll let you know when I get back."

Mrs. Salters exits with her shoulders dragging and a dry look coating her face. Something about this isn't right, and I hope I don't regret allowing her to leave.

5:22 P.M.

By the time I exit my office, the lights in the lobby are off, with a glare from the sunset peeking in from the window above. It's also quiet. Very quiet! There's not even a single person here— even Rachel has left for the day, and she's usually the last to leave the office. *Hm!* What's this? On Rachel's desk sits a small brown envelope with a golden bow wrapped around it, and my name is written on it. It's from Daniel. I recognize the handwriting. Why didn't Rachel tell me about this? Inside the envelope is a small card with an instruction.

> Tonight is all about you!
>
> 1. Go to Bloomingdales in Aventura and ask for Cindy. Don't question anything after that. Just say okay.
>
> Signed, Your Lover

Now, this should be interesting. I wonder what Daniel has up his sleeve. While repeatedly reading the card, I walk over to the elevator. As I stand there waiting for the doors to open, my heels clack against the floor as my hands begin to moisten. There's a rumbling in my stomach as well. These are signs of being nervous. But I'm not nervous. Why would I be?

Ding!

The door slides open, and there's nothing but dust floating in the air, but just like that…the nervousness disappears. I enter the elevator, press my back against the wall, close my eyes, and take a deep breath. Relax, Andrea. Deep breaths. Steady movements. Yes, just like that. Suddenly, as the elevator descends to the first floor, my thoughts impulsively take me back to the distinguished gentleman who I refer to as Derek. Fuck! I shouldn't have these thoughts, but I can't control them. They're happening more frequently than I'm used to, and they're getting more inappropriate. What does this mean? Nothing, Andrea. Yeah. It's harmless. Strangely enough, I don't mind it because, in my thoughts, I'm safe. I can do whatever I want to, and there's nothing anyone can do about it. Right now, I watch him take my panties off slowly and then put them in his mouth. He even chews on them like red licorice. I smile girlishly as I watch him do so. Then, he slides his right hand up my skirt where he begins to…

Ding!

First Floor.

The elevator doors slide open, and that same tingling feeling rushes up to the muscles in my stomach and lingers there for a moment. I take a second to gather myself before stepping out into the lobby. Shit! I can feel the warm wetness between my legs, quickly becoming a cold spot whenever I take a step. It's pretty uncomfortable too.

I exit the elevator, and to my surprise, there's no one around. Quickly, I walk towards the end of the hallway, slide my floral lace panties off, and throw them into my purse. That's much better.

"Goodnight," the security guard with a heavy Caribbean accent shouts as I make my way out of the building.

"Goodnight, William," I reply without turning toward him.

"William has already gone home."

I stop, turn to the man, and realize it's not William. He's much older and shorter than William. His skin is also darker, and he's plump.

"I'm sorry. I'm used to William being here."

"Yeah, he goes home at six," he says.

"Oh. Okay. Well, you have a good night."

Wait a minute. The digital clock hanging behind the security guard's desk says it's 5:26 P.M. How's that possible? My watch read

4:22 P.M. just a moment ago. Suddenly, there are a few seconds of confusion where I try to assess what the hell is going on. How did nearly forty-five minutes pass by like that? Something must be wrong with my watch.

"Where's your friend?" the security guard asks.

He shoots me an awkward smirk that's quite disturbing. What was that about?

"My friend?" My eyebrows pull together, puzzled.

"Yes." He smiles wider.

Wait. Is this plump man flirting with me right now? He can't be. How could he ever think that I'd ever give him a chance? Obviously, he's mistaken me for someone else.

"I'm not sure, but you have a good night." I hurry out.

The moment I exit the mirrored building, I spot the black Range Rover driving away on Second Avenue. Was that him? The distinguished gentleman from this morning? What is he still doing here?

The black Range Rover stops at the red light. From here, I can hear its engine humming in a silent pause. I wait, curious about the driver's next move, when my attention is drawn to the striking woman from earlier. She appears within my view, just twenty meters away from the car, retaining her captivating and enigmatic presence. It is indeed her, the same woman who stood before the mirrored building, engaged in conversation with the distinguished gentleman. At first, she seems oblivious to the Range Rover sitting at the red light, but a purposeful stride leads her in its direction, making me think otherwise. Her posture is as perfect as one can be, shoulders squared, and gaze fixed ahead. They must have been connected, entwined in something secretive.

Green light.

The black Range Rover makes a right onto Biscayne Boulevard, and so does the woman. That's strange. Swiftly, I trudge along the pavement at a rapid pace, making my way to my car, but really, I want to see what the woman will do next. The moment I turn the corner, I spot her coming to a stop in front of the parking garage, but the black Range Rover is nowhere in sight. What is she doing? It's as if she is thinking about something. Or maybe she's waiting on someone? Suddenly, my phone pings. It's a text from Daniel...

> By now I hope you received my package. So go ahead and follow the instruction. And trust me...you're gonna love what happens tonight.

I love it when Daniel offers these sorts of romantic gestures. It lets me know that he values me in some strange way. Daniel can be romantic when he wants to be, but when he's not, God is he distant. There is no in between with Daniel. He'd either give you everything at that moment or nothing at all. Occasionally, he would go missing, stating that he needed his space, and rarely did Daniel put his ego aside to show me how much he cared. There were times when it felt like he barely existed. Almost as if he was a figment of my imagination. But then he does something like this to make me forget any of my previous thoughts. A few seconds pass, and my eyes drop to my phone as I reply to Daniel's text.

> Exciting!! I can't wait to see you tonight.
> Delivered

As much as I should be thinking about my rendezvous with Daniel, it's the woman on the street that has a hold of my attention. Something about her keeps tugging at my intuition. It's as if I can hear a voice whispering deep within, suggesting I follow her. For a moment, my consciousness floats through a space filled with random specks of images, like trying to watch a movie on a damaged LCD screen. I don't even know how I got here. But when I turn back to the woman, she's nowhere to be seen.

CHAPTER 4

RARELY DO I COME to the mall because it tends to be a sensory overload, especially with all the stores scattered within long-distance walks. There is always something that I want and never anything that I need. And moving through the shoppers means getting closer to other people, which is something I'd rather not deal with at this moment. I can't help but envy those who rejoice in the act of shopping, like Francine Augustin— a client of mine still grappling with the scars of a traumatic past. Anything that Ms. Augustin wore, no matter the brand, cost, or color, she'd rock the shit out of it. Sometimes, I look forward to her visits because, truthfully, that's the only time I get motivated to go shopping. Ms. Augustin confesses that her love for fashion saved her life, and now, she wants everyone to know it whenever she walks by.

When Ms. Augustin was just six years old, her parents gave her up for adoption because they could no longer afford her. However, after doing my research, I discovered they abandoned her because they were selfish, choosing drugs over their daughter. Ms. Augustin went from foster homes to group homes and then back to several other foster homes. At fifteen, Ms. Augustin decided she was tired of the constant abuse and moving around, so she ran away and soon found herself dancing in the strip club at night and sleeping away the day in a storage unit until evening. Ms. Augustin was only fifteen. Still, those who noticed her assumed she was a grown woman—especially considering her bold curves, stern demeanor, and striking features. Ms. Augustin was smart enough to use it to her advantage, though, meeting all sorts of men, including an evil man named Gabriel Houlihan, whom everyone called Chino. As Ms. Augustin claims, this man was a monster who sought to control her like some puppet. He kept Francine by his side like a holster while making street workers and strippers out of the other women. Ms. Augustin tells me that those were some of her darkest days, but she did what she had to do to survive. Besides, the man had one of the most pristine homes she had ever seen—a mansion. According to Ms. Augustin, there were maids, a chef, and even an assistant catering to her every need. Chino ensured she had every clothing, shoes, or purse that her heart desired. But as impressive as that may seem, Ms. Augustin says it was all temporary, and it hardly offered her the happiness she was craving at the end of the day.

After spending five grueling years with Chino, Ms. Augustin's wish to escape from him came true when the Atlanta police arrested him for sex trafficking, racketeering, and several other charges. Chino was sentenced to prison for forty-five years. When that happened, Ms. Augustin went into the back of Chino's closet, found his hidden stash of cash, and walked away with nearly three million dollars. With that money, she started a new life, even becoming a fashion stylist for some of the most influential people in Miami. Beyond her incredible sense of fashion, I have always admired Ms. Augustin. More so because of her resilience and determination to be better than she was yesterday. But the fact that she can't reconcile her parent's disappearance is what makes her my client. What can I say? The greater a child's nightmare, the harder it becomes to develop a strong and healthy sense of self. Yet, I still hope to channel my inner Ms. Augustin as I walk into this mall.

By the time I arrived at Bloomingdale, daylight had dwindled to the gloom of gray clouds with the sun faded in the background. *Mmm!* It smells like heaven in here, and the floor shines like the surface of a lake at sunrise. People casually walk around the store dressed in the latest fashion made from the finest material. In the background is soothing music that takes the shopper's cares far away. On the second floor is where I search for a woman named Cindy. My guess is that she's big but beautiful, and she has a natural look too. Long hair, no makeup, and all the bare minimums that makes her a woman. Definitely someone I'd never expect to work in a store like Bloomingdale. Guessing how someone looks based on their name is something I like to do. Most of the time, I'm spot on. That's because names tend to match people's faces and characters. For example, a woman named Esther is often in her elder years, sweet and gentle, along with a soft heart. She's often short as well. Then, you have names that end with "C-A," such as Veronica, Bianca, Angelica, and Erica. They tend to be self-absorbed women who are deeply rooted in their appearance, coming off as bitches or someone with incredible narcissistic behaviors.

"Hi, can I help you find something?"

I turn around and face a bi-racial woman with hair thick as wool, stretching down to her lower back. It's blonde too. She approaches with all the charm radiating from her smile and the friendly sparkle in her eyes glimmering.

"Hi. Yes. I am looking for Cindy."

"I'm Cindy. How can I help you?"

This is Cindy? I was wrong. It wouldn't be the first time. She's nothing like the woman I constructed in my mind. She's much taller, slender, and more of a woman than she appeared in my head. She also exudes an energy that makes her perfect for this store clerk position.

"Hi, yes… you're just the person I was looking for. I'm here because my boyfriend sent me here. Daniel Cooper."

"And he said to ask for me?"

"Yes. He gave me this." I hand the woman the card.

"Oh yes. I'm sorry. I remember now. The name didn't ring a bell. But please, follow me."

The woman escorts me to a fitting room nicely decorated with gold drapes and white furniture. It's as if this were a private area of the store that very few people get to see. Then again, I hardly go shopping, so it may be. Against the wall, dangling from a black velvet hanger, is a green Yves Saint Lauren backless short dress. It's stunning. Short but stunning.

"Here you go. Try it on and if it doesn't fit, let me know." She says just before she exits.

I waste no time taking off my khakis and white blouse and slipping into the dress. The dress feels like feathers gliding along my skin as I put it on. My goodness, it's shorter than I imagined, and it's pretty revealing. This is more than I am used to, but I must admit, it's gorgeous on me. $3,410! Did Daniel pay for this dress? God, I love that man. His soul speaks to mine and radiates from my heart to my fingertips.

"How does it fit?" Cindy says.

"It's perfect."

The woman enters, and immediately her jaw drops as her eyes widen. This must be a good thing. In her hands is a box of shoes. Daniel must have gotten me those as well. He's such a charmer.

"Omigod! You look amazing, and I hope you don't mind saying this, but your legs and breast are perfect for the dress."

"Really? You don't think it's too short?" I ask.

"No, not at all. It's like you said… it's perfect. Here! He bought this for you as well. Such a romantic man you have there. Uh! I would kill to have someone do something like this for me."

The woman drops down on her left knee, grabs my right ankle, and slips the leather open-toe shoe onto my foot. They're black and detailed by a gold chain link. Just how I like it. And he even remembered my shoe size. Omigod, they are stunning. I don't even want to know how much he spent on these.

"Looks good. How does that feel?"

"It fits, that's for sure. I like it."

"Well, glad you do because they're yours." She chuckles.

Cindy then puts the other shoe on my left foot, steps back, and carefully scans me from head to toe as if I were one of her great masterpieces.

"My job is done here. Here you go."

Then, she hands me another small brown envelope with a white card inside it.

> Tonight is all about you!
>
> 2. You got your dress and your shoes and I hope you like it. Now, Veronica is waiting for you down at the makeup counter.

There is an explosion in my brain from everything that's happening here. It's the type that carries more possibilities than my conscience can handle. Daniel has never done anything as spontaneous and compelling as this. The fact that I don't know how this will end has my mind flaring with random sparks of electricity that runs throughout my body.

"Thank you."

The woman then hands me a red leather bag with a gold chain and exits the fitting room. I take one more look at myself, smiling as if I had just arrived.

Eyes fall over me as I make my way down the escalator to the first floor like I am on a runway. At the makeup counter is a woman smiling as if she were expecting me.

"Hi, I'm Veronica. Cindy told me you were coming down."

She was expecting me? Daniel has really outdone himself on this one.

"You ready?" She asks.

"Sure. Why not?"

The woman sits me down in the chair, looks at me, and then begins applying makeup over my gentle face. First, she picks up her tiny bottle of primer, leans toward me, and spreads it around my face. Next comes the foundation. She lays it over my forehead, my eyes, and of course, my cheeks.

I've never been one to care for makeup because I've always thought of it as somewhat frivolous and deceiving. Most people wear makeup because of societal expectations. Social media advertisements and magazines lead us to believe that subconsciously, we're chasing an unrealistic beauty ideal. That infectious mindset lets us think that our appearance is never good enough and that we lack something internally. Therefore, we find a way to reveal it from the outside, and for some, makeup is the easiest way to do that.

Nowadays, a woman's makeup tells me everything I need to know about their life and how society has treated them. An excess of blush, dark mascara, bright color lipstick, and a heavily coated face tells me that woman need it to gain self-esteem and relieve the fears of societal rejection. They're often very emotional, expressing themselves through scattered words and teary eyes.

Women who like to be explorative with eclectic colors and styles want to stand out because they can, but not because they have to. They're much more into their feminine side than the others, and it's probably because she hasn't gone through anything traumatic in her life. As a result, she is energetic, creative, fun, artistic, and yet always so mysterious.

Now, the women with just a sweep of eyeliner, maybe a coat of lipstick, and a minimum of anything else are the ones who care less about what others think and more about what they feel about themselves. She's been through enough not to worry about society's perception of beauty. Therefore, she focuses her time on other things, like being organized and self-sufficient, her alone time, or her next move to progress in society. Even remembering birthdays without being reminded is more important than the makeup she decides to put on. I know this because that's the woman I am.

"All done."

When I hop out of my chair, I feel like a new woman. God, Daniel, has really put some thought into this. Just as that thought crosses my mind, Daniel sends me a text. Meet in the next thirty minutes at this address. This is getting even more exciting. What will happen next? Whatever it is, I can use a lot of it after the day I have had.

7:43 P.M.

It's a quarter to eight when I pull up to a guard house at the entrance of an upscale residential community in Sunny Isles. A neighborhood? So, I'm meeting him at a house? Hmm! This is interesting. I was sure I would meet him at a restaurant or some establishment. Certainly not a house.

As I approach the gate, it hits me... what will I say to the guard? It's not like I've been here before, and nor do I know who to ask for. Screw it. I take a quick glance at myself in the rearview mirror and gently swipe my right index finger underneath both eyes. Left eye first, and then the right. Perfect! I pull up to the guard house.

"Good evening. How may I help you?" The security guard asks.

My mouth opens, but I can't find the answer to his question. However, it doesn't matter because before I can even respond to him...

"Oh hey. How are you? Go right ahead."

The corner of his mouth twitches upwards to a smile as he glares down at me. He nods his head and then draws the gate open. That was quite strange. What was that all about? Daniel must have told him about me as well.

Casually, I stroll through the private community— admiring each home in passing. All the homes here are immaculate and uniquely designed, from a massive brick home to a three-story glass house. It's quiet and peaceful, with a faint sound of the water in the background. No one is leisurely walking around the community like Ms. Bouyon.

Then, I approach a breathtaking white brick house that is simply the epitome of a seductive architectural creation. The design is intense and esoteric, with a stunning manicured yard. Is this the place? 2232... yes, this is the house, but I don't see any cars outside. Where am I? Before climbing out, I wait for a few seconds, hoping to see something to make it safe to step out. All the lights are on in the house. Daniel never has all the lights turned on. Maybe it's a surprise of some sort.

Then again, I don't think Daniel would ever bring me to someone's house. Why would he? Come to think of it, I haven't talked to Daniel throughout this whole scavenger hunt. What if it's not him pulling this whole thing off, and instead, it's someone else? Perhaps, I should call him now.

The phone continues to ring, but there's no answer. That's odd. Suddenly, just as I open the door to step out, a silhouette figure passes by one of the windows. Was that a woman? No, this can't be right. I check the address, and sure enough, it is correct. Another person passes by, and I believe that is a man. I think. Who are these people in this house? As time passes, I stare off into the unknown, allowing me to go further into my thoughts. There's a gradual loss of hearing that shifts into a whine or hum while not being able to hear anything around me. My body unwinds as my mind stays at ease. I can't make sense of what's happening, and I despise it when that happens.

Suddenly, my phone rings. It's Shannon, my childhood friend who's more like a sister.

"Hey, Shannon," I answer.

"Where are you? I thought you'd be here by eight."

Something about this whole situation keeps tugging at my intuition. It's as if I can hear a voice whispering, telling me to get out of here now. However, I can't help but think about the man and woman I saw pass by the window.

"Hello, Andrea!" Shannon shouts, pulling me back to reality and feeling oddly uncomfortable.

"Yes. Hey. What is it?"

"Are you coming? We're waiting on you," She whines.

"Waiting on me for what?"

"Hello! You said you wanted to come out for drinks. Remember?"

For a moment, my conscious brain can't process anything. It's like I'm standing in a thick black smoke, waiting for it to clear to see where I am finally going.

"Andrea?"

"Yes. I'm here. Okay. I'm on the way." I snap out of it.

I hang the phone up before Shannon thinks to say anything else, and when I turn back to the house, all the lights are off. Completely dark. I call Daniel again, but there's no ring at all this time.

CHAPTER 5

9:03 P.M.

AFTER ALL THE lefts, rights, and U-turns, I finally find the bar elbowed between a hardware depot and a grocery store. I can only imagine what the inside will look like. One hour. That's how long I will be here. Not a second longer.

Standing outside in front of the bar is a tall, husky doorman who's broad in the shoulders with thick muscular arms. He has the posture of a secret agent with eyes that dare anyone to speak to him. As I approach, he opens the door almost robotically and gives me a head nod as he does. I wasn't expecting that.

What a shock! The place is nicer than I presumed it would be. It's spacious and decorated with a Greek theme. The dim lighting gives the inside of the bar a tasteful ambiance that feels welcoming. Hundreds of conversations are going on at the same time over the music, and judging by the looks of it, this isn't your typical bar. On the other hand, the degenerate drinkers and single women walking around…now that's what makes the bar seem normal.

"Excuse me. Can I talk to you for a sec?" a random guy catcall.

I turn to him as he licks his cracked lips and then swiftly turns away. Not only is he sloppy, shabby, and creepy looking, but he's also married. I'm good at identifying them—even if they're not wearing a ring. Sometimes it's as easy as spotting a cheerleader in the men's locker room. Married men tend to notice women quicker than single men, and that's because they're constantly looking over their shoulders, hoping that no one who walks in will recognize them. It's always just one drink. That way, they can avoid having their wives figure out where they've been. My guess is that he's been married for quite some time. I'd say eight to ten years. But now that his wife is pregnant at home with their third child, he wants to come out to play.

"No, thank you."

"Come on. Give me a chance," he whimpers.

The left hand of a married man is often tucked away in his pocket, under his right arm, or fidgeting around—even if they aren't wearing their ring. That's only for the amateurs. Professionals are much different. Their eyes are much lower as they scope the scene tighter than a marksman. They're much bolder and always calm in their demeanor. The conversations are always short and straight to the point. This is their attempt to establish a clear distinction between themselves and the others. Their narcissistic personality helps them to feel like they're the center of the world. That's why the conversation is always about them, making it seem as if they're an open book. But the truth is, they don't want you asking the obvious question.

"You in a rush?" A short and stocky man with a scruffy beard and dark eyes steps in front of me. "If not, would you mind taking a seat? Maybe we can find out what we have in common over a drink."

"Sorry, my boyfriend wouldn't like that."

I must confess, he sounds more sincere than the other, but I'm not that type of woman. And I can imagine how Daniel would feel seeing me entertain another man. Besides, the random thoughts of the distinguished gentleman from work are already too much. I don't need any more distractions.

"Andrea! Over here!" she screams.

It's Shannon, and she's with two others—Courtnie and Darlene. Darlene is Shannon's younger sister, who has had a few run-ins with the law, and Courtnie, well, she's a long-time frenemy of Shannon's. Looking at the table, I can tell they've been here for a while. There are five glass cups in front of them, three of which are empty, and there's also a plate with one sushi roll left.

"Finally. You're right on time. Don't look too hard, but you see the guy in the black blazer—by the pool table?" Shannon's eyes glimmer.

From here, I spot a man in the back of the bar surrounded by three guys and two women, but they all seem to be just friends. The man is a few inches taller than Daniel and has a textbook build for his height. Beneath his black blazer and denim jeans, I can see he's pretty trim. His skin is tan, and he has a perfectly symmetrical face. He's probably somewhere around his mid-to-late-thirties if I had to guess. Also, he's Cuban. Or Puerto Rican. Hispanic for sure. Either way, he is handsome, from the depth of his eyes to the charming way he smiles when he laughs. His short curls are midnight black, and although I can barely see his eyes, I bet they're brown.

"Yeah. What about him?" I ask.

"That is a beautiful man."

"Well, go over there then, Shannon. Because if you don't, I will!" Darlene pounds on the table.

Shannon's eyes remain stuck on the man like some perverted college girl. I don't blame her, though, because even I shouldn't be staring at him in this manner.

"I will if he looks over here." Shannon turns to us. "But isn't it desperate to approach a man at a bar?"

"Yeah, if we were in the fucking fifties," Darlene laughs.

"I agree with Darlene. That's bullshit, and any woman who thinks otherwise either loves being single or isn't into men at all," Courtnie says before she takes a sip of her drink.

"Exactly. As women, how do we go after everything we want and need in life, but when it comes to going after men, we feel like it's not our place? Fuck that!" Darlene says.

"What do you think, Andrea?" Shannon turns to me.

Yes, Andrea. What do you think? My inner voice echoes Shannon's question, and beyond my control, I begin to bite my nails while looking at the man. He is quite the specimen. I can tell he's passionate too. I bet he's the type to wipe you down with a warm wet cloth after making love to you and then offer you something to eat afterward. I wonder if I'm right. He's not married either. I can tell by how he carries himself as if he doesn't have a care in the world. For goodness sake, he's not even focused on women trying to get his attention.

Shit!

He meets my gaze with a smile, and I slowly take my finger out of my mouth, blushing. Great. In most cases, I'd quickly look away, but at this moment, I don't. I can't explain why, but I feel safe when I look into his eyes which are filled with raw emotion.

"And what's Andrea going to tell you? We are talking about the same woman who's only been with one guy her entire life." Darlene laughs.

"So, she says." Courtnie shoots me a puzzling stare. "Speaking of, when do we get to meet this refined man of yours, Andrea?" She adds.

"We'll meet him when she's ready." Shannon jumps in.

"Yeah. One of these days. He's not ready for that."

"Okay then," Courtnie rolls her eyes.

I'm not too fond of those who try to understand me. But perhaps Darlene is right. Maybe I have been living a sheltered, boring life, doing everything the right way while everyone else has fun being bad. I have always wondered what it felt like to be the woman who other women despise, yet deep down inside, they envy. The woman who is free to do what she wants and not be concerned with what others think of her—someone like my old college roommate—Denita Richardson.

Denita never struggled between the woman she was and the woman she wanted to be because they were the same. When I met Denita, I was just starting to understand who I was. Unlike me, Denita never showed her emotions on her lovely face and rarely did anything without an objective. Everyone noticed Denita, but very few paid attention to her as I did. I was obsessed with knowing everything about her. The way she walked. Her thought process. The way she lived. The way she'd smile when she was flirting or just sitting there by herself. Everything! My fascination with Denita is possibly how I became a psychologist.

"Andrea…so what do you think?" Shannon interrupts.

"Well…he is good looking, and maybe worth whatever can happen. So, why not go for it if you're into him? Or at the very least, make yourself noticeable," I reply.

Darlene and Courtnie's eyebrows raise in surprise as Shannon smiles. I, on the other hand, have no idea where that response came from.

"Wow. I'm impressed, Andrea. I didn't expect that response from you. I thought for sure you would have said something prudish. Like—"If he wants you, he'll make an effort," Darlene flips her hair and chuckles.

"Speaking of…Shannon, did you tell Andrea?" Courtnie says.

"Tell me what?"

"We're thinking of going on a trip. Somewhere exotic. And you're coming!" Shannon's eyes light up.

"Is that so? And where are we going?"

"We're thinking maybe Jamaica or the Virgin Islands." The anticipation in Darlene's voice intensifies.

"What about Barbados? I hear it's a very nice island. Not to mention you can ride horses on the beautiful beaches." Courtnie takes a sip of her drink.

"Oh, please! You can ride a damn horse right on South Beach. We need more than that. We need somewhere spontaneous, exotic, erotic, and full of things to do. Like Thailand. There's a place where women can get men to be their sex slaves. Not just any men. Sexy ones!" Darlene smiles.

"One—ew! Two—do you have the money to go to Thailand?" Shannon says to Darlene. "Anyway…so Andrea, what do you think?"

And just like that, they look to me for a response as if it were the opening scene of a feature film.

"Sounds interesting. When?"

"How about this weekend?" Shannon says.

"This weekend? No. I can't do that. I'll need enough time to prepare for this trip. And I have to talk it over with—"

"Omigod! He just looked over here. And I think he saw me looking at him. What do I do?"

"Shannon! For goodness sake, will you go over there, or I'm telling you, he's mine." Courtnie slams her palm against the table.

"I can't bring myself to do it. I mean, look at him!"

As they continue their conversation, everything around me fades into silence, with the man taking control of my attention. Like the waves in the ocean, my mind roams without a destination, trying to read his story. Everyone has a story.

First, I establish a baseline by creating would-be facts that I can stand on. For example, his choice of clothing. Black blazer, white V-neck shirt, and blue jeans. Nothing over the top, but it's enough to let me know he's either well-established or trying to be someone he's not. Then, I seek to find some inconsistencies in the baseline I just created. Like right now—although he seems confident in himself, he's not paying attention to any of the women. I wonder why that is. Could he be into men? I doubt it. Maybe he's single. Nowadays, single men would rather be made a move on than make a move. However, he doesn't seem like that type. He's certainly more assertive than the average man. Nor is he a narcissist either. I can tell that by the eye contact he makes with the others.

Next, I observe his body language. Crossed arms and legs. Whether or not he's leaning forward or away. His smile. His stance. Suppose he's constantly moving around. That will all show his level of comfort with his surroundings. Observing how far or close he is among those around him will tell me if he's an extrovert or just a social introvert. Everything else will be filled by the words he formally expresses to others. Most of the time, I'm spot on, and other times, I'm just a minor detail away from the truth.

Oh crap! It's almost ten, and I still haven't spoken to Daniel all day. This is unlike him. Something isn't right about that. I should give him a call. Suddenly, just as I am about to call Daniel, in the distance, I spot a familiar face entering the bar. Oh, God! It's Robyn Simpson. A client of mine who I didn't expect to see anytime soon— especially not in a bar. Ms. Simpson has no sense of boundary, and her whole attitude never really made sense to anyone who didn't know her. At the age of thirty-seven, she's psychologically stuck at the age of fifteen. That tends to happen to people who go through trauma and never recover. Now, she would rather blame everyone else for her problem than take ownership of her own flaws.

I keep my eyes on her, trying to make sure she doesn't spot me through the crowd of people standing around. I hope she doesn't see me. Seeing clients in public is always awkward and tends to turn into a session of its own.

"Right, Andrea?" Darlene says.

Swiftly, I turn my attention to Darlene, not having the slightest clue as to what she just asked. So, I nod my head and smile amusingly. I need to call Daniel because I'd feel much better sitting here knowing everything was okay.

"I'll be right back. I need to make a phone call." I inform the girls.

I place my purse on the table and make my way out of the bar. However, just as I approach the front entrance, the man that Shannon has been eyeing all night grabs me by the hand and pulls me in close. My mouth drops open as I bask in his presence for a moment. He's very masculine and has a dark shadow of a beard to match his earthy brown eyes. I was right about his eyes. But why in the world is he touching me?

"What do you think you are doing?" My voice is hostile, but inside I can't stop smiling.

I quickly snatch my hand away from him, and then nervously glance over to Shannan and the others, hoping they don't see me. Lord only knows what they'll say. Good! They can't see us.

"Come grab a drink with me." His voice is raspy.

He's so close I can smell the aftershave on his face. It's the same one that Daniel uses, but it's much more invigorating on him. Andrea! What in the world are you thinking? Keep it together. Yes, I must keep it together.

"No thanks."

I turn to walk away, but he grabs a hold of my left hand and pulls me back in. Then, the man swiftly stops one of the ladies walking around with their black uniforms neatly ironed and tucked in.

"I'll have two Manhattan," he says while keeping his stare on me.

"Coming right up."

I can't seem to walk away from him. It's as if a part of myself has left me alone with the man and there's nothing I can do to bring that part back. My reaction to this man is very similar to my reaction to the distinguished gentleman. Hands slightly moist. Unable to speak. Insides continue to clench without anything to hold onto. And I feel like I am trying to remember how to breathe. Not only that, but I'm also oblivious to what I will do next. Do I just walk away? Could one drink be harmless? I am kind of intrigued to hear what he has to say. But what about Shannon? Wouldn't she be devastated to see me talking to the man she's infatuated with? What am I saying? Of course, she would. Besides, I'm sure Daniel wouldn't appreciate me having a drink with another man either.

"Thanks, but I have to go. Take care."

"Wait. Don't leave like that. I didn't expect to see you here," he says.

"Excuse me?"

"That's right. I apologize. Good evening. My name is Manuel, but everyone calls me Manny."

He extends his right hand, and the only thing I can think of is that he doesn't look like a Manny. The name sounds too socially inept for him. He looks more like a Mario, Sergio, or Julian.

"Okay."

"Well, aren't you going to tell me your name?"

A shifty smile draws on his face as he stands there, calculating his next move. His eyes sketch over my entire body…

Up and down.

Down and up.

I can feel him fantasizing about what he might do to me if he ever got the chance to touch me. Shit, Andrea! What are you doing, and how do you know this? I don't know, but I can feel that tingle between my stomach and my thighs beginning to build as he glares down at me. It's parallel to the feeling from this morning. I must stop this at once. Just stop it, Andrea! internally I shout.

"Andrea," I interrupt him.

Why did you tell him your name?

"Andrea? Really?" He chuckles.

I raise my eyebrows in a cold stare, but it has very little effect on him. He leans in and whispers into my ear as his lips graze my earlobe. His left hand suddenly rests in the middle of my back—just above my ass.

"Well, Andrea, I saw you looking at me, and I know you saw me looking at you too," he whispers.

His lips brush against my left cheek as he pulls back. I can feel his touch along my neck, down my spine, and even in my toes. Fuck! Why am I so damn sensitive? Better yet, why am I still standing here? I must leave now. Now, Andrea!

I step aside from the man, hoping to finally walk away, but he steps in front of me.

"So, let's quit the bullshit," he murmurs.

He's aggressive. I didn't get that from him during my reading. This is interesting. He leans in again, and this time he circles his finger on a hidden spot on my lower back. Chills cover my skin as I close my eyes for a moment and exhale. How did he know to do that? I quickly recover and remove his hand, and then step back, remaining as calm as I possibly can. This is too much self-control for one woman to possess in a day.

"What do you think you're doing?" I fumble miserably over my words.

Goodness sake! He smells so good beneath that blazer that tugs on his body so well. *Andrea, stop that.* Enough with the thoughts and go home! Yes. I must leave. But I have to admit, the fact that he is turning me on, and he doesn't even know it…makes this moment somewhat exciting. If I had on panties right now, they'd probably be ruined.

"Sorry. It won't happen again. Without your permission, that is." He smiles.

I stare at him unblinkingly, searching for the energy to walk away. Come on, Andrea. Just walk away!

Lord, please don't let the girls see me talking to Manny right now. Nervously, I glance over my shoulder, and there's a sigh of relief as they still can't see me from there. Now is the time to walk away before they do.

"You take care of yourself. Night."

"Here you go." The lady returns with the drinks just as I am about to walk away, handing both over to Manny.

"Will you at least have this drink with me?"

Manny hands me one of the drinks with a softness in his eyes and a gentleness in his smile. Then, he takes a sip of his drink as he looks at me. He can have any of the women at this bar, but he's chosen me. That makes me the lucky one because while all the others remain in the distance, I get to feel his warmth.

"So… about this drink?

I snap out of it.

"Look, I appreciate the gesture, but I'm not that kind of woman."

"And what kind of woman would that be?"

"A woman who would entertain another man while in a happy and healthy relationship."

"Then don't be that woman." He smirks.

I'm not moved by his sarcasm.

"Wow. You are really sticking with this, aren't you? Here. Take my card in case you change your mind." He hands me a card, but I don't take it.

Screw it! Finally, I muster the energy to turn away from the man and walk off. However, just as I do that, I find myself staring into the eyes of the woman. It's her! The woman from this morning standing outside of the mirrored building. And just like before…she's all alone.

CHAPTER 6

9:37 P.M.

Is she following me? What is she doing here? It's a bar, Andrea, so why wouldn't she be? She probably belongs here more than I do, and that form-fitting burgundy dress that perfectly accentuates her body, gives truth to that idea. I bet it's one of those Nichole Lynel designs. And this time, her hazel eyes are like the night, deep and mysterious. Her long glossy black hair, which once rested on her shoulders, is now tied into a top knot bun. She has on makeup, but it is minimal—a sweep of mascara, black eyeliner, and rouge lips that is every shade of sin. I wonder if she notices me. I doubt it, or else she would have reacted to the shock registered on my face. Thoughts run through my head as she sits there like she's utterly immune to the problems of this world. I don't even know the woman, but somehow, I envy her.

I head back to the girls, approaching the woman as I do so. She scans the venue in search of someone when her eyes suddenly meet mine. Every muscle of my body freezes for a moment as a silly grin sneaks onto my face. I would've been better off just turning away.

"You should loosen up," the woman says as I walk past her.

Wait. Is she talking to me?

"Excuse me?" I stop and turn to her.

"You seem anxious and uptight. I can see it all over your face and the way you walk. You should loosen up a little."

Unlike myself, her emotions are not easily visible on her gentle face. In fact, I doubt she's ever frowned in her life.

"I'm fine. But thanks."

"It's hard to see the things in you that others can or cannot see."

She's getting more beautiful with every second I look at her. Her watch—it's gorgeous. It's a solid white ceramic gold-tone watch with a round case completed with crystals...and it looks exactly like mine.

"Nice watch. Where'd you get it?" I smile.

"It was a gift."

What a coincidence. So was mine. Daniel got it for me one night while he was out of town on work. He said the watch was his way of letting me know he was thinking of me at that moment. But the problem is…I don't believe in coincidence.

"Well, I gotta get going. Have fun." I nod and walk off, and just as I take my third step, she says something that pulls me back into her.

"What were you doing following me?" she asks.

Shit! Did she see me? My body instantly turns cold. My heart drops to my stomach, and my legs refuse to move. How embarrassing.

"Excuse me?" I stutter.

"Yeah. Outside of the mirrored building on Second Avenue—I saw you following me. I didn't think anything of it, but now I'm curious to know what that was about." A brief smile stretches across her face as she takes a sip of her drink. Anyone else would freak out if they just ran into the woman following them. But not this woman. She has an ease that most women crave yet never seem to capture. It's almost as if she doesn't have any stress or care in the world. If I didn't know any better, I would say she enjoyed the fact that I was following her.

"I thought you were someone I knew. That's all."

"That wouldn't be the first time. Many have told me that I have a familiar face."

"I guess you can say that."

"So, this person you thought I was…where do you know her from?"

"Not here. Someone I know from back home," I lie.

"Where's home?"

"Thibodaux. It's outside of—"

"New Orleans. Yeah, I know. That's where I'm from as well."

"Thibodaux? You? I should know you then because the town wasn't that big."

"Perhaps. Then again, I didn't get out as much. My mother was pretty tough on me."

Oddly enough, I know what she means. My mother was the same. She'd walk through the gates of hell to ensure I didn't witness whatever she tried to hide from me. Secrets? Lies? Or possibly the truth.

"Hello!" Manny seizes my attention.

I turn to him, and there he is, looking at me with hardened eyes, searching deep into my soul for the woman he desires. Something familiar swimming in his eyes makes me slightly vulnerable and quite curious. But I need to leave now. Right now.

Adrenaline rushes through my veins like a bullet shot out of a barrel, giving me the will to walk away. Just as I do, the woman from the mirrored building walks up to Manny. Her walk is purposeful as her eyes remain focused on him and no one else. It's so intense that I can practically see her pheromones seeping through her pores. The moment she faces Manny, she pulls him in with a gentle gaze and a soft touch on his right arm. Between her unmatched beauty and dominating behavior, Shannon doesn't stand a chance.

Manny then steps forward, closing the space between the two of them. She smiles and slides her left hand down his right arm. He grabs a hold of her hand and, in an amicable manner, kisses it. She stares into his eyes and takes a sip of her drink. Damn! I'm mesmerized by the gift that she possesses as a woman. First, the distinguished gentleman, and now Manny? She's undoubtedly living a more thrilling life than I could ever imagine.

I return to the table, and immediately, the girls barrage me with questions. I should have expected this, seeing how long I've been gone.

"Damn, Andrea, what took you so long?" Shannon asks before I can take a seat. "I was just about to come look for you," she adds.

"I stopped at the bar after my phone call."

I've never been good at lying, but this one is somewhat true. I did call Daniel, but it went straight to his voicemail like the previous calls. It's either that or the phone rings endlessly. Strange? I know.

"Well, where's your drink?" Darlene asks.

"My drink?" *Yes, Andrea. Where's your drink?* "I changed my mind. They were taking too long. And now my head is spinning from the wait." I do suck at lying.

"You were gone all that time and couldn't get a drink? Okay. Seriously, were you taking a shit or something?" Shannon laughs.

How long was I gone? According to my watch, it's now 8:58. What? How is that possible? It certainly didn't feel that long, and why do I suddenly feel strange? My mouth is sticky with thick saliva, and everything moves in slow motion. I can hear and see the girls talking, but I can't fully comprehend what they are saying for some odd reason. Not to mention, I'm beginning to feel somewhat light-headed. *Wait…is this it? Am I about to die?*

"Andrea, are you okay?" Courtnie asks.

"Yes!" I squeal. "I mean, yes… I'm fine! Just feeling a little light-headed, but I'll be okay."

Come on, Andrea. Get it together.

"Oh shit! He's coming this way!" Shannon breathlessly murmurs.

I turn around and spot Manny approaching our table like a man on a mission. Even his walk is smooth. I think it's time I admit what I knew all along but was too afraid to admit. I want him. Even if it's for just one night. Stop it, Andrea! Fantasizing about men you have no connection with is not you. Yes, this is not me, and I feel guilty for even thinking about it. Quickly, I turn away before he notices my torn emotions.

"Okay, Shannon, play it cool. Smile, but not too much. Small talk only. Don't start running your mouth about anything you wouldn't usually talk about. As a matter of fact, just let him do all the talking," Courtnie directs Shannon.

"Here he comes," Darlene adds.

The closer he gets to our table, the more I notice the nervousness growing in Shannon. I am no better myself because I'm stuck in my seat, losing my mind. It's bizarre, and I can't explain why this weird feeling is happening. I really should get going. Now!

"Good evening, ladies."

They all greet Manny with perfect smiles. Shannon is the last to do so. As for me, I avoid making any eye contact with him, but I can feel his gaze pricking away on my skin like a two-inch needle. For goodness' sake, I'm starting to sweat in unusual places, and I can't keep my damn legs together either. And why the hell is my head spinning like this?

"Excuse me, Andrea," Manny says.

Immediately, the girls all look at each other, and their eyes and mouths drop wide open. Although they stare straight at me, they appear not to notice me at all. Like I'm some sort of stranger holding a gun at them. It's the kind of look that usually comes after something devastating happens. But I don't bother to look his way. Instead, I pull out my phone, not to check for messages but to seem occupied—what a miserable failure.

Shannon's eyes pencil in on me with her lips pursed and arms crossed over her chest. Next to Shannon is Courtnie, and her smoky eyes glint like she's just seen the corpse of her ex-boyfriend. I'm just as stunned as they are. From the corner of my left eye, I see Manny reach into his pocket, pull out a napkin, and place it on the table—inches away from my arm.

"This is for you. Hope to see you soon. Have a good night, ladies."

And just like that…he walks away. Shannon scowls at me with her big brown eyes as she shakes her head. Darlene gives Shannon a look, and Shannon looks back at her, completely dumbfounded. *Oh God, what has he done?*

"Umm…What the hell was that?" Courtnie breaks the silence.

"I don't know, and I don't care to." I finally breathe. "You know what? I'm not feeling too well. So, I'm just going to head home."

Without hesitation, I grab my purse and prepare to make a beeline out of the bar—but before I do, I glance at the napkin that Manny placed on the table. Written on the napkin is "215," and nothing else. 215? What the heck is that all about? *Just go, Andrea.* Yes, I need to head out before Shannon, Courtnie, or Darlene think to ask another question. As I make my way through the crowd, I avoid eye contact with Manny or the woman from the mirrored building. The last thing I need right now is any more awkwardness. It doesn't matter, however, because I don't see either of them anywhere. Not by the bar, near the pool table, or in the back. Nowhere! They're gone. *Screw it! I need to get home.*

10:10 P.M.

I rush out of the bar, and as I approach my car, I spot the woman from the mirrored building standing there. It's as if she's waiting on me. My face drops faster than bad news as my mouth hangs open.

"You headed out?" She lights a cigarette.

She's a smoker? I wouldn't have pegged her for one.

"Yeah," I reply.

She takes a drag of her cigarette, and for a moment, we lock eyes. My memory has never been the best, but I can't help but wonder if I've met this woman before. Could she be a former classmate of mine? Perhaps I've counseled her in the past? If I did, it would have to have been in one of the group settings I held at the center on 47th street. Or the one at Johnson Colonial.

"I'm waiting for a ride myself. You smoke?" she asks.

"No. Not anymore."

"Of course." She smiles. "Well, there's something about this brand that I like. It's from South Korea and has a soft, pleasant menthol aftertaste."

"Esse. Yeah, I know that brand. That was my go-to when I used to smoke."

"Really? Interesting. Well, I can't tell you why I smoke. I just do. I guess that goes for everything we do in life, huh?"

Something is puzzling about how she looks at me and smirks whenever I say anything. It's enough to make me question her, and if I had a pistol in my purse, my hand would be reaching for it.

"I guess so. Well, have a goodnight."

Just as I climb into my car...

"Hey! I didn't mess up anything for you there, did I?" she asks.

"What do you mean?"

"With Manny. The guy you were talking to. I didn't know if you had any real interest in him or if you were..."

"No! It was nothing like that. You're fine. So, you helped me out if anything."

"Well, good. I'm usually good at that."

"Good at what?"

"Helping people out," she says.

And just like that! Everything stops for a moment as my curiosity peaks beyond the point I am used to. My eyes are stuck on a red pickup truck parked behind my car, but the truck is just there in my vision because I'm actually lost somewhere in thought.

"What did you just say?" I question.

"Helping people out… I'm pretty good at that."

She takes another drag of the cigarette and steps closer to my car, smiling with closed lips and taking a good look at me. I don't budge as I do the same to her.

"You coming from work?" she asks. "What are you into?"

"I'm a psychologist, but I feel like you already knew that."

"You mean like dealing with crazy people?"

"We don't call them crazy. But yes, I help those with addictions."

"Got it. You know what? I think you and I have more in common than you think."

"How would you know that when you don't even know me?"

"You'd be surprised," she murmurs.

Rarely does anyone grab my attention like this woman. She's not like the average person who just wants to wake up and return to bed, and whatever they do in between is usually spent getting by with no real sense of freedom. That explains why I am still standing here.

"So, what do they call you? Doctor, Miss…"

"I'm sorry, but do you know me from somewhere?"

"Maybe. I noticed you this morning and thought the same thing, but it doesn't matter because nowadays, who knows anyone when we barely know ourselves?"

She's right. Then, something flashes beneath her deep-set hazel eyes, drawing down to her suspicious behavior. I can't say for sure, but it feels like she's hiding something. I can tell by the way she lookS at me. Wait. Does she know Daniel? Please, tell me she's not here to tell me about the man I love. *No, Andrea! Don't fall for it.* I won't fall for it.

"Well, you have a goodnight."

She tosses the cigarette off to the side just before I climb into my car. My keys jingle in my left hand as I attempt to focus on just one of the several thoughts circling in my head.

"By the way, I saw how you were looking at them," she says.

I look up and offer her a confusing look.

"Excuse me? Looking at who?"

"The man from this morning and the guy at the bar…I saw you. I also noticed the look in your eyes when you saw them too. I know that look all too well. That's the look of your wants, needs, and desires all coming together for a moment. The way your hands fidget and your feet shuffle beyond your control when you're around them is a natural response. Sweaty palms and loss of words, fearing you'll say the wrong thing. That's the confirmation. Yeah, I know those signs all too well."

I am speechless. I wasn't even aware that this woman noticed me like that, yet she's able to unveil my truth so quickly. My goodness! I haven't been fascinated by anyone like this since Denita Richardson.

"But I gotta admit…you have good taste."

It's probably the sudden shift in her demeanor or how she looks at me, but a curiosity hovers over me like dark clouds before a storm. This must be what Dr. Gonzales was referencing when he said that our lives mysteriously feel unfamiliar as the explainable becomes inexplicable, leaving normal to feel surreal.

"You mind if I ride?" she asks.

A ride? Why would she think I'd give a ride to someone I don't know? Someone who could be having a romantic affair with the man

I love. But then again, it is just a ride. Maybe I'll find out just how much she and I have in common.

"Earlier, when I was following you, why didn't you say anything?"

"Should I have?"

"Maybe. I'm just curious."

"Well, I saw no harm in it. Besides, you seem innocent, so I figured you had your reasons," she responds.

I can't tell if she's lying through her perfect white teeth, but the answer is close enough to pass as the truth. Or perhaps that's just something I want to believe. She steps closer to my car as if she's about to climb in.

"So…about that ride?"

Think about it.

Think about it.

"Where're you headed?" I ask.

"Not too far from here."

As I climb into my car and start the engine, I don't say anything but leave the car in park. Her reflection peers through the passenger side window, faintly batting her eyes while flashing an empty stare.

"Who are you?" I ask.

Everything about her seems wrong as I stare into her eyes, yet I can't stop myself from trying to understand why. It's as if I see something that I can identify with, attempting to drown out this persona I have created to fit into this world. She looks away for a moment and then turns back to me with a smile so innocent that it allows me to comfortably put my guard down.

"Madison."

Think about it.

Think about it.

"Okay Madison… get in."

CHAPTER 7

10:27 P.M.

An awkward silence fills my car as I drive down the wet pavement of A1A. A few minutes into the ride, I ask myself the obvious question—what the hell am I doing? How did I let myself get to the point where I am allowing a woman I know nothing about to come into my space and perhaps turn it upside down? I feel violated, and yet, I'm not sure why. I must drop her off before I get into trouble. *But don't you want to know about her?* No! I don't want to know anything else. Even if she does know Daniel. I don't want to know.

"Where are we going, anyway?" I ask.

"Just keep going down this road. Just a few more miles," she tells me. Then, she turns to me and says, "I know what you're thinking."

"Yeah? And what's that?"

She sighs and then turns to the window, staring into the eyes of her own reflection. Silence fills the car, and I hate it, especially on a rainy night like this one. This kind of toxic silence annoys me, brutally underscoring how much of a mistake I have made. Suddenly, the loud sound of a SUV honking at me pulls my eyes back onto the road. That's it. Next red light… I'm dropping her off.

Left onto Biscayne Boulevard.

Green light…

Yellow light…

I stop at a red light at the intersection of Biscayne and 123rd. On the corner sits a shopping center where I can drop her off. That would be malicious of me, but it needs to be done. *Damnit, Andrea! Just do it!*

"You're wondering about the men you saw me with today, aren't you?" she finally says.

Being caught off guard isn't a reaction I take well, but Madison takes me by surprise because she's right. I want to know all about her and the men I saw her with today.

"Uh, no, I wasn't thinking about that. But I guess since you mention it, maybe just a little."

"What do you want to know?"

"Um, I'm not sure." I take a deep breath.

I turn to her, and there's no trace of a smile across her reflection—just a steady but slightly ironic gaze. Why am I so curious to know all about this woman?

"Yes. I mean, I guess I was wondering if you—"

"If I fucked any of them, right?"

"No! Not really. Why? Did you?"

"I have a feeling that you already know the answer." She looks away.

From what it looks like, her smile is how she expresses herself more than words can ever begin to tell, and although it's forged, she's determined to fool me through it. I had a client, Ms. Rosana Rodriguez, who did the same. Ms. Rodriguez would smile no matter what she was doing or how she felt. As a result, it wasn't easy to know who the real Rosana Rodriguez was. The same could be said for Madison.

"You have to understand who I am, Dr. Clarke."

"Well, tell me then."

She turns to me, and for a moment, I can see the real side of this woman staring at me as if she were drowning deep in grief.

"For a long time, I struggled with different disorders. Eating, personality, stress, and even sleeping. I never told anyone. So, I had to figure it out all by myself. I began taking drugs, which led me to acquire an addictive behavior. However, unlike most women, mine wasn't due to a non-consensual sexual situation. Still, something triggered my problems around sex, leading to a massive disconnect between my mind and body. At times, I didn't feel like my body was mine, and having sex was just something to do. Like some sort of drug, but just better. My mind would switch from reality to a make-believe world of euphoria, overriding anything happening in my life. Or perhaps, that was my mind trying to connect to my body again. I don't know. It was all confusing until I met him.

"What do you mean?"

"Life is all about what you make of it, and for me, it happened to come from my experiences with men. These experiences eventually forced me into a reality where spontaneous and passionate encounters were not only craved but were also normal. I loved everything about it because it made me feel freer than ever. But it's gotten out of control. Now, I've fallen deep into a place where I can no longer make sense of my identity. A place where my extreme sexual behaviors collide with frequent opportunities, and managing those behaviors, becomes a total blur. Consequently, I have persistent thoughts about men that interfere with my ability to work, complete daily activities, and tell the difference between what's real and what's not."

Oh my! This is more than I imagined, and for some strange reason… I'm fascinated by it. There's no smile on her face, or shame, or anger. No expression from her at all. Her eyes are stuck on the road, but who knows what she's really thinking about. I'm not sure if I should feel sorry for her or not, but I do know that now, at this moment, I want to learn more.

"Why do you think that is?" I inquire.

Madison shrugs her shoulders, adjusts herself, and then turns to me.

"I'm not sure. For the longest, I felt like I wasn't normal when it came to sex because while all the other women talked about their orgasms, I was still trying to figure out mine. However, that didn't stop me from obsessing about it. There were moments I'd get really horny, and if I didn't do anything about it, I would go crazy. I know how this may sound, but the more I tried to control it, the more that obsession grew. To everyone else, I was an ordinary woman going through the motions of the day, but in secret, I was yearning to meet the company of a man who would give me what I wanted. Better yet, what I needed!"

"What's that? Sex?" I question.

"Not just the act of having sex, but the thrill of it as well. From that initial flirting where his full attention is on me to how he touches my body for the first time like some rare diamond. There's also that look in his eyes that I hardly saw from the ones I loved. Even the conversation, which gives me just enough to want more, is what I craved—going out, dancing, the thoughts of what will happen next. All of it. Sometimes, I felt empty afterward, but that only made me want to do it again and again. Every second of anticipation leading to the moment he enters my body gives me that rush of adrenaline.

"It's kinda weird, but there's this thing I like to do with the men I encounter. It helps keep things interesting and somewhat mysterious. Every time I run into a man I've slept with, I pretend we've never met before—always introducing myself to him like it was the first time. God, there's nothing like that initial touch or that first look. Sometimes we use the same name, and sometimes we don't. But we go about our lives whenever we're done as if we never met…until we meet again." Madison takes a deep breath.

I'm speechless and trying to understand what I've just heard from Madison without analyzing or judgment is a total failure. The worst part is that I can't tell if she's troubled by it. Perhaps, this is an area of her life with more confusion and complexity than she can truly understand. This wouldn't be the first time I've seen this. Plenty of my clients go through the same, but no matter what the case is… I am interested. So, I look at her as the center of my universe comes to a halt. This thing floating in my thoughts leaves me with a feeling of wonder. Not only that, but that strange tingling feeling rushes to the pit of my stomach once again.

"I guess that's what life is all about—making the best of every encounter," she turns away.

That would explain the instant connection between her and the distinguished gentleman—Derek. I can imagine him having his way with her in the most sinful way that any man can offer. The thought of it is vivid. One hand squeezes on her breast as his tongue glides around her nipple. The other hand travels up her legs and applies pressure on her stimulating spot. Circular motions, and then slow, gentle rubbing. *Andrea! Focus!*

"But to answer your question, yes! I fucked the guy from this morning." Her voice fades as if she's somewhat ashamed.

"And the guy from the bar?"

"Not yet. But probably soon enough." She hangs her head.

I could never do anything as spontaneous as the things Madison does, but it does seem empowering to do so. I wonder how it feels to live a life where I am not shamed into sexual suppression, all to be considered holy and worthy of love. A life where I can do what I want when I want and with who I want to.

Red light.

"I sound all fucked up, don't I? That's because I probably am. But it's the truth. And that truth is that I am powerless over my sexuality with no sense of control, and it's all because of him. Now, it's taken over me like a continuing path of bad decisions."

"I don't understand. Are you saying—"

"Yes. I'm addicted to sex." She looks away.

An obsessive sexual compulsive disorder? Although it makes sense, nothing about Madison shows me that she's troubled by any sort of addiction. She doesn't even carry herself like most addicts, and I've sat across from plenty of them. Most sex addicts lack confidence and often focus on how others will see them. That doesn't seem to be the case for Madison. Not only that, but the addicts I've worked with, were dominated by their sexual activity to the point it shows in their physical appearance. Dark wide-open eyes, messy hair, fidgety hands, teasing behaviors, and an element of defiance when they speak. Those are all subtle signs of an addict I do not see in Madison.

"Interesting," I murmur.

"What is?"

Crap! She heard me.

"Everything that you're telling me. I wouldn't have suspected that."

"No one ever does."

She sighs, looks away for a moment, and then turns back to me.

"You're intrigued by me, aren't you? I can tell. That's the reason you followed me. The reason you look at me the way you do. It's all because of how I choose to live my life, isn't it?

There is a feeling in my gut that tells me not to answer, but the voice in my head tells me to do so.

"No. I'm just listening. I'm not sure what to make of it."

A smile flashes across her face beneath the lamppost that I pass by. Even though it was only for a quick moment, it was still there.

"It usually starts off fine, but then you find yourself looking for a man who will put you in the realm between love and lust."

"What do you mean?"

She turns to me, and in her arrogant triumph, she smirks, narrowing her eyes, and tilting her head.

"Easy. Not all men are sexual. Most of them just like sex."

"Isn't that the same thing?"

"Would you consider a chauffeur and a mechanic the same?" she replies. "Most drivers only know how to drive a car, but a mechanic knows the ins and outs to make that car run. So, you see, some men drive cars while some make them go."

I take my eyes off the road and turn to Madison, staring at her as if I've just seen a monkey jump onto her shoulder. How does she come up with this stuff and make absolute sense of it?

"You say it as if it were that easy." I chuckle anxiously.

"Why wouldn't it be? Besides, the idea of a woman being comfortable with her sexuality shouldn't be scrutinized and shameful. It should be admired and explored."

"Yet, you feel as though you are screwed up because of it. Isn't that right?" I ask.

"You're right. But my issues go deeper than even you can begin to understand."

Madison has a point. Could this be the difference that I've been missing out on? An experience that dwells within my sexuality leaving me with something to remember.

So much of Madison reminds me of Denita Richardson because, like Madison, Denita was fueled by her sexuality, using it as a weapon. She could twist men around her finger while making women envy her. Denita flirted with guys just to get their devotion, and once she got it, she'd leave them alone. For her, it was all fun and games, but I think it was Denita's way of coping with something much more profound than she could identify with. Yet, I envy her, and as the rain comes pouring down on my car, one thing is for sure, Madison is no different.

Oh, God!

What about Daniel? How could I have forgotten about him? Suddenly, it feels like my heart is trying to explode in my chest as the chills run through my body, making me anxious. *Relax, Andrea.* I take a big gulp of air, followed by a deep breath, hoping it helps. I need to stop with these thoughts and get to him now.

"You, okay?" she asks.

I turn to Madison, and what I see in her eyes sends a surging pulse against my temple as a mild panic begins to grow. Something dawns on me. She said she was an addict because of him. Who could she be referring to? There's something about that I find puzzling. It's more so how she said it than why she said it that has me concerned.

"Wait…can you go back a second? You said it was all because of him? Who's him?" My voice hitches up several octaves.

She turns to me as a shrewd piece of despair covers her face with a look of manipulation and a twinkle of lies in her eyes. As a young girl, I saw that same look on my mother's face plenty of times. Not only that but there was this patient of mine, Tamar Osborne, who had that same look just before she told me about her obsession with cutting herself. Yes, I know that look all too well. I've even seen it once while standing in front of a mirror.

CHAPTER 8

10:44 P.M.

ONE TIME, I SAT across from a patient, Charity Goodwin, and listened to her tell me about the time she tried to kill herself by driving headfirst into a wall. At ninety miles per hour, her Toyota Camry hit the wall so hard that the EMT found parts of the engine in her trunk. Anger and depression drove Ms. Goodwin to the point of not wanting to live anymore. Fortunately, she survived that accident, but she'll never be the same—both mentally and physically. Ms. Goodwin's story left me stuck to my seat and filled with emotions, all while trying to understand the meaning of my own life.

Madison is nothing like Ms. Goodwin, but I sense that whatever memory she's getting ready to reveal will give me that same feeling.

"Madison… who's him?" I ask again.

"The man that turned me into the woman I am today. A woman who's not afraid to explore herself beyond what makes others uncomfortable. However, I'll admit, because of him, that's why I'm probably fucked up.

"It was almost a year ago, on a rainy Thursday night, when I met him in a place that I had no business being in and at a time in life when I was looking for a change. In need of some excitement to offer something different, I ended up at a massive black and white building on N.W. 27th Street and Third Avenue. The building had no sign and looked questionable at best, yet that didn't stop me from walking in. The door opened to a long hallway so narrow I could touch both walls by barely stretching out my arms. At the end of the hallway was another door with a dingy light bulb dangling from the ceiling. I could hear the music getting louder the closer I got.

"Just as I approached the stainless-steel door with no handle or lock, a woman with a clipboard in her right hand appeared out of nowhere. Her face, rigid with tension, was covered with makeup that belied her age. She wore a skimpy blue dress that covered her petite body like paint. The woman asked for my name, and I handed her an invitation card that someone had given me. She quickly looked at it, and without saying a word, she knocked three times on the door. The door slid open, and I stepped into the massive building, feeling like I had walked into a different dimension.

"The inside of the place was nothing compared to the hallway I had stepped out of. It was enormous and lush. Very pleasing to the eyes. White walls. Scattered around the place are statues of exotic animals. The floor, a distinct shade of black and gray, is polished with a glossy shine. A bouncing, dark, fluorescent red light shadowed the entire venue, giving it an unusual mystique. Indeed, I could feel this was no ordinary place, and anyone with righteous morals, should never find themselves there. Nonetheless, there I was, standing in the midst of it, anticipating what might happen next.

"Beneath the dry-ice smoke, twisting and turning through an array of lights, are several bodies intertwined like vines. Weaving, dancing, and holding hands as they stare into each other's eyes. Some looked like fools, while others looked like they were making love more than they were dancing. Judging by the wide-open eyes and heavy eyelids all over the venue, I'd say they were drinking or on drugs. The music was so loud that I felt my skin tingling from the vibration thumping in time with my heartbeat. Overdressed was an understatement because my long-sleeved green sequin dress and black heels were too much. For goodness sake, some of the men didn't have on shirts, and some of the women had dresses so short you could see their panties. Well, those who had any on, that is.

"For a moment, I looked around the venue, hoping to indulge myself in everything I saw happening. The dancing, the touching, the drinking, and the overwhelming thought of what would happen next. Then, as I made my way through the crowd, heading to the bar, I met the gaze of a refined, well-dressed man who stood near a staircase leading to the second floor. He was all alone and didn't seem to fit in with the others because, unlike the others, he was fully clothed. Fitted denim jeans, a blue button-up shirt, and a brown blazer is what he wore. His hair was dark and cut short with gray along the sides. He wasn't big or small, nor was he short or tall. He was just an average guy with daring eyes and a charming smile that was hard to ignore.

"From across the room, his eyes were focused on me as much as mine were focused on him. It's as if he and I were in a stare-off that neither of us wanted to lose. He twitched his lips upward to a smile, and I smiled back while softly running my index finger along my bottom lip. We used our eyes and bodies to communicate in a way I wasn't used to, causing me to blush. It was fun and innocent, yet it felt emphatic. I like to think of it as some sort of superpower.

"By the time I reached the crowded bar, he approached me face to face, grabbing hold of my left hand. He softly kissed it and then shook it. Our energy vibrated so uniquely that my stomach turned, and my skin became clammy. Everyone in the place continued to shout over the loud music. Yet, it felt like it was just him and I. Alone!

"What's your choice of drink?' he asked.

"'It depends on how I'm feeling at the moment.'

"'So, tell me then…how are you feeling right now?'

"'Like an old-fashioned.'

"'That's the drink, but what's the feeling?'

"I chuckled and smiled like some shy girl. Everything we said to one another was a perfect lead to something else. For nearly an hour, I sat there enjoying his company as if I'd known him forever. Our conversation was perfect. He listened and offered intelligent responses, all while gazing into my eyes. The attention he displayed, if I'm honest, was the most amazing thing I'd ever seen in a man. He could feel my energy just as much as I felt his as I flirted with him more than I had ever done with anyone else.

"'I want you to stay with me for the rest of the night,' he said.

"I just smiled and shrugged it off. Besides, between the drinks and the moment, I knew he would have said anything to have his way with me. Then, he wrapped his arms around my waist, pulled me in, and promised to give me the best night of my life if I did. He didn't seem like the aggressive type, but the way he took control of me and whispered in my ear turned me on. I had never been this connected to anyone who barely knew my name.

"'So, aren't you going to say something?' The corner of his mouth twitched upwards to a smile as he glared into my eyes.

"'I don't know about that yet.'

"'Okay. Well, come with me.'

"He led me to the middle of the floor, where we danced intimately beneath the dry-ice smoke mixed in with an array of colorful lighting. Our bodies were so close that I could feel the bulge in his pants pressed against my stomach. I closed my eyes and held onto him tighter, becoming a stranger to the woman who had walked into that black and white building. I wasn't sure why I did it, but I put my right hand into his pocket to feel the warmth of his bulge. It felt stimulating to do so with very little inhibitions. He wasn't the least bit surprised, judging by his subtle reaction. Instead, he gazed down at me, not moving his wrapped arms from around my waist. Then he whispered into my ear.

"'You can do more than that if you want,' he said.

"I smiled and melted in his arms. There was something about how he did it as if, for a moment, he was utterly absorbed by the feeling of our hands touching. It played out in his subtle smile and soft gaze. But then, as time dissolved, something about the man changed. I watched as the innocence disappeared from his eyes as his dark eyebrows sloped downwards to a stony expression. His smile drew into a hard line across his face. His touch made me feel less comfortable and more concerned.

"There was something about how he stared at me that didn't seem right. His warm persona, which was once captivating, had vanished faster than summer rain. Leaving would have been the smart thing to do, but I didn't. I stayed, watching him get more aggressive. When I finally tried to pull away, he held onto me tighter.

"'Please, stay with me for the night, I said?' he whispered in my ear.

"I didn't respond, fearing if I told the truth, he wouldn't accept it. It took almost ten minutes before I finally pulled away from him, and in a crowded room filled with people dancing around us, we stood there looking at each other like gunslingers in a duel. The look in his eyes was something I had never seen from anyone else before. Cold and empty. He stood there with a malicious smirk. I kept thinking, how could he be this sweet in one moment and then someone whose face is rigid with fury in the next?

"My phone vibrating in my purse is what got me to turn away from him finally. Without thinking about it, I hurried off to a corner, away from the dance floor, hoping to hear over the loud music.

However, that didn't help because the music was still too loud. Then, as I was steadily trying to listen to the person on the end of the phone, I was abruptly shoved into an area so dark that I could barely see my hands. It took me a moment to gather myself as my mind stumbled over itself, unable to comprehend what was happening. Screaming wouldn't have done any good because the music was blasting so loud, I could barely hear myself.

"'I said I wanted you to stay with me tonight.' His voice was stern.

"I couldn't see him, but I smelled the spicy scent of his masculinity, and it was apparent that it was him. Then, like some barbarian, he pressed his body onto my back, shoving the right side of my face against a cold wall. His left hand covered my mouth as his right hand pulled my sequin dress up. I kicked and twisted my body to break free from his hold as much as possible, but he was too strong. My heart rate accelerated, and the attempt to control my breathing was a miserable failure. Each breath I took felt like it would be my last one.

"His left hand uncovered my mouth and tugged on my panties, seemingly trying to tear them off. I couldn't see his face, but I felt him smirking with those evil eyes. His scruffy face brushed against my left cheek as I smelled the whiskey on his breath. At that moment, I gave up, hoping for someone to save me. However, that never happened.

"'So, is this really what you're going to do to me? Right here? Like this?' I asked while breathing profusely.

"He finally ripped my panties and forcefully pulled them off of me, and as he did that, he slid his tongue from my left ear, across my neck, and then over to my right ear.

"'What do you think?' he whispered.

"Then, something strange happened, and even as I sit here telling you this, I can feel my body getting hot—especially between my legs. I tried over and over to understand it, but I couldn't.

"While pressed on my back, he spread my legs open using his left foot. He then took my left hand and placed it on his erection.

"'This is all you,' he whispered.

"The thought of squeezing it so tight that his heart would stop beating crossed my mind. I even thought about yanking it off or brutally digging my nails into his erection until blood leaked down my hand. But I did none of that. Instead, I took a deep breath and held onto it, feeling the warmth of his blood rushing and the veins radiating in my palm. On the one hand, I was scared, but on the other, I felt invigorated and aroused at the same time. His hard, warm dick resting in my palm allowed me to recall thoughts I had forgotten. I could see it all coming together at that very moment.

"'I want you to feel me,' he said.

"I remained silent as he brushed the tip of his erection between my legs for fifteen seconds. Up and down. Then, over my ass, and back down, he entered my pussy— slow but persuasive. He jerked and moaned a tad from the feeling of sliding inside of me. It was as if he had been waiting for that moment all night. Oddly, my mouth dropped open from the initial feeling, leaving me to wander in a place where there were no colors, uncertainties, or emotions. Just pure pleasure.

"The more he thrust in and out of me, the less the internal battle went on. I couldn't believe what was happening. Even the scent of his cologne and the alcohol on our breaths made me weak in the strangest way." Madison smiles.

That's it! I am officially infatuated with this woman. I take a big gulp of air, hoping to subdue any physical reaction that may happen. Shit! I also have a strong desire to have my breasts caressed; because of Madison, my entire body feels sensitive. I bet even a feather could cause me to have an orgasm right now. I want to hear more, but I'm afraid of what will happen if I do. Yes, I have Daniel, but it wouldn't be anything like what Madison just described, and I'm okay with that. Right?

"Between my legs, just beyond a place I could not touch, it felt so fucking amazing. I wanted him to keep going because as the pleasure increased, so did my desire, and—"

"Madison, enough!" I interrupt.

I'm conflicted. I should feel bad for what happened to Madison, right? However, I'm only concerned about the slight throbbing between my thighs. Oh crap! I don't have any panties on. I completely forgot about that. The sweet scent of my excitement reminds me.

Think of something, Andrea. Think.

Random thoughts of flowers and short deep breaths should control my urges.

Deep inhale.

White orchids on a picnic table.

Yellow Tulips floating in the wind.

Soft exhale.

Ugh! That's no help! Madison's encounter has traveled through my mind effortlessly. It's as if I were the woman in that back room at the mercy of this man she speaks of. But why? Why are her words so invigorating? And why does it feel so…real? Get it together, Andrea.

"Uh, I'm sorry that happened to you. No one deserves to be violated like that." I adjust myself in my seat.

Madison chuckles. Then, she looks away for a moment and turns back to me with a smile from deep within, lighting her eyes and spreading into every part of her.

"Don't be sorry," she replies, "because something happened to me during those few minutes. Something that I was not expecting. The man gripped his right hand around my neck so tight I could barely breathe, and as he did so, I felt him go deep inside of me. Fulfilled is the best way to describe it. The more he thrust, the more my body weakened. Then, there was a brief silence through the blaring music, where my body began to tremble. My breathing faded as a release of tension circled in my stomach. I reached behind and pulled him in tighter, digging my nails into his lower back. I don't know if I was trying to stop him or yearning for him to go deeper, but it felt so amazing. This may sound crazy, but until that night, I had never experienced a sexual encounter of that magnitude. In just a few minutes, my body was overwhelmed with a feeling so intense that I could not stop myself from pulsating. An orgasm is what had taken over my body, and it happened in the last place I expected it to and with a complete stranger."

Indeed, I was right about Madison. She's nothing like anyone I've ever met. Not even Denita Richardson. I watch her bask in her thoughts of that night with nothing but bliss on her face. It's as if she just told me about the time she won the lottery. I never met anyone who could be satisfied with such a horrific experience as the one Madison just described. Yet, her memory has me completely glued to my seat, like the day I sat across from Ms. Goodwin.

"Well, it's not uncommon for victims to experience an orgasm in their moment of weakness. You may think that if you had one, you enjoyed it, but that's not necessarily true. The physical and emotional responses to sex can be entirely unrelated," I explain.

"Even beyond our mental control?"

"Of course! An orgasm is a physiological response as well as a natural occurrence. Sort of like pupil dilation."

"Maybe you're right, but the fact of the matter is, I enjoyed it. I know it's strange to hear, but it's the truth, and I had to have it again, and again, and again. So, you see, that's why I said it's because of him." She covers her face with a slight grin.

"Just this one guy?"

"And plenty of others. But there's nothing like him."

Something is puzzling about this. If Madison is unaffected by her addiction, then I am genuinely fascinated with this woman. Even more than I was with Denita.

"Do you know his name or anything about him?" I ask.

Madison turns to me and offers a forged smile, and what I see in her eyes is someone hiding something so deep that even she's unaware of. Could she be referring to Daniel? No. It can't be. Daniel would never do anything like that. He's too kind and caring.

"Does it matter?"

Now, her presence is starting to buzz around me like a pesky mosquito that I can't seem to swat away. Her smile, her movements, and the fact that she's sitting here, breathing, suddenly seem to infuriate me to no end. I must drop her off at once.

"Uh, you know what? Actually, I should get going now."

"Just ask! You have something you want to ask. I can tell. So, what's stopping you?"

She is right. I do have questions, but they aren't the ones that could help her.

"What makes you so sure about that?"

"I just am. Like I said, you and I have more in common than you think."

"Do we? How can you even say that when you don't know me?"

"I'm pretty good at reading people."

A brief moment of silence passes by, and I find myself at her mercy, wanting to know everything there is to know about her.

"Okay. Yes. I do have a question."

She sits upright, paying close attention to what I have to say.

"How'd you allow yourself to get to the point where you're so comfortable with a man that you barely know?

"I can't say for certain, but perhaps it's because he made me feel noticed and wanted. Like I was the only woman in a room filled with others. The way he looked at me was admiring, especially given his nervousness. His touch was a confirmation of what he felt for me, and although it was that one time, it was satisfying to know that he desired me. It was exactly what I needed."

"You mean what you wanted."

"No. What I needed."

"Okay. So, now being that it was that one time…emotionally, how do you just move on from it? To know that he doesn't even care about you or love you the way one should, doesn't bother you at all?

"Dr. Clarke, these encounters aren't only about the men. Who's to say I'm not the one who makes him entertain those questions?" She seductively smiles and leans back.

"You see, the fact of the matter is, biologically, we were all created for this, and you and I are no different. Every part of who we are is built on the sense of sexuality. Our minds. Our walk. Lips. Hips. Everything! Even down to the way we seamlessly connect with others. We want them, and they yearn to have us. Perhaps, you've been looking at it all wrong. Sex is the relationship between two individuals, aiming to bring the only thing that has not changed through evolution."

"Which is?" I inquire.

"Pleasure!"

Where does she get this information? It's so perfectly random and yet eloquently challenging. In my profession, I've never been one to tell an individual what type of lifestyle they should or shouldn't live, especially a sexual one, but Madison has a point. No matter what I can think of to show why that lifestyle is immoral, she seems to have a rebuttal that would lead me to believe otherwise.

"What is it that you want from me?" I sternly ask.

"Sometimes, we forget about the moments in our lives that define us. We choose to bury them deep in our minds instead of embracing them. You know what I mean?"

I don't respond. Instead, I wait for Madison to tell me what I need to know.

"I'm sure you understand. As I said, you and I are more alike than you think. You may not know it right now, but it's true."

I can't take this anymore!

"And what's the truth here? You thought you could come in and tell me about the man I love? Huh? Is that the truth you want me to believe?"

"Not at all."

"Then what is it? Why are you in my car?"

Why did I let this woman into my life? My deep exhale comes out short and quivering, and as I keep driving down A1A, unaware of where I'm headed, something quickly dawns on me.

"I know what you want me to say, but I won't. That's not who I am. Do you think I'm supposed to ignore my inhibitions just because you saw me looking at some stranger? I'm sorry, but I'm not that type of woman."

"No. That's not it. Besides, I know you're not that woman. That's why I envy you."

Why would a woman like Madison envy me? I turn and look her in the eyes, and as a slight pain drowns out her soul, I sense she's telling the truth. That much I can see. However, there's still something suspicious about her being here.

"You envy me? Why do you envy someone you don't even know?"

"The same reason why you may envy me. We're intrigued by a life that we want to live."

Once again, she has a point.

"Then what is it that you want?"

"I just wanted someone to talk to."

My ability to speak leaves me stranded, and as I stare into her deep-set hazel eyes, my heart falls to silence. Could that really be it? Does Madison need my help? This doesn't make any sense. But I wish it did because the lord knows how much clarity is needed right now.

"Tell me… what are you thinking right now?" she says.

I can only think about Madison and the man, hoping it's not Daniel she's talking about, and if she is, I want to know everything there is to know. Every bit of their moment. The kisses, the touches, and the way they made love in ways that I can only imagine. Then again, if she isn't referring to Daniel, then I want to know everything there is to know about her— all while living vicariously through her stories.

"Madison, even if I could tell you what I was thinking, why would I? It would be pointless?"

"Pointless?" She chuckles. "Maybe you're right, but then again, you never know."

Her eyes desperately search through mine…waiting.

"No. I can't. I can't do that." I take a gulp of air, trying to focus through the unwavering battle between my sexual thoughts and my total avoidance.

Left onto North Miami Avenue.

"Whatever. But just know this. Desires have a way of lingering somewhere in our mind that is almost incapable of being touched if it is never fulfilled. Then, it spreads like an infectious disease, making us continually wonder about the what ifs until we find ourselves lost in it.

And by that time, you'll be just as fucked up as I am. The way I see it, fighting the urge to seek pleasure is like some sort of sick self-preservation."

For goodness sake! Madison sure does have a way of making the immoral seem moral, leaving me to scowl at the fact that she could be right. It's as if she stowed a ticking time bomb in my mind, and now it's driving me crazy. Maybe if I ignore this feeling, it will go away. Screw this! I must drop her off at once.

Red light. Right on 108th Avenue.

"Pull over in there," Madison tells me.

The sky is completely dark with a full moon when I drive into the parking lot of the Crescent Cove hotel—tucked away along the beach. Closely, I watch as Madison stares into the dimly lit sun visor mirror. She swipes her left index finger underneath her eyes. Right eye first, and then the left one.

"Where are we?"

"This is where I call my special place. I shouldn't be here, but like I said, I can't control myself," she murmurs.

"Then why are you here?"

"What happens when our reality is mistaken for our perception? Or our perception becomes our reality? When everything that we believed in vanishes in an instant. More importantly, what happens when any of this occurs beyond our control?" Madison asks.

My eyes are stuck on her as the words make their way out of her mouth.

"I guess you adjust your life accordingly."

She shrugs her shoulder loosely and then reaches into her clutch for a tube of Chanel dark rouge lipstick. She slowly slides the shade of red against her lips—first the top lip, then the bottom. Red has never been my choice, but it looks enticing on her. Then, she places her YSL black clutch with gold trimmings under her left arm and exits the car.

"You're right. So, you see, I need this. It will relieve me in ways you can't even imagine. Or maybe you can," Madison walks off.

How does Madison do it? Fully open herself to men she barely knows and be okay with it? I wish I could be just like Madison. I don't know why, but I am fascinated with Madison's chosen way of life. It's raw. It's spontaneous. It looks exciting. That's what makes her who she is. Then again, why can't I live that way too? I shouldn't have to be stuck between the realm of my desires, especially where possibilities can be the realities of life. Besides, sexual desires are both common and expected. Not some sort of curse. Nor should I feel ashamed for something that comes naturally. Embracing that I want to be kissed, touched, or fucked at any moment should be acceptable and cherished. Andrea! What about Daniel? Right. Daniel.

Shit!

God, I feel terrible for having those thoughts. Then again, this might explain the strange feeling that's been tingling randomly throughout my body. This must be the excitement that I have been looking for. Besides, one time wouldn't take away from me being considered a virtuous woman, right? Nor would I want to leave Daniel. And, of course, there's no way I would allow it to turn me into a woman like Madison. However, I don't want to spend the rest of my life feeling like I missed out on some spontaneous experiences that may transpire while exploring my sexuality. Otherwise, I will be left with all these consuming thoughts of what-if, and how will I ever really know who I am and what I want with a lingering thought like that?

Wait a minute!

What if she's here to meet Daniel? No. It can't be. There's no way she would have me drop her off to meet up with the man I love. Even though I don't know what's going on, Daniel wouldn't do this to me.

What am I saying? Madison is a woman that I don't know anything about. Could this all be a coincidence? I believe not.

"No, Andrea. Please don't do it. Daniel isn't here," I murmur to myself. But what if he is? Looking around the parking lot, I don't see his car anywhere. Screw this! I need to find out. Quickly, I pull my phone out and call him. But there's still no answer. What the fuck? He hasn't answered any of my calls. Screw it!

I exit the car, and once again, follow behind Madison. My steps are light and careful as I attempt to be as inconspicuous as possible. With every step that she takes, I do the same. Madison then dips into the lobby, where a doorman with gray hair and a droopy face stands at the front. She doesn't even look his way, but the man tilts his black hat up to her and smiles. Then, she makes a left down a hallway and into a courtyard of gardens. I remain anxiously drifting in the background like a shadow. Madison is so calm and collected with the posture of a Victoria Secret model. Eyes front and shoulders back. The temperament of this woman is riveting.

By the time I step into the courtyard, I spot Madison making her way up to the second floor. Four doors down, she comes to a stop. Once she's there, she waits a few seconds, looks around, and enters the room, closing the door behind her. A rising feeling of weakness rumbles in my stomach, and below the clack of my heels, my heart beats to unsteady thumps. I press my back against the concrete wall and take a deep breath. What do I do now? I need to get out of here. This isn't where I belong. *Yes, get out of here, Andrea,* a voice whisper.

As I return to my car, something happens where the synapses of my brain are brought to a standstill. I can't will myself to move a muscle, and even worse, I don't feel anything. There is no excitement, nervousness, or confusion. everything is blurred, with the world around me getting quieter and darker. My eyes blink rapidly as my stomach begins to churn. What is happening to me? This is typically my body's way of shutting down during something traumatic, but it can't be that. Is the drink finally catching up to me? It must be. Either way, I need to leave. *Yes! Leave now, Andrea.*

But what if she is in the room with Daniel? *Ugh!* This is killing me. She's probably on the bed with her hands tied behind her back as he rests on his knees, in-between her legs, at the edge of the bed, pleasing her. First, grabbing onto her panties with his index finger and pulling them to the side. Then, he possibly grips onto her ass, spreading her apart, and then slides his tongue, slow and long, over her pussy and up to the middle of her back.

Goosebumps begin to crawl over my skin as I think of what Madison is doing inside that room. It's disturbing and arousing, but I know it's not with Daniel. I can feel it. And I hope that I am right.

1:22 A.M.

The feeling of emptiness disappears when I arrive home, and God, do I want to know more about Madison. She does what she wants, lives how she pleases and does not give a damn about society's perception of women. Even with all the backlash that follows that type of lifestyle, there is a beauty and purity that she could never live without. Madison claims she envies me, but deep down inside… she's the one I envy. Yes! I can do this. One time is all it would take. Just one time.

DECEMBER

THURSDAY

10

CHAPTER 9

7:05 A.M.

Knock! Knock!

FUCK ME! The loud thumping at the front door startles me, and quickly, I sit up with my eyes bug-wide open. Who could that be this early in the morning knocking? I remain in bed, waiting, as rain tapping against my window gets louder. Yet, the sun blooms on the horizon, but barely enough to get past my window blinds.

Knock! Knock!

There goes the knocking again. It's an ear-shattering, disturbing type of knock, like the ones that come with bad news. And because of the force of the knuckles pounding against the door, I can tell something is wrong. I feel it in the pit of my stomach as the world around me is eerily quiet. It's as if it ended last night and left me to dwell in the middle of a never-ending blackhole.

off me, and to my surprise, I'm naked. What in the hell? Did I go to bed like this? Perhaps I got hot in the middle of the night, and while asleep, I stripped out of my pajamas. It wouldn't be the first time that this happened. But the room is rather cold. And what is this on my legs? The inside of my thighs, directly across from each other, looks like some sort of bruise fading away. However, it doesn't hurt. What could this be?

Knock! Knock! Knock!

God, that better be Daniel because if it's anyone else, I'm calling the police. I throw on my robe, slip my feet into my satin slippers next to the nightstand, and make my way to the front door.

I spot a woman with short brown hair and a stern look through the peephole. Although her lips are tinted with a shade of burgundy, and her skin is flawless, something tells me she's not here to sell anything.

"Can I help you?" I ask without opening the door.

"Morning, I'm Detective Barringer with the Miami Police Department. Do you mind if I ask you a few questions?"

A detective? I take a gulp of air as every natural body movement of mine is put on hold. Just for a second. Why in the world would a detective be at my door? Oh, God! Please don't let this be about Daniel.

"Regarding what?"

"It would be easier if you just opened the door."

Take a deep breath, Andrea. Just relax. Everything is fine. I open the door, and immediately, my eyes settle on the gun pressed along her waist on one side and a badge on the other. The woman is emotionless as she looks at me with her bulging brown eyes in a very judgmental manner. It's as if she knows something about me that I'm unaware of.

"Andrea Clarke?" she asks.

"Yes. That's me."

"You mind if I come in?"

"I'd like to know what this is about first."

A distinctive look in the woman's eyes makes me question everything. Why is she here? Where is Daniel? Am I in some sort of trouble? What could it be?

"Is this about Daniel?" I ask anxiously.

Before she even opens her mouth to answer, my heart drops to my stomach, slow and bumpy, as my knees begin to buckle. I can barely make eye contact with the woman as the tossing in the pit of my stomach intensifies. I cross my arms and squeeze tightly, hoping to stop the trembling that will soon take place. Why am I scared? Or nervous. I must get it together before she mistakes my behavior for being suspicious. God, I wish I were wired differently. That way, I could control my reactions. But I can't. So, listening to what she has to say is the only option.

"Daniel? No, but I am working on a missing person case that I believe you may be able to help me with," she says.

Whew! It's not Daniel. Good, I can relax now. Then, her eyes glance over my shoulder, into my home, and begin to scan the place in search of something. Maybe a clue? Or perhaps some sort of evidence? I'm not sure, but whatever it is, it's enough to confirm the strange feeling twirling in the pit of my stomach.

"Who's the missing person?"

The woman takes a step closer, and her brows crease as her face tenses to a scowl with no trace of a smile.

"James Walker,"

James Walker? The name doesn't ring a bell at all. This makes this visit even more confusing.

"Sorry. I don't know who that is."

Her eyes squint off her puzzled expression, staring at me unblinkingly. It's as if I can see her mind surging with questions, and it's all because she doesn't believe me. I don't blame her, though, because sometimes truths and lies can be masked by personal feelings.

"I take it that you're not going to let me in?" she says.

Having nothing to say, I allow the silence to serve as a response. The woman then takes a couple of steps back and nods.

"Okay. Fine. Here's my card. Just in case." She hands me a card, and as I'm about to shut the door…

"I will be back. So, if you change your mind about what you know of James Walker, let me know."

"Like I said before…I don't know who that is."

"Okay. Well…thanks for your time."

I shut the door, and for a moment, I am weakened, standing here as if I'm paralyzed from the neck down. The woman's unwarranted visit doesn't make any sense. Why would she come here looking for a man I don't know? My back presses against the door as I take a deep breath and slide down until my chin rests between my knees.

12:50 P.M.

Fourteen calls, five voicemails, and over twelve text messages later, still no word from Daniel. Daniel not reaching back out to me is entirely frustrating. I need to be out there looking for him, but instead, I'm here at work, listening to all the nutcases tell me about their problems when I have one of my own.

Ding!

The elevator doors open to two women in the middle of their conversation. The moment I enter, they stop talking. One of the women is in her mid-fifties while the other is younger and much heavier.

"Going down?" the older woman asks.

They turn to each other and snicker like grade schoolgirls, unaware I can see them from the corner of my eyes.

"No, I'm actually…"

Wait a second. Eleventh floor? I must've been so deeply distracted by my thoughts of Daniel.

"I guess I am," I reply.

The door closes, and immediately, the silence creeps in on me. All

I can hear is the beating of my heart mixed in with the women's breathing. I spot the heavyset woman mouthing something to the older woman, but I can't make out exactly what she's saying.

Tenth floor...

"You work at the counseling center, right?" the younger woman asks.

"Yes. That's correct." My eyes are focused straight ahead—on the doors.

"A customer of mine told me about you. Christina Section. You know her, don't you?"

Ninth floor.

I can't see the woman's face, but I sense her questions are beyond curiosity. Her tone and the pace at which she speaks is how I know.

"I'm sorry, but I can't answer that."

"That's right. Duh! Confidentiality, right? Well, maybe I'll stop by sometime. I think I could use a good talk. I mean, who couldn't?"

Eighth floor.

"Sure. Our doors are always open."

"Great. By the way, I didn't get your name."

"Andrea Clarke." I turn to her, offer a crooked smile, and then turn away.

"Okay. Thanks, Dr. Clarke." Her voice drips with sarcasm.

Ding!

Seventh floor.

The elevator doors open, and just as I step out, I notice Rachel quickly recovering from something she doesn't want me to see.

"Dr. Clarke! You're back." Her voice peaks. "Your one o'clock is here."

Waiting in the lobby is a woman wearing fitted ripped white jeans, a yellow top, a fuchsia blazer, and a pair of pointed-toe nude stilettos.

She has a head full of curly black hair and cat-like brown eyes of a million hues. Childbearing hips define her bold curves, and her full lips blend perfectly with her detailing cheekbones. Patricia Walker is her name, and I forgot about her visit today.

"Thanks, Rachel."

Mrs. Walker called this morning, pleading to come in, and judging by her tone over the phone, I could tell it was important. I met Mrs. Walker nearly a year ago while serving as a witness on the trial of a former client of mine, Kara Turner. A thirty-eight-year-old woman accused of murdering her stepdaughter. After the trial, Mrs. Walker would come to my office occasionally, wanting to talk. At first, it was all about Kara, her best friend, but then it progressed to talking about other issues in her life. Mrs. Walker isn't a typical client because she doesn't have an addiction needing immediate attention or any real mental issue. She just likes to come in and talk, and her visits are always refreshing. Talking to her feels like having a conversation with a close friend, or better yet, myself. There's no pressure or feeling of having to put my guards up. With Mrs. Walker, I can just be…me.

"Good afternoon, Mrs. Walker. You ready?"

"Yes. I am."

"Come with me."

We enter my office just before one o'clock, and immediately, she takes a seat on the off-white upholstered sofa. Getting comfortable has never been an issue for Mrs. Walker. It's her being emotional that she struggles with. From what I remember, she believes it makes her look weak, and for a strong woman like Mrs. Walker, displaying weakness never does any good.

"Would you like something to drink?" I offer.

"You have tequila?"

We share laughter as I take a seat across from her. Everything about Mrs. Walker seems stable, from her smile to her clothing to how she positions herself upright on the sofa. Most people believe everything is okay when it's not, but not Mrs. Walker. So, I wonder why she's here today.

"Well, I'm sure that was a joke."

"I wish." She grins.

Several years before I met Mrs. Walker, she confessed she had a drinking problem. But she wasn't the type of person to get drunk and belligerent. Nor did she drink to cover her sorrow and pain. Mrs. Walker loved having alcohol as a choice of beverage. For lunch, she would have a martini. At dinner, she'd have rum with some sort of fruit juice. Then, she'd sit on her couch watching television with a glass of red wine at night. Oddly enough, Mrs. Walker has never been drunk. Imagine that. A person who loves to drink as much alcohol as Mrs. Walker does, yet never drinking enough to get drunk? Just another reason why everything about this woman seems stable.

"By the way, you smell amazing. Your perfume…let me guess. Dior, Hypnotic Poison?" I smile.

She snaps and looks at me as if she's just seen a ghost flash behind my back. Did I say something wrong?

"No. It's just that you're spot on, Dr. Clarke." She smiles, but it seems to be motivated by secrecy—nothing like a friend's nimble grin, but more like an enemy's smirk.

"I'm not sure how I guessed that. Anyway…please! Get comfortable. Take off your shoes and jacket if you want. You can even rest your feet up on the sofa. Whatever. Just make yourself feel at home."

She peels the blazer off her shoulders and slips out of her nude stilettos. Wow! Her arms are toned for a woman of her stature, and her collarbone curves contrast with a straight strap that could hold six quarters.

"It's been a while since you came in. How have you been?" I ask.

She pauses for a moment and stares at me without saying a word. There's no trace of emotion from her at all. Not in her eyes or the track marks on her angelic face. Her eyes are rigid and stern, and it's evident that something heavy is on her mind. I don't know what it is, but I know it's there.

"Mrs. Walker…?"

"Not so good, Dr. Clarke," she interjects.

"Want to tell me about it?"

Her eyes, slightly opened, wander around the room for nearly five seconds as her right leg begins to fidget. A smile creeps onto her face, but then it quickly vanishes as she takes a deep breath and focuses back on me.

"I thought I would be more nervous."

"You don't have to be nervous at all. So just allow yourself to feel at ease and receptive to the environment. No different than before."

"Is that so?" She shifts her body.

She's holding onto some sort of hurt, and I sense it in her tone and sudden inability to sit still. Depression? No, I doubt it. She's much too calm to be depressed. So, what could it be?

"I know I haven't been here in a long time, but my visit today is slightly different. So much so, I'm not even sure how this will go."

"That's understandable. How about this? You can ask me three essential questions, which hopefully will help you loosen up. Is that fair?"

She nods, and I smile. Like some of my other clients, there is something about Mrs. Walker that I feel connected to. Sometimes, there is a shyness to her that reminds me of myself. The hesitation in her body movements and the softness in her voice are things that I know all too well.

"Good. Go ahead. Ask away."

She shifts her body towards me and places her feet on the floor. Looking directly into my eyes, she puts her left hand on her lap and the other tucked underneath her chin. I can't tell if she's hurt, angry, or just has a lot on her mind. One thing is for sure… she's here for a specific purpose.

"Dr. Clarke, I never asked, but what made you choose this profession?" she asks.

"Well, I've always been fascinated with the human mind and how it works. I hate the sight of blood, so I decided to take the psychological path instead. Understanding how people think and how their thoughts affect their decisions, which then affect their lives, is intriguing to me."

"Interesting. I sense your passion for your work."

"I guess you can say I'm passionate about what I love."

"What about who you love?"

"Yes. That goes for them as well."

I think we're now getting to the crux of the matter because her voice ascends, and her tone is calm. This usually occurs when someone is out of the thought process and into the delivery phase.

"Do you have someone you love?" she asks.

"I'd rather not talk about my personal life, Mrs. Walker. I only allow you to ask questions that will make you feel comfortable."

"That question will help me feel more comfortable, Dr. Clarke. I believe some things are best learned through experiences. You can study your way through all the degrees you want, but until you've lived it, you probably won't fully understand what someone is going through."

"I see. And you have a valid point." I softly sigh, trying not to be so obvious. She sits there with a blank face, waiting. I turn to the large window for a moment and think about Daniel. I still haven't heard from him, and it's starting to get to me. However, I must remain positive. "All right. If it will help you. Yes. I have someone who I love." I turn back to Mrs. Walker.

"Passionately?"

"Yes. Passionately."

Mrs. Walker sits back on the sofa, smiles for a moment, and then gradually returns to a blank expression, having the emotion of a wet branch. She crosses her arms over her bosom and turns away. It's as if she is avoiding something…or someone.

"So, what if you lose that passion for that person? Is it replaced with hurt, curiosity, or even worse…anger?" She turns back to me. "Could you still love that person then, Dr. Clarke?"

Of course. Mrs. Walker must be here because of her husband. In the past, Mr. Walker sat in with Patricia for a session, and although they seemed perfect together, I knew that things weren't as blissful as they appeared to be.

Oh shit! James Walker. Of course. How could that have slipped my mind? I completely forgot about him. Could it be the same James Walker the detective asked about this morning? It has to be. Why else would Mrs. Walker show up at my office today? Out of nowhere? *Wait! Did she do something to Mr. Walker?*

"Yes. I believe you still can. Love isn't a force that just disappears. There are moments where you will find yourself upset, or troubled with doubts, or even downright angry, but those emotions don't negate love."

"Dr. Clarke, are you speaking from experience or research?"

"Both."

Mrs. Walker presses her lips together, raises her eyebrows, and nods her head, apparently satisfied with my response. She returns to her relaxed position, putting her feet on the sofa again. I must know why Mrs. Walker is here, and more importantly, if she has anything to do with her husband's disappearance.

"Is that why you're here today? Because of your husband?"

"I thought this would be much easier, seeing as I'm not the emotional type." She chuckles shrewdly.

I remain quiet, waiting for her to finish that thought. She takes a deep breath, looks over to me, and finally tells me what's brought her to my office today.

Mrs. Walker tells me how a few days ago, she left work earlier than she usually did. It was an ordinary day when she arrived home that afternoon. However, when Mrs. Walker entered the house, her thoughts collided with her intuition like freight trains at two hundred miles per hour. That's because the rug in the foyer wasn't where it was when she left that morning, yet she ignored it. But then, she noticed something else that was strange. The carpet she vacuumed the night before had been embedded with footsteps. What was more bizarre was the pillow she saw on the floor near the doorway. Calling the police would have been the smart thing to do, but Mrs. Walker was sure this was no break-in. It was something else. As she made her way up to the second floor, she felt the humidity of hot water lingering in the air and a familiar scent. Mrs. Walker says her husband tends to leave water running when he's in a rush.

I can relate to that because Daniel does the same. "So, I take it that you have suspicions about your husband?"

Her face instantly turns stern from her eyes to her mouth, and there is a tenseness she can't mask.

"Dr. Clarke, when you're truly in love with someone, you don't think…you know." Her cat-like eyes widened.

"And what makes you so sure of this?"

"Because I don't believe in coincidence. Everything that we think is a coincidence will somehow connect to another event."

Funny she says that because I feel the same way. She places her feet on the ground and reveals an unyielding smile. Her eyes painfully pierce through me with a lethal stare.

"And that's why I'm here today, Dr. Clarke, because I think you can help me figure this whole shit out."

"Well, Mrs. Walker, I am here to assist you the best I can."

She sits up, chuckles, and then leans forward, abandoning her ability to blink. I can't say for sure, but there's something she's not telling me, and it's getting my curiosity to focus like a lion stuck on a gazelle.

"Yes, I'm sure because I believe you have answers for me about my husband that no one else does. And that's a fact!" She leans in.

What?! All of a sudden, I notice a struggle occurring within Mrs. Walker. Her hands clasp together and rest on her right leg, shaking uncontrollably. Even her eyes have the type of hatred I haven't seen from her before, so nervously, I look away—over to the clock on the wall hanging over her left shoulder, taking a gulp of air as I do so. What in the world is happening right now? I am baffled, and although I can't say for sure, it feels like I have something to do with the sudden change in her behavior.

"I'm sorry. I don't understand. How are you so certain that I have the answers you're looking for?" I adjust myself in my seat to get comfortable.

She leans back and calmly crosses her legs. Right over left. A sweltering feeling slowly fills the room, and it's making the fear in my chest grow, waiting to take over completely. What do I have to be fearful of? There isn't any danger here. Am I nervous, though? My right foot tapping against the floor as my heart races suggests I am. *Control yourself, Andrea.* Yes. I must control myself.

"Because Dr. Clarke…while walking into that bathroom, I noticed a few things that confirmed my thoughts about my husband."

"Which are?" I ask, taking another gulp of air.

"The blue tie with silver horses he wore that morning before he left the house…was laying on the bathroom counter. And that familiar scent upstairs was my perfume—Dior, Hypnotic Poison, which is strange because I didn't use any of it that morning. Oh, one more thing. Next to the door, on the floor, was your card with an appointment time-stamped for today. Five o'clock. So, you see… that's why I am here, Dr. Clarke."

CHAPTER 10

1:15 P.M.

MY MOUTH IS WIDE OPEN, and as I remain stuck to my seat, Mrs. Walker's burning eyes stare at me. Like lightning on a pitch-black night, the white around her pupil becomes covered by red veins. Her breathing is deliberately slow as she bites on her lower lip with a closed mouth. If I didn't know any better, I would say she's fighting back the urge to scream.

What is going on? Where there once was contentment…there is now emptiness. Everything is blurred as the faint sound of the traffic outside the large window goes mute. I don't know why, but her aggression, which seems to be directed at me, makes me feel like I am being choked with a damp towel. Does she know something that I don't?

I've never been comfortable with conflict. For some reason, I seem to bite my nails beyond my control, and my body heats up, causing beads of sweat to form against my forehead like dew on morning grass. That's rather strange, seeing as how the room is quite frigid.

"You okay there, Dr. Clarke?" she asks.

Control yourself and calm your nerves, Andrea! Yes, that's what I must do. I promptly remove my index finger from my mouth, control my breathing, and look into Mrs. Walker's eyes. It's a struggle at first, but if she notices my internal battle, then she has a special gift.

"Yeah. I'm fine. But Mrs. Walker…"

She leans in, places her elbows on her lap, locks her hands together, and then offers a creepy smile with her stern gaze.

"Yes?"

Gradually, the silence seeps into my pores like poison, paralyzing my ability to speak or move. Come on, Andrea.

"My business card?"

Mrs. Walker sits back, and although she appears calm, her teary eyes say far more than she can comprehend.

"Not just an ordinary business card. It had a handwritten appointment time on it for today at five o'clock. That's what I found on my bathroom floor. So, when I saw it, I didn't know what else to do but come see you."

"So, is that why you're here?"

"I figured if we talk long enough, you'll be able to tell me something I should know."

"Mrs. Walker—"

"Please…Dr. Clarke, call me Patricia."

"Patricia, I'm not sure if I can help you with what you're looking for." My voice is stern. That's better, Andrea.

"Dr. Clarke, I'm not accusing you of anything if that's what you're thinking."

That's a relief. Her fiery stare was beginning to feel like a blade digging deep in my side.

"But I do need your help. My husband is missing, and I don't know what to do. I've had no word or anything from him."

"And that's why you had the police come to my house."

"I only gave the woman the card. She must've taken it upon herself to come to you. But she hasn't told me anything yet. So, here I am."

"What is it that you think I can do?"

"I don't know! But the fact that I found your card on my bathroom floor lets me know this is a good place to start. Why else would it be there? So, either my husband is coming to you for therapy…or the woman that was in my bathroom is."

"How are you so sure there is another woman?"

"That's for you to tell me. You have a five o'clock session today. Who's it with?" She narrows her eyes at me.

"That's impossible. My last session is at 4:15. Besides, even if it were true, you know I couldn't tell you that."

Her head falls back on the sofa as she stops to take a deep breath, letting it all out in one sigh. Then, she takes a moment to gather herself, fighting back the tears. God! Why am I dealing with this right now when I could be trying to locate Daniel? And why the hell isn't he answering my calls anyway. I'm losing it and thinking about this isn't helping either. Remain calm, Andrea.

"Look! Can you at least tell me if my husband sees you for therapy? That's all."

Her burning stare fades, leaving her as a woman in despair. Dammit, Andrea! Please don't do it. This is not safe, and you could lose your job. But a simple yes or no to her question won't hurt, right? I sigh and cave into her innocent brown eyes, glaring into mine. I shouldn't do this, but what the heck! Dammit, Andrea!

"No. He's not." I answer.

"Okay. Then please tell me if the person coming in later is a man or woman. I don't need a name."

"No. Stop it! I can't help you with that. Even if such a person existed, I couldn't tell you anything about them. I'm sorry, but I can't—"

"Stop saying you're sorry and just help me!" Suddenly, her eyes shift to the side as the first wave of tears drip from her eyelids and fall onto her cheeks. She bites her lip tightly to hide the pain, or perhaps it's so that no unwanted sound escapes from her mouth.

"I can only tell you this. I've never scheduled a session past 4:30 p.m.

"Okay. What about the name Madison? Does it sound familiar?"

Madison? How did she allow her scandalous ways to lead back to me? Wait a second. I barely know Madison, so how is Mrs. Walker here looking for her? Something isn't right, and all of this can't be a coincidence. Daniel and James go missing, and suddenly, Madison appears in my life? I'm not sure who, but someone must be up to something.

"Madison?"

"Yes. Do you know her? I overheard him say the name once while coming into the house. I didn't think anything of it at the time, but as I think about it, maybe she's the person who knows something. What do you think?"

"I can't do this. I'm sorry, but I will have to ask you to leave if you're not here for a real session."

"Fine! You've confirmed exactly what I thought."

Infuriated, Mrs. Walker stands up abruptly, pushing the sofa back as she does so. Her hands visibly shake as she steps into her nude stilettos, nearly falling over. Then, she grabs her blazer and purse and heads for the door. Just before she steps out, she turns back to me with a lethal stare that painfully pierce right through me.

"As a woman in love, I thought you'd understand, but I was wrong. I'll find him my goddamn self."

Part of me wants to stop Mrs. Walker, but what would I say? That I know Madison? No, I can't tell her that. Besides, I'm sure she'll find answers to all her questions sooner or later. Or, at the very least, find Madison.

Knock! Knock! Knock!

"Come in."

Dr. Lanier, my overbearing director, enters with a blue folder in hand as his eyes show the kind of concern my uncle used to have.

"What was that all about?" He fixes his glasses.

"What are you talking about?"

"The woman who just stormed out of here. She looked quite upset."

"Oh. That was nothing."

"You sure about that? Didn't look like nothing to me."

I release the tension through a shallow breath as Dr. Lanier stands there momentarily, looking at me as he does with his patients.

"Dr. Lanier? Is there anything else?"

He approaches my desk, letting his eyes roam the room before saying anything. Then, he throws the blue folder on top of the pile already sitting on my desk—folder 0023.

"What's this?" I ask as he turns to exit.

"A gift."

"Come on, Allan. I can't take any more patients right now. I thought we talked about this."

"No, we didn't. Remember? You missed our meeting. But no worries. You're a professional, so I'm sure you'll work it out."

I despise him, and the fact that we work together makes my skin crawl. He's an overweight, ill-mannered, disturbing, lazy, repulsive-looking man with a severe case of dandruff. The worst part is having to look at the foamy white substance he always has stuck in the corners of his mouth. Dr. Lanier is probably the type to spend countless hours at home masturbating to some sort of weird porn.

"Speaking of being a professional, Dr. Sumpter is still waiting on a visit from you." He turns away.

"I'm fine."

"Andrea, as I stated before, what's the good of understanding everyone else if we fail to understand ourselves? You're great at what you do, but everyone needs someone to talk to, and you're no different. Give her a call." He exits my office, leaving the door open behind him.

I lean back in my chair, staring out the large window as I tumble into the dark pit of my mind. It's almost two o'clock, and I still haven't spoken to Daniel. I'm beginning to believe that something is wrong. It's unlike him to go this long without talking to me. What if he's…dead. No. Don't think like that, Andrea. Perhaps, he took a trip and forgot to tell me? No. That's unlike Daniel, too. This is so frustrating and confusing.

I watched Mrs. Walker go to the length of coming to my office to find her husband, and yet I haven't done anything besides call and send a few text messages. At this point, my only option is to find him myself, which means calling the police. I grab my phone and make the call with a trembling finger.

"9-1-1, what is your emergency?"

I can't move my lips as I remain stuck for the moment, unsure if this is really what I want to do. It will confirm the truth if I tell the operator why I am calling. Daniel is gone. No, I can't bring myself to do it. I cannot accept the fact that he is no longer here. So, I hang up. But what will I do now?

The air is so tense I could drown in it, suffocating in the reality that has come to be. Five seconds go by when it suddenly hits me. I'll look for Daniel myself, starting at his job. Of course. If there's anywhere Daniel would be, it would be at work. Why didn't I think of that before? But wait! I can't leave right now. Frances Adams will be in at three o'clock.

Ms. Adams is a client who desperately wants to have a child and has done all she can. From sleeping with random men to going through two in vitro procedures, unfortunately, she's had no luck. The whole process has brought her to depression, and that's what brings her to my office. Ms. Adams believes her psyche is stopping her from having children—even though she's been told otherwise. Isn't it strange that a woman who longs for a child will struggle while a woman who doesn't have them effortlessly?

Knock! Knock!

"Dr. Clarke?"

What does she want now? "Yes, Rachel?" I answer.

Rachel enters my office, and I sense something is on her mind. That's judging by the look on her face and her ginger steps. But she doesn't know how to say whatever it is. Oh, God! It's about Daniel, isn't it? My heart immediately begins to race as my legs shake.

"What is it, Rachel?"

"Nothing. I was just making sure everything was all right." Her voice is filled with sympathy.

Deep inhale…

Soft exhale.

My heartbeats return to a steady pace, and I can relax for now. I've processed that there is nothing wrong with Daniel.

"Yeah. I'm good. Why do you ask?"

Then, as she's about to say something, my phone rings. Quickly, I reach for it, hoping Daniel is calling, but it's not. It's Ms. Adams, and knowing her, she's calling to tell me she'll be here soon. Ms. Adams always arrives early.

"You know what… I'll just come back later." Rachel takes a step back and then exits.

"Hello, this is Dr. Clarke speaking."

Ms. Adams tells me that she is still in New York and can't make it to today's session. This must be a sign. I can now go to Daniel's job and not have to rush back here. The building is on the corner of 42nd Street and Biscayne Boulevard. That's less than thirty minutes away. My next client does not come in until 4:15 P.M., leaving me plenty of time. I sigh. In disbelief that it's come down to this. Am I going out to look for Daniel like some sort of desperate psychotic girlfriend? This is beyond the woman I am, but what else can I do? God, I hope he's there.

2:18 P.M.

I pull into the parking lot of a tall yellow building where Daniel works. Looking around for Daniel's blue Audi A7 is a miserable failure because I don't see it anywhere. It's a relatively small parking lot, so maybe he parked it somewhere else. Do I need to do this? I take a deep breath, look around the area, and then exit my car. Yes, I do.

The inside of this building is classy in the most tasteless way possible. The carpet looks like it was installed in the eighties—the beige walls age without the slightest touch of personality. Don't get me started on the odor. I can smell the scent of all the people who have walked in and out of here. It's also quiet, but a security guard comes from around the corner just as I make my way to the elevator doors.

"Can I help you?" the man says.

"Hi. Yes, I'm here to meet with someone at Visitrol?"

"Okay. Fourth floor."

"Thanks."

He steps aside as I make my way into the elevator, and there's no one in here besides time. But what is my game plan? What will I say when I see him?

Ding!

The doors open onto the fourth floor, and I make my way down a long hallway. Visitrol is the third door on the left. I walk as if my brain is struggling to tell my foot which steps to take next. Even though I haven't opened the door yet, I can already feel his presence. Slowly, I approach the dull, dark wooded door with a silver handle and no lock. I take a deep breath and then open the door. A young woman sits at the front desk—no older than twenty-four. Her long braids and arched eyebrows that look down on her sweeping eyelashes are how I can tell.

"Hi. How may I help you?" she asks.

"Afternoon. Is Daniel Cooper here?"

The young woman glances upward, her mouth pursed but slightly open, and her eyes squeezed together as she ponders my request. I would have thought she didn't understand English if I didn't know any better.

"I'm sorry, but no one by that name works here. I started last week, though. So maybe he no longer works here?"

That can't be right.

"Are you sure?" I inquire.

"Yes. I'm sure. It's a small office."

"Is there another location?"

"No, ma'am. This is the only office."

The door behind the woman opens, and a man with rugged features steps out. His eyes are a familiar brown, but his stare, which is unwavering and shameful, is not. He looks at me for a moment, then quickly looks away as if he's just seen a ghost. That is weird. There is a seriousness to him that raises my attention and brings chills over my skin, leaving me motionless and unnerved. There's also a lump in my throat that makes it hard to swallow.

"Hey! How are you?" He approaches.

Wait a minute. It's Paul. Mariah Salters' husband. How did I not notice this at first glance? That explains why he looked at me like that. I guess Mrs. Salters' story was just a thought, not a memory. What is he doing here, though?

"I'm fine."

His eyes swivel to the young woman for a second and then back onto me, where they stay longer than he can control.

"Have you been helped?" he politely asks.

"Mr. Salters, is there someone by the name of Daniel Cooper who works here?" the young woman asks Mr. Salters.

"Daniel Cooper? No. We don't have anyone by that name here. But if you want—"

I snap out of it.

"Know what? Never mind. I think I'm at the wrong location."

"You sure?"

Without saying another word, I exit the building and stride over to my car. What do I do now? The more I try to make sense of it, the more there are paths than clues. Perhaps, I genuinely don't know anything about Daniel. But how could I have been so stupid and naïve? There must be some explanation for all of this, and I feel it has something to do with Madison.

Suddenly, there's a buzzing coming from my purse. It takes me a moment before I realize it's my phone. I don't recognize the number, but it doesn't matter because before I can answer, the phone stops ringing. Shit! What if that was Daniel? I'd kick myself in the ass if it were him. Wait a minute… what's this? Detective Barringer's card. It must've fallen out of my purse. This must be another sign. Maybe she can help me find Daniel.

Without a second thought, I call Detective Barringer and anxiously wait on her to answer. For nearly fifteen seconds, the phone rings, but there's no response. I call again.

"Come on, pick up." Still no answer. Just a voicemail. It would be my luck. Then, just as I'm about to leave a message...

"Andrea!" a man's voice calls my name.

Swiftly, I turn in that direction, thinking it's Daniel, but my energy immediately seeps out of my body like a broken pen when it's Mr. Salters I see standing there. Shit! I swallow a gulp of air as he approaches with a grin on his rugged face. Until today, I hadn't seen him since he sat in one of Mrs. Salters' sessions. That was a few months ago. But here he is, coming my way with a softness in his eyes and gentleness in his smile.

"You got out of there kinda quick. I didn't even get the chance to say bye." He grins.

"Yeah. I'm kind of in a rush."

"I see. So, tell me…what were you really doing in there?" His fingers run through his short and wavy dark hair.

"Why does it matter?"

"Just curious."

"Is there something I could help you with?" My voice is stern as I stare into his eyes.

"I was wondering if you and I could sit for lunch and talk."

"About what?"

"Mariah. I'd love to know how you think she's doing?"

He looks at me like a starving dog glaring at a piece of meat through a glass window. Some might find it charming, but I find it disturbing. Then again, this isn't the first time. Something about him has my mind running in circles until there is no room for anything else.

"You okay?" I ask, pulling him away from his unwanted stare of intimacy.

"Yeah. You know… there's just something different about you.

It's more than just your look because you've always had that. Is it your eyes? Or maybe it's—"

"Mr. Salters, please be careful about what you say next."

He smiles and nods. "You're right. So, about that lunch…will you join me?" He steps in closer.

Most women would love having lunch with a man like Mr. Salters. He's charming, and when he listens to you speak, he stares into your eyes intently. Also, he has a look that stops you in your tracks. However, my soul scowls at the thought of it. Besides, he's a man who happens to be married to a woman whom I've been helping to deal with his erratic behavior.

"Sorry. I can't. I already have plans. Besides, there's nothing for us to talk about."

My phone rings just in time to pull me away from Mr. Salters. It's Shannon calling. I quickly answer.

"Hey. Are you almost here?" my voice perks up.

"Almost where?"

Mr. Salters watches me with an awkward grin as I walk away from him.

"Disregard that. I had to get away from some guy."

"What'd he want?"

"Nothing important. What's up?"

"I'm free. You want to do lunch," Shannon asks.

Having lunch with Shannon right now isn't something I need to be doing, but the Cuban café across the street does offer a perfect view of the yellow building. Perhaps if I wait around, I'll see Daniel. Screw it. It's just lunch. What's the worst that can happen?

"You know what… I'm in the mood for some Cuban."

CHAPTER 11

2:37 P.M

I ENTER THE café, choosing a seat towards the back, strategically positioned near a window. The restaurant is pretty empty for lunch time, with only a small group at one table, a man sitting alone at another, and a couple hanging at the bar. From my vantage point, I have an open view of the entire café, allowing me to survey its occupants with ease. Yet, it is the towering yellow building across the street that truly captivates my attention. Every entrance and exit becomes my domain, and if Daniel dares to make a move, I will be the first to know.

According to Shannon, she should be here in ten minutes, but knowing her, she'll be here in twenty-five. That's one of the many things I've learned about Shannon these past twenty-five years. Expect the unexpected. It's been that way since we were kids. When I was twelve, Shannon thought it would be a great idea to steal a pair of denim shorts from the mall. I was the only one who got caught. At sixteen, she took me to a frat party where I took enough shots to put myself in the hospital with my stomach pumped. I'm sure this lunch won't be anything like those experiences, but again, with Shannon, you never know.

"Hello." A man of commendable height pops up out of nowhere. "I'm Zach, and I'll be your waiter. Will it be just you?" he asks.

He chuckles softly, no doubt noticing the shock on my face before I can hide it. I can't help it. His physique takes me by surprise. He has the body of a swimmer—tall and lean, and I can tell he's just now growing into those developed features of his. For goodness sake, he doesn't have any facial hair to go with his boyish smile, yet he looks as manly as any man I've come across. His voice is low enough to send chills through my body. I remember a former client, Ms. Stephanie Álvarez, telling me that there's something special about how a young man looks at her. It's engaging, honest, and filled with intentions. It's enough to make you feel youthful, giving you the type of confidence that can't be achieved on your own. That was according to Ms. Álvarez. I never questioned it, but at this moment, I now know what Ms. Álvarez meant.

"Hi, Zach. Nice to meet you." My voice sounds slightly seductive.

Wait. That was weird. I'm not sure where that came from, and judging by how he's looking at me, he must be thinking the same.

"So, will someone be joining you?"

Part of me wants to tell him no, but what is the point? At any moment, Shannon will walk in and take a seat, and I won't have any reasonable explanation for lying. Besides, the last thing I need right now is to worry about some young man when I am still concerned about finding Daniel. "Yes, I'm meeting someone here."

Ugh! But why'd you have to say it like that, Andrea? Yeah. Why did I? It sounds more like I am waiting on someone I am romantically involved with than it does just Shannon. Get it together, Andrea.

"It's a friend of mine. She'll be here soon." That's better.

Internally, I smile from ear to ear because him knowing that this lunch date is nothing romantic makes me feel much better. Not that it matters anyway.

"Okay. Cool. Well, would you like a drink to start with?

Chardonnay, perhaps?" He chuckles.

I can't tell if he's flirting or just doing his job, but the way his eyes are hard-rimmed and fixed on me as he offers a soft smile tells me that he has something on his mind. It's the type of stare that comes with intent, and whatever his objective is… it's working. Then again, it could all just be in my mind.

"Chardonnay is my go-to drink, but not right now. Thanks."

"Okay. Once again, I'm Zach. If you need anything, just let me know. I'll be back around."

I nod. Then, just as Zach walks away, I notice a distinctive tribal tattoo on his right arm. That tattoo…I've seen it before but don't recall where.

"Hey, Zach! You know what? I'll take that glass of chardonnay."

He stops in his tracks and turns back to me.

"Okay. Chardonnay it is." He winks.

A wink? I was right. He's not just doing his job. And where the hell is Shannon?

Nearly five minutes later, Shannon enters and takes a seat across from me with a toothy smile and enough energy for the both of us. This is typical for Shannon. Especially when she is eagerly excited to share something. I wonder what it will be this time.

"I'm sorry about that. I took the back road thinking it would be faster, but I was wrong," Shannon explains.

"It's fine."

"So why Cuban? I don't think I've ever heard you suggest it." She takes off her jacket.

"Trying something new, I guess."

"Hm! Okay." As Shannon reaches across the table for the menu, she stops in a long stare.

"What?" I question.

"You're wearing mascara?"

"Yeah. So what?"

"So, when did you start doing that?"

I shrug and look down at the menu. However, that's not enough for Shannon as the left side of her glossy lip tugs upward to a sinister smirk. It's as if she's just come across juicy gossip or discovered a secret about me.

"What?! I don't know. I just did it."

"Well, I like it. You don't look like that much of a prude today."

"Thanks."

"Here you go!" Zach places the glass of chardonnay down on the table. Along with the drink, he puts down a basket of Cuban bread.

"Thank you."

"No problem." He stares at me.

"Can I get a mojito and a glass of water?" Shannon orders.

"Coming right up." Zach walks off.

"So…what's new with you?" Shannon asks.

This is the part where I am expected to open up and tell her everything that's happening in my life, including Daniel's disappearance and my sudden impish thoughts. But knowing Shannon, she'll only make things worse with all of her questions and worrying.

"Nothing really. Just stuff."

"What kind of stuff? Come on. You can tell me."

She's right. I can tell her, but I'd rather not. My mother was the only person I could truly confide in, but after she died, Shannon somehow stepped into that role. She isn't the best at giving feedback, but she listens with intent while using positive body language, which is rare to find in most people. That's how she became the only person I could be completely vulnerable with. So, yes, there was a time when I'd share intimate and personal details about myself. However, as strange as it may be, the only person I feel comfortable to do so with now…is Madison.

"Mostly work-related stuff. It's all boring, though. Besides, I can't talk about it anyway."

"You sure?" she asks.

"Yes. I'm sure. I'm good."

"You're good?" She scoffs. "Who are you?"

I chuckle, but honestly, I am as removed from this conversation as the hostess standing up front. The worst flaw a person can have is that of self-deception. Many of my clients are like that, and right now, I have a feeling that I am too.

"So, listen to this."

Shannon begins to tell me about her petty grievances with a co-worker while I pretend to be tuned in. Head nods, a fake smile, a touch of empathy here, a chuckle there, and a few helpful suggestions does the trick. Then, Shannon tells me about a call she received from her father. Now I *am* alert. Shannon's father, Mr. Ricks, was the type to act on impulse and then create the reason for his actions after the fact. If he was feeling good, he would do good things, and if he was feeling negative in any way, he would do bad things. No one knew which side of Mr. Ricks they would get on any given day. Most people were afraid or intimidated by Mr. Ricks, but I wasn't. I saw the gentle and caring side of him, and he saw the same thing in me every time my mother would drop me over at Shannon's house. Mr. Ricks was my introduction to me wanting to understand my body. Things would happen to me when I was around him. Things that didn't happen around anyone else. I would get sensitive in parts of my body, and between my legs, I felt like I was peeing. As a young girl, I couldn't help but stare at Mr. Ricks as if he were a sundae during a hot summer day. He was my little secret, and I was his.

"Andrea!" Shannon blurts.

I snap out of it.

"What? I'm listening."

"Then what do you think? Should I go up to the prison to visit him?"

Did I mention that Mr. Ricks is fifteen years into his thirty-five-year prison sentence? Armed robbery and kidnapping. For someone like Mr. Ricks, prison is where he belongs.

"I can't make that decision for you, Shannon."

"Well, if I do, will you come with me?"

Just as I am about to reply to Shannon, I meet the gaze of the distinguished gentleman as he walks into the café. It's him, Derek, and he's just as tempting as I remember. So much so, it's now difficult to breathe as my chest pounds to an unknown beat. The room spins counterclockwise, and I can barely feel anything in my fingers and toes. What is he doing here?

"You okay?" Shannon asks.

"Who me? Yes. I'm fine."

I take a gulp of air, and then a sip of my drink. My goodness, even his walk makes my insides tingle. He takes a seat three tables down. Every so often, he looks over at me, as if he wants to make sure that I notice him. My God! No woman deserves to have a man like that all to herself. He's too much of a specimen for that, and undoubtedly worth every second of my stare. I wonder if he sat there on purpose. To make me feel uncomfortable or to simply tease me. This must be some sort of game to him, and if it is, he's winning.

"Hello, Andrea! So?" Shannon persists.

Once again, I snap out of it, pivoting my attention to Shannon who just happens to be looking up from the menu. It's a good thing she didn't notice me.

"Um, sure. I'll go with you. The last time I saw your dad, I was fifteen years old. He'll be surprised to see me now." I take a sip of my drink.

Shannon continues on about her day, but after a few seconds, my attention returns to the distinguished gentleman. Shamefully, I begin to imagine him sitting here with me instead of Shannon as his hand touches mine. I release a soft moan, but then quickly grab ahold of myself before Shannon notices.

"What was that? Did you just moan?" She laughs.

"What? No! I caught a chill. It's cold in here."

Impulsively, my eyes shift back to the man. *Dammit, Andrea.* Shannon notices and quickly turns around to see what's taken my attention, but luckily for me, the gentleman has strangely disappeared. Where'd he go?

"What were you looking at?" she asks.

"Nothing." I recover, taking a sip of my drink as I do so.

I can't seem to stop myself from having these impulsive thoughts whenever I see random men like the distinguished gentleman. The thoughts are happening more frequently than I'm used to, and it's starting to get the best of me. They roll through my brain like a train, with no intention of stopping. It's troubling, because on the one hand, I should only be concerned about finding Daniel and nothing else, but then on the other hand…there's a voice in my head begging for me to explore myself. I remember Ms. Álvarez telling me that every woman has a voice in their head that is often ignored. A voice that tells a woman all the secrets about the man who can trigger a thought in her mind like no other can. The secret is often told through the way he walks, or the way he positions his hands, or sometimes the way he breathes. According to Ms. Álvarez, a man that walks with haste, whose eyes are all over the place, and who is constantly doing something with his hands isn't the man you want to be with. However, a man that walks in long coordinated strides, focused on what he's doing, and taking calm soothing breaths—he is the one. Ms. Álvarez is a special woman indeed—especially for a woman whose issues go beyond any sort of counseling I can provide.

"Excuse me for a moment. I need to use the restroom." I jump out of my seat.

"Don't you want to order first?"

"Shrimp scampi salad please."

I make my way to the restroom, roaming my eyes around the café for the distinguished gentleman, but he's nowhere to be found. He must've left.

I enter the restroom, walk over to the mirror, and stare at myself, wondering why I'm feeling like this. Hot, bothered, and slightly weak. Better yet, why am I here wasting my time with Shannon when I should only be focused on Daniel. Nine seconds. That's how long it takes before I realize that perhaps I'm overreacting. Everything is going to be just fine. Nothing happened, and I'm still the woman I was before I walked into this café. In fact, I'm going to walk out of here and go find Daniel.

You got this, Andrea.

Yes, I do.

I grab a few sheets of paper towel, throw a dash of water on them, and bury my face into it.

You are in control.

Yes, I am in control. My breathing settles down and my mind abandons every immoral thought I can think of. Now, the only thing on my mind is Daniel. *Whew!*

All of a sudden, when I come up from the paper towel, I spot the distinguished gentleman in the mirror—standing right behind me.

Quickly, I turn to him and jump back against the countersink. My brain stutters for a moment as every part of me goes numb. He's right in front of me—just a couple of steps away, and I'm at his mercy.

"What are you doing in here?" I snap.

"Would you rather I leave?"

"Yes. You shouldn't be in here."

If I could only just say what I want to say. *Fuck me! Right here! Right now!* However, I'm not sure if that's me or the voice that Ms. Álvarez was talking about.

Stop it, Andrea.

"Okay. I'll go," he politely says just before he turns to walk out of the restroom.

"Wait!"

He stops and turns to me steadily.

"Yes?"

The words are on the tip of my tongue, but they just will not leap from my mouth.

"Well?"

"You said my name the other day. Do you know me?"

"Knowing someone's name doesn't mean you know them. It's knowing the minor details about that person, which are usually neglected by others, that makes you know them. Like knowing that someone likes chocolate just as long as it has peanuts in it." His tone is playful.

Hold on! How does he know that? My mouth is slightly open as I stare at him unblinkingly. Only my mother and a few others know this about me. Then again, I'm probably not the only one that doesn't like chocolate without peanuts. Either way, he's making me nervous, no, scared to hear that he knows this.

Think, Andrea. Think! Where would you know this man from? If I could just get my heart to stop racing and my mind to calm down for a moment, then maybe I could remember.

"Oh, you're good. Real good." He drops his gaze and shakes his head as he slowly approaches me in coordinated strides.

"I think you have me mistaken for someone else."

"Do I? Let's see…skinny caramel macchiato with a hint of almond extract, right?"

He takes a couple of steps forward, slowly and persuasively. His demanding gaze forces a rush to go from my chest and down between my legs. I'm no longer nervous or scared. Instead, I'm intrigued.

Keep it cool, Andrea.

He leans forward, unbuttons the top button of my burgundy satin blouse, and then travels my body with his roaming eyes. I am too paralyzed to stop him. I can only wonder what he will do next.

"Are you not a woman who loves being touched everywhere except for her toes?"

His fingers graciously tiptoe across my collarbone like a little man walking across the street. I'm stuck under his charm because he's right. The feeling of my toes being touched never felt good to me. Softly, I inhale and hold it.

He unbuttons the second button.

"Sometimes when it rains, you cry because it reminds you of the days you spent with your grandma."

I'm in awe as goosebumps grace my skin. That isn't a lucky guess. Someone must've told him that because there's no way he would know this. His index finger slides down to my cleavage. I exhale silently as the rush wandering between my legs begins to swirl. I can even feel myself heating up, making my panties gradually wet. It's happening again, and I can't stop it. He smiles, leans in closer to my lips, and unbuttons the third of five buttons on my blouse. His eyes are hooded yet drowning in lust as he looks at me. That's for a moment. So, instead, I just accept it and stare at him in complete shock, wondering where he's planning to take this.

"But I guess when you have others…how can Alton alone be memorable?" He leans in closer and whispers against my lips.

Alton? I repeat internally.

On any other day, I would run out of here, but in this moment, his presence holds my entire body captive, and he knows it. Desperately, I want him to throw me against the wall, and fuck me like the night Madison experienced at the secret venue. God, this is too much for me to deal with in one day.

"I don't know what you want, but I'm here with someone. One scream, and she'll be in here with a gun in hand." I lean back.

Suddenly, the door opens, and an older woman enters. She stops in her tracks the moment she sees us. I step aside and quickly button up my blouse as the woman looks at me guardedly. He chuckles and then exits without saying another word. At last, I can breathe normally again as my heartbeat returns to a steady rhythm.

"Are you okay?" she asks.

"Yes. I'm fine. Thank you."

"You look like you've seen a ghost."

I feel like I have as well. But at least I know his name now. Alton.

By the time I return to Shannon, she and Zach are laughing. Knowing Shannon, they could be talking about anything from fruits and vegetables to memories of an ex.

"There you are. I thought I was going to have to come get you myself," Shannon says.

"Sorry about that. I ended up taking a call as well."

Oh crap! My phone is on the table next to my purse. I hope Shannon doesn't notice it. God, I really do suck at lying.

"So, did I interrupt anything?" I continue.

"We were just talking about our dislike for seafood. I don't even know how we got to talking about that, either." Zach laughs.

"Well, I eat seafood, and this looks great." I stare at the shrimp scampi sitting on top of a bed of fresh spinach.

"Trust me, it is. Well, I'll leave you two to enjoy."

He smiles and gently trails his index fingers along my left hand as he walks away. Shannon must have not seen it or else she would have said something. Was that an accident? No. It couldn't have been, because the way my skin tingles from his touch and my heart erratically beats in my chest lets me know that was no mistake. On top of that, there are butterflies, no, monkeys in my stomach, jumping around. It's such an enthralling feeling.

"Guess what? I have good news. Actually, it's great news!" Shannon says. Here we go.

"What is it?" I cautiously ask.

"So, you know how we've been going back and forth about our girls' trip?"

"Mmm-hmm."

"Well, we've decided on a location. You ready for it? We're going to Cabo!" she squeals. "Now this is going to sound crazy, but we have to leave by Monday morning. Five-day trip," she quickly adds.

"Monday morning?! You mean a couple of days from now? No. Shannon, I can't do that. What about my job? I have people that I have to see all next week."

"I know. I know. But can't you do something about it? Besides, it was your idea to go to Mexico in the first place, and this is the best time for it."

"Wait. What? My idea?"

"Yeah. You told us at the lounge that you wanted to go to Mexico.

How could you forget? You were adamant about it."

I haven't the slightest idea what Shannon is talking about. Perhaps, she has me mistaken for Darlene or Courtnie.

"Well, it still shouldn't involve me leaving on the drop of a dime either. For goodness sake, Shannon."

"I'm sorry, but it was super cheap. And we happen to be staying at one of the most beautiful resorts in the country. The same resort that will be featuring Jazmine Sullivan on Wednesday night."

"Jazmine Sullivan? Are you kidding me?" I can even hear the excitement in my voice.

"Yes! So, does that mean you'll be ready Saturday?"

Perhaps a trip to Mexico is exactly what I need right now. *Yes, you do.* It will be fun, and I can get away from all the stress and bullshit for just one moment.

Let's go!

"Okay. Okay. I'll see what I can do, but I can't make any promises."

"Great. I bought your ticket already, and the entire week is planned. But no pressure. We're going to have so much fun."

Like a toddler during recess, Shannon can hardly sit still. It's as if she wants to run and shout to everyone. But instead, she quickly makes a phone call to Darlene. Suddenly, as I dive into my salad, I glance out the window. That's when I spot a blue Audi, pulling out of the parking lot of the tall yellow building. Shit! Was that him? That had to be Daniel. I quickly jump out of my seat and run out of the café, but I'm too late. He's gone…

CHAPTER 12

4:12 P.M.

I FEEL MYSELF slipping to an unknown place that is troubling. It's the dark corner of my subconscious mind that welcomes me to the horrors of guilt and panic. Not to mention the disturbing thoughts that make life more confusing and challenging. I'm aware of this pit because plenty of my clients have wandered off to this place. Some of which have yet to return.

It's a quarter past four, and a pang of regret surges through me for agreeing to have lunch with Shannon. Now, as I watch the minutes slip away, I'll be late for my crucial four-thirty session. Punctuality is a personal virtue I hold dear, and being late contradicts the very essence of who I am. I have precisely fifteen minutes to make it back to my office but considering the maze of construction throughout I-95, I fear it will consume a full twenty minutes. The frustration springs within me, fueling a decisive resolution. *"Screw it!"* I mutter, firm in my course of action. Determined, I prepare to seize the next exit, surrendering to the lesser-known back roads that might offer a path to salvation.

Exit 6 places me on 47th Street, where I make the first left onto Northeast Seventh Avenue. Hopefully, this cuts four minutes off my drive. I travel nearly ten blocks east of the highway when I finally come to a red light on Seventh Street and 29th Avenue. On the corner is a black and white building. The building is enormous and eye-catching, and yet, it looks abandoned. There's no sign on it either.

Ring!

My phone rings, pulling my attention back to the road just in time to catch the light turning green. I frantically reach for my phone, thinking it might be Daniel calling.

"Hello?" I answer.

"This is Detective Barringer returning a phone call."

I wasn't expecting her. What should I do now? I have to say something, or else who knows what she will do next?

"Hello?"

"Hi. This is Andrea Clarke. We spoke earlier when you came to my place…"

"Yes. I remember. Are you calling about James Walker?"

"No. I'm calling because I have a similar situation of my own. It's been a couple of days since I last saw my boyfriend, and I don't know what else to do."

"Sorry to hear that. Have you reported this yet?"

"No. I didn't think much of it at first, but now I'm kinda scared that something is wrong. It's not like Daniel to go this long without speaking to me. I've called his phone, and I'm not getting anything. Also, I just left his job, but they haven't seen him either."

"I see. Is there anything else you can tell me? The clothing he was last wearing. Favorite hang spots. What kind of car does he drive? Is there anyone you think might want to hurt him?"

"There's this woman. Madison. She randomly approached me the other day, and I found it strange. I have a feeling she might have something to do with this."

"Madison, you say?"

Beyond my control, I feel my chin beginning to tremble like a spoiled child. I'm not the emotional type, but the walls that usually hold me up are starting to collapse. *Hold it together, Andrea. You got this.* Yes. I got this.

"Yes. Madison. I don't have any other information about her."

"All right. I'll look into that. What's your boyfriend's name?" she asks.

"Daniel Cooper."

"And his birthday?"

"March 30, 1985."

"I'll take a look at this, and if there's anything else I need, I'll be in touch."

4:32 P.M

I arrive at my office two minutes late, but luckily, Ms. Kiner is not even there. This should come as no surprise because this is typical of her. She usually shows up late with the strangest excuses. Once, she arrived twenty minutes late and told me she had nearly drowned at the pool. Then, this one time, she completely missed her session because her car caught on fire while driving on Dixie Highway. Ms. Kiner struggles with telling the truth, and although that's not why she comes to my office, I make it a point of reference to squeeze it in.

I swiftly grab her file off my desk, and just as I take a seat, there's a knock at the door. That must be Ms. Kiner.

"Come in."

A few seconds pass by, and the door doesn't open.

"I said come in!" I sit in silence, staring at the door handle, waiting for it to turn. But it never does. What is she doing?! I get out of my seat and answer the door.

Oh shit!

To my surprise, when I open the door, I find myself staring into

Madison's eyes. It's her! And she's standing in front of me with her deep-set hazel eyes beaming into mine.

"Madison? What are you doing here?"

Without saying a word, she enters my office and strolls over to the large window. She's calm, confident, and vastly different from the other women. The longer I stare at her, the more I want to explore things about her that I wish I could see in myself, starting with how she walks. Loose but confident. Her hips twist as if she's not controlling her own body, and unlike the others, she doesn't walk like she's clenching a tennis ball between her legs.

Then there's her sense of fashion—which again reminds me of Jessica Hayden. Ms. Hayden also believed that what you wore was how you presented yourself to the world, especially when human interaction is limited. That's why Ms. Hayden dressed as if she were headed somewhere of importance every time she stepped out of her house. The same can be said for Madison, who's dressed in a white form-fitting, long-sleeve dress. The dress has gold foil embellishments and is accompanied by a stunning pair of gold Yves Saint Laurent heels. Her hair sits in a bun, making the dress look even more incredible. And she has the same watch that I have on.

"Is there something I can help you with? I have a client coming in soon."

"The word help is such a complicated word, isn't it, Dr. Clarke?"

"What do you mean?"

I take a couple of steps towards the large window. Madison intently stares into my eyes, and she's quite intimidating in her own way.

"So…you had an interesting visitor today, huh?" She smiles.

"What are you talking about?"

"What do you think?"

I've come to the realization that Madison isn't so much of a stranger as I initially thought. She knows too much. I must know her from somewhere because this cannot be a coincidence. However, the question is…where do I know her from?

"Why are you here?" I inquire.

She turns away from the large window, hands at her sides and eyes gazing out in front of her. Silence fills the room like air in a balloon. Then, she turns to me and presses her back against the window as her eyes travel around my office. After a moment, she focuses on a picture sitting on my desk. It's a picture of me standing in the French Quarter on my trip to New Orleans.

"I like that picture." She walks over and takes a closer look. "So…have you heard from him yet?" she asks.

My stomach knots up, and for a moment, my breathing discontinues. Madison turns to me, places the picture frame on the desk, and then smiles. Her suspicious behavior is less amusing as time goes on. I feel like I am falling into a trap, and if that's the case, it's probably too late to escape from it now.

"Are you referring to Daniel?" I ask, bracing myself for her response.

There's an acceptable distance between us before I take a couple of steps toward her. I want to be as close as possible when she responds to my question.

"So…"

She looks up and nods her head. Immediately a cold tingle rushes through my body, leaving me weak in the knees. I feel as if I am about to black out at any moment.

"What do you know about Daniel?"

I take a big gulp of air, suppressing the urge to jump across the room and snatch her by the hair like I desperately want to. But I can't do that because that's not who I am. I'm much too mild-mannered and reserved to do such a thing. However, why am I okay with this? Should I not be okay? Is something wrong with me? Who am I kidding? Of course, there is.

"If I were you, I wouldn't concern myself with that." She turns to me as her eyes sink beneath the sunlight beaming from outside.

"Who are you to tell me what not to be concerned with? What do you know?" I demand.

"Everything. That's what you want to know, right, Dr. Clarke?"

I step closer.

"You don't know shit, so whoever the hell you are, leave me the fuck alone." My voice stains with rage.

"If you're so sure about that, then tell me, where is Daniel? Why hasn't he answered any of your calls? Did you think about that?"

She's right. Daniel hasn't returned any of my calls or texts, and now, his phone won't even ring. I was right. Madison was up to something this whole time. All that talk about being a sex addict was about Daniel. *Fuck!* Madison must know something about him that I don't, and I need to find out what that something is.

"I can tell you this, Dr. Clarke—he's not just ignoring your calls. He's probably gone! So, face it."

I turn away from the large window, unsure if I should continue to listen to Madison. This doesn't sound like Daniel.

"So, is that why you're here? To tell me about him and ruin my life?"

"There's nothing I can tell you about him that you don't already know. I'm here because I need your help…and you need mine."

"Why would I help you?"

"Because by helping me, you would be helping yourself."

The wheels in my head spin rapidly, with everything becoming more confusing when she talks. She sounds confident, and judging by her eyes, she's telling the truth. Maybe I can hear her out for a moment. Besides, I believe Madison is the person that I need to talk to. I'm not sure if I want to know everything she has to say, but what choice do I have right now? Perhaps Madison and I do have more in common than I thought.

"Well, if you're talking about counseling, you'll have to follow our protocol for new intakes, so you're going to have to come in for a—"

"It's already been done. Also, I'd like our sessions to stay between us," she interjects.

That can't be right. I would have remembered getting a file with Madison's name on it. Unless it's the file that Dr. Lanier placed on my desk earlier. File 0023. I promptly walk over to my desk and grab the file. I'll be damned! The name on the file reads Madison. Just Madison. How did they allow her to move forward without a first name? Or last name—whichever makes sense. Madison turns away from me and walks over to the large window, and once again, she gazes out at the city's skyline with drips of rain falling onto the window. Like me, she seems to have an appreciation for the view. Yet another thing we have in common.

"I love this view. It's peaceful, and I can truly think without any distractions." Madison takes a deep breath.

The room is quiet, and as I intently watch her stare at her reflection, I notice an internal struggle with Madison. I can tell by the look on her face. It's the same look I saw from her in the car, but this time, I can feel it just as much as I can see it.

"Madison…"

Slowly, she turns to me with an unsettling smirk and a twinkle in her eyes.

"About my visitor today…do you know James Walker?" My heart

stops beating for a moment.

"Well, like I said before, Dr. Clarke...I need your help."

"What exactly does that mean? Actually, you know what? Never mind. I have someone coming in at any moment, so we'll have to do this at another time."

Madison doesn't move a muscle as she looks away from me. That look... I've seen it somewhere before. They are eyes with a stillness that reflects everything while seeing nothing. Behind them is a secret more intense than the normal thought can hold. Yes, I know those eyes quite well. Those are the same eyes of my mother's.

"In a moment, Dr. Clarke," she walks over to the sofa and takes a seat, crossing her stunning legs right over left. Her eyes, narrow and captivating, stare into mine and put me in a moment beyond my reality.

"Why didn't you just tell me this in the car?"

"I didn't have to."

I sigh silently. Why am I putting up with this when I should be trying to find out where Daniel is instead? Speaking of which, where the hell is Ms. Kiner? She should've been here by now.

"Okay...we can talk. But I want to know...is this about Daniel?"

Madison shakes her head no. Whew! I feel better about that. However, I'm not sure if I believe her.

"So, tell me then...why are you really here?"

"It's complicated. I'm dealing with an issue so deep within me that it's shredding me from the inside out, to the point that I can no longer make sense of who I truly am." Madison takes a deep breath. "And I have no one to turn to because no one else will understand." She turns her focus out to the large window once again.

Something dawns on me in the middle of my thought, pushing me to take a closer look at her. It's puzzling, but something about this woman is very familiar.

"So, why me?"

"Because I know you will understand."

"How can you be so sure of that?"

"Well, the fact that I just referred to Daniel and you didn't kick me out lets me know you want to know more."

"You said this wasn't about Daniel."

"Yes, that's true. But there's still something I think you should know."

"What does that mean?"

"Take a seat, Dr. Clarke."

I compose myself and take a seat across from Madison. According to the clock hanging behind her, it's almost a quarter to five, and I can only imagine Mrs. Walker showing up to find Madison sitting here.

"So, what's this issue that you're dealing with?"

"It's more complicated than I would like it to be, and it's all because of him," Madison says.

"Him? Would this him be…Daniel?" I ask nervously.

"I'd rather not say his name."

My stomach shrinks, and my heart feels like it's about to explode out of my chest. Why does Madison continue to play these games? I don't know if I want to hear any more of this. I'll allow Daniel to tell me everything that's going on—assuming I ever find him. Then again, maybe she's not referring to Daniel. Nevertheless, I can't deny the truth—she might know Daniel in a way that I don't. Or, in a way, I probably should. No.

"Why are you telling me this?"

"Because it's time I face the truth."

She pauses for a moment as a blank look covers her face, but somehow, I can still feel her energy racing through my core. It is vigorous yet flustering. This truth of hers isn't about her sex addiction because she's already told me about that. Even if Madison is a sex addict, I refuse to believe that's why she's here.

"Is this about the conversation we had in the car?"

"Partially."

My eyes shift to the window and stare out for a moment, trying to make sense of Madison's sudden appearance. How did she make her way into my life at a time like this?

"What are you thinking?" she asks.

I turn back to her.

"I think that, although many of the issues and problems can stem from sexual engagements, it's still a surface issue."

"What does that mean?"

"It means that isn't the problem that actually needs identifying."

"So then, what can it be?"

"I'm not sure. Sometimes those with an appetite for random sexual encounters can be commonly linked to various mental disorders—possibly psychosis, manic episodes, substance abuse, or dissociative identity disorder. Then again, it can also just be who you are. But if you want my honest opinion…I don't think that's why you're here, and that's what I'm most concerned about."

"Is that so?"

"Yes. I think it's something else, and you know it as well. Besides, the man you've described…doesn't sound like the Daniel I know."

"I never said a name, Dr. Clarke. Then again, you and I might know a different side to the same man." She shrugs and raises her eyebrow as I take a deep breath.

Damnit! I want to jump across the table and snatch this woman by the hair with rage. However, I won't allow myself to believe that she's talking about Daniel. She can't be.

"Sometimes the truth may be hard to hear, but it's still worth it. And my truth isn't something I'm proud of, but it's all because of the man I've come to love that I spend countless minutes of the day seeking the need to be touched and fucked like some sort of junkie. Even though part of me wanted him to myself, I knew it would never happen," she murmurs.

"Did you ever stop to think it's because he belongs to someone else?"

"Maybe. So, now, seeing as I don't have him anymore, I look to find it in someone else. Anyone. And when I try to suppress it—"

"It ends up doing more damage than before," I interrupt.

"Yes. Exactly," she whispers.

Interesting. Madison is faced with the same issue that both Denita Richardson and Ms. Tori Collins, a former client of mine, were dealing with. Like those two, Madison seems to have lost track of herself while desiring and worshiping men in a way no spinster should. The sad part is it will never be enough. Women like Denita and Tori are fascinated with seeking a man's initial touch because there is nothing like it. That's according to Denita. It's as if it were some sort of drug. I suspect the same could be said for Madison.

"When did this begin?"

"Just over a year ago."

That was around the same time I met Daniel. Could she be the reason why he had to travel quite often? There were times he'd go missing for days and sometimes weeks. I always found it strange but never questioned it. *Andrea, stay focused.* Yes, I must remain focused. "I see."

"And now it's like there's nothing I can do to stop it," Madison says.

"That's because sexual behaviors do not simply cause the sexual instinct to disappear. It finds different ways to express itself—some happen to be positive and creative while others are negative and destructive."

"That sounds about right because now… I am in trouble," she murmurs.

Madison uncrosses her legs, sits upright, and crosses them left over right. Are sexual behaviors in women still as negatively viewed as they used to be? What if women like Madison are the smart ones, while women like me, a virtuous woman who'd rather wait until marriage to fully explore her sexuality, are doing it the wrong way?

"What sort of trouble?" I inquire.

God, I can't believe I just asked that. And why in the world would I want to know anything about this woman? I have every reason to believe she's hiding something, but I can't seem to figure it out.

"It's the kind of trouble that will change my life, and right now, there's only one thing I can do about it."

Madison closes her eyes, uncrosses her legs, and takes a deep breath as she prepares to visit a buried thought. It's a thought that digs up emotions and stirs up what was once believed to be settled. The point where things must have taken a turn between her and whoever this mysterious man is.

I can tell that for a woman like Madison, falling in love doesn't come easily. It comes with bumps, bruises, and all sorts of wrong turns. That's until she met this man who twisted everything she believed in and made her fall in love. Perhaps Madison is not a sex addict; instead, she's a woman who fell for a man who took control of her sexuality, and now that he's gone, she's looking to find it in someone else. Whatever Madison has done because of his actions…must be why she's here.

"And what's the one thing you can do about it?" I ask.

"Accept and face the truth." She opens her eyes, and immediately, I see the wandering in her stare.

"Which is?"

"I fucked everything up."

Looking into Madison's eyes almost feels like staring into a mirror, which I seldom do. So much of Madison makes me question myself and everything. This must be what she meant when she said by helping her, I would essentially be helping myself. My God, what have I gotten myself into?

5:02 P.M…Now!

NO ONE MAKES ME feel like I belong in this world more than a person who doesn't. The beauty of being a psychologist is that I get to meet a lot of those people. Most of them are confused, struggling to find the meaning of life while trying to measure their worth through the perception of others. Some of them are lost souls, crying for help because they've somehow allowed their past to twist how they think and behave. But then, there's Madison. A woman with enough flawless imperfections to make her seem perfect. Her honeyed voice, which comes out in whispers, gives me comfort as her familiar scent, an earthy and creamy almond, takes me to rejoicing moments. There's something about her that is different and yet very familiar.

CHAPTER 13

6:22 P.M.

"Dr. Clarke!"

A voice calls my name. Immediately, I snap out of it, turn my head in that direction, and spot Rachel with her head poking in the doorway.

"Rachel," my voice weak, "What are you still doing here?" That sounds better.

"I was going to ask you the same," she replies. Rachel looks at me with puzzled eyes, her brows creased and face tense, staring at me as if her brain is suffering a massive, short circuit. Then, she shifts her eyes to Madison, and for a moment, there's a silence that goes beyond acceptable.

"Rachel…" I remove my glasses. "I'm busy here. Is there something I can help you with?"

She turns her attention back to me with the same tense look.

"Rachel?"

"Oh, sorry. Never mind." Rachel's eyes squeeze together as she steps back and shuts the door.

The sun has nearly faded behind the city's skyline, and as the sound beyond the large window goes mute, something flashes beneath the surface of Madison's hardened expression.

"Sorry about that. Continue as you were."

"Where was I again?" Madison asks.

"You can pick it up from wherever you want."

She takes a moment before she revisits the memory, and as she does so, I brace myself for what will come next.

Silence...

Madison speaks...I listen.

I listen...as Madison speaks.

"As I was saying. Although I didn't know what to expect, I knew I couldn't wait any longer as my body became flooded with tingles, making it easily noticeable. I told you about the night when he shoved me into a dark corner of the venue and fucked me like I was a woman that belonged on the street. It was invasive and humiliating, but I loved every part of it. But then, there's the night it all changed. Just a couple of days ago.

"Initially, I did not know what to expect when I walked through his door that night. Would he tie me up like a hog, fuck me like a slut, and then whip me until the pleasure turned to pain? Or would he lay me down, rub oil over my body, and then make love to me like I was his only one. I had no idea, and because of that, an explosion in my brain spread to parts of me I couldn't touch at that moment. I could barely keep still, my nipples were sensitive, and a faint pulse was starting to get the best of me between my legs. This wasn't normal and blaming it on the wine was pointless because I had only taken a sip.

"'You okay?' he asked as our hands remained locked.

"He cared about me. I could hear it in his voice and see it in his gleaming brown eyes. It was unlike the cold and empty look I saw the night I met him. My breathing was uneasy and shallow, and I could feel my pulse pounding everywhere in my body with any sudden movement that I made. I didn't understand why that was happening because it was not like I was nervous. In fact, the moment his front door shut, my worries and morality had forsaken me, and all that was left was time and opportunity.

"'Yes. I'm fine.'

"'Then why are your hands moist?'

"Immediately, I pulled my hands away from his hold. Standing in front of him while his lips twitched upward to a smile made it difficult for me to think, let alone speak. The last thing I wanted was for him to mistake my anticipation for uneasiness. It's too bad he couldn't feel somewhere else that was much more moist.

"'It's okay. I got you.' He grabbed ahold of my hands.

"The way he and I met wasn't ideal, but that didn't stop me from having these strong feelings. I had been with plenty of men before him, and none of them ever made me feel the way he did so quickly. Inside and out, I wanted to discover more about myself through his sexuality. But I wouldn't allow myself to be the woman who mistook that night for more than what it was. A night meant for nothing more than two people experiencing pleasure with no rules, inhibitions, or expectations. Just pure pleasure. So, I became the woman I wanted to be instead of the woman I was, unable to tell which one wanted it more.

"He pulled my hands up to his mouth and softly kissed each one. Left hand first, and then the right one. I had the urge to show him just how comfortable I was, but every thought that came to mind made me seem desperate. First, I thought about putting my hand down his pants and feeling him up until he was completely hard in my palm. As tempting as that may have been, it probably wouldn't have worked for the moment. I also thought about taking my clothes off right then and there and then telling him to fuck me. Then again, had I done that, I would be in control just like I had been with all the others. Whatever I was going to do had to be subtle, and it needed to be done quickly.

But it didn't happen because he pulled me in out of nowhere and slid his tongue across my lips like a lollipop.

One moment I'm thinking about something, and then in the next, butterflies fill my stomach. It was happening, and it felt like time was suspended as the world stood still for everyone except us. His sweet breath was on my lips, and I could taste every bit of his tongue. In complete silence, the sound of our lips pressed against each other was mesmerizing. Every so often, he'd deeply inhale and then softly exhale into my mouth. It felt different and connected us on a level I hadn't been with any of the others, and even if he didn't feel the way I did, it was still enough for me. His right hand slid up and down my lower back as his left hand firmly held onto my neck. I softly exhaled into his mouth, and he swallowed it."

Why is Madison telling me this in such vivid detail?! I can't sit still as I continue to feel myself in her thoughts. It's even causing a slow build up between my legs. My skin tingles, and silently, I can't stop taking deep breaths as I try to control my urges. Even sitting here, I can feel how sensitive I am between my legs just by crossing them. But I need to hear more.

"My heart fluttered at the sight of his lips showering my collarbone and my neck with soft kisses. I couldn't pull myself away from him even if I wanted to because I was lost in the moment. My senses were utterly seduced, and just thinking about him inside of me gave me chills. The more time passed, the more he seemed different from the man I encountered at the venue. That night, he was much gentler and loving. Very passionate with his hands and attentive with his eyes. Indeed, he was completely different. His long index finger on his right hand trailed up my left thigh, raising my skirt along the way.

"'I guess you did come prepared,' he whispered.

"I was smitten by every word he said, and the fact that I couldn't formulate my own forced me to respond with a coy smile. I was bursting with emotions that were not typical of me. Emotions that took strength to lower my shield and allow him to be with the woman that I would often hide from. The cage to my vulnerability opened, and he walked right on in, locked the door, and made himself at home.

With the others, I only wanted to be fucked and worshiped. But with him, I wanted to make love, hear all his stories, and discover what we had in common. I needed him.

"His hands slowly inched towards the center of my legs, where I deeply needed to feel his fingers.

"Do it! Please, touch my body. Touch my pussy in any way you want! Just touch me! I internally moaned.

"I took a deep breath, held it for a moment, and then waited for his charming smile to cover his face once he felt how wet I was. Slowly, his fingers slid between my thighs and then inside of me. My mouth dropped slightly open from his touch. I closed my eyes and felt him strumming his fingers on my spot like strings on a violin. Gracefully and sensually. With every touch, I couldn't help but moan. It was a moan that he whispered to be a lovely sound.

"He bit on my bottom lip while strumming his fingers against my clit, and then began gently sliding them in and out of me. I gasped from the pleasure and scowled at the thought that he could touch another woman like this. There was no way he could have. His control over my body made me feel like I was the only woman he wanted. It had to be true. I know it was. There was just no way he could be this attentive, loving, gentle, or thirsty for anyone else. Even though I barely knew him, I loved the feeling of knowing that. I didn't even know who I was while I was around him. With all the other men I had been with, I was never torn or timid. I was bold, expressive, and decisive. But for some strange reason, I was puzzled and entirely at his mercy when it came to this man. My thoughts and feelings were in a constant battle that neither wanted to lose.

"'Relax,' he whispered.

"Two of his fingers grazed that spot inside my pussy in a breathtaking come-hither motion while his thumb slowly circled around my clit. I held onto his robust forearm as I looked into his eyes, with my heart racing the more he touched me. Indeed, I was ready for him this time.

"'You should get more comfortable,' he murmured while his fingers circled inside me, adding more pressure as he did so.

"Then, he peeled the pink blouse off my skin with his left hand and tossed it onto the stove. He unclasped my bra and left it hanging on my shoulders without removing his hands from between my thighs. The small details of his actions fondled my mind and made me even more sensitive to his touches. The feeling of his skin touching my shoulders brought tingles from my toes to the roots of my hair. The stubble in his beard brushing against my neck had me soaked and panting.

"All of a sudden, he pinned me against the stainless-steel refrigerator, and with the metal against my back, he pressed his body on me. Chest to chest. His left hand softly caressed my shoulders, arms, and waist as if he were searching for something. A tingling sensation made my knees weak, but I held it together, hoping he didn't notice. He then turned me around aggressively and began kissing across the back of my neck, along my shoulders, down my spine, and over my ass—all while his fingers remained inside me, twirling in circles. I never expected the woman that walked through his front door to fall for a stranger with unrestricted emotions, but she did, and oddly enough, I loved it. Because with him, I didn't feel any guilt or shame for exploring my thoughts, feelings, or my sexuality. It all came naturally with him, and I was stuck to that feeling. It gave me a sense of relief and freedom that didn't come easily with the others.

"Without warning, he turned me around, placed his hands in the pit of my arms, and hoisted me in the air. I wrapped my arms around his neck and my legs around his waist, holding onto him as if he were the last man left on earth. Or better yet, as if he were mine.

"'I like this side of you,' he said.

"I never thought I could be considered aggressive with him, given our first encounter, but at that moment, I was. An aggressive woman. That's what made the encounter so exhilarating. I could be anyone I wanted to be. I knew nothing about him, and he knew nothing about me, but he was my everything for that moment, and I was his.

"'Now what?' I asked.

"He slowly removed my bra from my shoulders and softly kissed my breasts—the right one first, then the left. Everything he did was done with methodical precision.

"His left hand firmly gripped my ass as he held onto my wrist with his right. His tongue brushed around my nipples in slow circles. Watching him leave wet trails over my breast turned me on even more. From there, he seized my nipple with his teeth while sliding his tongue around the tip—offering a satisfying pain. There must be a nerve in my breast that connects directly to my pussy because I could feel him there as well, moaning and tasting my body. It was enough to make the muscles between my legs tighten up where I was completely moist. I was so fucking wet that I could even inhale the unique blend of my arousal mixed in perfectly with the scent of red wine.

Now, I'm completely distracted and subconsciously restless. Shit! Why am I touching my neck? And if that's not bad enough, my leg can't keep still as Madison goes on with this story. Why am I doing this? Quickly, I stop. Everything is warm. Me, this room, my thoughts. Everything! Oh, God. That build up is turning into a throb, and rubbing my thighs together, only makes it worse. Relax. Just relax, Andrea. That's not helping either.

"He raised me higher and placed my legs over his shoulders, spreading them apart to admire my gift to men. I felt his breathing just an inch from where I yearned for him to taste, but again, I had to wait. My legs hung over his shoulders like chains on bars with no struggle. It drove me wild to hear how wet I was every time my legs came together and then spread apart.

"'May I?' he politely asked, looking up at me.

My voice was frail when I replied, "Yes!"

"He licked his lips. Smiled. And then, his tongue, moist and warm, circled between my thighs, long and slow, before he pushed it deep inside me. There I was, sitting on his shoulder and dripping on his curvaceous tongue. Even his lips and his beard were covered with my eagerness. Watching him was just as satisfying as his actual touch. It's as if he wanted all of me in his mouth. I was so captivated by that moment, but at the same time, scared as well. Maybe not scared, but more so worried because I kept thinking…*what if that was the only time I'd have him to myself?*

"'I love this,' he murmured.

"Unable to bear the sight of his tongue flickering against my clit, I shut my eyes tight and pushed my hips forward, nearly falling off his shoulders. I loathed the fact that I had to wait any longer for him to be inside of me. I wanted him so badly! More than any man I have ever wanted before.

"'Fuck! What are you doing to me?' I murmured as the feeling became more pleasurable.

"'Making you cum.'

He heard me.

"'In your mouth?' I exhaled.

"'Right now.'

"The moment he said that I lost control and gave in. My head fell back, and my mouth dropped open as a wailing moan escaped. My legs were shaking uncontrollably as I remained stuck, panting for more.

"'You want me to come in your mouth?' I moaned.

"'Right fucking now!' he said between licks.

"Again and again, his tongue circled on the spot that made my body weak. Kissing it. Licking it. Simply making out between my legs while his fingertips softly grazed along my back and down to my waist. What he was doing to me was not normal. It was…different, making me lose a handle of my sense of reality. My insides began to pulsate as I took a big gasp of air. And just like that, it happened. He got what he wanted and freed me from my remaining inhibitions, making the moment even more intensifying."

"Madison!" I interrupt.

I can't take any more. I feel my nerves, brain, and hormones changing, along with my thoughts and emotions. Even worse, my insides are pulsating as it repeatedly tries to clench onto something without my control, and I shouldn't be feeling like this. Especially not right now or right here— while in a session? Not to mention, I still don't know where Daniel is. However, from what I'm hearing, it doesn't appear that she's talking about Daniel. That's a sigh of relief.

"Yes, Dr. Clarke?" she smirks.

I look up at Madison, and the corners of her lips twitch up to a smile, her eyebrows slightly raised, all while she crosses her legs— right over left. I sense Madison is aware that everything about her encounter with this man makes me want to explore myself. And she's right. I want to be like her and disregard what others may think without feeling ashamed of my actions. I envy her for that. The way she does what she pleases with no harassing thoughts. *Ugh!* I wish I could be just like her. Andrea! What about Daniel? Fuck! Why must that voice continue to interrupt my thoughts and bring me back to reality?

I must hear more from Madison. Perhaps then I'll find out everything I need to know, including where it went wrong for her. Surely it can't all be great. Right? Why else would we be here?

CHAPTER 14

"Is something wrong, Dr. Clarke?"

"No. Everything is fine. Continue." I direct Madison.

"Are you sure you want me to continue with this?"

Madison only asks because she can see that I have succumbed to the desires circling in my head. The motion of one movement to another was like water flowing in the river, leaving me with no option.

"Yes. I'm sure."

Two summers ago, I decided to visit a spa that was like none that I had ever been to. That was the only time I've ever had anything close to what Madison described. I heard about this place through Courtnie on the night she returned from the hospital following a drug overdose. If you ask her, she'd tell you that I was more interested in watching paint dry, but the truth is, I paid close attention to every detail of that visit. So much so that I decided to visit the place for myself. The spa is located in Hialeah, just off 68th street and 24th avenue—a block from the Palmetto Hospital. The door to the spa is inside the gray and white five-story commercial building. Fourth floor. It's a typical transparent glass door with a yellow and green lotus flower covering half of it. Not usually where you'd expect to find a spa, but nothing about this place seemed out of the ordinary. In fact, the moment I walked in, I felt a calmness abandoning all the tension within my body and a scent that took me away to a better place. Just as I took a deep breath, a bold woman with long dark hair and freckles—

"Dr. Clarke…"

"Yes!"

Just like that, Madison pulls me back into her world where I can once again lose myself. My eyes quickly wander the room in search of anything to help make sense of this moment.

"Would you like me to continue?" She whispers.

"Um…yes. Go ahead. Pick up from where you stopped."

Once again, Madison uncrosses her legs, sits upright, and crosses them left over right. This time, though, it's much slower.

"Well, Dr. Clarke, the next thing I remember is him taking me off his shoulders and placing me down on the counter. He stared deep into my eyes as he grabbed ahold of my left leg, sliding the heel of my feet along his body. All the way to his mouth. Then he placed my toes in his mouth. I like my feet being touched and kissed, but it felt more intimate at the moment. No one had ever touched my feet the way he did. It was as if he wanted every inch of me. I softly moaned as my head fell backward and my eyes slightly closed. He placed me down on my feet for a moment. I was utterly drained and mesmerized by the entire design of this man. His physique. His touch. His tongue. His smile. More importantly—his smell had all gotten the best of me. He is the man every woman needs to encounter just once in their life.

"Then, he took a step back and untied the drawstrings on his blue pajama pants without taking his eyes off me. I kept my eyes steadily fixed on the outline of his bulge, waiting for it to jump out like a jack in the box. This was the moment I had been waiting for.

"'Come closer,' he commanded.

"I stepped forward until only a couple inches remained between us. He looked me in the eyes as I looked into his eyes with temptation.

"'Get down on your knees and take my pants off!' he said.

"Without questioning him, I dropped to my knees and followed his order, sliding his pants down.

"'Slower.'

"I surrendered to his every demand and melted into nothingness. So, slowly I pulled his pants down to his ankles. He stepped out with his left foot first, then with his right. His erection was just an inch from my lips when I finally looked up. I gasped at the sight of it as I nibbled on my bottom lip. It was desirable and…gorgeous. Lengthy enough to satisfy my thoughts and thick enough to leave me silently panting. The dark complexion only added to his beauty. It's also smoothly shaved down with an irresistible girth—all the way to a lovely tip. Wrapping my hand around him was all I wanted to do at that moment.

"'You see what you've done?' he looked down at me.

"'Well, consider us even.' I smiled.

"It was begging for me to touch it. So much so that I felt a warm, tingling pulsation on my clit. I couldn't think of anything other than my desire to be filled. I pondered on what I could do at that moment as it remained so close to my mouth. Hold it in my hand? Caress it between my lips? Or better yet, put it inside of me.

"'Anything else?' I asked.

"During our first encounter, he took over my body physically, but that night, he did the same mentally. It was a moment that caused an absorbing feeling to run through my entire body. All the stress and problems inside me were released through an intensifying pleasure— causing a quivering and exhilarating experience.

"'Yes. I want you to touch yourself,' he insisted.

"Touch myself? I wasn't sure why he wanted me to do that when he could do it himself, but I would have done anything for him. So, I did it. I pressed my fingers between my legs and began to touch myself in a circular motion— all while his erection remained inches from my mouth. The more I stared at it, the more I wanted to touch myself. I took a deep breath, then placed two of my fingers inside of me while sliding my right hand over his body.

Along his stomach.

Over his thighs.

Against his chest.

"The smooth ridges of his skin fit perfectly against my palms. Like my hand was meant to touch him. Finally, I was able to graze my fingernails along the veins of his erection.

Up and down.

Down and up.

"'Shhh…I want you to listen,' he said.

"In the silence, I could hear my pussy overflowing with moisture as I circled my fingers around my clit. He closed his eyes, smiled, and then glared back into my eyes. I supposed that was a sound that made him fall further into the moment.

"'That's a beautiful sound, isn't it?' he asked.

"I nodded and closed my eyes as an incredible sensation overwhelmed me.

"'No. Look at me.'

"I opened my eyes, slipping beneath his intent brown eyes and gazing down at me. While looking up at him, he slowly slid the tip of his dick over my lips the same way I would apply my Chanel rouge lipstick. Left to right, and then right to the left. I smiled as a taste of coconut water with a pinch of salt fell onto my tongue. He bit his bottom lip and closed his eyes, allowing the sensitivity of his dick in my mouth to take over. And it quickly got the best of him.

"'Open your mouth wider,' he demanded.

"My mouth opened wide, and he tapped it against my tongue three times before resting it slightly between my lips. He was in my mouth, and it only motivated me in a way I wasn't expecting. I wanted him so deep in my mouth that I would forever remember his taste. So, I gripped it with my left hand and felt the warmth of his blood pumping. It was hard and smooth. The veins coursing through his erection were so powerfully detailed that I traced along each one with my tongue. Following that, I slipped a couple of inches forward, pursed my lips, and kissed the tip of it.

"So eager to taste more of him, I circled his dick with my lips and finally took it deep in my mouth. The heat radiating from his erection swarmed the inside of my mouth like smoke in a chimney. Whenever my tongue slid around it, his body jerked wildly. It turned me on to see what I was doing to him.

"He was getting warmer while growing inside my mouth, and it was such a fascinating feeling. I slid his dick against my tongue and then pushed it to the back of my throat. I couldn't fit that much of him in my mouth, so I sucked on the tip like a popsicle I had not had in a long time. God, it felt so fucking good. His hips would wriggle and shift the faster I went, confirming that I was doing something right. I sucked, and he groaned. I licked, and he jerked. I loved watching him.

"He closed his eyes and tilted his head back as his body collapsed against the steel refrigerator doors. My left hand traveled over his body as I continued to slip him in and out of my mouth. Every so often, I'd tap it against the sides of my cheeks. It was exciting and unlike anything I had ever done.

"'Don't move!' I murmured.

"My mouth, warm and wet, went far down on him while my tongue curled along the base of his shaft. I stopped breathing, and my eyes began to water up. When I pulled back, I panted for air, smiling deviously. The suspense had grown tiring, and I could not wait any longer. I was over the idea of being a good girl and wanted him to see the real me. The side of me that I encountered for the first time at the age of twelve. So, I stood up and slid my skirt off but left my heels on for the sake of the moment. Then, I turned around, bent over onto the white granite counter, and looked back at him, biting my bottom lip. I was ready for him to fuck me. No hesitation. No thoughts or concerns, before or later, or fear and anxiety. Just he and I, melting into each other for two intense hours.

"He stepped forward, grabbed both my wrists with his left hand, and held them together behind my back as if he were arresting me. Then, he propped my right leg on the counter with his right hand, causing me to drip down my leg. I was spread wide open, bracing myself to feel him enter my body just as I did that rainy Thursday night. I knew exactly what I was expecting.

"Eyes closed. Mouth opened. Breathing stopped. Mind blank. His hard dick, warm and long, slid inside me and filled the void. With him, there was a fine line between pleasure and pain that added incredible pressure *to my hidden spot. He moved slowly but methodically, finding the perfect angle for my body to quiver.* His warmth inside of me brought flashbacks which made the moment more exhilarating.

"'Stop moving! Just take it,' he whispered.

"Hearing him say that made me want him even more. *He made it safe enough for me to live in my truest sexual form, and from that came a* wave of warmth that rose from my clit to my pelvis once again. There's a pulsating feeling that grows by the second, but this one didn't *just peak. It lasted for a long time.* I squeezed my pussy tighter on him, hoping to intensify the feeling as my breathing surrendered again.

"He thrust his hips uncontrollably, fitting himself perfectly inside of me. As he stroked his erection in and out of me, *he released my wrist and grabbed my hair instead. Shockingly, he slid the index finger of his right hand into my asshole.* I nearly stopped him because it took me by surprise at first. Never *had anyone done that to me, but after a few seconds, I was all for it. It's like I could feel everything even more than before, enhancing the feeling times one hundred. I could feel the tip of his dick grazing against the ridges inside me every time he went in and out. Immediately, he began biting on the back of my neck and shoulders—all while fucking me.*

Again and again, he touched a spot inside of me that others had not been able to reach. Every time he pulled away from me, I yearned for him to return. He groaned. I'd moan. Sometimes we'd do it together.

"When he fucked me faster, he did it with precision. When he did it slowly, he was aggressive. What he was doing to my body didn't make sense and was strangely unfamiliar. How he executed his motions allowed me to see how much of a professional he was.

"'Damn, I feel you cumming,' he whispered directly in my right ear.

"'Yes!' I moaned.

"'There you go. Just relax and let it come.'

"He went faster, knocking on that hidden spot over and over. Then, he pushed himself as deep as he could and held it there for a few seconds. His right hand squeezed my ass for leverage as his left hand again grabbed my wrists and bound them together. It was a mental and physical pleasure as I felt him fully inside me.

One.

Two.

Three.

"A sharp tingling rushed from my toes through my thighs, then up to my stomach, where it exploded like a broken glass window. My muscles were relaxed as if I had taken a dose of Prozac. My body became sensitive, and a lingering piercing feeling caused me to lose track of my breathing. The same feeling I experienced on that Thursday night at the venue occurred at that very moment.

"How did he do that? That was all that I could think about. Honestly, it shouldn't be so easy for him to pull an orgasm from me like that because up to that moment, no other men had done what he'd done to me. He pleased me to the point that every time I took a step, I would think of him. It was to the point that *I was aware of every molecule in my body. And when I looked into his eyes, I knew there was something that I probably wouldn't ever see again.*

"After nearly forty minutes of making love, we laid on the floor, naked, staring up at the ceiling. I was drained and unable to move a muscle, but it was such a magical moment. I could have just laid there on his floor all night. But then…he told me something that would change the rest of my life."

RING!

Crap!

My phone rings as I try to catch my breath. Yet, I am unable to move a muscle. Furthermore, the silence between each phone ring is nerve-wracking, and it feels like it's getting louder. Madison must feel the same way because her demeanor suddenly changes. She no longer smiles as she avoids making eye contact with me. Yet, she blinks uncontrollably. Madison then takes a gulp of air and turns to the large window. I wonder if she's aware of her fading disappearance. The phone continues to ring. I jump out of my seat, hurry over, and answer, turning my back to Madison as I do so.

"Hello?"

There's no response.

"Hello…"

Nothing. No background noise or breathing.

"Daniel? Is that you?"

The call drops, and I turn back to Madison, who sits with her eyes wide open, yet focused on nothing. It's as if she is a corpse.

"Madison?"

She snaps out of it and looks at me with a devious smile. Then, she crosses her legs, right over left, spreading her arms along the top of the sofa. I return to my chair and sit across from Madison, glancing over to my office door, which is slightly open. That's strange. When did that happen?

"Dropped call?"

"Yes, it was."

The worst flaw a person can have is that of self-deception. That sort of mentality can easily take the fears and emotions of who we think we are and then put us into conflict with who we really are. That would explain her behavior, which stems from her sexuality. And whatever it is, it's making it difficult for Madison to tell the difference between what's real and what's not. Even as detailed as that memory was, I can't help but think there's more…

CHAPTER 15

Tick...tick...tick...

Madison's mouth is slightly open, and her eyes are fixed on a spot behind my head.

"Madison..." I call her name.

It takes a moment before she blinks and returns her attention to me.

"Yes, Dr. Clarke?" she replies.

"As detailed as that was, I can't help but think there's more to why you're really here."

Her eyes have an emptiness to them that I have only seen in the mirror. Almost as if the world around her is slowly disappearing. It's a never-ending dark void consuming her mind with truths when she'd rather tell lies. I know that feeling all too well, but unlike Madison, I tend to mask it with normal human emotions.

"You're right. There is." She breathes.

Madison sits up and crosses her legs as her eyes narrow to a cold stare. I've never seen that look in her eyes before. The free-spirited woman who does what she wants and goes where she pleases...has a hardness that she can no longer disguise. She can't hold onto the idea that everything is okay. How can she when nothing ever is.

"It happened so quickly, and it was beyond my control, and now, I'll have to live with it forever. You must understand, Dr. Clarke; even though that night was filled with ecstasy and pure pleasure, I was still in a hopeless place. Somehow, the more I thought about him, the more my brain spiraled out of control. Our lives were headed down different paths, and we wanted nothing more than to be transparent with each other. He was more adamant about it than I was.

"After we made love that night, I laid on his floor, naked, and taken by the moment we'd just shared. It felt like time had lost its way and left us wandering in its absence. The feeling was so unfamiliar and stretched throughout my body in cold tingles. I turned to him and softly outlined his lips with the tip of my fingernail while looking into his brown eyes. He smiled, moved in closer, and then grabbed my right hand. I had an urge to kiss him, but before I could purse my lips, he told me it was over in a whispering voice.

"'Excuse me?' I asked.

"'I thought you should know…we can't do this anymore. I'm sorry, but it wasn't supposed to be like this,' he said.

"It caught me off guard, leaving me speechless and unable to move. Although I already knew the truth, hearing him say it felt like a wooden spear piercing through my chest. He glared at me and then released my hand.

"'I hope you understand.'

"The truth is, I wasn't okay. He snuck into my mind like a thief in the night and stole something meaningful to me—my dignity. Even though I told myself not to mistake this night for more than what it was, I was still devastated. And he knew that. I would have rather he had taken a knife to my throat instead of telling me why he could no longer see me. It was because of the other woman. A woman he felt that he needed to give his all to, and because of me, he couldn't. So, for the next fifteen minutes, I listened to him go on and on about this woman. He spoke to me about her as if I was a stranger sitting on a park bench. Like we didn't finish making love all over the place.

"'Hey! You okay?' He snapped his fingers inches away from my face.

"I recovered, turning to him with a forged smile. What else could I have done? Cried? Fought? Screamed? Maybe. But I could hear my mother's voice echoing in my head, saying, 'Don't let anyone see your weakness because they'll thrive off it.'

"'Yes. I'm fine,' I replied. "I understand. How about one last drink? You sit here. I'll get it.'

"Honestly, I was dying inside as I went into the kitchen to pour us a glass of wine. I didn't want to accept that we could never be. How could he be so connected to this other woman that he'd leave me? What was it about her? The thought alone drove me crazy. I mean, sure, she was well put together, but so was I. Her eyes glistened like an old copper penny. Her hair, like mine, is naturally black, and some days it's woven into a braid, and other days it's either out curly or pulled back into a ponytail. What in the entire fuck did he see in her that he couldn't see in me?

"I'm embarrassed to say this, but I did everything I could to be just like her, hoping he'd love me the same. Her endless smiles. Her graceful walk and posture. The way she expressed herself through her bold style. Her mannerisms. The more I tried to become the woman he could fall in love with, the more I lost sense of who I was.

"Here you go.' I returned with a glass of wine.

"At last, he stood up, grabbed the glass from my hand, and chugged down half of the wine. Then, without looking at me, he said something I'll never forget.

"'Okay. It's time for you to leave.' He tossed my blouse over to me.

"Just like that, it was all over. Everything went blank the moment I heard him say that. I froze and sat in the pit of it, staring off into the distance. His lips were moving, but I couldn't hear his voice. The rapid beating of my heart against my chest was all I heard.

"'Hello? You going to say something?' he asked.

"Four seconds. That's how long it took for me to snap out of it, turning to him with a face of utter nonchalance, as if I were simply thinking about eating a slice of upside-down pineapple cake.

"'Okay. I'll be on my way then,' I coldly replied.

"'Good.'

"I held my glass up towards him and smiled. What he saw in me was a calm woman unfazed by his words. However, internally, I was surrendering to an unfamiliar pain.

"'What's this for?' he questioned.

"'Just one last drink. Cheers.'

"I tapped my glass against his before we chugged our drink. Then, he placed his cup on the table, put on his pajama pants, and made his way to the front door.

"'Well, maybe I'll see you around.' He winked.

"I nodded, and before I could say a word, he ushered me out as if I were a pest control inspector. No "I'll miss you," "I love you," or even "I'll be thinking about you." He didn't say anything as he opened the door, stepped aside, and waited for me to exit. The moment I did, he shut the door and left me to rot in the pit of misery. I stood on his doorstep for a moment before finally making my way to the car, and once I entered, my heart twisted and sunk with nerves. I took several deep breaths to calm myself down, but that didn't work. I could still hear his voice repeating in my head, telling me it was over and that I needed to leave. And although I could hear him, I still couldn't process his last words.

My hands clasped tight against the steering wheel as a tear came down my right cheek. The moment I pulled out of his driveway, I wanted to look back and see if he was standing there, watching me, but I couldn't allow myself to do it. I knew that if I saw him there, I probably would have run back to him like some desperate idiot.

"I came to a stop sign down the block—not too far from his house. My stare was off ahead with a blurry vision of kids playing on the street. However, I barely noticed them because I was stuck in the maze he placed in my mind, trying to figure my way out. But I just couldn't.

"Five seconds. That's how long it took before the pain poured out like water from a dam, spilling down onto my cheeks. I felt numb. I felt lost. I could even feel my chin muscles quivering like a child left in the cold. How could he take what he wanted from me and then toss me away like an unpaid bill? I kept thinking about what I should do because it wasn't fair. Some way or somehow, I needed him to know that as well. Surely, the way I handled the situation isn't how the woman he loved would have. At the very least, she would have made him listen to what she had to say, and that's what I needed to do as well. So, I quickly circled back around, preparing myself to tell him exactly how I felt, but when I got there, I saw him pulling out of his garage. He was in such a rush that he didn't even notice my car parked a couple of houses away. I had no idea where he was headed, but something made me follow him.

"Ten minutes into the drive, he made a right on 116th—followed by another right onto Biscayne Boulevard. Obviously, he wasn't headed to his office because it was in the opposite direction—nearly twenty-five miles across the county line. He pulled into a hotel tucked away along the beach by a quarter to nine. The hotel looked more like somewhere unfaithful men turn good women into mistresses. Indeed, this was a hotel he'd been to before, yet a place he'd never bring the woman he loved.

"He parked his car a fair distance from the entrance, toppled out, and then changed shirts. I watched him sluggishly make his way into the hotel, and after six staggering steps, he bent over and vomited. The glass of wine had taken over him, or perhaps it was something else I had given him. That would explain why he was unaware that I was following behind. Part of me wanted him to see me, just to terrify him, but the other half wanted to know what he was up to. So, I remained in the back, waiting until he was near the entrance before stepping out of my car.

"My steps were much quicker than his because before I knew it, he was just making it out of the lobby. There he was, in the middle of the courtyard, trying to walk up a wooden staircase that went up to the fifth floor. I could see him struggling to keep his balance as his legs swayed left to right, and no matter how many steps he took, he was no closer to where he wanted to be.

"After his slow and sluggish climb to the second floor, he slumped onto a door—just a few feet from the staircase. I was sure he would fall out right there, but instead, he abruptly turned in my direction. Quickly, I dipped behind a pillar, and it's a good thing I did, or else he would have seen me.

I peeked from behind the pillar and saw him banging on the door. No one answered. He waited another twenty seconds before knocking again. Still, no one answered the door.

"He looked defeated, barely functional, and completely chaotic. Certainly, this was not the man I'd come to know. Then, he reached into his right pocket and pulled out a room key. He was so intoxicated that he could barely open the door. It didn't matter, though, because, for that moment, he was alone. And if there were ever a time to confront him, this would be it.

"I walked up to the room door he had just entered, but I had no idea what to do next. Would I knock? And if I did, would I scream and curse at him? Would I hurt him? Or would I simply find a way to hold him in my arms in hopes of making love?

"As soon as I arrived at the door, my brittle knuckles knocked four times against it and turned me into a despairing woman. After that fourth knock, I noticed the door was slightly open. I found that strange because the man I knew would never leave his door like this. I looked around and then unwisely entered the room. The room was cold and smelled like a refreshing blend of lemon blossoms, green tea, and laurel leaves. There was a peculiar silence that filled the space that made it even eerier.

"When I took a couple of steps further into the room, I saw him slumped over, struggling to breathe like a fish out of water. I closed the door, approached him, and stood over him, smoldering underneath a stone-cold expression.

"Every word I had rehearsed and every thought that came to my mind had become silenced by pain. That's the thing about anger. It has a way of hiding like a snake in a garden, ready to strike when someone least expects it.

"'Help me.' His eyes shot open, and he quickly grabbed ahold of my left ankle.

"I tried to kick him off, but he held on tight.

"'Let me go!' I scold.

My foot brutally swiped across his face, and after many attempts, I was able to break free of his hold. He began gasping for air, and instead of helping him, I just stood there watching him fade away like the morning mist of a summer's sunrise. The more he struggled, the more I anticipated seeing the light go out of his eyes as he lay on the floor begging for help.

"'Please, help me,' he murmured painfully.

"I took three steps back and stared at him with a smirk on my face. It was strange, but I felt satisfied. It was riveting and soothing all at once. Besides, what could I have done? The man who just told me it was over and that I had to move on now needed my help. How ironic was that?

"Suddenly, he crawled to the other side of the room with all his might, nearly making it to the phone. I watched him muster enough energy to get up, but I yanked it away just as he reached for it.

"'You fucking bitch,' he screamed.

"Then, something took over me, awakening the evil side that I spent years burying deep within my soul. Red eyes. Shaky hands. No blinking. Lagging heartbeats. The dark monster dwelling inside me came out and sought to destroy anything in its way. What had become of me came with no plausible answers, and I could no longer watch him lay there as helpless as roadkill on the side of the road. So, I did what needed to be done. I pulled the belt off his waist and wrapped it around his neck, holding onto the brown leather so tight I could feel the blood draining from my fingers. His mouth opened wide as he attempted to scream for help, but only the faint sound of a squeal came out as he gurgled on blood clogged in the back of his throat. Even if he could scream, I'm sure no one would have heard anyway. Besides, what would anyone be able to do for him if they could? Help? I doubt it. By that time, my desire for his death was greater than his need for survival.

"Everything became silent as his breathing turned into shallow gasps. A feeling of relief transpired throughout my body as my stare remained straight ahead, somewhere where things made sense. Besides, I didn't want to watch his eyes bulge out of their sockets as I held onto the belt.

"The more he jerked, the harder I pulled. Seventeen seconds.

That's how long it took for his breathing to fade like footsteps down a stairwell. And just like that…he was gone.

"I was panting from all the strength I'd put into holding the belt, and when I finally released it, I saw a stillness in his bug-wide-opened eyes. They were covered with red veins, and his face was mottling with pale colors. He looked calm. It was as if he were dreaming of riding a white horse on the shores of Tulum. One second, he was looking at me with anguish, and the next, he's a corpse on the dirty hotel floor, rotting away. I thought that night would have haunted me, but that would prove to be a lie. The truth is, I felt nothing. There was no joy or pain, no sadness or happiness. Everything that led to that moment, the lies, the hurt, and the senseless way I'd come to know him…was all carried out at that moment. A moment that I decided to bury deep in my mind. Until now…"

7:12 P.M.

Oh, my fucking God! What has Madison done? My breathing is shallow as an eerie silence hangs in the air like the suspended moment before a falling glass hits the ground. My palms are sweaty, and the adrenaline coursing through my system shuts down my logical thinking ability.

"So…what are you telling me?" My voice is trembling.

"Yes. He's dead."

The stern look on Madison's face brings chills down my spine, and then over my skin like ants on a caramel toffee. My stomach twists in knots, making breathing a difficult task. I can feel the whole world crumbling around me. Did I just hear her say that? What do I do?! Her mouth doesn't twitch at all, and her eyes are as unmoving as a stone statue. How could she ever think that I could help her? I need to call Detective Barringer and tell her what Madison has revealed to me. Yes, I must do that.

"Dr. Clarke…" She walks over to the large window.

I snap out of it and stand to my feet, and pace back and forth, feeling as if I am the guilty one. I knew the day I met Madison I should have turned away. Why doesn't this faze her at all? She should be the one pacing back and forth as her nerves abandon her. Not me. Instead, she focuses on the reflection from the large window with a frivolous smile.

"Madison, you must tell the police what you've done."

"That's not an option. Now, like I said before, I need your help. That's why I'm here." She turns to me.

"My help. What would I be able to help you with?" I take a seat.

"That night, after I watched his life slowly fade from his body, I sat there with my chin between my knees, thinking about what I would do next. Leaving him in the room would not be the best idea because it could lead back to me. So, I had to come up with something, and I had to do it fast.

"That's when I noticed a sliding door behind the heavy taupe curtain. Beyond the door is a balcony looking out to the ocean. I ran over to the sliding door, opened it, and immediately felt the ocean's breeze kissing along my body as it whooshed by. There was a stunning view of the moon in the distance, reflecting off the ocean waves. The promise of life in the darkness with a sense of warmth from the stars made me rethink my actions. I couldn't continue with the absurd idea floating through my mind. However, I knew there was no turning back.

"Directly below the balcony was a wall of shrubs that ran along the back of the hotel. The darkness that robbed you of your ability to see had replaced it with a paralyzing fear. So, it was perfect. I could dump his body, and no one would see me. Nevertheless, whatever I was going to do, I had to do it quickly.

"I grabbed him by the ankles, dragged his lifeless body onto the balcony, and then mustered the strength to stand him upright against the wall. I contemplated my decision for nearly two minutes, looking all around to ensure no one was watching. I waited, and waited…and then, I did it. I pushed his body over the balcony, headfirst, falling two floors down. The sound of his body thumping against the ground like a bag of rocks gave me chills that ran through my spine.

"Once I had him over the balcony, I had to ensure the room was in order. No broken furniture. No bodily fluids. No items on the ground. Nothing could be out of place. Everything had to be perfect.

I placed the chair he knocked over back underneath the desk, straightened the sheets he pulled off the bed, and cleaned the area where he threw up. I even wiped down everything I touched, which took me over an hour."

"Madison!" I stop her. "Enough. You have to tell the police because there's nothing I can do to help."

"No! You have to help. Especially now that you know."

Like a cell phone in the middle of nowhere, my brain searches for the signal to make the right decision. However, it's a total failure because nothing comes to mind. And when my mind cannot decide…my heart does it. Nothing good ever comes from my heart making decisions.

"What could I possibly help you with?"

She remains standing at the large window, staring at the ant-like people walking up and down Second Avenue. There is no sadness, no fear, no joy, or resentment in her eyes. But deep down, I know something is stinging her with guilt.

"I wore my solid white ceramic gold-tone watch that night, but somewhere in between everything…it must have slipped off my wrist," Madison murmurs.

"A watch? You want me to go back to the spot where you killed a man to find a watch? Are you crazy?"

"No. It's not the watch I need help with." She grins.

"Then what is it that you need help with?"

She turns to me.

"After I finished cleaning the room, I felt lost and flustered. I couldn't even think straight. All I wanted was to get out of there. And that's what I did. I quickly returned to the car, avoiding eye contact with anyone. For the most part, I think I was successful. However, something dawned on me after I climbed in my car and drove away."

"And? What is it?"

Madison walks back over to the sofa and sits, crossing her legs right over left as she does so.

"I never went to move his body."

"So, he's still back there?" My eyebrows rise.

"That's what I need help with, Dr. Clarke."

Hold on tight, Andrea. My heart nearly jumps out of my chest, and my senses are on high alert. The colors are brighter, and I can smell everything, yet I can hear nothing. I wish I had the strength to run out of there, but I can't do it. Why am I conflicted? This shouldn't be something that I struggle with. It's obvious. I must call the police.

"Are you crazy? That's not something I can help you with!"

That's it. I must call Detective Barringer at once. I can't have her thinking that I am an accessory to murder—especially if Madison is referring to Mr. Walker. Abruptly, I walk over to my desk, grab my phone, and call Detective Barringer, turning away from Madison as I do so. The phone rings, and as I wait on her to answer, Madison looks at me with nonchalance. Perhaps she thinks I'm bluffing. It doesn't matter because the Detective doesn't answer. Screw it! I'll call 9-1-1. But what will I say? That there's a woman named Madison who just told me she killed a man? Yes! Of course. But where's the body?

Behind the hotel, Andrea. Duh! That's right. But how will I be able to prove it was Madison? Shit! Think, Andrea. What should you do?

"Madison, have to turn yourself in." Slowly, I turn back to her.

"Like I said. That's not an option. I just need your help. Together, we can put this whole thing behind me. Besides, I've already told you too much." Her eyes are narrowed, rigid, and cold.

A sudden fear sneaks into my soul, suffocating my spirit like a pillow covering my face. Beneath Madison's smile and free-spirited mask, she must have been planning this all along. All of it. That's why she's here.

"Even if I could help, why would I? Better yet, why should I?"

She slowly approaches me with an unnatural look in her eyes.

"There's so much more to what you want to know. More than you can even imagine. Trust me…by helping me… you would be helping yourself."

I can taste my saliva thickening, making it harder to swallow, and as I look into Madison's eyes, it seems as if this is the end of the road. This whole time she let me think I was in control when she's been steering me easier than a brand-new car. They are my thoughts and my choices, but it's her hands on the steering wheel.

"Okay. Now what?"

"We get rid of his body. Meet me in the hotel parking lot in a few hours—one o'clock, to be exact," Madison says.

Wait a minute. This may be a way for me to get the proof that I need. No Andrea! You can't do that. Why not? Think about it. *Shit!*

Madison walks over to the door, and before she exits, she looks back at me with a devilish smirk.

"For now, enjoy yourself." She says just as she exits.

Enjoy myself? What is she talking about? The door closes, and there's a stillness stuck in the middle of emptiness, tugging at my intuition. What have I just gotten myself into? I'm beginning to realize that I'm not normal. Nothing about me is. The fact that I am considering helping Madison move a dead man's body gives truth to that. I need to walk away from this now. Everything hinges on what I do next, and it can never be undone.

I walk over to the door, close it, and take a deep breath. When I turn around and lean against it, I spot a laminated red card lying on the floor—not too far from my chair.

That wasn't there before. The card is decorative and looks more like an invitation than a random piece of paper. On one side of the card is a notice that says to be there at 10 P.M. This is interesting. Madison must have been planning to go here tonight. There's no telling what sort of place this might be. It can be anything from a simple bonfire gathering to an intimate dark place filled with ecstasy. But she can't possibly be thinking about going now that she has a dead body on her hands. Right? How could she do this to Mr. Walker? And now she wants me to go to the hotel to help with this chaotic situation? Oh my God. The thought alone doesn't even sound real echoing in my head. I need to do something about this. Right now!

I quickly toss the card in the trash and make a call to Detective Barringer. Once again, there's no answer. *Crap*! Following that, I call

Daniel's phone again, but he doesn't answer either. Lord, please let Daniel be okay. It's late, and I need to get out of here.

I grab my purse, and as I make my way out of the office, I take another look at the card sitting in the trash can. Hmm. I didn't notice the back of the card before. *"An Immoral Experience"* is written at the top with a happy face in the center. At the bottom is an address. Intently, I stare at the card, thinking of all the possibilities of what might happen at this place. *What are you saying, Andrea?!* How can I even consider this thought when I have all this shit going on? A moment like this is not the time to be curious, Andrea. Exactly! Then again, Detective Barringer may need to locate Madison, and if she does, this would be a great place to start. So, maybe I'll hold on to the card…just in case.

Tick. Tick. Tick…

CHAPTER 16

8:02 P.M.

BY THE TIME I pull into my driveway, the sun has switched shifts with the moon. *That's strange.* The lights in the house are on. Did I leave them on this morning? Or perhaps Daniel is here? No, it can't be him. Daniel never has the lights on when he's in the house. So, cautiously I climb out of the car and make my way to the front door, and before I enter, I peep through the window blinds. That doesn't help because I can't see anything.

There's a slight panic growing as I reach to unlock the door, and depending on what I see when it opens, I may go into complete terror. Slowly, the door opens, and I wait a few seconds before entering, hoping to hear something. Sudden movements, a door closing, or maybe feet tramping along the floor. There's nothing. The place is calm, quiet, and in order. Perhaps I did leave the lights on.

A few steps into the house, I notice a folded piece of paper sitting on the coffee table. It's a handwritten letter with just three sentences.

> Sorry, I can't do this anymore.
> It wasn't supposed to be like this.
>
> PS: It's still our secret

A letter? Did Daniel walk out of my life, leaving me with a fucking letter? Is this supposed to comfort me? And what the hell does he mean by *It's still our secret?* So many questions circle in my mind, yet there are no probable answers. The frustration and confusion of this situation forces me to scream, hoping to relieve some of the anger, but it doesn't do any good. He would have been better off stabbing me in the side with a dull knife because this hurts even worse. It's an emotional hurt that I've always praised myself for disregarding, but this one has an unpleasant warmth. *Relax, Andrea. Just relax.*

My mind races as my thoughts take me to some unknown place where my brain's response and function have different ideas about the same world. In this world, it's colder and darker than before, surrounded by dingy doors with missing keyholes. There is a key to one of the doors, but it feels like I'll never find it. And had it not been for that voice in my head, I wouldn't even try. *Fuck! I need a drink.*

Knock!

Knock!

Knock!

It's a quarter past eight. Who could that be? With the bottle of wine in my hand, I pause for a moment, waiting to see if the knock will continue. Eight seconds. That's all it takes before the person decides to knock again.

I pour some red wine into my glass and then make my way to the door, taking a sip along the way. Through the peephole, I spot Detective Barringer standing there. This time, she's not alone.

"How can I help you?" I answer.

"Good evening. This is my partner, Detective LaVeaux. May we come in?" she asks.

Part of me wants to say no because this is the last thing I need for the night. However, if I do, she'll only be more suspicious of me. So, what choice do I have? I roll my eyes, step aside, and let them into my home. As soon as Detective Barringer enters, she immediately scans the room with her judgmental eyes. It's as if she's determined to find something. Or someone.

"May I use your restroom?" the man asks.

I turn to him as something flashes beneath his unyielding stare. There's an attempt to explore his eyes, his gait, and even his posture for the truth, but nothing comes to mind. He must be trained to position himself so that no one can figure out his motives.

"Sure. It's down the hallway. Second door on your left."

"Thank you."

He looks at Detective Barringer for a split second and then heads to the bathroom.

"Look, I know you're here because of my call earlier, but everything is fine now. So, you can disregard what I said."

"Well, the thing about a missing person report is…once it's reported, we have to follow up with it until the person is no longer missing."

"He's not missing. He's gone!"

"What do you mean?"

I hand her the folded piece of paper, and she looks over it thoroughly. She doesn't say anything. I can't tell if she's confused or skeptical because of the blank expression covering her face. There's no smile. No blink. Nothing. It's as if she's waiting for me to reveal the truth that I'm hiding.

"Sorry you're going through this." She hands me the letter.

I take it from her and toss it on the floor. Just a foot away from the front door.

"It's fine. So, do you really need to be here? There's nothing else for me to talk about."

"That's not necessarily true," she replies.

Could she know about Madison? *Oh, God. What if she does?* My stomach shifts uneasily, my hands clasped tightly on the wine glass, and suddenly, I find myself gnawing on my bottom lip. The tension grows by the moment, and if it continues, I'm afraid I won't be able to hold on any longer.

"Mrs. Walker said she talked to you today," she approaches.

Shit! That's it! I'll just tell her what she wants to know. I turn away from the woman and take a deep breath. I'm not even sure if she noticed, but it doesn't matter because I needed it.

"She did." I turn back.

"I advised her not to, but she went ahead and did it anyway. However, I'm glad she did because she told me something interesting." Detective Barringer casually walks around the room.

There is a seriousness about her that disturbs me, making the hair on my arms stand to attention as a platoon of chills marches down my spine.

"Yeah. And what's that?"

"She told me that her husband has been to your office before. In fact, he sat in one of your sessions with Mrs. Walker, where you also talked to him."

I can't move, I can't even breathe, and I'm frozen in my stance. But why? *Relax, Andrea.* Internally, I sigh and then mask my face with normal emotion, trying to surrender to the better and calm version of myself. The one with a subtle smile with warm things to say. Besides, there's nothing I need to feel guilty about.

"So what?"

"So, this morning, you said you'd never heard of him. You don't find that to be strange at all?" She turns to me, and there's no trace of a smile.

"No. Because it's not my business to remember the names of my client's significant other. So, when you asked if I knew him, I told you the truth. I don't. Besides, I'm a professional. Without a proper court order, I don't have to disclose private information to anyone. Including you."

"You're right, Ms. Clarke, but I'm confused. Do you or do you not know James Walker?"

The silence interrupts my thoughts, and I can't think of anything for a moment. The more I try to think, the more my brain becomes a spinning top, always finding more questions than answers. *God, I hate silence.*

"Ms. Clarke?"

I snap out of it, shifting my eyes to the hallway for a moment and then back to Detective Barringer. *Remain calm, Andrea. You've got this.* But the question remains…why don't I just tell her the fucking truth about Madison? Why am I protecting that psychotic bitch?

"I don't know him. He may have come in for a session once or perhaps even twice. I don't recall. I'd have to check my files to remember the notes, and even then, I couldn't share that information with you. Now, are we done? Because I have my own problems to deal with at this moment."

I take another sip of my drink. This time, it's much longer, hoping it will somehow calm me down. I am most in control when I am calm, and wine tends to do an excellent job of that.

The woman scrunches her face at me. The pressure between us will never depart. And because of that, I need more wine.

"I'm an easy person to talk to. So, if there's anything you want to tell me, now is the time to do so." She follows me into the kitchen.

"Not that it's any of your business, but like Mrs. Walker, I just found out that the man I love has been with another woman, and now…"

"…he's missing? Can you tell me again what his name was? Because I could barely hear you over the phone earlier."

"I said he's not missing. He's gone. And his name is Daniel Cooper."

Her eyebrows pull together, and her eyes squint. The look on her face lets me know that she doesn't believe me, giving me chills to the very core. And where the hell is the other detective? It shouldn't take him that long.

"Ms. Clarke—"

"Look, I've told you everything I know about Mr. Walker, and I don't need your help with anything else. So, if that's all, I would appreciate it if you left."

"Is that Pinot Noir that you're drinking?"

"No. Castelvero Barbera."

"Hm…Never heard of it. Maybe I'll try it out sometime. By the way, if you don't mind me asking, how'd you find out about your boyfriend seeing another woman?"

I look away for a moment and slide my right hand through my hair, wanting to yank it out of my scalp.

"She told me herself." I turn back to her.

Her eyes sink beneath a disguise, waiting for me to say more. Instead, I make my way back into the living room.

"She did? Interesting." She follows behind.

"Yes. She did. The woman I told you about…Madison. She told me."

"That's right. Madison." Her voice perks up. "And what's her last name?"

"As I said before, I don't know. But it doesn't matter, anyway."

"Actually, it does. Mrs. Walker mentioned that name as well. I wonder if she's the same woman you're talking about?"

Mrs. Walker told the police about Madison? This must be serious. I knew it was, but certainly not like this. That's it! I've said enough already. Yet, I don't understand why I haven't told her the truth about Madison. Had I just told her what Madison said, this could have been over.

"I don't know her last name or anything else. Now, if you don't mind, I'd like to be alone."

The man finally returns from the bathroom and stands next to Detective Barringer. He doesn't look suspicious, but what does suspicious look like when you've already done what you came to do?

"All right, then. We'll be leaving now," Detective Barringer says.

As they're heading out, she spots the letter on the floor and picks it up.

"You mind if I take this with me?" she asks.

"No. I'd like to hold on to that for memories and motivation."

"Motivation? What kind of motivation?"

"To do whatever the fuck I want to," I take a sip of my wine.

She smirks as she scans the letter carefully. Then, she takes a snapshot of it with her phone. Should I have let her do that? *What's the worst that can happen?*

"Okay. Goodnight, Dr. Clarke," she hands the note over to me.

And just like that, she and the man exit.

I shut the door and wipe the beads of sweat from my brow, and with a trembling left hand, I hurry over to my phone and call Daniel.

However, there's still no answer. This time it goes straight to voicemail. What do I do now?

I stare at the ceiling as if an answer will somehow come falling. Every muscle in my body feels like it's giving up to gravity, and all I want now is to lie in my bed and drift off to a place where reality is overrated. A place where I am in complete control.

Wait a minute…the laminated red card. I completely forgot about it. I wonder what that's all about. Perhaps, I should go tonight and finally take a chance on being spontaneous. If Madison was planning on going there, then I can only imagine it's a place I'd never go to on my own. Besides, who knows where it could lead me or what would happen when I get there. I guess that's the best part about it, right? *Right!* Then again, the card might not even be for tonight. It just says to be there at ten o'clock on the dot with an address at the bottom that only gives the street intersection. No date. No building numbers. Nothing else at all. This is very interesting.

It's almost nine o'clock. Good. That's just enough time to get myself together and put on my favorite dress. My eyes smile, followed by my mouth. Before I can move a muscle, every nerve in my body and brain is electrified, making the moment even more real. God, the anticipation is as captivating as any feeling I've ever felt. Maybe this is the night I've been secretly yearning for, and I can already feel my nerves vibrating from the anticipation. The adrenaline coursing through my veins feels good. This is what it must feel like to be Madison. But I'll have to admit, it's strange. I know I should be hurt about Daniel leaving me the way he did, but I'm not. Instead of crying and sulking over it, I feel free. More than I have ever felt before. Now, I just need to walk out that door. Walk out that damn door tonight, Andrea! *You can do it this one time. One time only.*

9:04 P.M.

Tick. Tick. Tick

While pacing around the house, I catch a glimpse of the wrought iron clock hanging on the living room wall, and it's almost time to head out. Calm down, Andrea. Yes, I need to calm down. I really can't believe that I am actually going through with this. God, I hope this dress isn't too much, but it'll have to do. The dress is the color of a raven's feather, completely exposing my back. I figured if there were ever a time to look like a desperate and horny woman, then this would be the dress to do it in. Now, I just need my burgundy Saint Laurent stilettos, and that should do it.

It's a quarter past nine, and with every shift of the little hand, my heart races a tad faster. *Calm down, Andrea!* Easier said than done. How can I? I've somehow convinced myself to go to some unknown place where anything can happen. Who might I run into? Is this place even safe? What if it's some sort of brothel house or swinger party? Then again, it could be a speakeasy. *Why must I continue to do this to myself? Just stop it, Andrea.*

Tick. Tick. Tick

The heels of my four-inch stilettos tap against the wooden floor as I anxiously pace around the house. Ten o'clock on the dot! Right? I grab the card to check the time again, and this time, I notice something new. A tiny print at the bottom of the card states that phones and watches are not permitted. What? How did I not see this before? What kind of place wouldn't allow phones and watches? *I guess this place.* Now I'm really on edge. My hands are moist, my stomach churns, and I feel like I have to use the restroom for some strange reason. These are all signs of being nervous. But then, as I pace back and forth, I catch a glimpse of myself in the foyer mirror, angling my face in ways that flatter me the most. The woman in the mirror does the same. Intently,

I stare at her and examine the things which she cannot see. Thoughts. Emotions. Feelings. And it feels as if I haven't seen myself in a very long time, but I think I finally understand who she is.

It's time! I take a deep breath, place my black clutch beneath my right arm, and take one last glance at myself before stepping out. Hmm…something is missing. But I don't know exactly what it is. Suddenly, my clutch falls from my arm, and everything spills onto the ground. Including a tube of Chanel Allure rouge lipstick. Red lipstick? How'd this get in here? It's certainly not mine because I hate red lipstick. Madison must have left it in my car, and I mistakenly put it in my purse. Back and forth, the gold tube rolls, and as I watch it do so, I feel compelled to try it on. At least this once. Why not? It looks racy on Madison, so maybe the same could be said for me. *Screw it!* I pick the lipstick up off the floor, turn back to the mirror, and slowly, I cover my bottom lip with the alluring red lipstick and then my top lip. My lips then press together, giving me an even coat. *Looks nice.* Yes, it does. I like it.

9:31 P.M

The phone rings just as I am about to exit the house. It's Shannon calling. I would answer, but I'm not in the mood to talk right now. I'm focused, staring off into emptiness as something dawns on me. For the first time, I didn't look at my phone and expect it to be Daniel calling. I'm shocked! Have I already accepted that he's gone from my life? It seems so. How am I no longer concerned with it? Better yet, why? Then again, after tonight, he probably wouldn't even recognize the woman that I am.

TICK…TICK…TICK…

Here I go. I grab onto the knob, but suddenly, an internal struggle makes it impossible to turn it. Should I do this? *Open the door, Andrea!* My inner voice influences me. Impulsively, my right hand slips forward as I lean my body into the door. I take another deep breath and then step out of the house. *Relax, Andrea. You need this.* Yes, I need to do this.

"Hello, Andrea!" Mrs. Bouyon, wrapped in a colorful muumuu, yells out to me as she walks her dog, Duke, down the sidewalk.

"How are you doing, Mrs. Bouyon?" I make my way to the car.

"You look very nice! Where're you going?"

Quick! Make something up.

"Uh—I'm off to a gathering." That didn't sound too convincing. Then again, why do I need to convince her?

"Sounds like fun. Are you going alone? My son Jeff is still around if you need him. He can fix your porch light if you'd like."

I mean, seriously…how does this sixty-something-year-old lady always seem to be walking her damn dog when things in the neighborhood are happening?

"Yeah. I'd appreciate that. Have Jeff give me a call. Only for the light."

"Will do."

"Goodnight."

I hurry to the car with twenty-five minutes left to get there, and according to my GPS, I'm seventeen minutes away.

I climb in, shut the door, and notice Mrs. Bouyon standing in my rearview mirror, watching me. What does she want? I turn and shoot her a dry smile. She waves back but refuses to walk away. Goodness' sake, she's annoying. I close my eyes and take another breath, but this time, it comes out in quivering gasps. *Drive, Andrea!*

9:44 P.M.

I pull onto 125th street, and according to the directions, the place is located near the Art District in Wynwood. My navigational system tells me that I'm only twelve minutes away. That means I'll arrive at precisely 9:56 P.M., four minutes ahead of schedule.

On this side of town, the skies are overshadowed by a blanket of dark clouds, buildings covered with graffiti, and vagrants wandering the streets searching for food or money. Truly, this is not where I like to spend my time. God, I really hope I don't regret tonight.

Eight minutes later, I come to a stop at the red light on the corner of Seventh Street and 29th Avenue. Directly on my left side is a black and white stripe building with no sign. It's the same building I saw earlier, and the one Madison told me about where she had her encounter with James Walker. There's a throng of people waiting outside the building, yet I don't see Madison anywhere. The crowd seems like a typical group of ordinary people. No one appears strange or creepy, and what makes it even better... I don't recognize any of them. Now, I just need to get out of the car and make this night happen.

You ready? Once again, I take a glance at myself in the rearview mirror. Gently, I swipe my right index finger underneath both eyes. Left eye first, and then the right. Yes, I'm ready.

As the line begins to move up, my heart hammers unkindly, and my brain short-circuits with thoughts. Looking at some of the women, I can at least confirm that I am appropriately dressed. That's good because God knows I would hate to be the only one wearing something extravagant and scant. I hate standing out like a sheep amongst wolves. Wait! What if I see one of my clients in this god-forbidden building? What do I do then? Perhaps, I should turn around now. *Stop it, Andrea!* Yes, I must stop questioning myself and just go! That's precisely what Madison would do.

9:59 P.M

The closer I get to the building, the more I can hear the faint sound of music blaring in the background. I can smell cologne and perfume intertwined with the city's pollution. The group of people has dwindled down to just twelve. One by one, they ring the doorbell, the door opens, and they walk in. This is already turning out to be nothing like I've been to before. When it's my turn to ring the bell, I pause, look around, and then push the button. As nerve-wracking as it may be, I am excited as I desperately await the mystery that lies past these doors.

The door opens, I walk in, and a sexy, petite, fair-skinned woman steps in front of me.

"Hello. Can I help you?" She smiles pleasantly.

The woman, who reminds me of a former client of mine, Taylor Mack, is wearing a tight, skimpy red dress with a gorgeous pair of turquoise geo pumps. Like Ms. Mack, I can tell she is the type of woman others love to hate. It's her confidence combined with her tone that makes that happen. She is an adult, of course, but has the energy of a young child.

Behind her is a long hallway so narrow that I could touch both walls by stretching out my arms, and at the end of the hallway is another door where a dingy light bulb dangles from the ceiling.

"Do you have an invitation?" she asks.

The red card, Andrea. I hand the woman the card. She takes it and, after one quick glimpse, says, "Of course. Okay, come with me." Her smile widens even further. "Come. Come," she excitingly says.

We approach a stainless-steel door with no handle or lock, and she knocks three times against it. The door slides open, and the woman steps aside, allowing me to enter. Oh. My. God! The inside of this place is not what I envisioned it to be. White walls. Statues of panthers, lions, and other wild animals are everywhere. Polished marble flooring with shades of black and gray. Red lighting bounces around the room, giving it an unusual mystique that makes this encounter a tad comforting in the strangest way. This looks like a forbidden place not written in *Alice in Wonderland*.

After two steps inside the immaculate home, the woman shuts the door and bolts the locks. What the hell have I just stepped into?

"Champagne?" Another woman appears out of nowhere.

This woman is tall and very thin, her hair is brown and messy, and she has bulging eyes bound by an excessive amount of eyeliner.

"Thank you," I reply, taking the glass off the tray.

"Drink up. Follow me," the woman politely demands.

She's so unlike the bubbly woman because she lacks personality. Nevertheless, I follow her down a long, wide corridor with white doors on each side. I wonder what's happening beyond those doors.

"I'm so glad I got to meet you," she says.

Me? Why would she say that as if she's heard of me? We dip into a large room that looks like an old hangar full of writhing bodies. It is nothing like I've seen before.

In the corner of the room, I spot a woman pressed against the wall as a man passionately kisses her exposed breast. Her panties hang on her right ankle. They're either blind to the fact that I can see them, or they just don't give a damn. Something tells me I should stop following my guide, turn around, and head out, but I don't. I continue to trail behind this woman who I've never met before.

"What is this place?" I ask.

She laughs for a second, stops, and then turns to me.

"Whatever you want it to be. Heaven to some…and Hell for others. A place where reality is overrated."

"What does that mean?"

"Look, all I know is that people love it here. Some never want to leave "The house." But I'm sure you already knew that." She smiles.

"The house?"

She turns and faces me, walking backwardly. The music gets louder, and the energy around me thickens. I can feel something happening to me. What is in this champagne?

"Yes! The house! A place that is like no other. You can do a little bit of this…or a whole lot of that." She points to a man dancing passionately on a woman, squeezing her ass while kissing her neck. My jaw drops slightly as I watch enviously, waiting to see what he does next. They aren't the only ones either. It's everyone. They're dancing, drinking, and standing in each other's faces as if they're about to make out at any moment. There isn't a single soul just standing around, looking stuck up, as I would typically see anywhere else in the clubs of Miami.

"Beautiful, isn't it?" the woman says to me. 'Come."

"Where are you taking me?" I ask.

"You'll see."

I would simply die if I were to run into any of my friends or my clients. I scan the room, hoping to see Madison, but she's still nowhere around. Everything is moving fast, and the place is massive, so there's no telling where she could be. Assuming she's even here.

The music quiets down as I follow the woman down a staircase. My hands shake slightly, and for some strange reason, a large knot appears in my throat when I try to swallow. Am I nervous? No, that's not nervousness. It's a feeling of being intrigued. Or thrilled.

"By the way, just let me know if you need anything else. I'll be upfront the whole night," she tells me.

"Okay. Thanks."

"Anytime. Relax and enjoy yourself." Once we arrive at the other door, she opens it and steps aside. Then she turns to me. "You deserve this." She smiles." Oh! And thank you."

Thank you? What was that all about?

Walking into this section of the building is slightly intimidating because not only are the people very attractive and well-dressed, but they're all so stimulated by one another. I feel like the new kid at recess, as it seems many of the people here already know each other.

"Hi, we saw you outside and wanted to introduce ourselves. This is my wife, Tina." The man, who seems like your average Wall Street douchebag, politely says to me.

"You're so beautiful," the woman declares. "This is our first time here. What about you?"

Unsure of what to say, I simply nod my head.

"So, what's your rule?" he says.

"My rule? What do you mean?"

"Well, as much as this place is about ecstasy, everyone also respects boundaries. So, what's something that you want people to know?"

I can see how Madison would struggle to stay away from a place like this. Even temptation hugs my body like a brand-new leather jacket, and it's starting to pull me in.

"I haven't really thought about it."

"Can I touch you?" The woman asks.

What do I say now? Madison would probably tell me to just go with the flow at this point. Hell, I can even hear her voice whispering in my head.

"Um, I guess. Sure."

She steps in close, sliding her hands up and down my arm while staring at me with this intense look of lust. She then brings her hands over my shoulder and begins caressing me. It does feel good, but I'm not so certain this isn't awkward.

"You want to join us?" she asks.

I have never been around so many unregenerate sex-craving people in one room—simply doing whatever they feel like doing in the most respectful manner at that. They're kissing, touching, holding, and some of them even do it all at once. Yet, it's all classy and tasteful.

"Not right now. I'm still trying to get a feel for the place."

"We understand." She steps back. "Maybe later?"

I nod in agreement. The woman then leans in, kisses me on the right side of my face, and then makes her way to another couple.

Oh, shit!

Off to the side, I spot a woman straddling a man with a dress so short that she might as well take it off. My goodness! Is it not too early for that? I guess not. I can't tell if they're having sex, but the fact that everyone casually stands around watching them as if they were simply in an office meeting makes it even more strange. Hell, I can't blame them. Even I can't take my eyes off them.

Next to the two, is a woman on a wrap-around sofa, sitting on a man's lap—engaged in what looks like a deep conversation. Fortunately, she has on panties. That much I can see. However, the way he stares at her, biting his lips as they dive deep into the conversation, is what turns me on. It's like he's giving her all his attention, yet he wants to also devour her. I don't know what they're talking about, but damn, do I wish I could hear them. Indeed, this place is beginning to make my body warm up with tingles. A sense of euphoria takes away the negative feelings I may have had before coming here. All my worries, concerns, or anything that doesn't bring pleasure is starting to fade away.

Deep inhale...

Soft exhale.

Further in the back, a man with dark skin dances between two women. They dance as close as three people can without having sex. One of the women is whispering in the man's ear while the other softly kisses him over his back. They are so tightly pressed against one another that they have no choice but to move to each other's rhythm. I can feel something beginning to happen between my legs as I watch them, entangled with the tempo of the music. Clearly, this is a sight to see.

All of a sudden, I meet the gaze of a familiar face standing off by a table. We lock eyes for a moment, just enough to make me feel safe. He waves, and I smile faintly. Wait. Is he waving at me? I look over my shoulder just to ensure there's no one there. So, he must be waving at me.

"Looks like someone is happy to see you," a woman passing by says to me.

It's the guy I met the other night at the bar. The one Shannon was infatuated with. However, I don't remember his name. Come on, Andrea. *Think! What's his name...*

CHAPTER 17

11:10 P.M.

SAY HIS NAME, SAY HIS NAME…Isaac?! No, that's not it. Why can't I remember his name? Is it Alex? No. Manny? Yes, that's it. Manny. What is he doing here? I suppose the same could be said about me. Oh, God, now he's coming this way. I must remain calm. However, the closer he gets, the more my attempt to seem unruffled fails. It's my darn hands. I just don't know what to do with them. Do I place them on my sides? Do I just cross my arms? Fold my hands together? What?! Immediately, my subconscious slaps me back to reality. Relax! Just in time.

"Hey, beautiful. Nice to see you again. I'm glad you made it." He pulls me in for a hug.

"Yeah—good evening to you, too." I slightly pull from him.

He witnesses my shock at his embrace register on my face before I can hide it, and then he chuckles.

"What's so funny?" I ask.

"I could be wrong, but you seem…nervous—especially for someone in this venue."

"What's that supposed to mean?"

"Look around you. This isn't the place to be bashful now, is it?"

He's right. One of the women dancing heavily on the man now has her breast fully exposed to everyone. The couple that approached me is now making out with a woman as a man, who appears to be her partner, just watches. As much as I want to explore myself, I don't know if I can have it like this. In front of strangers? Where anything can possibly go wrong? It's already bad enough that I'm contemplating having sex with a stranger.

"You know what… you're right. Maybe I don't belong here," I tell him.

Just as I turn to exit, Manny grabs hold of my right hand.

"Wait. Don't go. You can't leave."

I turn back to him, and I feel myself loosening up for some reason. "Why not?" I ask.

"Well, for starters, the doors don't open until two."

What? The gears in my brain can't turn fast enough to process what he's just told me. "What do you mean the doors don't open until two?"

"I can't tell if you're joking or not." He looks at me strangely.

The words are on the tip of my tongue, but they won't come out. Therefore, I stare into his brown eyes as my voice falls silent, and then…

"I'm serious." My tone is more calm than worried.

"That's just one of the rules of the house."

So, I'm stuck in a house with people whom I have never met in my life for the next four hours? What have I gotten myself into?

"Besides, why get all dressed up and drive over here for nothing? I say you forget about everything else and enjoy the moment." he continues.

Maybe he's right. I did come here for a reason, and I've never been anywhere like this. So, why not? Who knows where the night will take me? However, two o'clock? That's another three hours and forty-eight minutes. You can handle that, right? I hope so. God, I can only imagine what Shannon would say if she saw me right now.

"So, tell me… what's the deal with the doors not opening at two or the fact that there's no clock in here?" I ask.

"Is that a real question?"

"Of course, it is."

He grins, looks away, and then turns back to me with a faint, boyish look.

"Okay. Well, we don't associate ourselves with the rest of the world for these next few hours. The concept of time, money, and whatever else are irrelevant here. We do what we want, how we want, and enjoy it."

I'm in complete awe as Manny continues to explain the dynamics of this house. It's unbelievable. The way he eloquently breaks down every rule of the house brings chills along my spine. Manny explains rule number one—while inside the house, there's no talk about what's happening outside the world. Number two—clothes are optional. Number three—the mentioning of names is not required. "In fact, we encourage aliases," Manny tells me. Number four—there's no contact with those in the house while outside in the world. He continues to speak as I listen intently. Rule after rule. By the time he's done with the details, I'm dumbstruck. It's no wonder these people seem so elated. They can do whatever it is they truly want to do.

"Wow. That's…interesting."

"But very worth it." He smiles.

What kind of person would come up with such a place as this? A place that allows people to feel isolated from the rest of the world. Do whatever they want while being whoever they want to be. A place with perfect rules to help maintain a sense of predictability and consistency. Indeed, this is no ordinary thinking to come up with such a place.

"You say it as if you knew I would be here. Like you were waiting for me?"

"Me? No." He smirks.

Then, shoot me an awkward wink. "Come on. Let's get a drink."

Manny takes my left hand and leads me to the translucent glass bar, holding onto me as if we came together. How is he so openly expressive with someone he barely knows? What is it about humans that often allows us to be more intimate with strangers than we are with the ones we love? The better question is what allows our mind to effortlessly submit ourselves to the immortality dwelling within. Stop it, Andrea. You're questioning everything again. Just relax. Yes, that is what I must do. Once we approach the bar, the bartender walks up from behind wearing black slacks, no shirt, and a white bowtie.

"So, who runs this place?" I ask, hoping I'm not breaking any of the rules.

Manny turns to the bartender without acknowledging my question. "Can I have two of the specials? Thanks."

He turns back to me. "No one knows. Some say it's a group of people. And some say it's a woman. A woman who no one has ever met," Manny says.

"Interesting."

"Like I said, we don't associate ourselves with the rest of the world."

"Even if that were the case, surely someone must be liable for what happens here, right? What if there's an emergency like a fire or someone gets hurt? What then?"

"That's all taken care of and accounted for. We got you." He winks.

He smiles and then turns to the bartender. Wait a minute. The bartender. That's the same guy from the Cuban café. Zach. I remember that tattoo on his arm.

"Here you go," he says as he puts the drinks on the counter.

"Thank you," Manny says. "By the way, Aiden, this is our friend."

Wait, did he just break a rule? I thought names were not allowed. And his name is Aiden? At the café, he said his name was Zach.

"Hello." He leans in and extends his right hand to me. I place my hand in his, and we shake as I stare at him, but it doesn't seem like he remembers me. He's much different than he was before. At the café, he was friendlier and very animated, but here, he seems much more serious.

"What's in the drink?" I ask.

Aiden turns to Manny, and Manny nods. What was that about? Did I just break a rule?

"I can't tell you. But just know it's special. Trust me, you'll like it."

I look into his eyes, hoping he'll remember me from the café, but he doesn't.

"Okay. I'll let you know what I think."

"Please do," Aiden says.

Manny places his arm around my waist, pulling me in tighter. Is he jealous? I laugh bashfully, and then slightly pull myself from his hold.

"Do you mind taking a seat with me?"

"Yeah. We can do that."

He holds my left hand again and walks me to a white sofa near a black door. Manny sits me down and then takes a seat beside me. His eyes remain on me as his elbows rest on his lap, tucked beneath his chin.

"What is it? Why are you looking at me like that?" I blush.

"Just glad that you're here. That's all." He moves in closer.

I'm stuck in my seat from both being nervous and excited. And one thing is for sure, I'm falling deeper into the moment.

"So am I. This place… it's just so different from what I'm used to. Everyone here is so…open, expressive, free of anything that may happen in their lives." My eyes roam the room.

"Yeah. This place gives insight to someone looking for more to life. It boosts self-esteem, untangles emotional dilemmas, and provides some sort of support."

"So pretty much, this is therapy." I chuckle.

"Yeah. You can say that."

Out of nowhere, Manny grabs ahold of my chin with his left hand, turns my head to him, and intently stares into my eyes.

"May I kiss you?"

I faintly nod, but it feels like I hardly have a moment to react before he leans forward and places his lips on mine. Like two puzzle pieces coming together. His lips—rich, smooth, and moist—brush against mine first. Not innocently, like a tease, but with passion and demand. Had he done this two minutes ago, I would have pulled away, but right now, I can't. My senses have been seduced, and I can no longer think straight. I open my mouth and taste his warm breath, and I am weak to the soft touch of his lips against mine. I can't believe this is happening. My lips are touching another man's lip. Manny is only one of the handful of men I can remember kissing. One is Daniel, of course, and then there's Eric, Gerard, Allan, Pierre, who I kissed on a bet when I was fifteen, and Curtis, my college neighbor. There's also Terry McAllister, my eighth-grade dance partner. However, I'm not sure if I can consider that, seeing as Terry meant to kiss me on the cheek.

"See. You can trust me," he whispers against my lips. I smile, my heart fluttering at his words traveling through my mouth and into my mind.

Then, Manny grabs the back of my neck, holds on to it firmly and continues kissing me. This time, his tongue explores my mouth for a few seconds, where our hearts pound and our breathing accelerate. As incredible as this kiss feels, it just doesn't feel real. Fuck! What is wrong with me? Why can't I just do this without thinking about anything else? Don't think, Andrea. Just do! Yes, just let go and let loose.

The moment intensifies beyond what I am familiar with as my heart shoots to the back of my throat. Slowly, I pull away from him. He's confused by my reaction. I can tell by the raising of his eyebrow.

"Is everything okay?" Manny questions.

"Yes. Everything is fine."

He chuckles.

"I have a question for you," Manny says.

"What is it?" I turn to him.

"What brought you here?"

"It's a long story, but you can just say I was following my instincts."

He closes his eyes, takes a deep breath, and shakes his head as if he's either confused or frustrated with my response. "I've never met anyone like you. It's interesting on the one hand and frustrating on the other."

"Frustrating?"

"Yes. I've never seen anyone so comfortable yet…so nervous at the same time. Most women come here dying to explore the possibilities before they even walk through that door. But with you… it's different."

"Is that so? Well, I can't explain why that is. Sometimes, I feel like I can just go with the flow, and then in the next moment...I don't."

"You're afraid of how others will see you or feel about you. Or perhaps, you're nervous about what being your true self will do to you."

"Maybe."

"What is there to be afraid of other than not being who you want to be?"

"Well, for starters, there's being raped, degraded, and treated as property. Or even worse, becoming addicted to a place like this. There's absolutely no way of knowing what can happen here. Certainly not with the rules you've listed."

"This isn't the place for that. Everyone here knows how to play within the lines. Look around you."

I take a sip of my drink and look at everyone around the room. They all seem to be in the moment with no regrets. Overjoyed with pleasure, all while looking innocent in their own way. Some of them laugh while they dance spontaneously. Others are making out and touching each other provocatively. Whatever it is that they're doing, it makes them feel good. There's even a man against the wall with a woman's right leg hung over his left shoulder. I can't stop watching them, nearly drooling at the thought of that being me. What have I gotten myself into? Nothing you can't handle. I hope so.

"How should I trust that?" I turn to him.

"Don't trust it. Just trust me."

My mind is blank as I stare at him. There's something about Manny that makes me want to meet the pure side of myself. The side of me that needs to feel pleasured and whole. Our energy vibrates in a way that makes it easy to trust him. I'm not in love or anything, but I am smitten. Besides, what am I to be afraid of? Myself? My sexuality?

I search my mind for a response, but to my surprise, my heart answers for me instead.

"You said endless possibilities? What does that mean?"

"Whatever you think of… I'll make it happen."

He smiles, and I smile back. His eyes never move off me.

"So, anything I can think of? Like even being tied up and made love to in a way you've never made love to anyone else?" I seductively smile.

Where did that come from?

"Like I said…Anything!"

"All right. Well then, how about we finish our drinks?"

"Yeah. I'd like that," he replies.

I take another sip of my drink, and immediately my right leg begins to quiver as Manny's eyes trace my body. My heart rate increases, so I take another sip of my drink. Followed by another.

He stands up. "Here, let me help you relax?"

Manny grabs ahold of my ankles, swings me around, and places my legs onto his lap. I chug down the rest of my drink as his fingers glide over my legs softly and sensually.

"Is this okay for you?" he asks.

I nod my head as the hair on my arm stands to attention from his tinder touch.

"Yes."

Then, he slowly makes his way to my thighs, pushing my dress further up, stopping just before he can see what I have on underneath. I take a deep breath and wait to see what he will do next.

"How's that?" he asks.

"It's good." I blush.

From the corner of my right eye, I notice the bartender staring at us from across the room. Why is he looking at us like that? No. Wait. It's me that he's looking at.

"How about this?"

Suddenly, I feel Manny's hand—strong yet gentle—inches from my panties. I close my eyes for a moment and take a deep breath…

Inhale…

Exhale.

A pulse starts between my legs as his thumbs work from the center of my thighs and then out, searching for my spot.

My body unwinds as he touches me, and the more he whispers into my ear, the wetter I become. Long deep breaths. Heart rate rises. Blinking uncontrollably. Dry mouth. For goodness' sake, I can't even sit still. I'm sure by now he notices my eagerness. Curse my damn oversensitive skin. I can't seem to stop jerking from any of his touches, and it's quite embarrassing. I need another drink.

Manny's hand grazes the sensitive place between my thighs. My eyes close as I softly moan. This is happening. Someone other than Daniel is touching me. The pleasurable contraction deepens in my pelvis, causing me to tremble. Great! Now he can definitely tell that I'm at his mercy.

"Like I said…you can trust me." He smiles.

That's easy for him to say. He isn't the one being overwhelmed by all sorts of feelings and thoughts. Or sitting here with wet panties on.

Manny leans in, and once again, he places his lips, wet and warm, against mine. I have no urge to stop him this time because I want it. I need this. He breathes into my mouth, and I give in. My heart bounces in my chest as chills run over my arms, feeling like a plume gliding on my neck. As we kiss, his left hand explores my back, and when he gets to the zipper, he slowly pulls it down. Oh, My God! Is he actually doing this right here? Right now?

"There you go. Relax," he whispers.

Never have I experienced a man's touch like this—not even with Daniel. It's as if Manny wants me more than any man has ever wanted me. The feeling is invigorating, different, and simply intriguing. I moan into his mouth as his hands travel down my spine, and then between my legs. I can't believe he's doing this. More importantly, how does he know the spots on my body that will trigger these reactions?

"You like this feeling?" Manny asks.

"Yes! I do," I whisper back.

A tingling sensation flows through my body just before his finger grabs onto my panties. I am so embarrassed by the amount of moisture built up between my legs that I want to stop him. I can feel it, and I'm not sure I can control the moment from going further than it already has.

"Here you are." Aiden hands us the drinks.

Manny grabs them, and Aiden walks away. But not before he winks at me. That was weird. Could it be that he now remembers me?

"Here you go." Manny taps his drink against mine.

"What are we toasting to?"

"To you."

I take a sip of the drink while looking into his eyes. This drink is a bit stronger than before and has a sour tang with an aftertaste, leaving the alcohol lingering on my tongue. Based on Manny's reaction, he must think the same thing.

"I'm not sure what this is, but I'm not a fan of it," he says.

"Neither am I." I chuckle.

"Would you like something else?" Manny asks.

Perhaps I shouldn't. I feel fine, but my head is beginning to spiral a tad. I can see smoke forming artistic curls within the illuminated lights.

"No thanks. I'm fine."

Then, Manny puts his drink down on the ground and stands up.

"Come with me." Manny grabs my left hand.

Part of me is curious about where he's taking me, but the part that brought me here just follows him instead, not knowing what to expect…

CHAPTER 18

ACROSS THE ROOM, not too far from the bar, is a black door with a gold knob. That's where Manny leads me. This is it. The moment I have been yearning for is about to take place beyond that door.

We enter a long and narrow hallway with closed doors on each side. The walls are gold with black trimming, and all the doors are different colors. There's a red door, a blue one, green, yellow, pink, and even a silver one. Each has a gold doorknob with a missing keyhole. As we walk down the corridor, I can smell the scent of testosterone and estrogen seeping through the small crevices and into the hallway. It's like the scent of the wind just before a storm. What in the world is this place?

Suddenly, while passing by a purple door on my left, I notice it's slightly open. The sound of moaning and skin slapping against each other sneaks out. I stop and let go of Manny's hand.

"What are you doing?" he nervously asks.

I walk up, look through the hinged gap, and spot a man naked behind a woman bent over on all fours. The woman's frail body lacks imagination—flat chest, pale skin, and no curves. However, that's not what takes me by surprise. The plastic bag over her head as he fucks her does that. I can't tell if she's begging for air or having an orgasm, but she reaches back and grabs onto his waist, forcing him to go harder. He pulls on the bag a little tighter, yet she begs him to keep going. I can barely see their faces; thus, I push the door open a little further.

"No. You shouldn't do that. Come on," Manny whispers.

"She has a plastic bag over her head. I've never seen anything like that. Is it some sort of fetish?"

"It's called erotic asphyxiation. Restriction of oxygen will cause a more intense orgasm.

"Really?"

"Yes. The sudden loss of oxygen to the brain causes the body to weaken, making the feeling more pleasurable and the hidden spots more sensitive."

"And how do you know this?"

"Like I said, anything you want can happen here. Now come." He grabs my hand demandingly.

"Wait. Did you hear that?" I ask.

I hear the sound of people chatting, chuckling, or mumbling inside the room. Yet, I don't see anyone. Slowly, I push open the door a little more and spot five women and four men standing there, watching the two individuals fuck each other to the brink of death. A rush of warmth flows from my stomach to between my legs like waves against the shores. Oh, my goodness. This is so mesmerizing. I have never seen anything like it.

"Are you just going to stare at them all night?" He finally pulls me away from the couple in the room.

At last, we stop at a turquoise-colored door—the fifth door on the left. 215 is written on the door. So that's what he was referring to when he wrote it on the napkin. Manny opens it, and immediately, I am taken by surprise. It's a bedroom with no windows. The slightly cold room smells like pinewood with a hint of vanilla incense. Around us, I can hear the faint sounds of moans through soft music.

"Come," he steps aside.

Internally, I can't stop smiling as I walk into the dimly lit room. Manny shuts the door just as I cross the threshold. A queen-size bed sits in the middle of the room on top of a white shag rug. There's also a wooden bedside table with a swanky lamp that's obviously there for decoration. Black padded panels cover the wall with gold buttons. Oh my God! There's a large mirror plastered on the ceiling above the bed. The mirror has that tarnishing of age around the gold frame with splotches on the surface. Still, it's enough to reflect the entire room. Not only is there a mirror plastered on the ceiling, but there's also one on each side of the room. Oddly enough, this all looks familiar. This must be the room Madison detailed in one of her stories.

"Here we are," he takes me by the hand and casually pulls me over to the bed.

Manny then kisses me on my forehead, across my shoulder, and then along my neck. Soft and slow. Then, he looks into my eyes and gradually removes my dress. There's no stopping it now, and even if I wanted to, nothing in my mind or body could help me to do so. Besides, the caressing tingle covering my skin tells me this is...right.

"You okay?"

"Yes."

"Good."

It's really about to happen. I step out of my dress and stand with only my panties and heels on—nothing else. On most occasions, I would feel the need to shy away from my nudity, but in this moment, I don't. A look into Manny's eyes gives me all the motivation I need, and internally, I'm panting as I yearn for him to touch me.

Then, he pushes me onto the bed and stares into my eyes with a burning look. The bed is irresistibly soft, like flowing in clouds. I sink into the mattress and squirm my body against the white silk duvet. My black hair spreads around me as I stare at the woman in the ceiling mirror— smiling and biting my lip. At this point, he can do anything he wants with me. Finally, I can follow what feels good rather than do what I think I should do.

"Turn around and relax."

Liquid droplets fall onto my skin, and when I open my eyes, I see he's standing shirtless, pouring oil onto my body. He squeezes some of the oil into the palms of his hands and rubs it over my shoulders.

Around my neck.

Over my breasts.

Against my stomach and sides.

A little further, down to my thighs.

He massages my body gently and sensually, touching areas long forgotten. It's so soothing and comforting. Certainly not what I had in mind when I decided to follow the red card tonight but screw it. I'm here now.

"How does this feel?" he asks.

"Amazing."

His index fingers grab onto my black panties, slowly pulling them down to my knees. I don't stop him, and it feels good not to do so. This is it! I'm finally free of my inhibitions. Now, I just want to feel pleasure.

"What now?" I teasingly ask.

Suddenly, the door opens, and I quickly sit up. I can't see the face of the person standing in the doorway, but through the velvet of darkness is a silhouette of a man. A tall man with narrow hips and broad shoulders.

"Would you like some Champagne?" He solicits. It's Aiden. I can tell by his voice.

"No. We're fine," Manny replies. "Sorry about that." Manny turns to me.

Just as Aiden is about to exit the room, the synapses in my brain spark a fire in my body, fully awakening the sexual spirit resting deep within. The tingling feeling I felt the past few days rushes up to my stomach and lingers there for a moment. "Wait!"

Aiden stops in his tracks and turns back to us. He heard me. I wasn't sure he did.

"Excuse me." Alton says.

"You mind if he stays?" I turn to Manny, holding onto his forearm.

Did I just say that? Manny looks at me, over to Aiden, and then back to me with his mouth slightly open. It's as if I can see his brain stuttering for a moment, trying to process the words that just came out of my mouth. I don't blame him because I am just as confused.

"You want me to stay?" Aiden asks.

"You said whatever I want, right?" I turn to Manny.

He's at a loss for words, but I don't feel guilty for some strange reason. Yes, Manny is quite the man, and his touch on my body feels incredible, but there's something about Aiden that I'd love to explore as well.

"Right. Anything you want."

"Stay!" I command Aiden.

For nearly five seconds, the two remain still, looking at me, then over to each other, and then back at me. Aiden closes the door and walks over to the other side of the bed—Just above my head while Manny remains at my legs.

"What would you like for me to do?" Aiden inquires.

"I'd rather feel than tell."

Aiden's fingers glide through my hair, tracing along my scalp in slow and intense circles. Each touch sends an electric thrill coursing through me, as if the delicate tips of his fingers ignite a fiery response. The feeling even lingers in my nipples with a heightened sensitivity. In the same moment, Manny slips off my heels, one by one. His hands move deliberately with grace before he gracefully slides my panties off, allowing a thrilling vulnerability to consume me. I stand there, utterly exposed and bare, every inch of my skin laid bare for their hungry eyes. Surprisingly, the rawness of my nudity doesn't faze me; instead, it stirs a deep desire within me, a longing for uninhibited pleasure.

Manny and Aiden massage my body using different motions and pressure. Aiden works his way from my hair to my shoulders and down to my breasts— slow and gentle. Manny's hands glide over my stomach, between my legs, across my thighs, and down to my feet— diligently and briskly. The combination of the two of them touching me weakens my body. I am at the mercy of two men in a way I have never been before. Fuck! This is such an unbelievable feeling. Once again, I look up and see myself in the mirror, and the woman smiling back is just as content as I am.

Aiden then removes his slacks and boxer and climbs onto the bed with my left shoulder resting between his legs. Now, he's focused on my breasts only, massaging them in a seamless circle. The tip of his erection keeps brushing against my left shoulder. I'm not sure if he's doing it on purpose, but it's turning me on even more than I already am. I don't think Manny notices as he remains focused on my thighs. It touches my shoulder again, but I move closer to Aiden this time, hoping to feel all of it.

Manny then steps back and removes his clothing. Whew! Now we're all naked, and I can't stop beaming inside with excitement, unsure of how this is even happening.

It doesn't take long before Manny falls to his knees, spreads my legs apart, and begins to lick and suck on the spot that's been yearning for his attention. I grab a fistful of the silk duvet and hold on tight as Manny teases me with his fingers, sliding them up and down for nearly a minute. Then he places them inside of me in a steady, upbeat motion. All while sucking on my clit. The muscles in my stomach are starting to contract, and I can't tell if I am getting wetter, or if it is just his tongue. All the other times I had this done, it felt like just something to do. Nothing like this. However, with Manny, it's different. It's as if I can feel myself pulsating against his lips as he touches all the right spots. I can even hear him moaning between my legs, enjoying it just as much as I am. And it's driving me wild. Perhaps it's the drink, but a sense of euphoria comes over me like a gust of wind.

Aiden then grabs ahold of my hands and clasps onto them like shackles. The next thing I know, he has his lips on mine, allowing me to moan into his mouth. The more I moan from Manny licking on my clit, the more Aiden kisses me— slow and soft. Comforting in ways no man could ever offer.

Then, Aiden makes an acrobatic move, where he mounts on top of me, straddling my stomach. He isn't a small man, but I can barely feel his weight on top of me. My breathing is just fine, and there isn't any discomfort. His hands grip my oiled breast just before he slides his erection between them, looking into my eyes as he does so. I can feel the strength and warmth of his hard dick against my breast as he massages them over it in a slow circular motion. All while sliding it back and forth. Our naked bodies are all entwined, leaving me in a complete trance.

I look up and watch the woman in the mirror glide her hand over Aiden's chest and chiseled abdominals. It's as if I am watching someone else being pleased. Fuck!

Manny's tongue rapidly flickers against my clit as he squeezes on my thighs. I grip Aiden's leg as Manny keeps going. I am completely soaked, and my heart speeds to a pace I can't control, all while Aiden's erection inches toward my mouth, lightly touching my chin each time he slides between my breasts. A constant rush sends shivers throughout my body, and it continues to knock at the door of my orgasm.

All of a sudden, my legs go numb. I take a deep inhale as my body begins to shake uncontrollably. Madison said this happened to her the night she was with the distinguished gentleman, and here I am.

Deep inhale...

Then comes a slow vibrating wave that starts in my toes, curves into my back, and flows to my hardened nipples. It's never been this intense, and I can't tell if it's because of Manny or Aiden.

Soft exhale.

"I want you to tie me up."

Between my legs, I spot Manny looking up at me with his mouth hanging open and eyes wide. His face turns rigid as a board. After a few seconds, he grins with excitement radiating from his eyes like a bright light bulb. My body is covered with oil and beads of sweat when Manny stands up and steps away.

"Aiden. Get off her." Manny demands.

Aiden does just as Manny says, hopping off me in a swift motion.

"You said anything, right?" I murmur.

"Yes! Anything." Manny chuckles. "Aiden, grab her arms."

The two of them rotate my body on the bed, placing my head near the headboard. Manny grabs my ankles and ties them to the bedposts with a leather belt, and as he does that, Aiden binds my wrists together above my head. I'm not even sure where the straps come from.

However, there is an explosion of impish glee in my brain as I await what's about to happen next, and it is beyond my imagination.

Manny climbs onto the bed, kissing his way up my legs as he does so. I take a deep breath, and then for a moment, there's a silence before he slides his dick inside of me— slowly filling my body at a perfect angle. Fuck! I feel every inch of him— including at the bottom of my stomach. His weight between my legs, on top of me, is comforting. The look on his face is covered with eagerness, scrunching his lips as he narrows his eyes with intent. There's a pleasure that continues to build in the very deepest part of my pussy. The muscles tighten as all of his strength and emotions pierce that spot. My God, I even feel him getting warmer and harder. As Manny continues to thrust his erection in and out of my pussy, Aiden sensually kisses all over me.

Around my breasts.

Up to my collarbone.

Down to my waist.

Across to my navel.

Onto my lips.

"Is this what you wanted?" Manny whispers.

"Yes. Don't stop!" I moan into Aiden's mouth.

Five minutes! That's all it takes before I'm filled with a tremendous sense of pleasure that tingles and pulsates between my legs. It begins with a slow vibrating wave in my toes, arching into my back and flowing out of my mouth into a quivering moan.

Manny then takes his thumb and circles it over my clit as he fucks me, applying pressure to a spot that is already sensitive. No one has ever done that. As bad as I want to feel Aiden, Manny is more than enough. I can't take it! I want more. I break free of the straps on my wrist, grip his waist with my left hand, and pull him in deeper. Then, my right hand impulsively grabs onto Aiden. His erection, smooth and thick, rests in my palm perfectly. I am reminded of the time Madison put her mouth on a man and went as far down as she could, curling her tongue along the base of his shaft. So, without a second thought, I pull Aiden in and kiss the tip before putting it in my mouth. My lips, draped with the Chanel rouge lipstick, complement the complexion of his dick perfectly as I slowly go as far down as I can. He squirms just a tad and then jumps back, but I quickly pull him back for more. The more Manny fucks me, the more I want to taste Aiden. My breathing is gone to an unsteady rhythm that I can't seem to control. The room that was once frigid is now warm. This is what I needed.

Aiden looks down at me as I lick along the length of his dick while staring into his eyes. This is unlike me. I've always felt physically inferior to the men I was with, but here, I have the power and control to guide what pleasure or pain I feel.

"Keep going!" I moan as Manny touches a susceptible spot inside of me with his warmth.

Once again, I gaze into the eyes of the woman in the mirror plastered on the ceiling. Her eyes, inkling with a stillness of soft glimmer, betrays the idea that I could have this type of pleasure for just one night. One night only? No. Instead, staring into her eyes, I find my place of comfort, and it's nothing like what I saw in her eyes before tonight. That woman was always consumed with pointless thoughts. Not enough confidence. Worried about others' opinions of her. Focused on blatant imperfections. But now, the woman in the mirror above is poised ahead of her wants and needs. Unafraid and unapologetically free. A woman in charge of her sexuality. Perhaps, Madison was right. Maybe she and I have something in common that goes beyond what I could have imagined.

Tick…Tick…TOCK!

DECEMBER
FRIDAY
11

How long have I been asleep? There's no clock anywhere, so it's impossible to tell. If I had to guess, I'd say it's a quarter to one. No later than two. *Oh, shit!* I'm still in "The House?" Did I have sex with two men? *Wow, Andrea.* If it weren't for this lingering feeling between my legs, I would have thought it was a dream. Besides, the images popping in and out of my mind are too vivid to be my imagination. *What a night!*

I should get going now, but Manny's arm rests on my thighs, and that also helps bring me back to reality. The room is filled with an absolute stillness in the air that sinks into my veins like poison. No sound of music. No voices. No moans. Just a silence that allows the memory of tonight to sear into my brain forever. This kind of silence usually troubles me, especially in a moment like this, but oddly enough, it works in my favor this time. I can fully accept the action of the woman I was at that moment and think through what I will do next. *Oh, shit!* Madison. I forgot about her. I must get going.

Carefully, I scoot Manny off me. Luckily, he doesn't wake up. Not even a little bit. Good! The last thing I want right now is to have a conversation about what just happened or what we do from here on. I sit up and take a moment to process everything. Nothing seems out of place, and I feel perfectly fine. *Wait a minute.* Where's Aiden? His pants are still hung on the headboard, and his shoes are beside the bed. Surely, he didn't walk out of here naked. Did he? *Andrea, that doesn't matter because you need to get going.* Yes, I must get going.

I climb out of bed and quickly collect my stuff. Near the door, I find my dress. On the other side of the room is one of my shoes, and the other is next to the wall, near the bedside table. But I can't seem to find my panties. *Screw it!*

Quickly, I get dressed and then exit the room. Even the hallway has an unnatural silence. The smell of pheromones that once lingered in the air is no longer there. Instead, it's replaced with an unfamiliar scent. Almost smells like eucalyptus. Which is strange.

As I make my way down the narrow hallway and into the main room, I spot a few people lying around. There's a couple on the sofa, a few on the floor, and three at the bar. One thing is for sure, they're nothing like the energetic folks I saw when I came in. Not only that, but there also aren't many of them either. I can only assume it's after two. *Are you kidding me?*

When I get to the main door, all the bolts are unlocked, and it's slightly open. The woman that stood here when I entered is nowhere to be found, and just as I am about to exit…

"Hey. I didn't know you were still here," he says.

It's Aiden, standing there in his underwear and a bowtie while holding a bag of trash. My legs refuse to move, too shocked or embarrassed to look at him. He has a boyish smile going on that makes it even more awkward.

"Uh, yeah. Don't know how I fell asleep for so long."

'I don't blame you. That was intense."

TICK…TICK…TICK…

"Yeah. It was. Well, I need to get going."

"You actually shocked me."

"Yeah, but can we not talk about it? I enjoyed it all, but it's not something I want to discuss."

That has to be a broken rule. Talking about what happens inside "The House" even while inside of "The House." If it isn't, then someone needs to make one.

"For sure. I understand," Aiden says.

I turn to exit.

"See you next time?"

Next time? Why would he assume that I would return to this place?

"We'll see about that."

I scurry on out, and the moment I exit "The House," I feel like myself again, taking in a deep inhale of Miami's polluted air. However, it's quiet out here. No cars zooming by. No police sirens or helicopters in the sky. No one is walking around. This part of the city is always quieter at this time of night, though. Perhaps that's another reason I prefer to move through the night.

By the time I get into my car, it's 4:22 A.M. How in the world is that possible? That couldn't have been more than just a couple of hours. I start the car and put it in drive, but my foot remains on the brake as I stare into the eyes of a woman in the rearview mirror. The woman's eyes project a glare that shivers me to the core. Her eyebrows raise, filled with glee, yet a twinkle of concern. It's as if she knows that my actions will be followed by a consequence that is yet to come.

"Whatever. I'm fine and enjoyed myself," I murmur to the woman in the mirror. She nods back with a smile.

Besides, it was exhilarating and exactly what I needed. So, anything that happens because of tonight, I'll consider it worth it.

CHAPTER 19

4:41 A.M

I HATE SURPRISES. Finding an extra fry in the bag is fine but discovering key evidence to a murder, while searching for a watch, isn't the type of surprise I'm okay with. All the more reason why I shouldn't be headed to meet Madison at the Crescent Cove Hotel.

This is so unlike me, which is why I should turn around. Come on, Andrea. Just turn around. For some strange reason, even if I wanted to, I couldn't do so because I promised Madison I'd be there. Hell, she may not even be there at this time. Who knows? If she's not, how would I get in touch with her? It's not like I have her phone number or email. She usually just shows up out of nowhere and does so whenever she wants. Does she even own a car? The last time I saw Madison, she was strolling down third avenue. And the time she ended up at the Crescent Cove hotel, it's because I dropped her off. It's like she's a ghost. God, what am I doing?

The sun is starting to rise by the time I pull into the parking lot, and it's not even as full as it was the last time I was here. I'm not sure if that's good or bad, but it's certainly not enough to stop me from exiting the car.

The moment I step out and shut the car door, I instantly feel surrounded by a tension that's so harsh and pervasive that I can barely move more than a few feet in any direction. Even my breathing is out of my control. I can't believe I've allowed Madison to lure me back here. It's almost four hours after the time Madison told me to meet her. By now, I'm sure she's gone. But what if she isn't? What if she's somewhere around here waiting on me? This is ridiculous. Why am I here to help this woman move a dead body? Could it be because I am interested to see for myself? Or perhaps I want to know the truth. Was it actually James Walker's body that Madison dumped back here? Or was it someone else? Perhaps Daniel?

I climb out of the car and carefully head to the hotel lobby, avoiding eye contact with anyone. Luckily for me, there's no one around, including Madison. As I make my way into the lobby, I still don't see anyone. Not even the concierge. I should head back to the car now. Besides, why would Madison be waiting in the lobby for me?

Turn around, Andrea, I whisper to myself, but instead, I head into the courtyard. As I take my fourth step, I spot a heavyset man with a head full of gray hair coming from the other end. Based on the man's gait and his uniform, he must work here. I can't allow him to see me. So, I quickly make my way out before he does, but then a sudden realization hits me. What if she's at the back of the hotel? Maybe I should at least check.

Through the shadowy gloom behind the hotel, I crouch against the concrete walls, taking shallow breaths as I do so. Some of the rooms have their lights on as I pass by, so I'm careful not to make a sound. However, no one can be that silent, not even me. What am I doing back here? I need to head home before it's too late. If it weren't for this aggravating feeling stuck in the pit of my gut, I would. I'm not sure why it's driving my curiosity crazy, but I feel it has something to do with Daniel. What if Daniel didn't leave, but instead, he's the one that Madison killed? It would all make sense. His sudden disappearance. Madison's random pop-ups in front of the building, in my office, at the bar, everywhere. All of it makes sense. On the other hand, if Madison killed him days ago, how could she be sure that the body is still back here?

Halfway through the back of the hotel l, I spot a woman on the second floor, just above me, stepping onto the balcony from the darkness of her room. What the hell is she doing up at this time of night! Quickly, I jump against the wall. I can see the woman, but I doubt she can see me. She looks out to the ocean as she lights her cigarette.

Stay calm, Andrea. Stay cool.

I spot something on the ground in the distance, maybe fifty feet away. I can't tell if it's just trash, a broken tree branch, or even a body. However, one thing is certain. It doesn't belong there. Could that be it? The dead body? If I could only get over there without the woman seeing me.

Five minutes go by, and a man comes out of the room and joins the woman for a smoke. Screw this. I'm leaving. Slowly, I turn around and walk back to the front of the building. And just as I do, I spot Madison's watch halfway in the dirt. The solid white ceramic gold-tone watch with crystals is exactly like the one I have. Madison must have been here, or perhaps, it's been on the ground this entire time. I grab the watch and continue through the shadows of the hotel, gliding against the wall as I do so. That's it! I'm out of here.

8:27 A.M.

I awake to another morning of Duke's barking, but as annoying as the bark is, the sound of the water running is more troubling. This again? Running water could only mean one thing, but it can't be. Could it? I quickly jump out of bed, slip into my slippers, and enter the bathroom. There's no one here. Of course not. But how does that explain the running water? Did I do this? Was I that tired? Perhaps I woke up, came into the bathroom, and turned the water on? Seems reasonable. Studies have shown that couples in sync tend to pick up on each other's habits. Maybe it was me, and if so, I must get myself together.

As I turn the water off, I notice my nails are filthy. Not only are they short, but now they're dirty too? I begin to wash my hands, staring into the wall-mounted mirror hanging over the sink as I do so. Unlike the previous encounters with the woman in the mirror, this one is different. I see the woman I am instead of the woman the world sees. Hmm…but perhaps it's time that I do something with my hair. What could I do to it? Cut it shorter? No. I don't think that would work. Color it? Maybe blonde. No. You're right. Black? Yes. Black. Okay. Black it is. I think that'll work. I can even add extensions to make it longer. I've never done that. Yes, that's what I will do. I'll call Rachel now to let her know I won't be coming in.

"Good morning, Dr. Clarke." Rachel answers.

"Rachel. Can you do me a favor? I'm going to take the day off, so could you let my patients know I will have to reschedule our sessions?"

"Okay. Is everything alright, Dr. Clarke?"

"Yes. Everything is fine."

"Okay. I'll get right to it then."

"Thanks, Rachel."

Just as I end the call… "Dr. Clarke?"

"Yes, Rachel?"

"A detective stopped by this morning. Detective Barringer. She didn't ask a lot of questions or anything, but she seemed quite determined. Is everything okay?"

"What did she want?"

"Information about one of your clients."

Why would she show up to my job and not my house? She must be up to something. Wait a minute…she can't possibly think I would… "What information did you give her, Rachel?"

"Nothing. I told her that I couldn't give her anything."

"Was Dr. Lanier there?"

"No. He'll be in at ten."

"Okay. I'll handle it. In the meantime, can you keep this to yourself?"

"Sure."

"Thank you, Rachel."

"But Dr. Clarke, the client that the detective asked for—"

"It's okay. I'll handle it. Have a good day."

I hang up before she thinks to ask another question. I don't want to deal with any of that right now. I just want to get to my new look.

10:27 A.M.

I would consider myself lucky to find an appointment on the same day I want to change my hair, and that's only because of Darlene. She recommended this place. When I enter the beauty salon, I'm shocked that there's barely anyone here. Just two other women. The place is relatively small and very intimate. It's a modern design, styled comfortably with gold trimmings along the white wall.

"Hi. How may I help you?" a woman says in a bubbly tone as she pops in from the back.

"Hi. I'm looking for Krystal Wilson?"

"That would be me," she says.

Her voice certainly doesn't match her look. She must be Creole.

"Hi, nice to meet you. I believe my friend Darlene spoke to you. My name is Andrea Clarke," I tell her.

"Oh, yes. She did. Nice to meet you" She shakes my hand. "So, what are you looking to get done today?" Krystal asks.

"I'm not sure. I just want a whole new look."

"Anything in mind at all?" She chuckles.

"Black. Maybe jet black. I also want length. At least down to my shoulders.

"Not a problem. I can do that," she replies.

She sits me in the chair closest to the front door and then swivels the chair around to a large mirror enclosed by a black wooden border. Intently, I stare at the woman in the mirror who I've come to know all these years and begin to debate this impulsive decision. Should I do this? I think so. Yes, I should. Krystal taps me on the shoulder, taking me from the discussion with the woman in the mirror.

"You ready?"

We continue to stare at each other. She and I—the woman in the mirror. My gaze is locked on her as she awaits my approval. I wait…and wait…and then…"Yes. Let's do it."

2:22 P.M.

Time dissolves into itself, and before I know it, Krystal is finished with my hair. She hasn't turned the chair around to face the mirror yet, and I can already feel the difference. There's extra weight on my head and a smell of new hair that brushes against my back, neck, and shoulders. I'm sure it's beyond what I could have imagined. Then again, I might look stupid. God, I hope that's not the case.

At last, Krystal swivels the white padded chair around to the mirror. Slowly, I open my eyes and intently stare at the woman in the mirror whom I've come to know all these years. A woman with long black glossy hair smiles back at me.

Wow!

Black hair looks good on the woman staring back at me. Even her cheeks seem to be inflated and fierce, highlighting those pretty eyes of hers. Indeed, no beauty in the universe could hope to compete with this woman in the mirror.

"I...I love it!" I declare.

My hair hasn't touched my shoulders in years, and this jet black is everything. I don't know what took me so long to do this.

"Honestly...what do you think?" I ask Krystal.

She removes the nylon cape off me and runs her finger through my hair gently. Goosebumps cover my skin as her touch soothes me. Immediately, I feel that incredible tingling rush between my thighs, over my neck, and in the pit of my stomach. This feeling is happening more frequently, and although it's strange, it is certainly welcomed.

"Think you should've done it a long time ago. You look amazing," Krystal tells me. I can sense she's being genuine through her smile and the way her eyes are pinned on me. "Why today?"

"I'm not sure. It just came out of nowhere."

"Well, whatever motivated you to do it, I'm glad it did, because this look fits you."

2:30 P.M.

I exit the shop, and for the first time in a while, I feel like I belong. It's as if I were one of the pretentious women that frequently walked up and down Third Avenue. It feels liberating and motivating. However, there's something else missing, and I know just what it is. I need to—oh shit! A black Range Rover pulls up ahead, and it looks just like the one that the distinguished gentleman drives. I can't say for sure, but quickly, I pull out my phone, not to check for messages or make a phone call, but to seem busy long enough for the car to get closer. That must be him, and if it is, it would certainly be great to have him see me like this. This time... I'll be ready.

The Range Rover parks along the curb—near the end of the walkway where I am standing. Discreetly, I glance over to the car, but the dark tint makes it hard to see anything. But I know that's him. I just know it is. The passenger door opens, and as it does, a woman steps out, reaches over, and kisses the man. I try to catch a glimpse of him, but it's a miserable failure.

"Bye, honey. I'll call you when I'm done," the woman says to him.

Maybe that isn't Alton after all. I didn't take him to be a married man. He's too much of a specimen to be tied to just one woman. Not to mention, she doesn't look like she'd be his type because she's nothing like Madison. Although her eyes seem impossible not to be a prisoner of, her nose is too long, and her lips are pretty small. She has no shape to her. It's like watching a lumber of plywood walk.

"Dr. Clarke?" the woman says.

I snap out of it and turn my attention to the woman just as the black Range Rover drives off. Shit! I don't know if that was Alton or not. I doubt it was.

"Dr. Clarke, is that you?" The woman approaches.

It's Christina Section. A former client whom I haven't seen in months. How did I not notice her at first glance? I must've been too focused on Alton to notice her. She approaches me with a vibrant smile that can take the burden off anyone's shoulders. Nothing like I remember.

"How are you?"

"Christina. Hey. I'm good. What about yourself?"

"I'm good. Now! Actually, I'm doing great. Thanks for asking."

Last year, Mrs. Section came to my office because she got so down in life that she contemplated suicide. Twice. There was no apparent reason why a woman with so much to give would want to do such a thing, but as we went through the sessions, it became evident that Mrs. Section was yearning for more in life than she could be offered. A few sessions and a couple of prescriptions of Brexpiprazole, and she's good as new.

"You changed your hair. It looks great," she says.

"Thank you. I just got it done."

"Let me guess…Krystal?"

"Yes. How'd you know?"

"I figured. She's amazing. I'm actually on my way to see her now. My husband is tired of my wigs." She laughs.

Husband? She's still married?! After everything she went through mentally, I figured no one would have the patience to deal with her bullshit. I guess some men just love crazy women. However, that answers my question. There's no way that could have been Alton.

My phone rings.

"Excuse me for a moment," I tell Mrs. Section. "Dr. Clarke speaking," I answer.

"Hi, Dr. Clarke, it's Zara. I'm at your office right now, but I wasn't aware that you wouldn't be in today. We rescheduled my appointment for today a couple of weeks ago. Remember? And I really need to speak to you."

I forgot about Mrs. Thompson—a thirty-four-year-old woman desperately holding onto the past. Right now, I have the urge to tell her to fuck off, but I've already canceled on her twice.

"Well, you have a good day, Dr. Clarke," Mrs. Section says to me as she walks away.

"You too."

Look at her. Even the way she walks, graceful and full of poise, shows how well he treats her. Her shoulders are held high as if she's walking down a runway. Her footsteps, though short, are ginger and straight. I can only imagine how he—

"Dr. Clarke, are you still there?" Ms. Thompson interjects.

"Yes, I am. Uh, listen Zara. I'm sorry, but can I have Rachel—"

"No. No. No. Please don't do this, Dr. Clarke. I need to talk to you today. Please!" Her voice trembles.

I sense her frustration barreling through the phone, and although I know where our conversation will lead to, I know what I must do.

"Okay. Fine. I can be there in thirty minutes. Is that good for you?"

"Yes. Thank you, Dr. Clarke. Thank you!"

2:50 P.M.

Fifteen minutes…

My hands remain firm on the steering wheel as I focus on the road ahead. And as I come to a red light before jumping on the I-95 south ramp, my phone rings again. It's the same number that called me three times this morning. Detective Barringer. I take a good look at the phone, and before I can answer, the call drops. I wonder what she wants now.

Green light.

It's 3:03 P.M. by the time I arrive at my office, and when I step out of the elevator, Rachel stands at her desk with her back towards me.

"Hey, Rachel!"

"Good after—" Rachel turns to me, and immediately, the folders in her hand fall to the ground as her eyes widen, her jaw drops, and her eyebrows elevate. "Dr. Clarke!! Your hair! It's amazing. I love it!"

That's right. My hair. I completely forgot that I had changed my hair. "Thank you."

"It's…different!" She grins, picking the folders up off the ground.

"This is the first time I've done anything to my hair in years."

"I know, and it's about time! No offense. I mean, before, you were a pretty woman, but now…you look amazing! Gorgeous."

Rachel smiles and then looks at me with a look that I am not used to. It's the kind of look that's filled with intention, and quite honestly, it's somewhat puzzling because it's the same way Aiden looked at me last night.

"So, where's Ms. Thompson?"

"Oh! Right. She's in the restroom. I'm headed to the mailroom. Did you need anything?"

"No. Thank you."

Rachel looks at me again, but this time she does something with her eyebrows, raising one higher than the other while grinning. Nearly batting her eyes.

"Well, I should get to my office before she gets out,"

"Yeah…uh, okay," Rachel fumbles over her words.

As I make my way to my office, I can't help but think that she's watching me walk away. I wonder if I'm right. I turn around, and there she is, looking at me, just as I presumed.

"I'm sorry. I'm headed to the mailroom now," she quickly says. "Dr. Clarke, I don't know what's going on with you, but even your walk is different. Very loose and confident. Almost as if you had no care in the world. I'm jealous."

I nod subtly, but internally I am grinning like a kid in the candy store. After all, this new look does seem to be working in my favor.

3:05 P.M.

The moment I enter my office, I spot Ms. Thompson standing in front of the large window, looking aimlessly. She's not even aware that I've walked into the room. I sigh. I can see this is going to be an exhausting session.

"Afternoon, Ms. Thompson."

She abruptly turns to me, nearly stumbling over the boxwood topiary tree. I can practically see the blood rushing through her pale skeletal frame.

"Dr. Clarke?" Her eyes widen.

"Yes?"

"Your hair. You look different. Very different," she says while examining me thoroughly. "It's nice, though."

"Thank you."

"And I'm sorry for being in your office. I promise I didn't touch anything." She approaches.

"It's okay, Ms. Thompson. Just don't do that again. Okay?"

"I promise. I won't."

"Great. Well then, have a seat."

"So why the change?" Her tone is shaky.

"No specific reason. Why? Are you uncomfortable with it?"

"No. It's fine. It just caught me off guard."

"Don't worry, Ms. Thompson. It's me. So, please…have a seat."

She takes a seat on the sofa as I sit across from her. For goodness sake! Ms. Thompson would look much prettier if she just tried for once. I don't know why she'd rather look like a desperate woman who hasn't slept in days. Wrinkled floral dress. Dry thinning hair. Parched lips covered with dead skin. That's how she leaves the house? It's no wonder she has problems.

"Okay, Ms. Thompson, what's your issue?" I bluntly ask.

"Excuse me?" She sounds offended.

Did I just say that out loud? My thoughts must've carried over to my lips.

"I'm sorry. I didn't mean for that to come out like that. Let's just pick up from our last session. Okay?"

She nods, and five seconds later, her shoulders loosely gulp up in a long draw before she sobs in the palm of her hands. I was right. This is going to be a long session.

"Why the tears?" I callously ask.

"Sorry. I don't know what I should do, Dr. Clarke. It's been a rough few days for me with all the moving around."

"You mean with Tony?"

"Yes."

If I could only shake the shit out of this senseless woman, it would save us all the time in the world.

Six years ago, Ms. Thompson met a guy named Tony. They dated for three and a half years before he decided to break it off. Two years later, Tony met another woman named Jasmine and married her eight months after that day. In the same venue where he and Ms. Thompson talked about getting married. Now Ms. Thompson, unable to let go of the thought of Tony being with another woman, is in my office with all sorts of depression. It's funny how life works sometimes.

"Moving around? What do you mean?" I ask, slightly annoyed.

"He's leaving the state, and I don't want to stay here anymore. And before you say anything…please consider my feelings, Dr. Clarke," she cries.

Ms. Thompson wants me to coddle her feelings like a newborn baby, but what I really want to do is tell her, "Get the hell over it, you stupid bitch!" However, that wouldn't serve its purpose, now would it, Andrea? Probably not. Besides, I like Ms. Thompson. Now and then, I see a little of myself in her. Reserved, but always troubled by curiosity. Constantly smiling, just so that no one notices what she's going through. Indeed, there's something about her that I can see in myself.

"I see. And you feel like if you stay, things will only worsen. Like you will lose any progress you've made with him," I appease her for the moment.

Her sobbing recedes to sniffles as she looks up at me.

"Yes. Exactly. Now he has me in a predicament that's just not fair."

It's official. She has reached the point where I dreadfully try to avoid meeting my clients. It happens when their created thoughts become their reality. Consequently, this is the point where my tolerance reaches zero.

"Ms. Thompson…listen to me. I'm telling you this as a friend. Not as your psychologist." I take my glasses off and lean forward, hoping she will find the truth in my tone. "Don't you think it's about time you let this go? Tony is not thinking about you, and you deserve to be happy as well. Understand what I'm saying?"

Ms. Thompson looks at me with those huge blue eyes, seemingly disturbed by my words. She opens her mouth, but her voice trails slowly as if her speaking ability is fading.

"Yes, Ms. Thompson?"

There is also a sadness in her eyes that is difficult to ignore, but it doesn't stop me from doing just that.

"You're right," Ms. Thompson murmurs.

Wait! Did that work? Was that all I had to tell her? I wish I had known that all along.

"I've never heard you speak like that, Dr. Clarke. It was cruel, insensitive, and inconsiderate of my feelings. But when you put it like that…you are absolutely right."

The confusion that had her crying is now over. A tear dangles on her eyelid before falling onto her right cheek. Her emotional mask is off, and I can finally see who she really is.

"Ms. Thompson, it may be best for you to—"

My jaw drops as the door swings open like it's been hit by a gust of wind. Madison? No, not now! She Stands in the doorway as if nothing about this was out of character. What am I saying? This is Madison. Of course, this is who she is. She does what she wants to do when she wants to do it. As Madison and I find ourselves in a stare-off contest, Mrs. Thompson swiftly turns to Madison and then back to me. Mrs. Thompson is just as nervous as I am, except she seems more concerned for me than I am for her.

CHAPTER 20

3:32 P.M.

Oh God! Not now.

"Madison, what are you doing here?" My voice is harsh.

Ms. Thompson turns her attention to Madison, regarding her suspiciously, with her mouth slightly open and eyes widened, and then quickly turning back to me.

"Everything okay, Dr. Clarke?"

"Yes," I say to Ms. Thompson. "You need to leave. I'm busy!" I turn back to Madison.

However, Madison casually walks over to the large window and stares at the reflection bouncing off the glass. There is no anger, no sadness, no joy, or resentment from her at all. Her face is as emotionless as it would be during the moments she's dreaming.

"Dr. Clarke?" Ms. Thompson says, sounding concerned.

"It's okay." I turn to her. Then, I snap my head back to Madison. "Again, you need to leave. Now!"

Time stops and lingers in the middle of nowhere with the silence, thick and heavy, covering us like a woven blanket. Madison rests her back against the large window. There isn't a trace of softness in her eyes like I've seen before. Her lips bear the resemblance of a smile, just enough to show that she's somewhere in her thoughts. Whatever they may be.

"Dr. Clarke, I'll just come back another time. It's no problem," Ms. Thompson stutters.

"No. Stay! You're fine. Madison, will you please leave, or else I'll have to get someone in here to remove you."

"But Dr. Clarke—" Ms. Thompson begins to say.

"I said you're fine."

Ms. Thompson's right leg frantically shakes, her fingers jump rhythmically, as if in spasm, and her eyes bulge like an invisible man is choking her. Before I can stop her, she grabs her bag and dashes out of my office, closing the door behind her.

Now it's just Madison and me, stuck in a grueling silence thicker than molasses.

"You can't just show up whenever you want to. That's not how this works."

"It's fine. Besides, I'm sure I did her a favor."

She walks over and takes a seat on the sofa, crosses her legs, and then takes a long deep breath. Her lips, covered with the Chanel dark rouge lipstick, contort into a forged smile. I can never get a read on this woman.

"Your hair. I see you changed it." She leans in. "Was I the motivation?"

"Excuse me?"

"Your hair. It's just like mine." She leans back, and once again, she turns to the large window.

She's right. My hair is a straight match to Madison's long and glossy hair. My mind is reeling with confusion. How did I not realize that? I look away for a moment, unable to comprehend or process the thought of that happening. Was I subconsciously thinking of Madison when I decided to change my hair? I must have been because even the length is precisely like Madison's.

"Madison? What is it that you want?"

She sits up and looks into my eyes. As she does so, I see her world slowly disappearing—even her demeanor shifts to an unpretentious woman. Madison doesn't say anything for a moment, then pivots her body towards the large window and slowly begins biting her fingernail nervously— like some misbehaving child. I'm not sure she's even aware of what she's doing. The biting of the nails can happen without someone even realizing it—especially when they're scared or full of guilt. I've never seen this side of her. I wonder what it could be that has her like this? It must have something to do with last night. *Of course!*

"You spoke to a detective?" she murmurs.

What? Is that why she's here? Surely it can't be. And how does she know I spoke to Detective Barringer?

"Why do you ask?"

"Don't worry, Dr. Clarke. I know you did what needed to be done," she murmurs.

She tilts her head slightly to the left, turning her weak smile into a cold look—the kind of look you'd see in the eyes of someone who's killed a man.

"Madison, if you're here about last night…I got caught up with something, and time slipped past me. Despite that, I'm glad it did because that's not something I want to be part of."

"I understand. But it's fine. I took care of it."

"You did?"

She stands up and walks over to the large window once again, taking a drawn-out deep breath along the way. Just as she's about to speak, there's a brash knock at the door, pulling me away from Madison.

"Dr. Clarke?" Rachel opens the door and pops in, her brows creased and face tense. "Is everything okay?"

My thoughts accelerate, and I want them to slow down so I can normally react without Rachel noticing there's something off about me.

"Dr. Clarke?" Rachel calls out.

Finally, I turn my attention to Rachel.

"Yes, Rachel. Everything is fine. Thank you."

"You sure? Ms. Thompson told me that—"

"Rachel, I said I'm fine!"

With her eyebrows raised, Rachel stares as if she's seen my ghost appear out of nowhere. Then, she looks over to the large window where Madison stands paralyzed by a thought of her own. I can only imagine what's running through her mind.

"Okay," Rachel says.

Slowly, she steps out and shuts the door behind her. I walk over to the door, lock it, take a moment to myself, and then turn to Madison with my back pressed against it.

"Okay, what is it that you have to tell me?" My voice is stern.

Madison gracefully walks back over to the sofa and takes a seat. She turns to me and crosses her legs gradually. Right over left. Her fingers intertwine just before she places her hands on her lap with no form of a smile. Her presence is starting to make me uncomfortable.

Madison speaks as I listen…

I listen as Madison speaks.

"Last night, I didn't arrive when I expected to, but it was still the right time. The sky was covered with a special kind of warm and quiet darkness. This kind of darkness robbed me of fear and replaced it with an unusual amount of confidence. No guilt, nervousness, or panic could come within its shield. Even though I knew what I was there for and didn't know what to expect, I felt safe enough to continue within the comfort of that darkness.

"In the back of that hotel is where I stood with all these thoughts circling in my head. Would I find him back there? What would happen if someone saw me? Are there any cameras back here? And if I did find him there, what would I do next? So many thoughts, yet not enough time.

"Eight minutes. That's how long I stood there before I finally made my way through the darkness of that back hotel. I was as cautious as possible—calm and steady in my movements. Making sure no one noticed me along the way. The further I walked through the darkness, the more my eyes adapted to my surroundings. I began to see much clearer than before. Also, I knew I was getting closer to him because all of a sudden, I smelled the most disgusting pungent odor I'd ever smelled— like rotting flesh burned inside a septic tank. I nearly heaved at the thought of seeing him, let alone his smell. Two minutes. That's how long it took for me to get to him, and there he was, tumbled over into an awkward position and empty like a big wad of dough. The top of his head was caved in and covered with dry blood. His brown eyes stared into the dark sky while his mouth hung wide open. Even in the darkness, I could see how empty his body was and how loose his skin looked. I never saw a corpse in person. How no one else found him is a mystery to me.

"After a few moments, I held my breath and did it. I grabbed him by the ankles and shifted his body into a straight position. He was much heavier than I imagined. My stomach began to churn more, with nausea clawing at the back of my throat. His cold and clammy body nearly made me weak. However, I knew I needed to hold it together.

"From the back of the hotel to the ocean shore was roughly sixty yards. I knew if I moved quickly enough, I could get him into the water before anyone noticed.

"My will to get rid of his body gave me the strength to drag him across the back of the hotel, through a garden, and into the ocean like a worn-out rag doll. What could have been only ten minutes felt like forever. I was exhausted and mentally tired by the time I reached the shore. But I had to keep going before it was too late. Quickly, I removed his clothing and then removed mine. Then, I pulled him into the water, and his body instantly floated like a dry log. I swam as far as I could, hauling his body along the way. The further into the ocean I went, the harder it became to pull on him.

"I was so far into the water that I barely saw lights coming from the hotel. It was at that moment that the panic began to take over me. My breathing became more rapid and shallower. There was a moment when I thought of drowning myself to get it all over with. But I couldn't do it. I had to keep going. So, I held his body underwater for nearly six minutes, struggling for the first four minutes. I could not believe my hands were all over his dead body. On his head. His shoulders. His chest. I even touched his mouth at one point. That's when I lost it, and chunks of my partially digested dinner spewed out as the panic began to rise. My heart was going crazy, like a rabbit trying to make a run for it. Those six minutes turned into fifteen minutes, and it felt like forever. But it worked. His lifeless body disappeared into the ocean just like I had hoped it would."

What the fuck! I halt at Madison's expression. Her face is shuttered with a gaunt impassive stare. Although I already know what she has done and what she was planning to do last night, it still comes as a shock to me. My bowels churn, and swallowing becomes a lost trait. Who am I kidding? There's no way I could have helped Madison do such a thing. I'm disgusted just thinking about it, but I feel just as guilty as she does for some odd reason. No. I feel more disturbed and squeamish. Why did Madison have to tell me this?

My stomach violently shrinks, and quickly, I run over to the trash can, fall to my knees and heave until there's nothing left. Suddenly, my office phone rings. I don't usually get calls on that phone unless it's Rachel or an emergency, but whatever the case is, it's exactly what I needed to interrupt this moment.

"Hello?" I answer.

"Hey, girl, it's me. Shannon."

I sigh with relief, glad it's not Detective Barringer.

"Shannon…hey! Why are you calling my office phone?" I ask.

"You weren't answering your cell phone."

Shannon can be over the top, but at this very moment, I can't help but shake my head with a soft smile drawn over my face.

"I must've left it in the car. What's going on?"

"I just wanted to let you know that Mexico is all set. I'm emailing the details to you now. I'll call you later. Gotta go." She hangs up before I can get another word in.

I put the phone down, but I can still feel the disgust building like an unstoppable snowball in the pit of my stomach. There's also discomfort in my chest, making me want to run or hide. Whichever gets me further away from this moment. *Relax, Andrea. One deep breath. Two deep breaths.*

When I turn back to Madison, she's gone! Where did she go? Suddenly, the discomfort in my stomach moves into my chest, making me feel like I've taken in too much caffeine. Another classic sign of anxiety. Why do I feel this way? Panic attack? Perhaps. Maybe it's time I take Dr. Lanier's advice and see someone because things aren't making sense.

Think.

Think.

Think…

Mexico! How'd I quickly forget? Yes. A trip to Mexico is what I need to help decompress and figure everything out. A weekend of relaxation and getting back to myself should do it. Besides, I sense the woman inside desperately wants to go just as badly as I do. God, I love Shannon.

Immediately, I call Rachel to let her know, but there's no answer. The time now is a quarter after four. Rachel couldn't have already left for the day. Could she? I exit my office and make my way up front to Rachel's desk, but she's not there either. She would have—

"Dr. Clarke?" Rachel appears out of nowhere.

"Rachel! You scared me."

"Sorry. I didn't mean to." Her eyes show a gentleness like the expression I've used with patients desperately needing my help. The ones I've felt pity for.

"Yes. I'm fine. I need you to do me a favor. Can you reschedule all my appointments for next week?"

"Sure. Is everything okay?"

"Everything is fine. And you can stop asking me that. Please tell everyone that I have to reschedule due to personal matters. I will reach out to them soon."

"All right, Dr. Clarke. I'll do that right away."

"Thank you."

I turn to walk away.

"Dr. Clarke?" Rachel stops me in my tracks.

I turn back to her, and she stares at me with a look of complete and utter dismay. It's as if she is about to break out into tears.

"What is it, Rachel?"

"Did you hear?"

Oh no! It's Daniel.

"Hear what?"

"Patricia Walker...they found her husband. He's dead."

Mr. Walker is dead? Madison was referring to Mr. Walker this whole time.

"Are you serious?! What happened?"

"I can't say for certain, but they discovered his lifeless body drifting in the waters around the Biscayne area," Rachel reveals, her voice tinged with uncertainty. "Decomposition had taken its toll, and that made it hard for them to identify him at first. And they said they found an alarming presence of benzodiazepines coursing through his system."

"How'd you not hear about this?

I shrug and look away for a moment. Rachel doesn't know I'm already aware of it because of Madison, and I like it that way. However, benzodiazepine found in his stomach? I didn't know about that. Madison must have drugged him as well.

"You think Mrs. Walker did it?"

"No. I don't think she would do that."

"You never know. Benzos? I'm sure she got some from you, right? Think about it. She hasn't been here in nearly four months, and the day after she does, her husband is found dead in the middle of the ocean with an insane amount of drugs in his system? You don't find it strange?" Rachel says.

If it weren't for the fact that I knew Madison was behind all this, I would have thought that Rachel was on to something.

"Right. Well, can you make sure to make those calls? Thanks. And send some flowers over to Mrs. Walker?"

"I surely can, and I'll send the flowers right away. By the way, do you plan on telling me where you're going?" She smiles.

Rachel crosses her arms beneath her breast, biting into her lower lip, and for a moment, we stare into each other's eyes. This is yet another look from Rachel that I am not used to. But what's the harm in telling her? Besides, it's so unlike me to be this spontaneous. No planning, no scheduling, no meeting…no nothing! Just up and go. I can get used to this.

"Yes. I'm going to Mexico."

"Mexico? That's nice," she says while doing a random dance.

Suddenly, a random flash of Mr. Walker pops into my head. It's pretty vivid, too. Madison's story is playing out in my mind. I see him standing there, scared, as the tension grows on his face. Strangely enough, I can hear his voice screaming and groaning in my head. There's even an image of Mr. Walker's clothing. Navy blue pants, white button-up collarless shirt, and brown oxfords. I'm not sure Madison told me what he wore that night.

"Dr. Clarke?"

I snap out of it.

"Yes. I'm going to Mexico."

"Right. You just said that."

"I did?"

"Yes. Just a moment ago. Are you sure you're okay? Ms. Thompson ran out of here like a bat out of a cave. She said she couldn't come back until you were in your right mind."

"Me? In my right mind? Whatever. Rachel, how about next time, you don't let someone like Madison just walk by you and enter my office like that."

"What do you mean, Dr. Clarke?"

"What do I mean? The woman you let enter my office and interrupt Ms. Thompson's session."

"Dr. Clarke…there was no other woman who went in there."

"What are you talking about? I'm referring to the woman you saw when you came into my office just a moment ago. Madison."

"But Dr. Clarke…there was no one in your office besides you."

Everything moves in slow motion, and although I have complete control of my hands and feet, I can't move them. Rachel glances upward, her mouth pursed but slightly open and loose. Her eyes are stuck on me as if I am a danger to her well-being. I take a step away from her. Something must be wrong with Rachel. I've seen this before. A chemical imbalance that forces the mind to move faster than she can keep up with. Delusional. Everything Rachel says will only make sense to her— almost like if she were on a phone call, talking, with a dial tone on the other end. This is exactly the look I saw in Ms. Sarah Wildmon before she went off the deep end.

"Dr. Clarke!"

"Okay, Rachel. I need to leave now."

Quickly, I grab my stuff from my office and make my way out. Rachel follows behind like a lost puppy without saying anything. She looks at me as if I am losing it, but something is wrong with Rachel, and I need to get out of here before I find out what it is.

6:48 P.M.

The sun is starting to set when I arrive home, and I want nothing more than to just relax. I don't want to think about anything, because the more I do, the more paths there are.

It's a quarter after seven by the time I enter my house. Immediately, I make a beeline to the bedroom, taking off clothing along the way, down to my black bra and sheer plum panties. *You know what would make this night better? A hot bath? Yes. A hot bath.* I can certainly use a hot bath right now.

The water fills the tub as I go into my secret stash of medicine— located in my vanity drawer. However, I don't see my bottle of benzodiazepine or temazepam. Where the hell is it? Think, Andrea. Could Shannon have taken it? She loves to dig through my stuff. Wait a minute. Madison? No. There's no way Madison could have been in here, right? Shit! What if she was?

As I'm about to close the drawer, I see two pills lying randomly at the back. It makes me feel uneasy. I don't remember ever taking my pills out of their bottle, let alone finding them in my drawer. This must be Madison's doing. Is she planning something against me? I need to contact Detective Barringer right away and tell her everything before things get worse. I try to calm myself down, but how can I? The situation feels really serious. What about Daniel? Should I be worried about him? No, he's not important. He probably took the pills himself. I didn't think of that before. But what does it mean? *Andrea, just relax for a moment.* The voice in my head tells me not to worry, but it's frustrating and mysterious.

Deep inhale.

Soft exhale.

I scoop the pills up and swallow them— one by one, and then turn to the woman in the mirror, staring at her for a few minutes. This time, there's no questioning of who she is nor is there any sort of objectifying. Instead, there's a genuine connection with the woman in the mirror, pleased with what I see. Her smile. Her complexion. Her imperfection. Her wants, desires…everything! It's all connected to me in a way that allows me to be envious of the woman, and the fact that I am makes me pleased.

I step into the tub, submerging myself in hot water. The warmth comforts me almost like a man's touch, and it's peaceful and soothing. My body function slows down as the sound of the water against my skin tickles my senses. My limbs, which feel like music flowing through them, move through the water sensually. Butterflies fill my stomach with a fluttering sensation, getting deeper as time goes on.

Deep inhale.

Soft exhale.

My breathing is steady as I squeeze body wash into my hands. Then, my hands, lathered with soap, slide between my breasts, and firmly press on them. I begin to apply pressure from underneath while squeezing tighter, and I feel the urge to keep going.

I close my eyes, and as my hands travel across my body, I come to a place in my mind that I rarely ever visit. A place where I lose the ability to think but gain an exceptional strength to feel. There's no thought of today or anything else. At this moment, I only want to feel. I want to feel love, joy, and pleasure. I just want to handle all of myself in ways I haven't done before. And had it not been for the progression of time, I could stay here all day.

The feeling builds as my hands melt into my body like ice-cream in a warm porcelain bowl. *Don't stop!* After a few seconds, I prop my feet up on the sides of the tub, spreading my legs apart. The urge takes over me as I gently slide my left hand down between my legs, grazing the spot that makes my body quiver. My mouth drops open, my head falls back, and my eyes close. Pleasurably, I moan as my right hand relentlessly presses against my breast. *Go further in.* I hear my consciousness graciously whisper. My index finger moves in a slow circle on the spot that causes my body to jerk. *Do you feel yourself?* Yes. I moan between every other heartbeat. Even as my body remains submerged underwater, I can feel myself getting wetter. I'm much thicker and more slippery than the water. *Keep going*, the voice whispers in my head again. The deeper my fingers go, the tighter my right hand squeezes on my breast, tugging on my nipple as well.

In college, Denita Richardson told me about her fascination with pleasuring herself. In that room, Denita took off her panties, opened her legs, and detailed exactly how she would do it. I had never seen another woman touch herself until that moment, but I couldn't turn away. I was captivated by it. Denita took her index and middle finger on her left hand and pressed down against her clit, adding intense pressure. She explained how it would only strengthen the sensation. She was right because it feels incredible as I do it right now. While adding the pressure, she would rub her clitoris in big circles instead of small ones. Big circles brought more sensation all over and not just that one spot.

Yes! I gasp from the feeling of my fingers pleasing me, jerking a couple of times in between. Then, I spread my fingers apart, turn the water on, and allow the warmth of the running water to intensify what I'm feeling.

Denita also said she'd think of someone when she pleasured herself. And she did. I watched her close her eyes, bite her lips, and allow the memory to take over. It was as if I was no longer in the room with her as she became immersed in the thought. I could put myself in the moment of last night where I was fucked and touched by Manny and Aiden, but instead, it's Alton—the distinguished gentleman who appears when I shut my eyes. He's standing there in a dimly lit room. I can tell by the white drape hanging by the window that it's my bedroom. My senses run wild as I take in this moment. In the glowing silhouette is where he appears, standing in the doorway. I remain stuck like a wet log—surprised by his abrupt appearance.

He's wearing black cotton sweatpants and a gray shirt that has college lettering written over the chest. His fingers, long and dark, motion for me to come over, and without thinking, I step out of the tub, dripping wet, and slowly approach him. He grabs me by the hand, leads me to the bed, and lays me down. Every second I spend with him makes a permanent mark in my vivid imagination to the point it feels like reality.

He then peels the shirt off his skin and tosses it over the headboard as he stands over my naked body. Still…he says nothing. I wait for his next move, anticipating the moment I feel him inside me. I can even smell his scent, which is a billowy smell of lite sweat on a clean body, unlike our moment in the elevator. His lips rest on my forehead as his index finger slowly trails across my face. Then, he slides his index finger down to my shoulder, moving down to my inner thigh. Without warning, he turns me over on my stomach in one swift motion. The moment gets the best of me as I begin to pulsate deep within. Even God can't stop what's about to happen as he slithers between my toes…

Along the arch of my foot…
Around my ankle…
Up my legs…
Behind my thighs…
Over my ass.

Oh, my goodness! My fingers move faster as I begin to pant. Please don't stop. Denita was so right about this, because this is amazing, and it feels all so…real. His touches. His look. His breath against my skin. All of it. Then, he removes his pants, and although I can't see it, I know it's irresistibly thick. Just as Madison described.

He says nothing.

I remain quiet.

He reaches over, opens the window next to the bed, and then extends his right hand to me. I grab hold of him, and he pulls me closer in a swift motion. We gaze into each other's eyes before his hands tightly grip my waist and hoist me up. His smooth yet firm body is molded to mine, sharing his heat with me as easily as I share my desire. I can feel every part of his muscle in my palms as I wrap my legs around his waist. Something takes control of me and causes me to bite his shoulder, fighting the urge to wail. His left hand grips my ass for a moment until I feel the warmth of his erection brushing against my pussy like a paintbrush. I hold onto him tighter as he slowly enters my body like I was his missing piece.

One second…

Two seconds…

Three…four…five…

My eyes shoot open as an electrical current run directly through me and lingers in my pelvis for a moment. The moan finally comes out quivering as I stare at the ceiling in complete shock, staggered by the tingling feeling. Oh my God! That was amazing. My fingers have me pulsating and relaxed simultaneously, and I want nothing more than to have the real thing. Right now!

CHAPTER 21

8:53 P.M.

SMEAR IT ACROSS MY LIPS, and that should be the finishing touch I need. Looks good. I've never been a fan of lipstick, especially red because it always reminds me of my mother, and I hate anything that reminds me of her. However, this Chanel Allure rouge isn't bad. And after trying on seven different outfits, I've settled on this burgundy leather Fenty corset dress. Now, I'm ready to take on the world and have a good time. The question is, where will I go?

Las Olas on a Thursday night sounds like it could be fun. On second thought, a trip to Fort Lauderdale isn't something I'm up for tonight. Maybe I'll bar crawl in Wynwood. There are a few spots that I've been wanting to visit, but the chances of running into someone I know is very likely. And tonight is a night I'd like to be discreet.

What about "The House"? An internal voice whispers.

Going to "The House" tonight doesn't sound like a bad idea either, but I don't have an invitation. Doesn't matter because as desirable as it may be, I want something a bit…normal.

It's a quarter to nine, and Shannon hasn't called yet. Good. I was hoping to step out alone tonight anyway. There's a beauty in going out alone. Maybe it's the only child in me, but I've never had a problem with it. It's liberating and easier to maneuver through the night without someone else trying to steer you to their plans. Not to mention, you can do whatever you want without anyone judging you for your actions. Besides, tonight is about something more than just having fun with the girls.

In most cities, a quarter to nine is the perfect time to go out, but in Miami, that's early. According to one of my clients, Ms. Jasmine Speights, a former track star with a serious drinking problem, there's a bar located off Biscayne and 79th Street named *The Anderson*. Ms. Speights said the bar is decorated in shades of red. It's sexy, intimate, and the bartenders there make the best drinks. She only dates women, but Ms. Speights confessed that on a few visits to the bar, she'd been turned on by a few of the men as well. Sounds like a good place to start my night off.

The stars illuminate the dark sky like millions of broken pieces of glass by the time I step out of the house. This is a good sign because in a city like Miami, I rarely get to see the sky like this. Even on a night like tonight, the stars don't shine as they did back home in Louisiana.

Just as I head to my car, a silver Chevrolet Impala pulls into my driveway with the headlights beaming in my eyes.

"Hello, my dear!" Mrs. Bouyon says.

Of course. Mrs. Bouyon would be walking her dog at this time of night. Sometimes I wonder if she's spying on me because this is too frequent to be a coincidence.

"Good evening, Ms. Bouyon." I wave back, hoping she walks away afterward, but she doesn't. Her steps are much slower as her eyes remain focused on the car in my driveway. That's Mrs. Bouyon for you. Always looking to pry into someone else's affairs.

All of a sudden, the driver-side door of the Impala opens, and out of the blinding lights a figure slowly walks towards me. I can't see their face, but judging by the height, shape, and strut, I can tell it is a woman. I squint my eyes to catch a better look, and to my surprise, it's

Detective Barringer. I wasn't expecting her. Especially not at this time of night.

"You look nice. Going somewhere?" Detective Barringer says.

"Actually, I am."

"Well, you mind if we take a ride? Down to the station? Won't take much of your time."

There must be something puzzling about my posture or the look in my eyes because her hand draws to her waist and touches a pair of metal handcuffs.

"Am I being arrested?"

"No. You're not. But I'd like to get some things ironed out. So, what do you say?"

"Andrea, you alright?" Mrs. Bouyon asks.

I forgot she was over there. Now, everyone will know about my run-in with Detective Barringer.

"What's this about?" I ask.

"James Walker. Just looking to see if you could help us."

Beyond my control, my fingers begin to twitch as if there is music only I can hear, and my left foot repeatedly taps against the pavement. I look over to the right, and then to the left, unsure of what I'm looking for. What am I doing? I must get a hold of myself. Immediately, the twitching of the fingers and tapping of my foot stops as I take in a gulp of air. Then exhale deeply.

"All right. Fine," I turn back to Detective Barringer.

10:51 P.M.

There is an absolute stillness in this god-awful cold room. The ceiling is no taller than seven feet, and the claustrophobic white walls are stippled with chipped paint. I suspect the discolored lightbulb hanging above the stainless steel table is to intimidate anyone in my position. I've been here for over an hour, sitting in a chair as comfortable as a park bench while staring at the grimy walls. Where is Detective Barringer? She said this wouldn't take too much of my time.

Finally, the door opens. Just a little bit. However, no one enters. That's strange. What's even more strange is that I don't feel nervous, nor am I scared. Not one bit. Usually, a slightly opened door, combined with a grueling silence, would have my nerves running wild. However, in this moment, there's a calmness to me that I don't believe I've ever felt. My heart beats to a slow and steady rhythm. My hands and feet aren't fidgeting all over the place, and there's no uncomfortable churning in the pit of my stomach. Any other time, I'd probably feel trapped and imprisoned in my mind, but tonight I feel as calm as a Buddhist monk after several hours of meditation. Still, if Detective Barringer doesn't come in the next two minutes, I'm leaving. This is not how I imagined my night would be. I should be in a bar with hundreds of conversations being held in loud voices over the music. A place where the crowd is full of energy. People looking for something in each other that they lack in themselves. A place that is very similar to "The House," but with more restrictions. I can picture men making their way through a throng of warm bodies just to speak to me, and then me teasingly smiling back. From there, who knows where it would take us? But instead, here I am, in this cold dimly lit room with no windows. The room is so quiet that I can hear the paralyzing ticks of the clock hanging on the wall above the door. And it's only getting louder the more I stare at it.

"Sorry about the wait, Ms. Clarke. Had to finish up on something." Detective Barringer finally enters, holding a mug in one hand and a blue folder in the other.

She takes a seat across from me, looking into my eyes without saying a word. Her stare isn't as cold, but it's an empty one. It's the kind of stare that tells me she knows something that I don't. I know that because I've seen that stare before.

"So, why'd you want me down here?" I ask.

For a fraction of a second, the corners of her mouth twitch upwards to a faint smile, and then quickly disappear as her conscious mind asserts control again.

"For starters…Madison. We can't seem to find this woman. Any chance you might know where we can find her? We'd like to ask her some questions."

"I'm not sure."

"Didn't you speak to her?"

"I did, but there's nothing that I know of that would lead you to her."

Detective Barringer looks at me like she is unsure of what I'm saying. Doubt! That's what that is. And I can sense it radiating from her like heat off a stove.

"Okay. So, when you spoke to her, did she tell you anything about James Walker? Anything at all?"

"No. Why would she? She only told me about Daniel." The lie slips between my lips as easily as melted butter on a hot knife. Yet, I'm not sure why.

"Daniel…your boyfriend, right? And what was his last name again?" She scoots in closer.

"Cooper. Daniel Cooper."

"Have you been in touch with him since the last time we spoke?"

"No. I haven't, and don't care to."

She nods her head, sits back, and then plops the blue folder onto the desk. Right in front of me. There is still no sign of nervousness flowing anywhere in my body.

"Daniel Cooper. And you said his birthday is…March 30, 1985. Correct?"

"Yes."

"Right. Well, I searched our entire database, and I didn't find any match for that name and birthday. However, you know who I did find with that same birthday?"

I look over to the door as if someone would be coming in to rescue me, but it's just to take a moment to myself. Then, I turn back to the detective as calm as I was before she walked in.

"James Walker! Isn't that a coincidence? Oh wait, I forgot. You don't believe in coincidence, do you? What did you say again? Everything that we think is a coincidence, will somehow connect to another event someway or somehow. Ironic. Isn't it?" She grins.

"Where are you going with this?"

"I think you know. So, how about you just tell me everything? Start from the beginning."

She opens the blue folder and slides a picture of a badly decomposed man. My guess is that this is James Walker.

"There's nothing to tell."

She leans in and rests her elbows on the table with a burning hard stare, yet it has little effect on me.

"You sure about that?"

I remain silent as the walls begin to close in on me. Detective Barringer has asked every question she could, and I've told her all that I can. I have to get out of here.

"What more do you want from me?" I inquire.

Maybe I shouldn't have said that. *Calm down, Andrea,* my inner voice whispers.

"You wanna know what I think?" She hops out of her seat, her face tense, and lips pursed, towering over me from across the table.

"Whatever it is, it has nothing to do with me."

"So, why did you lead me to believe that you knew nothing about

James Walker? I know you met up with him at the Crescent Beach Hotel."

Detective Barringer walks around the table, and as she does, the soft clicks of her heels hitting the tiled floor strikes a nerve. Then, she takes a seat on the table facing me with a stern look on her face.

"Again, I don't know what you're talking about."

She rests her left hand on my shoulder, leans ever so slightly, and looks into my eyes with a stern look.

"Oh, I'm sure you do. Now, tell me what happened to Mr. Walker! Everything we know about this case has you involved. His last known location? You were there. His last contact? You. We know you've been seeing him for over a year. And the handwriting on the letter you showed me the other night at your house, the one your boyfriend wrote, was the same handwriting on a note you wrote to Mrs. Walker."

This must be what it feels like to jump off a skyscraper with no parachute. My brows tip up, muscles stiffen, and my hands grip onto my seat tightly. Did Madison set this all up? Could she have been this meticulous and calculated to pull this off? It would only make sense. However, the more I think about it, the more my brain falls out of sync with reality. I'm not sure if it's the fear or the uncertainty of the moment, but something is beginning to steer my emotions in the wrong direction. Even random moments with Daniel flash in my mind, but they aren't memories I remember. There's one of us in the park. In a dimly lit lounge. There's even one of us riding on a train. How is this even possible?

"Ms. Clark!"

I snap out of it.

"Okay! Look, I don't know what's going on, but I'm not the person that needs to be sitting here."

Get ahold of yourself, Andrea. Yes. I need to relax.

"Then tell me who needs to be sitting here?"

"Madison!"

"Madison?" Her mouth purses but stays slightly open and loose. "How is that you're the only one who knows Madison? Even your secretary had no clue about this client of yours. So, if you want me to help you…tell me where I can find this Madison person, Andrea. Help me help you."

"She never told me where she lives, let alone her last name. I only know her by the name Madison."

God, if Dr. Lanier finds out this is happening, there's a chance I could lose my license. I handled everything completely wrong with Madison, and it's all because of my stupid fascination with her. *Fuck!* I failed to acquire the proper basic information, deliberately misrepresented her, and to top it off, I should have never gotten that close.

"What did she tell you? You have to tell me because it's not looking good for you."

The ticking of the clock continues to get louder as my breathing comes in short bursts. If that's not bad enough, my heart hits my chest so hard that my ribs feel like they will break, and my eyes are stuck wide open. I can see the tension growing in Detective Barringer's face as her thoughts accelerate. I feel like I'm going to blackout at any moment.

"Andrea! If you want me to help you, you have to tell me what you know. Now!"

Detective Barringer walks back to her chair and takes a seat, folding her arms across her chest. For nearly thirty seconds, silence becomes our only form of communication until I slowly look up to her, taking in a deep breath. Then, I cross my legs, right over left, and narrow my eyes to a cold stare. My hands intertwine just before I place them on the table.

"Am I under arrest?"

"Excuse me?"

"Simple question, Detective. Am I under arrest for any charges?"

"You know what I think? I think you have something to do with this. I think you met Mr. Walker through your sessions with his wife, and then you started seeing him. You knew everything about him already through Mrs. Walker, so it was easy. However, Mr. Walker got tired of you and decided to cut it off. But you wouldn't have that, would you? You couldn't stand to know that you were nothing more than a useless piece of meat that he used to have fun with. And now you're throwing in this Madison person to throw us off. Isn't that right?"

No one will ever understand those who don't want to be understood, and I have a feeling Detective Barringer is starting to realize that as she glares into my eyes. Slowly, I swipe my right index finger underneath both eyes. Left eye first, and then the right.

"Am I under arrest?" I smile.

Detective Barringer lowers her head and sighs. She can't even bring herself to get the words out.

"No. You're not. But just so you know, this is not over with. I will be coming for you sooner than you think. I will not stop until I have the complete truth in front of a jury."

"Thank you." I exit without saying another word.

DECEMBER
SATURDAY
12

12:03 A.M.

After nearly two hours of sitting in that room with Detective Barringer, I thought I would have fear sit on my conscience like a pillow over my mouth and nose. However, there's nothing there. No fear. No nervous feeling. Completely free of any of the troubling thoughts I'd usually have. Now, all I want is to discover what I set out to find tonight.

Finally, I arrive at the bar that Ms. Speights told me about, and the place is just as she described it. An intimate setting illuminated by red and purple lights. The music flowing through the speakers is a soothing sound that touches my soul. This is exactly where I belong, and luckily for me, there's an open chair at the bar.

"I'll be right with you," the woman behind the bar says as I take a seat.

Madison conveyed her wisdom on capturing a man's attention, revealing the intricate dance of allure. "You must reveal a little," she said, her voice a seductive invitation. "But be subtle, teasing. Begin with a glance, a smile that lingers, then a fleeting turn of your gaze before returning to him, your hidden desire echoing internally." According to her, this subtle display would ensnare the attention of any man.

She emphasized the significance of body language, cautioning against crossed arms or needless frowns. Instead, she encouraged a warm smile and an open demeanor. To stimulate a man's intellect, she advised offering a fragment of oneself as a tantalizing gateway to deeper conversations. The occasional touch on his arm or shoulder, she insisted, would further dissolve barriers. Madison's message was clear: If you desire him, do not keep yourself closed off.

My eyes drift around the room in search of someone to serve as my target, trying to indulge myself in all that Madison has reminded me of. A guy sitting on the other side of the counter has been eyeing me since I sat down. I wonder what he's thinking right now. Perhaps, how I look naked? I bet I'm right. I wonder if he can tell I'm thinking the same about him.

"Sorry about that. How can I help you?" the female bartender interrupts.

"Uh, I'll just take a whiskey sour."

"Coming right up."

He's captivated by my stunning looks. He is unaware that I've noticed him looking at me, and the fact that he's sitting there with another woman makes it even more intriguing. His eyes are focused on me—with intent. By smiling girlishly, I let him know that I notice him. He looks away for a moment, says something to the woman sitting next to him, and then turns back to me with a smile. I doubt the woman notices our interaction.

Then, he shifts his posture, hoping I observe his physique. *Nice.* I must admit, it does create that tingling feeling inside of me. I uncross my legs, and then cross them back— right over left. Softly, my index finger runs along my bottom lip without looking his way, and then twitches my lips upward to a smile. I like to think of it as a special power.

"I'm sorry, but that was a whiskey sour, right," she asks, puzzled.

"Yes. That's correct."

"By the way, are you here alone?"

"For the moment, I am."

"Cool. Well, I'll keep you company for this moment then. Coming back with that drink." She walks off.

I suppress the urge to smile, but it's a failure. I'm not sure if it's because of the bartender, the man across the way, or my thoughts, but I can't help but to blush. It's not the kind of blush that is blatantly exhibited, instead, it's the kind that shows the soul. The kind that reveals the delicate person I am within.

"Peach martini," a male bartender says, holding out a martini glass towards me.

"No, actually I ordered a whiskey sour."

"It's courtesy of the gentleman in the blue blazer."

He puts the martini down on the counter, right in front of me, and then walks away. I have no idea who he is referring to. It's not the guy at the end of the table because he doesn't seem bold enough to do such a thing. Besides, he has a brown jacket on. Casually, I look around, trying not to come off desperate, but I don't see anyone around wearing a blue blazer. The anticipation is killing me, and as much as I want to find this man, I won't play that game. Instead, I'll just wait until he comes to me.

"Here you are, beautiful." The woman returns with my drink. "By the way, I'm Erica."

"Nice to meet you. I'm—"

There he is. The man in the blue blazer, sitting in the back, in a VIP booth, staring at me as if I were the only woman in the room. Mr. Salters? I quickly turn my head to the side to avoid his gaze.

"You okay?" the woman interjects.

"Yes. I'm fine. Oh! I'm Andrea."

"Andrea? Okay. I wouldn't have guessed that. Shit! Can you give me a second? I'll be right back."

"Sure."

She hurries off. Immediately, my attention shifts back to Mr. Salters. This time I smile. What is he doing here? He waves, and I wave back. Then, he motions me to come over. Perhaps he wants to talk about Mrs. Salters. This would be a good time to warn him about her thoughts of killing him. Then again, this isn't the place for that, so I doubt that's what he wants. Again, with just his index finger, he motions for me to come over. No, I can't do that. Can I? *Why not, Andrea?* Yes, why not? Fuck it. Besides, I came here to have a good time. I grab my drinks and cross over to Mr. Salters through a throng of warm bodies. The man sitting there with the woman has his eyes locked on me as I pass him by.

"So, you wanted to see me?" I step into his booth.

"Yes. I did." He smiles.

He sits there, holding onto his drink. A glass of Johnnie Walker whiskey with two cubes. Those deep clever eyes of his observe me with nothing hidden behind them.

"Are you alone? Or will someone else be joining us?" I ask.

"I'm alone. Please, have a seat."

He scoots over and makes room for me to sit on his left side. I hesitate to sit down at first. Five seconds at most. *What the heck! I'm already here.* I take a seat so close to him that I can smell his pleasant natural scent while feeling the warmth coming from his body.

"I'm surprised you decided to come." He smiles and then quickly covers it by taking a sip of his drink.

"You speak as if you knew I was coming."

"I did." Mr. Salters leans in closer, taking another sip of his drink as he does so. His shoulder touches mine as I gaze into his eyes. I sense this is the beginning of something.

Every so often, my eyes scan the room, hoping that no one I know walks in and notices me with Mr. Salters. He, on the other hand, isn't the least bit fazed by our close interaction.

"So, what's new with you?" Mr. Salters asks.

"With me? And here I was thinking you wanted to talk about your wife." I offer a devious smile.

"We can. But first, let's talk about you." He leans in a bit more.

"Well, everything is usual. You know? Work, life, growth, and finding a way to enjoy the moments in between it all."

"Sounds fair."

"Yeah. It is. But enough about me. Where's Mariah?"

"Stop it! You and I both know that you can't talk about my wife." He chuckles.

Suddenly, he puts his hands on my left thigh and softly, yet slowly, makes his way up. Then, he nibbles on my earlobe before he whispers…

"Just relax."

Mr. Salters looks around for a second, turns back to me, and then uncrosses my legs. Even if I wanted to stop him, I wouldn't know how to because this feels so fucking good. Both physically and mentally.

My heart beats against my chest to an unfamiliar rhythm as the tension quickly drains from his body. I'm stuck and unaware of the time passing me by. With no thoughts coming to mind, I stare into the abyss as his nomadic fingers slide over my left thigh. Chills skitter over my skin, and my breathing comes out quivering.

"There's something about you that even you can't seem to understand," he whispers in my ear.

"And what's that?" I close my eyes.

His hand climbs to my waist, and then slowly moves around to my back, finally returning down the side of my left thigh. It's as if my skin is already accustomed to his touch, and the feeling is quite reminiscent.

"You're addictive. Like a drug that's not only good for the body but also good for the soul. You take something out of me that I can never find in anyone else."

"Not even Mariah?"

"No one." He sternly says.

The muscle in my pussy jumps, hoping to clench onto something. Beyond my control, my hands clasp together as they firmly rest on the table like a good little girl's. In my head, I can hear Madison's voice,

"Your desires will linger somewhere in your mind that is almost incapable of being touched if it is never fulfilled." The thought alone is turning me on. I can only imagine what she would say if she knew I was letting this happen.

"Mr. Salters—" I remove his hand.

"Shh! It doesn't matter what you say at this point."

My mouth stays open, refusing to take a deep breath. His hand, robust and warm, return to squeeze my right thigh. Any more touching, and I'll have to remove my panties. Oh God, now he's touching my panties, tugging at the top of them. Is he really going to do this? Right here? Right now? There's a warmth building in between my legs as butterflies fill my stomach.

"You want me to stop?" he asks.

I don't say anything. Besides, the look in my eyes—as I sit here completely wet—should answer his question. How in the world did this situation happen so quickly? For goodness sake, this is the husband of one of my clients. But I must admit, the immoral side of this situation is turning me on.

"How far do you plan to go with this?"

He smiles. "Would you like for me to show you instead?"

Poor Mrs. Salters. She's been waiting to be touched by her husband like this for so long, and here he is doing it to me in the middle of a bar.

"Listen to me. I want you to cross your legs," he whispers.

He takes a sip of my drink with his left hand, while his right hand remains in between my legs. I look down at his hand, gesturing for him to move it in order for me to cross my legs.

"No! Just cross your legs."

I do as he asks of me, managing to cross my legs right over left with his hand squeezed in between my thighs. He grabs the black cloth napkin off the table with his left hand and places it over my legs—disguising what is taking place underneath. My heart dances with absolutely no rhythm as I squirm in my seat. *Have mercy!* What took me so long to come to this moment?

Suddenly, his middle finger hooks onto my panties and pulls it to the side like curtains. He slides two of his fingers to my warmest spot and applies pressure, causing me to jerk in my seat from the initial touch.

A couple sitting next to us looks over, and yet, he doesn't budge one bit. Instead, he waves at them with his left hand.

I bite on my bottom lip as he circles his index finger relentlessly inside of me. Tingles on my skin. Firm breast wanting to be fondled. Hypersensitive neck needing to be kissed. Constant deep breathing trying to control the urges.

"You have to settle down or else someone is going to know what is happening here," he calmly says.

That's easy for him to say. Not only do I feel how wet I am, but I can smell the blend of an earthy citrus bergamot and my peach martini coming together as well. All the while, his finger, curved inside of me, caresses a spot aching for his touch. I feel myself slipping by the second. So, my eyes drift all around the room, hoping it will help distract me from squirming in my seat. All of a sudden, I meet the gaze of the distinguished gentleman. Alton? He's sitting at the bar—in the same exact seat where I was, looking at me with an intent gaze and subtle smile. Is this real? What is he doing here?

I turn away for a moment, and then back to him—all while Mr. Salters continues to touch me.

If I didn't know any better, I would say he sat there on purpose. Just to make me feel uncomfortable, like this is some sort of game. And I must admit, it's working. Like me, Alton has that special power.

I snap my head away from him, knowing that if I continue to look his way, I will lose myself. So, instead, I turn to Mr. Salters for a moment as he continues to touch me in a way that Alton can't. That's only for a few seconds, because then I turn my attention right back to Alton and shamefully think of him touching me instead of Mr. Salters. Suddenly, as I release a soft moan, Alton gets out of his seat, and makes his way out of the bar. *Fuck!* I quickly grab ahold of Mr. Salters' wrist and uncross my legs.

"What's wrong?" Mr. Salters asks.

Without saying a word, I remove his hand from between my thighs, and hurry out of the bar. I scan the entire parking lot, but I don't see Alton anywhere. I'm too late.

Maybe this is good. I'm not sure what I would have said anyway. For goodness sake, he just witnessed me being touched by another man. What could I say?

"Looking for me?" He pulls up in his black Range Rover.

"Maybe." I smile.

"What are you waiting for then? Follow me."

This is it. It's a quarter after one and that can only mean one thing. I'm going to have the night I so badly sought to have. This night should be different from the other night because it's with Alton. A man that I've desperately yearned for since the day I laid eyes on him. Yes, I can do this just one time. One time only…

CHAPTER 22

I'M COMING to the realization that there is nothing I can do to turn back now, and I am completely fine with that. That's exactly why I left the house tonight. Under normal circumstances, I would never dream of shadowing a stranger into the unknown depths of the night. After all, what do I truly know about Alton? But this moment feels inevitable, as if an invisible force binds us together in a way I've never experienced before. My body shivers, goosebumps mingling with a tingling warmth that both unnerves and enthralls me. It intensifies my eagerness to share this peculiar juncture with him. It's a sensation altogether different from the one I encountered at "The House." Yes, the encounters with Manny and Aiden were pleasurable, even breathtaking, but with Alton, there's an electric promise of something far more exhilarating.

For the last twenty minutes I've been trailing behind Alton, and with the way he drives, I'm surprised I can keep up. Luckily, there aren't too many cars on the highway at this time of night. Water droplets splash onto the car windows just as he exits I-95 onto Sample Road—making a left to Coconut Creek. Is it about to rain? Now, this is becoming like some sort of scene from a romantic movie. I can feel the blood rushing through my skin, raising my temperature and making it hard to control my focus. There's even now a tingle between my legs that builds more and more by the second. Fantasizing about Alton is all I can do in this moment, but the more I dwell in these thoughts, the more they feel like memories.

We pull into a beautiful neighborhood with palm trees surrounding us. The homes are quite diversely constructed, and off in the background, there's a lake. For some strange reason, I vaguely remember this neighborhood. Especially seeing as how I knew there was a lake before even seeing it.

Alton makes a left onto a street with a dead end. Pine Hills road. I know this because— actually, how do I know that?

Soon after taking that turn, he pulls into the driveway of the first house on the right. It's a home constructed of steel and glass with a gray door that has as much personality as a blank page. There's a large palmetto tree in the middle of the short lawn. Bordering the house is a hedge of erecting Podocarpus.

Smiling, he steps out of his car and turns to me. My hands are stuck to the steering wheel, and my feet are locked on the brakes. He approaches my car and gestures for me to exit. I take a deep breath. This is it.

Inhale…

Exhale.

Now what do I do? *Grab your keys and get out!* Of course. I do just as the voice in my head instructs, pulling my key from the ignition and placing it into my black clutch. Patiently, Alton waits for me to step out of the car. I take another deep breath, and then stash my clutch underneath my seat before I step out. My heart plays some sort of game. One second, it's racing, and then the very next moment, it's back to beating a regular rhythm. Alton takes my left hand, and escorts me towards the house.

"Sorry about my driving. I tend to drive fast when I'm excited."

"I can tell." I chuckle.

We stand on the doorstep, in front of the gray door, as he fiddles the key in his hand for a second or two.

"You ready?" he says.

There goes my heart again, racing to an unsteady rhythm as he looks into my eyes with that charming stare of his.

"I'm here, aren't I?"

He nods, opens the door, and walks in. I follow behind. His home is welcoming and nicer than I would have imagined, yet, this doesn't strike me as odd. The walls are white with a shade of gray and the floor is a dark polished hardwood. There's a large window that's low to the ground and high to the ceiling. Unlike at my place, there is no clutter of shoes or a stack of mail on the table. No clutter of any kind. There's a floating stairway leading to the second floor with no sign of soppy portraits of him anywhere, either.

My God, the place is spotless. It looks almost too spotless in some strange way.

"I'll get us drinks. Be right back," Alton says.

While he's in the kitchen, I aimlessly wander around the house, unsure of what it is that I am looking for. It doesn't matter, though, because there's nothing that would cause me to leave.

"You okay out there?" he shouts.

My eyes continue to wander throughout his spacious open-designed home when they fall on a magazine sitting on the dark cherry coffee table.

"Yes. I'm fine." I reply.

Although the magazine looks like it doesn't belong there, that isn't what grabs my attention. It's the name written on it that does. Terrance Section.

"Actually, I need to use the restroom," I reply.

"Sure. Go ahead."

I head up the floating stairway, and at the top of the staircase are four doors—three of which are open. One of the open doors, the one closest to the staircase, is a bedroom. But it looks much too basic to be where he sleeps. Of course. That must be where he puts his guests, and right across the way is the bathroom. Then there's the last door on the left that grabs my attention. It's the only closed door, and it has a unique bronze handle on it. That must be his bedroom because the last door on the right is just an office.

"Use the one in the hallway," he shouts from downstairs.

Shit! Just as I was about to open the closed door.

"Okay. Thanks."

I make my way to the bathroom and shut the door, standing here, motionless, as I stare at the woman in the mirror smiling back at me. *You know what's about to happen.* Do I? *Yes! I do.* Perhaps I should freshen up just a bit. Besides, after sitting at the bar with Mr. Salters, I think I may need to.

I reach underneath the sink and grab a washcloth, turn the faucet on, and run the cloth through hot water. Three drops of the hand soap sitting on the counter is all I need. I pull my panties down, step out of them, hike my skirt up, and place one right foot on the counter. The wet warm cloth feels soothing as I gently wipe her off. Again, I run the cloth through the running warm water, and press it between my legs one more time. This time, as I wipe from front to back, I look at myself in the mirror. God, I have a feeling Madison is right. This night is going to relieve me in ways I can't even imagine. I can't tell if it's my hormones racing or the feeling of this warm cloth against my pussy, but something is causing me to behave and think totally outside of my normal self. And unlike the night at "the House," there's no alcohol involved. This is just me being the woman I am.

Now what do I do with this wet cloth? I pull open the first drawer, but it's already filled with toiletries. I close that drawer and slide open the second drawer, and to my surprise, I spot a beige bra. A woman's bra? What is it doing here? Better yet, who does it belong to?

Knock!

Knock!

I swiftly shove the bra back into the drawer and toss the wet cloth into the tub.

"You alright in there?" he asks.

Calm and collected, I step out of the bathroom as he's standing right there, holding two glasses filled with wine.

"You didn't have to knock. I was going to come out at some point."

"Thought you might need help with something."

"Something like what?"

"I don't know. Whatever it is that you women do inside the bathroom when you all mysteriously have to go." He takes a chug of his drink.

"Aren't you the funny one!? Thank you, but I think I can handle myself."

Alton stares into my eyes. It's an eerie sort of stare. It's as if he's searching for something that isn't true within my words.

"Is that my drink?" I ask, pointing my index finger to the flute glass in his left hand. What a good way to deflect from the moment.

"Yes. And if I remember correctly, you said this is the one you like last time. Castel—"

"Castelvero Barbera?"

"2004. You thought I forgot, didn't you?"

I am not even sure if I'm a woman who likes wine enough for him to know that. How does he know so much about me?

"Forget? I'm curious as to how you know this at all. It seems like you know so much about me, and yet, I know nothing about you."

Again, he stares at me awkwardly for a moment. As if I have a huge bloody pimple in the middle of my forehead. This time, it's a shorter stare.

"That's not good—especially seeing as how I'm really not a hard person to get to know. If you allowed yourself to, beyond the gimmicks, you'd know everything there is to know about me." He smiles.

I take a sip of the wine...*Mmm!* Crisp, smooth, and tasty. He steps in closer as his brown eyes twinkle with lust. I can feel his whole body trying to claim me, wanting me, owning me in this moment. The thoughts are beginning to swarm through my mind as they usually would. *Not now, Andrea!* But how did I surrender to this moment? *You wanted this.* Yes, that's true, but why? *Because you're a woman. You have desires that should be touched and needs that ought to be fulfilled. That's what makes you...normal.* Keep it cool, Andrea. The last thing I want is for him to mistake my anticipation for nervousness.

Just a few days ago I was fantasizing about marrying the only man I've ever loved, and here I am now thinking about how Alton will feel inside of me. My lips shiver as I search for the words, but nothing comes to mind. Therefore, a stretch of silence comes between us. I hate silence.

"You like it?" he asks.

I nod, and take another sip of the wine, hoping to free myself of my useless thoughts. It works. The drink swiftly stimulates the primitive part of my brain that regulates the basic human functions including body temperature, inhibitions, and, of course, my hormones.

"Come. Follow me." Alton grabs a hold of my left hand and leads me to the closed door.

I can faintly hear my heart thumping against my chest like sticks against drums. The moment he turns the doorknob, everything stops, leaving me desperately alone in the bosom of time. This is it!

"I want to ask something of you, and all I want you to do is agree to my request." He turns to me.

"Without even hearing what it is first? How can I do that?"

"Simple. Just agree to agree."

"But what if it's something I can't do?"

"It's me. You should be able to trust me completely by now. Besides, you must know that I wouldn't put you in any situation that wasn't favorable to you."

Two of his fingers softly slide down the side of my neck, then across my collarbone, and then over my shoulder. He gazes down at me with an intense look. His expression is sincere and approving. "You know what? For the first time, I can look into your eyes and see you for who you really are. And I like it. You are one fascinating woman," he murmurs. "I can't say that I've ever been more captivated like this by you or any woman for that matter."

Between his words and melodic voice, I feel some sort of combustible reaction building in my body. He leans in and kisses me, faintly inhaling air from my mouth. Surprisingly, there's not a nerve in my body that wants him to stop. It's as if the sexual spirit in me has awakened from a nap. He sucks on my lower lip, trailing his tongue inside my mouth.

"I like the way you react when I kiss you," he whispers between my lips, holding gently onto my lips with his teeth.

"Why's that?" Seductively, I smile.

He chuckles. "Do you really want the answer?"

"Yes. I love details."

He looks both charmed and confused. "Okay. Well for starters, you're so pleasing to the eyes," he kisses around my neck. "Also, my lips against your skin feel soothing."

He's right.

He gently nibbles on my shoulders. "Of course, I can't forget about the goosebumps that rise on your skin each time I kiss you." He places his lips on my collarbone. I watch him, and yet, this feels strangely familiar. "Does that answer your question?"

"Yes, but I was already aware of the answer."

"I know. I just felt like playing along. Like I've been doing this whole time." He wraps his arms around my waist. "But tonight, please, let me make love to you. No fucking! None of the bullshit. Just me, and you."

There's the tingly feeling in between my legs happening again, and this time there's warmth that comes with it. I have a strong desire to be touched, and—*Oh shit!* My panties! I left them on his bathroom floor.

"You okay?" he asks.

"Of course," I murmur.

He smiles and grabs a hold of the doorknob.

"So, what's this request of yours?" I ask.

"I'll tell you soon."

At last, he opens the door and leads me into the spacious bedroom. Oh my, is it nice. Stepping across the threshold into the room feels like walking into the best place on earth. The room is not too cold nor is it warm. It's perfect. There's a large window behind the king size bed that opens out to a view of the lake in the background, reflecting the stars from the sky.

He pulls me into his chest, and I feel his bulge pressing against my stomach. The feeling takes me by surprise, leaving me more intrigued.

"This is an incredible view."

He laughs.

"What's so funny?"

"You. You're an interesting person."

The massive king-sized bed is made of dark black wood with four establishing columns at each corner. Everything is black. The bedding. The furniture. The sixty-inch plasma television mounted on the wall that is cloud gray with blotches of black squares. The ceiling is vaulted high with a crystal chandelier hanging above the bed.

"And so are you. Why is everything so…dark?" I ask.

He sits me down on the bed and peels the shirt off his body. His eyes light up as I stare into them, making me want to touch him in that moment.

"Like I told you before…that's the way I like things. Black is an impressive and elegant color. It represents the man that I am. A man who walks to the beat of his own drum. Someone who's not afraid to be alone."

"Is that so?" I chuckle.

"Yes. Now, if you'll excuse me for a moment. I'll be right back." He heads into the bathroom.

I fall back onto the plush king size bed and sink in, swinging my arms back and forth as if I were making snow angels. God, this bed is so comfortable, and as I lie here, the sound of water running puts me further into the moment. Slowly, I close my eyes, my smile softens, and unexpectedly, my fingers trail over my neck. Across my collarbone. I can't wait to feel Alton touching me instead.

I sit up, reach behind, and unzip my dress. The moment I stand to take it off, I notice a glass case sitting on a shelf. Inside the case is a decorative trophy, and judging by the figure sitting on top, it must be a football trophy. Next to the case is an autographed ball. Is that his signature? I walk over and notice the name is the same as the name on the magazine downstairs. Terrance Section. An eerie feeling floods my stomach like a broken levee. Who is the man in the bathroom? *Don't worry about that, Andrea! Let it go.* How can I do that? *Because he wants you! And you want him.* I scowl at my inner voice for making so much sense. Besides, knowing his name won't change anything. But the fact remains…who is he really?

After five minutes, Alton pops out of the bathroom, wearing nothing as water drips down his body.

"Didn't mean to keep you waiting." He approaches me.

And just like that, my concern about his identity disappears. I would have waited hours to see him stand there, naked and wet, as he looks at me with a charming smile. I want him now.

"It's okay. I…um…I was just…I'm fine."

I should consider myself lucky. On a night where my hormones are racing with a strong desire to be touched, I happen to find myself with a specimen as fine as Alton, Terrance, whoever the hell he is. It doesn't even matter at this point. *Unbelievable.* I take a deep breath and walk over to him.

"You are doing something to me that no man has ever been able to do. The crazy part is…you have no idea." I bite on my bottom lip.

"Is that right?"

I nod as every nerve in my body and brain is electrified. It's the anticipation of being in this moment, in this way, that takes me to a place where I have no inhibitions.

He takes me by the hand and brings me into a steamy bathroom. Then, he slowly slides my dress off my body. "Don't say anything."

He places his gentle left hand on my breast, leans in, and softly kisses my neck as his right hand travels to the middle of my back. It's a slow process, but I enjoy every second of it.

Alton then kneels on one knee and begins to glide his tongue around my navel. Five long and generous licks bring butterflies to my stomach. I inhale, and my mouth drops open, watching his tongue move across my body. *How does it feel?*

"Good." His breath hitches.

Oh shit! He heard me? I didn't mean to say that out loud.

"Take these off."

He removes my left shoe, and then my right. Had it not been for this necklace around my neck, I would be completely naked. I'm usually timid in the presence of my nudity—but with him, I feel comfortable and stimulated. I can't stop smiling, aware that at any moment, his lips will be touching the spot where I am most excited. The thought alone has me so wet that I can feel it.

He then takes my right foot, places it into his palm, and showers it with tender kisses, massaging it as he does so. The more I watch him, the more a stimulating prickling feeling covers my skin. Almost as if I'm being tickled from within.

"You never cease to amaze me," he murmurs.

After a few minutes, Alton stands up, pauses, and looks me in the eyes with a boyish smile. Every few seconds, my eyes drift to his erection, and then back to him. I want to feel him inside of me. So much so, I'm pulsating from the thought of it. *Touch it.* No, I can't do that. That would show my excitement. *Touch it!* she adamantly says. I'm sure he can feel my desperation to use my hand, and the willpower it's taking me not to. Fuck this! I wrap both hands around his erection, feeling the veins that are so boldly detailed and commanding the smooth skin in my palms. I step in closer and slowly brush the tip of his erection against my clit. Up and down. Down and up. He takes a deep breath, closes his eyes, and bites on his lower lip. I'm making him weak, and it's so motivating to see it happen. I bite on his chest, and then move to his neck—all while I continue to cover his erection with my eagerness.

"You are—"

"Shh." I press my lips against his, and then grab ahold of his hard and warm dick.

Put it in your mouth. No! Not right now. *Do it!* Just as I'm about to drop down below his waist, Alton turns me around and bends me over onto the counter. He tugs on my black hair with his left hand, and with his right hand, he grips onto my thigh, slowly kissing over my back—down my spine. As his lips travel from my shoulder, across to my back, I can't help but feel like I'm stuck in some sort of déjà vu.

Suddenly, I feel him breathing between my legs. There's a building up of energy just before it turns into a warm tingle. I moan softly while I bite on my bottom lip. God, I want him so bad, and judging by the never-ending chills covering my skin, it's obvious that my body is enjoying every bit of this moment.

Deep Inhale.

Softer exhale.

Alton grips my ass, spreads it apart, and explores my pussy like a paintbrush against a canvas. Up and down, down and up. A long lick from my clit up to the center of my lower back. A slow pulsating sensation builds with each lick. He blows between my legs; I inhale. He slaps his right hand against my ass, I exhale.

"Damn! I love how you taste. Since the first time," he says, flickering his tongue between my legs.

My eyebrows pull together, confused by what he just said. Since the first time? What does that even mean? However, before I can respond to him, I feel his tongue twirling in seamless circular motions as he squeezes my behind.

My God!

The sound of my wet pussy against his tongue is stimulating

enough to keep me in the moment. He licks, I quiver. He twirls his tongue, I moan. He sucks, I weaken. Then, he pushes his tongue deep inside of me. *What the fuck!*

How am I already feeling the urge to cum? It's like every part of my body wants in on the action, too. This is so embarrassing as my body keeps jerking. Fuck! I'm going to explode over his mouth any second. *Don't fight it.* She's right. I squeeze my eyes shut, grip onto the counter, and let the feeling come to me. My heart races to an unsteady beat. My moans forsake me, leaving me speechless.

"Please don't stop."

Suddenly, he stops just as I am about to reach that point where my body is relieved of the pleasure. I abruptly turn to him, panting and wanting more, and before I can ask why he stopped, he pulls me in tight and wraps his arms around me. Then, his lips press against mine, softly, delicately. This is it. He's about to slide himself inside of me and I can't wait another second.

"So, about my request," he says.

I glance upward, my mouth pursed but slightly open. My eyes, narrowed, are stuck on him, trying to understand what it is that he wants from me.

"You never told me what it was."

"Andrea…I want you! Just you! Understand what I'm saying?"

What is he referring to? I'm totally confused.

Unexpectedly, my mind reels with random images of Alton, but I am unable to process them. Alton and I lying naked on the grass. He and I making out in a public bathroom. There's even a flash of us riding in his black Range Rover. Even one of us standing outside of the mirrored building. I'm noticing things I didn't notice before. Like the scar on his left shoulder. Why didn't I see it until now?

"Hello?"

"What do you mean by *just me*?" I snap out of it.

"I want you to be you! No alter ego. No games. Just you, Andrea. No Madison!"

What the fuck! I take a big gulp of air as I remain stuck with my mouth wide open. Suddenly, bells are sounding off in my head like fireworks on the fourth of July. Breathing is almost impossible, and I am speechless. My eyes are fixed on him, but it's as if I'm looking through him instead of at him.

"You okay?" he asks.

"No. What did you just say?"

"Look, it's not that I don't enjoy the discreet relationships that we have, but for once, I would just like to have all of you. I want to feel something more between you and me. Just for this once." He gives me a subtle kiss on the lips. "So just for this moment, can we be ourselves? You and me. Terrance…and Andrea."

The wheels in my head swiftly spring out of control as the thumps in my chest reach Mach speed. I stare at him in disbelief. What is happening right now? This doesn't make any sense.

I pull his arms off my waist and step back. Everything changes in that moment. My body is back to normal with no urge to be touched. Alton now looks like an average man instead of the specimen that he once was. And there's this feeling inside of me begging me to leave.

"What is it?" he asks.

His eyes desperately search mine, waiting on me to say something, but I can't even move my lips to speak. I am helpless, and I feel trapped.

"Andrea…what's wrong?" He steps forward.

"Who are you?" I step back.

"What?! What are you talking about? You know what… just forget I said anything."

He grabs ahold of me, but I quickly pull away from him, and take a step over to the right, along the counter. Noticing my uneasiness, he steps back, staring at me in disbelief.

"Why are you lying to me? I saw the trophies and the mail around the house with the name Terrance Section. So, who are you?"

He takes another step back and looks at me suspiciously.

"Are you serious right now? Because I can't tell at this point." His eyes are almost as still as the eyes of a mannequin.

"Yes, I am! You know what…never mind."

I quickly grab my dress, throw it over my clammy body, and then grab my shoes, trying to move as fast as I can. That only cause more problems.

"Andrea, wait! For just one minute, put aside the games, and tell me the truth. Have you really been so wrapped up in this whole charade that you don't even know who I am?"

My eyes drown in Alton's eyes, and then travel down to his feet. Everything about this man feels familiar, but I can't make sense of it. *You don't have to.*

"Shut up! Just shut up!" I yell out loud.

He jumps back and braces himself as if he's afraid of me. How can I blame him? I'm frightened of myself as well.

"What games are you talking about?"

He hesitates to speak, baring the face of a man who's lost a loved one. This is the kind of silence that normally troubles me, especially on a rainy night like this one.

"Please, just tell me," I murmur.

"This is beyond wild right now. I don't know what to say." He pauses for a moment. "Andrea, it's me! Terrance."

More images of him pop in and out of my mind like a broken reel, yet they don't feel like they belong to me.

"I gotta go!"

I put my shoes on and hurry out of the bathroom. Terrance follows behind me.

"Andrea, wait! Please, wait a minute."

I don't stop. Quickly, I exit the bedroom, heading downstairs.

"Andrea! Andrea!" he yells out.

I continue on to the front door, and just as I'm about to step out… "Madison!" he yells.

I stop, turn around, and look up at him. The sound of his voice echoing in my ears pierces through my soul like shiny daggers.

"Don't call me that!"

"Then why'd you stop?"

He's right, Andrea.

Why did I stop?

You know why.

Terrance reaches toward me. "I don't know what's going on with you, but—"

Something dawns on me as my reality explodes into pieces like a broken mirror. I can't even tell the difference between what is real and what is not. How is this fucking possible? Things that were never in my view are appearing like ghosts. Pictures of Terrance and a woman, his wife, my former client, Mrs. Christina Section, are all over the place. How did I not see them before? *Because you didn't want to.*

"Your wife is Christina?" I approach a wedding picture.

"Yeah. You already know that. That's how we met. During my wife's third session with you. Last year. Remember? That day, you came up to me at the coffee shop and asked if I knew the difference between cappuccino and macchiato. And I said…"

"The difference is in the foam and milk."

"Right. I hesitated to talk at first because, well, you just finished having that intense session with Christina and I, but the way you smiled at me, I knew it was okay. That's when you said…"

"…Just call me Madison." I stare off into the distance.

It's like I am being set up and everyone is in on it except me. I feel the same as when I was a little girl watching my mom go through one of her schizophrenic episodes. Scared and confused, buckling under the strain. Come on Andrea. Get it together.

Just leave, you stupid bitch. Leave now!

"Stop it! Leave me alone!"

"Andrea, what is it? Let me help you." He approaches me.

"No! Get away. I'm fine."

I step away from him and hurry out the door. My abnormal consciousness and the function of the mind seem to be disrupted. This would explain— Oh, God! I need to get going and get to the bottom of this, because if this is true, then I am in serious trouble.

CHAPTER 23

THERE IS A MOMENT when time simultaneously stops, and then it moves on quickly. In that split second, the brain desperately scrambles to think of all the possible outcomes. However, nothing happens. It is the moment when the mind finally shifts into consciousness from a realm of sleep. The moment things make sense or leave you temporarily incapacitated.

2:13 A.M

By the time I pull up to the forty-seven-story building, my head lightly spins as I try to comprehend what has just occurred. How did Alton mistake me for Madison? Was this Madison's plan the whole time? Pretend to be me and take over my life? That would explain everything. Her random appearance. How she knew so much about me. The House. Manny. Aiden. Mr. Salters. Alton. Daniel's disappearance? Omigod! Could she be the reason Daniel left? Fuck me! Madison set this all up. But why would she?

Ding!

I've never been here this late. It's eerily quiet, dark, and it feels like someone is watching me. There's also a stillness in the air that seems to suck the sound of my steps into nothingness. If only this were a dream, it would all make sense. But seeing as it's not, I must get to the bottom of this, and for some reason, I have a feeling it starts here.

I enter my office and hurry to the folders sitting on my desk, rummaging through for Madison's file. *Come on. Come on.* It's not here. Where the heck could it be? It must be on Rachel's desk. I swiftly make my way out of my office, but it opens just as I reach the door.

"Andrea?"

I step back and nearly stumble over my feet, startled in that split second with eyes wide and mouth hanging slack. It takes a moment before I can breathe again and notice it's only Dr. Lanier.

"What are you doing here?" he asks.

My brain stutters for a moment, staring at him as if he's waving a gun in my face. Yes, what am I doing here? I look over to the pile of folders scattered on my desk, then back to Dr. Lanier.

"I, um…I came in to look for something."

"Look for something? At two in the morning?"

"Well, I'm leaving soon, so I wanted to get this out of the way before I did."

"Leaving soon? Well, where are you headed to?"

"Mexico."

"I wasn't aware of that. What's the occasion?"

"Get away. Just a few days to clear my mind."

"Got it. Maybe you do need that. By the way, is everything okay? I received an e-mail from one of your clients, Jennifer Allen. She said something was rather strange about you."

Ms. Allen saying anything about me is strange in itself. Ms. Allen is a thirty-six-year-old unconventional psychotherapist who would rather solve problems by sitting in a garden of marijuana.

Four months ago, the west wing of Johnson Colonial Hospital accidentally collapsed, killing seventeen and injuring fourteen. The scene was so horrific that the hospital had its entire staff receive counseling. It's a standard move following any traumatizing event. Ms. Allen counseled half of the team who witnessed that tragedy, and after hearing all their stories, she came to me. It's prevalent for a psychologist to seek therapy of their own. We are normal, too, and like everyone else, we get overwhelmed by the common issues and problems that the rest of the world experiences. Nevertheless, I've never been one to have a therapist or psychologist. That's because I don't know what someone else will tell me that I can't figure out on my own. As for Ms. Allen, it has always been a mystery why she bothers to come to my office.

"Strange? What did Ms. Allen say?"

"Not totally clear about that. But she said you were…different. Not in an enjoyable way. She wouldn't go into details, but she felt somewhat uncomfortable when she saw you the other day. She also said it might be good for you to see someone."

What?! I didn't see Ms. Allen the other day. What is she talking about? Nothing about Ms. Allen appears to be…normal. But then again, are any of us ever? We are talking about the same woman elevated by an ideological system set around the values of peace and love. For goodness' sake, she wants to be made love to every day under the canopy of trees. She told me this in our first session. Like Madison, Ms. Allen would randomly tell me about her insatiable sexual appetite.

"Well, I'm not sure where that's coming from."

"And what about Ms. Thompson? Mrs. Martin? Mrs. Salters? There have been others who have noticed a change in you. They don't know what it is, but there's something. Even Rachel has said you've been acting strangely. Staring out the window. Arriving late. Missing appointments. Talking to yourself? She also mentioned a detective coming by for you. So, tell me… what's going on?"

I'm completely stuck— mouth buckling, eyes tearing up. *Hold it together, Andrea.* For the first time since I can remember, I am lost. No mask of coping left as my eyes stare at Dr. Lanier unblinkingly, unsure of what to say next.

"I think it all has something to do with one of my clients. Madison."

"Madison? What's the first name?" He folds his arm over his plump stomach, looking at me suspiciously.

"There was none. Just Madison. It's the file that you handed me the other day."

"That's impossible. That file belongs to my sister-in-law's stepdaughter. And her name is Tamara Ross."

My face falls faster than a brick in water. Instantly, chills crawl over my skin like millions of ants. My mouth hangs with my lips slightly parted. The thoughts are accelerating inside my head even more. I want them to slow so I can breathe, but they won't.

"That can't be. The file I saw said Madison." I head back to my desk.

"Not the one I gave you. That's why I gave it to you. Tamara is too close and needs help, so I suggested you take her on as a client instead. Are you sure you're okay?"

I frantically dive through the folders again, and lo and behold, there's folder *0023*. Tamara Ross. How is this possible? I specifically remember seeing Madison's name on this folder.

"Andrea? You okay?"

"Stop asking me that! And what are you doing here?" I abruptly turn to him.

"I'm often here around this time of night. Especially when things at home are a bit rough between me and Olivia. And when I was on my way out, I noticed your office light on."

"I'm fine."

"You sure? It may be time you see someone."

"I said I'm fine. Now, will you please leave me alone?"

He looks at me, stuck, as if he is genuinely concerned and unable to will his lips to move. Then, he heads to the door, and before he exits, he turns back to me.

"Okay. But we'll talk about this soon. And I expect an explanation and a solution at that time."

He exits and closes the door behind him. Immediately, breathing becomes difficult as my chest pounds to an unknown beat. The room spins counterclockwise, and I have no feeling in my hands and feet.

I fall to the floor, facing the ceiling with wide-open eyes. What in the world is happening? Suddenly, I begin to see images of men appearing in my thoughts. It's not just their faces but images of them touching me. Vividly. The thoughts aren't random, and in fact, I believe these are memories. A memory of Mr. Salters appears where he and I are making out in the parking garage of this building. His clothes are the same ones he wore earlier in a session with Mrs. Salters. A green half-sleeve button-up shirt and brown khakis. I remember it like it was yesterday. In fact, I remember how he looked at me, eyes narrowed and twinkling, licking his lips, opening his legs wide just so I could see his bulge— all while Mrs. Salters poured out her feelings. It was both disturbing and stimulating.

There's even a memory of Eddie showing up—a longtime friend of mine. *No way! Not Eddie. Please say it's not so.* He seems somewhat intoxicated in the vision. His eyelids are weighing down on him. His mouth is open as if he's going to belch at any moment, rocking side to side. It's not a pleasing sight, yet he's on top of me. Sweating. Groaning. My soul scowls at the thought that I could have been intimate with Eddie at any point in my life. How? Why? Eddie is not the cutest, nor is he the brightest. He's Puerto Rican but speaks no Spanish. Not to mention, his weight is also an issue, and he always works my last nerve whenever we're together for more than an hour. So, there's no way I'd ever take it there with him.

Where are these memories coming from? They continue to appear in and out of my head like some broken reel. Kissing. Fucking. Making love to me in ways that make my body warm up just thinking about it. A slight tremble starts to occur as the memories get incredibly real. An electric kick flows through my veins as my eyes tighten from the sensitivity that captures my entire body. I can't stop the thoughts even if I try. Thoughts of Manny, Aiden, and even a man whose name I don't even know. There's also a well-built man dressed in jeans, a navy-blue t-shirt, and a yellow hardhat crossing the street on his way over to me. I remember him, but what's his name? *What's his name, Andrea?* Patrick. Yes, that's it. I remember his dark skin and his African roots chiseled into his face, looking into my eyes as I touched myself.

Bit by bit, I fall further into my subconscious, where I now have an unwarranted flash of a woman standing over me. The woman, short with a curvy frame, is outlined by the sunlight hugging her naked body. She then drops down on her knees, right in front of me, looking up at me with a smile. Her wild curly hair is between my thighs as she kisses the spot that makes my body shiver. A puff of smoke suddenly fills the room as her small hands glide along my inner thighs in such a sensual manner. Oh my! It's Ms. Allen. Wait! Was I intimate with Ms. Allen as well? Yes. I was. That would explain why she mentioned I was acting strange.

Shit!

Daniel! No. It can't be. Oh my God! I remember now. It was dark and loud on the night we met. He wore a black blazer, a V-neck t-shirt, and ripped black jeans. We locked eyes from across the room, and it didn't take long before he approached me. Of all the men in the place, he's the one that piqued my interest. Something daring and forbidden about him made me want to explore him, and nothing would stop me. He asked me my name, and I told him. Then, he laughed and said, *"I thought your name was Andrea…Dr. Clarke."* I took a sip of my drink while batting my eyes, smiling deviously. *"Well then, call me…Daniel."* He followed this with a chuckle. It's all coming back to me. Daniel wasn't his name, just like Alton isn't Terrance's. James Walker. Oh, fuck! What have I done?

Knock!

Knock!

"What do you want now, Frank?"

"Hello, Dr. Clarke."

"Madison!" I sit up, startled half to death.

She walks over to my desk and takes a seat, crossing her legs right over left. Her presence makes the hair on my arms stand to attention. Even my heart wants to explode out of my chest. And if that's not bad enough, my body is starting to sweat in weird places.

"What are you doing here?" I ask.

"I thought you'd be more excited to see me."

She strolls over to the large window and stares to God knows where. Her silence is uneasy and eerie, suspended in the air like the moment before glass shatters onto the ground.

"What happens when our reality is mistaken for our perception? Or our perception becomes our reality. When everything that we believed in…vanishes in an instant. More importantly, what happens when any of this occurs beyond our control?" Madison turns to me.

Slowly, I stand, but I feel like a toddler trying to take their first step. The beats in my chest drop to a steady rhythm.

"What is this all about?" I ask.

"Come on, now. You know. But you're afraid to say it, aren't you? Go ahead, Andrea. Say it."

I stare at her with my eyes wide open as the whole world crumbles around me. I don't remember Madison ever calling me by my first name. My stomach twists in knots and breathing becomes uncomfortable. I wish I didn't have to breathe at all, as every part of my body goes numb.

"You aren't real, are you?"

"Bingo! There it is. No, I'm not."

"How is this possible? How are you…you?"

"You allowed your unconscious feelings and behaviors to emerge as a result of working with all your clients. For so long, you suppressed it, and you could've stopped it, but you didn't want to, did you? And now…here we are." Madison approaches me.

"Countertransference…" My breaths come in gasps, and I feel like I will black out any moment.

"Yes. Countertransference." She walks to the window. "Remember the woman you counseled who felt guilty for not answering her mother's phone call? All because she was too busy making out with a co-worker in the classroom. Her mother died that night, and she'll forever live with the fact that had she answered that call…she could have done something. What was her name again?"

"Kimberly Madison," I murmur to myself.

"Yes! Kimberly Madison. God, she had the most perfect body I'd ever seen. Nice long legs, slim waist, and long black hair that flowed down to her shoulders. Five foot five, slender, with a face that no one could forget. Nice smile too. You would not have ever known she had a sex addiction by looking at her. But that's what made her even more intriguing, isn't it? You loved hearing all the stories of her encounters. Just like you did with Denita Richardson."

"No. That's not true." My stomach knots up.

"Yes! Instead of helping her deal with her mother's loss, you were more intrigued by her stories. Her encounters. So much so that you studied her. Worshiped her. You even had her describe details of her sex life that no other professional would have had her do."

"It was only to provide best practice therapy." I step back.

"Come on, Andrea. It was more than that. You wanted to be her. Go where she would go. Do what she would do. And it's all because deep down inside…you were already just like her."

My heart falls to silence, and I can't seem to move my lips. It's as if I'm stuck underwater, drowning in the reality of the truth. For the first time, everything makes sense. Madison is a cumulation of all the clients I've counseled and everything I admired in those I didn't. Staring into her eyes is like looking into the mirror I rarely ever do. She is me, and I am her.

"Why couldn't I tell the difference?"

"Well, that's the part. You get to figure it out on your own. Perhaps, you didn't want to, and by the time you could, differentiating between the woman you are and the woman you wanted to be… became almost impossible.

Kimberly. Mrs. Walker. Mrs. Hicks. Amber Porter. Ms. Niah Phillips. Ms. Rebull. Ms. Valdez. Danielle Brown. Ms. Mack. All of them. You took a piece of them to make me who I am. All so that you could live the life you want."

It feels as if someone is choking me. How did I lose myself in Madison like this? Better yet, how was I not even aware of it? All I want to do is curl up into a ball and wait for this to be all over.

"And what about Daniel?"

"Like I said before… he's gone. And you can stop calling him Daniel and call him by his real name."

"James Walker," I whisper.

"Exactly. James Walker. What happened to Mr. Walker wasn't planned and was out of our control. You got too involved with him and fell in love. Even to the point where you contrived this romantic life that made no sense. It would help if you had allowed me to be with him, but there's nothing we can do about it now."

"But kill him? Why would I do that?"

"I think your time with Mrs. Salters would explain that. You couldn't tell the difference between your life…and her thoughts."

Time keeps slowing down the more everything comes back to me. All these memories are too much to take in. Quickly, I run over to the off-white sofa and fall onto it, burying my face in my palms. This is too much to take in.

"I'm going to prison. It's only a matter of time before they come to get me. And Mrs. Walker…she knew. Oh my God! My life is over. Why didn't you tell me this before?" I shout.

"You were having fun. There's something special about allowing yourself to live freely and to the fullest with no restriction, you know? And the men we lived freely with…*Mmm*! Like Manny. He was so passionate and caring. Aiden—oh my God, he was everything. Eddie. Ms. Salters. Tony. Mr. Ortiz from the coffee shop. Terrence! Fuck! We can never forget about Terrence. Then, there's the guy we flew in from Atlanta. Remember? He was okay. The same goes for your neighbor's son, but he might have made things a bit awkward."

"My neighbor? Jeff?"

"Is that his name? Hmm."

Madison takes a seat in my chair— across from me. She crosses her legs as she always does. Right over left. Then, she takes her Chanel dark rouge lipstick and glides it over her lips—top lip first, and then her bottom. Her fingernails tap against each other in the silent room, making the panic in my chest grow.

"You're in control, Andrea. You don't need me anymore, so embrace it. Cherish it. You are entitled to every experience that leaves you feeling more alive and connected to yourself than you've ever been. No matter who it's with, the best thing you can do is to understand, accept, and take charge of your sexuality. That's what makes you a woman," she whispers seductively.

"Stop it! I'm not like you!" I jump out of my seat in total disbelief.

"You are me."

"Madison…someone is dead. I killed someone. Don't you understand that?" My breathing is more rapid and shallow.

"Relax. No one knows anything. If you continue listening to my voice, everything will be fine."

Madison walks over to me in the most graceful steps a woman can take and glares into my eyes without saying a word.

Then, she does it. Her lips press against mine as my inhibitions free themselves into her body. The tips of her fingers touch my chin and slightly lift my head. Electricity runs over my skin, travels through my core, and then sinks into my stomach. I can feel her more than I have ever felt anyone else—more internally than physically. My God! No one understands Madison like I do.

Madison is no longer there when I pull away and open my eyes. She's gone. I find myself thinking of Madison's initial question. *What happens when our reality is mistaken for our perception? Or our perception becomes our reality? When everything that we believed in…vanishes in an instant. More importantly, what happens when any of this occurs beyond our control?* You live life accordingly and stop fighting the inevitable.

DECEMBER
MONDAY
14

7:15 A.M

"COME ON, BITCH! Wake up!" Shannon pulls the comforter off my shoulder and then jumps on top of me—straddling my waist. Her grating voice pierces my ears as she shakes me by the shoulder. On top of that, I hear Duke's barking.

"Wake up! Wake up!" she shouts.

Shannon's childish behavior reminds me we're about to set off for Mexico. She's excited. I must admit…so am I.

"How did you get in?" I ask, pulling the comforter away from Shannon.

"I have the key. Duh! Now come on, get up!"

"The sun is barely up. What time is it?"

"Quarter after seven. We have a flight to catch in approximately three hours. So, get out of bed!" Shannon pulls on the comforter again, but this time she takes it entirely off the bed.

"Andrea…no panties? Ooooo."

"Would you cut that out? I'm up. Okay. Now, will you leave so I can get myself together?"

Shannon doesn't budge.

"Shannon! Come on."

"Fine. Fifteen minutes. After that, you're leaving this house just as you are."

Shannon exits the room but leaves the door open. I sit up and stare at an unknown spot, thinking about last night and everything else that has taken place. Then, it hits me. Perhaps I should leave as soon as I can. There's no telling if Detective Barringer will be here to arrest me at any moment. And this time, I'm afraid I won't be so lucky.

"Hey Andrea, now I know why you're in bed with no panties," Shannon says, standing in the doorway, eating a banana in one hand while twirling my panties on the other.

"Found this in the living room. What were you doing?" she adds.

"Would you stop that? Those are my underwear. Not some toy."

"Why are your panties on the living room floor anyway?" Shannon takes a bite of the banana.

I quickly wrap the comforter underneath my arms and storm over to her.

"Give me that!" I snarl, snatching it off her finger. "Because it's my house."

"And when did you start smoking again?" She picks up a pack of cigarettes off my dresser.

Esse. My favorite brand. Madison must have grabbed these for me. She has a way of doing things like that.

"I smoke from time to time. Nothing serious."

"Whatever. Just hurry up. Ten minutes."

9:12 A.M.

"Remind me again, why did you bring so much stuff? You do know that we're only staying a few days, right? It's as if you do not plan on coming back or something?" Shannon says.

I shrug, but internally…I think that may be a possibility.

"Surprise! First-class seats. What do you think?"

It's no wonder Shannon was so eager to get on the plane. The seats are large and lustrously polished with 11-inch television screens and Bose headsets.

"This is nice. Where are Erin and Darlene? I thought they were coming as well."

"They fly in later. But for now, I need a drink."

"Same here."

Really? You? Okay. I have just the thing. I'll be right back."

Shannon grabs her purse and makes her way to the cabin restroom.

"Attention all passengers, thank you for flying Delta Airlines flight 7362 to Cabo, Mexico. At this time, we ask that you buckle your seatbelts if you haven't already…"

Just as I lie back and shut my eyes, the man in front of me grabs my attention.

"Psst! I couldn't help but overhear that you wanted something to drink. It just so happens that I have a bottle of whiskey in my bag. I'd gladly share with you if you want."

"Is that so?"

I can barely see the man's face through the crevices of the seat, but I sense he's older. That's judging from his grayish hair. My guess is that he's in his mid-to-late fifties. And his voice, in a richness of tones, rumbles like a storm deep inside of him.

"So, what you headed to Cabo for?" He passes the whiskey to me.

"Just looking to have a good time."

"Well, Cabo is surely a spot for that."

"I hope so."

I place my lips around the bottle and chug the liquor down my throat. The drink is so strong that I can feel it burning through my system. Not only that, but it also leaves a nasty aftertaste.

"That's what I'm talking about. Get the party started now. By the way, the name is Ray."

The man stands up in his seat, and finally, I get a good look at him. He's an older man, just as I thought, but through his seasoned face, I can see the young boy who told the most incredible stories. He extends his hand toward me.

"It's nice to meet you, Ray."

I shake his hand.

"Well, aren't you going to tell me your name?" He holds my gaze for a second too long. I smile, look away for a moment, and then turn back to him while moaning internally.

Like Ray, every man found something about Madison they could identify with. From her beautiful lips, seductive behavior, and stunning glossy black hair to her dangerous bedroom eyes. You name him, and he'd easily swoon under Madison's alluring presence. That's just it! Madison can have any man she wants…and I am no different.

"I'm Madison."

"Madison? I like it. Nice to meet you, Ms. Madison.

Printed in Great Britain
by Amazon